Lost American Fiction
Edited by Matthew J. Bruccoli

The title for this series, Lost American Fiction, is unsatisfactory. A more accurate series title would be "Forgotten American Works of Fiction That Deserve a New Public"—which states the rationale for reprinting these titles. No claim is made that we are resuscitating lost masterpieces, although the first work in the series, Edith Summers Kelley's *Weeds,* may qualify. We are reprinting some works that are worth rereading because they are now social documents (*Dry Martini* and *The Cubical City*) or literary documents (*The Professors Like Vodka* and *Predestined*). It isn't that simple, for Southern Illinois University Press is a scholarly publisher; and we have serious ambitions for the series. We expect that these titles will revive some books and authors from undeserved obscurity and that the series will therefore plug some of the holes in American literary history. Of course, we hope to find an occasional lost masterpiece.

At this point six titles have been published in this series, with three more in production. The response has been encouraging. We are gratified that many readers share our conviction that one of the proper functions of a university press is to rescue good writing from oblivion.

M. J. B.

Stephen French Whitman

Predestined

A Novel of New York Life

With an Afterword by
Alden Whitman

SOUTHERN ILLINOIS UNIVERSITY PRESS
Carbondale and Edwardsville

Feffer & Simons, Inc.
London and Amsterdam

Library of Congress Cataloging in Publication Data

Whitman, Stephen French.
  Predestined; a novel of New York life.

  (Lost American fiction)
  Reprint of the ed. published by Scribner, New York.
  I. Title.
PZ3.W5955P5   [PS3545.H7574]   813'.5'2   74-8672
ISBN 0-8093-0701-4

CONTENTS

PART ONE

EILEEN

CHAPTER I

IT was said that Felix Piers inherited his good looks and attractive manners from his mother, who had died in his childhood. The son had at home an old, faded photograph of her, by aid of which he made himself believe that he remembered her. She was portrayed in a beaded zouave-jacket and a voluminous skirt, wearing a chignon, leaning over a flower stand, before a fringed curtain looped up with heavy tassels. Despite her clumsy-looking dress she appeared charming, and in her face was beauty of so peculiar a quality that one was puzzled by it. What sort of woman had she been? The boy, noting her dark eyes and crinkling black hair, had always felt tender satisfaction at the thought that he resembled her.

On the other hand, none could perceive what attributes Felix had obtained from the husband who survived her.

This gentleman, Sheridan Piers, was bony, sallow, "plain-looking," his eyes pale blue, his mouth hidden by a gray mustache, his face—which had been shortened by false teeth—wearing invariably a saturnine expression. He attracted none of his acquaintances to intimacy. Even when young, for the most part he had shunned companionable customs.

3

Shy and retiring as a boy, by disposition always solemn and austere, he had experienced in his life but one great happiness—an idealistic passion for the brilliant, ardent woman he had married. At her death, which occurred when she still possessed all her powers of fascination, he thought himself despoiled of everything that made his life worth living. When told that his intense grief would wear away in time, he repulsed his comforters with the fury of a priest before a shrine to which some one has offered sacrilege. He was determined never to mourn her less intensely.

He was rich; he had no business; he lived a life of leisure. His mind was not adapted to profitable intellectual pursuits. His time was taken up with petty occupations. He was one of those persons for whom living has been made easy through inheritance, who never feel any positive incentive to achievement, who are content to spend a lifetime aimlessly, from time to time wondering at their ennui and discontent. Growing old, he fell into the melancholy ways of solitaries.

He travelled; he made elaborate collections of curiosities that might, perhaps, have been of use in museums; he accumulated rare books wherein the pages all remained uncut; he lined his walls with gloomy paintings that would have been appropriate in the chapels of cathedrals. But when he was on his travels the beauties and the gayeties about him roused in him no response. With a sombre countenance he looked at sunsets on Italian lakes, Swiss mountain peaks at dawn, the Paris boulevards in the golden dusk, Norwegian fjords by moonlight. Before each exquisite scene he forced himself to think: "If she were here!" In New York, amid his books and pictures, during the long evenings his thoughts were all introspective and regretful. Reviewing his unprofitable, lonely life, he told himself that its poor quality was traceable entirely to fate, which had deprived him of his wife. "If she had lived!" He asked himself unanswerable riddles: Why must we have sorrow? Why do we survive for years to mourn a loved one? Why do we attain happiness just for a moment—just long enough to realize its worth? Sometimes he exclaimed proudly: "Have I forgotten her? Have I ceased to mourn her? Am I like those people who get over grief?" His wife had furnished his life's one romance; and faithfully he kept fresh his sorrow at the loss of it, as if by so doing he were paying back in part a great debt that he owed her.

Monotony and solitary living made him, at last, morose, hypochondriacal, "peculiar." He found the world a poor place; he began to look forward curiously toward a future life, and wondered: "Shall I meet her there? How shall I find her?" He was drawn to investigate doctrines of immortality, was excited at the thought of "spiritistic phenomena," and finally fell into the hands of trance-mediums and those adroit magicians who, in a darkened room, seem to materialize the dead. His name, his secret thoughts and habits, the intimate details of his family history were drawn from him by clever charlatans, and passed about through that profession which preys on the grief of the bereaved. In "private séances" he seemed to see, emerging from the shadows of a cabinet, the vague simulacrum of his wife; sometimes he heard her speak; sometimes he touched her, kissed her, and then—his normal senses overwhelmed by emotion—believed that he recognized her face. She told him she was "waiting for him." At last he shut himself up the more; his world was a world of shadows—a place thronged with invisible presences; and when he went abroad he looked with impatience on the activities of healthy life, with which he no longer had anything in common. He had become an eccentric. His former associates told one another that his mind was diseased.

But all admitted that he had acted the part of a good father. He had given Felix "every advantage."

In childhood, Felix was a quiet boy, dreamy, full of imagination, fond of looking by the hour at pictures in old books, attracted by gentle scenes and beautiful ladies, responsive to affection, easily moved in respect of his emotions. As soon as he learned to read, into juvenile literature he plunged headlong. New worlds were revealed to him. In fancy he floated through nebulæ which took the uncertain, gorgeous forms of other lands and epochs. His solitary musings were then all of ancient Britons, of Carthaginians, of Aztecs, of peoples tattooed, painted, crowned with feathers, clothed in shaggy skins, encased in armor, following faithfully his own small figure through the fog of wild enterprises. Walking home from school, swinging his strapful of books, perhaps he was the King of the Incas, covered with gold ornaments, crested majestically with green plumes, passing judgment—in a hall of skulls—on some arch-enemy. "Away with him, to the tormentors!" Felix bumped into people on the street.

When he was fourteen years old he was sent to a big boarding-school in the country.

That was a rolling region. There patches of woodland, dim purple in the distance, were spread on the declivities of hills; there, in the valleys, were laid out fields of yellow, of rich green, of white, of terra-cotta color after ploughing time. The school buildings—all of red brick with blue slate roofs and gables—stood round a great grass circle. In the evening, when all the trees were motionless and seemed enveloped each in a separate, gauze-like haze, the sky would slowly turn from dusky blue to yellow. Down by the still lake, which lay beyond the foot-ball field, at that hour the swallows would come out, sailing and skimming here and there, low down, while uttering shrill cries which rang as if the sky were a hard dome of veritable amber. Sometimes the boys, returning from the tennis-courts, managed to strike down and kill a swallow or two with their racquets.

This placid lakeside was a favorite of Felix's. His dreams at that time, affected by his text-books, were based on models purely classical. In the flash of a window-pane on a remote hill-top, struck by the last rays of the sun, he saw the bright shields of the

Lacedemonians. At the rumbling of thunder he thought of Attic shepherds falling on their knees in fear of the sonorous voice of Jove. Gray brushwood smoke adrift above the valleys brought up before him scenes of ancient warfare—the pillage and the ruin of old cities. He was in the Wooden Horse when it was trundled into Troy; he led the sack; he was prodigious in a brass helmet crested with red horse-hair. And "Fair-cheeked Chryseis!" Now, in the background of every such sally of imagination hovered some fair-cheeked maiden observing all his feats of valor fondly.

Taunted by his school-mates for his dreaminess, in self-defence he plunged into their gay activities. The habit of excitement grew on him. He became of all the school the most ingenious in devising spectacular and humorous escapades. He furnished gayety for every one, and so became popular.

By his instructors he was thought precocious, talented, and promising. But he grew restless under continuous restraint, erratic in his moods, subject to all wandering impulses that took his fancy, apt to forget completely, in an access of nervous gayety, his duties. He learned, at length, barely enough to "scrape through" into college.

He went to live on a college campus—a tranquil place, full of great elms, of rambling white stone buildings, of winding flag-stone walks where undergraduates in odd head-gear strolled, pipe smoke above them, their arms over one another's shoulders. Every hour there was thrust through the silence the sound of a clear bell calling to lectures. In the evening the voices of young men, singing with a harmony of many parts, stole from afar across the grassy stretches with a clarity as if across still water. Later, one heard the confused, uneven songs of revellers returning home to bed.

One day a Freshman friend of Felix's proposed to him in the street:

"Let's have a drink."

They entered a café in the town. Felix concealed his curiosity, ashamed that he had never before been in such a place.

Along one side of the café ran a bar, behind which three pyramids of glasses were reflected in large mirrors. A man in his shirt-sleeves stood there talking to a rough-looking fellow who leaned across the rail, a glass of beer in his dirty hand. On the other side of the room one saw a row of wooden tables, their round tops marked with gummy spots and rings. There was sawdust on the floor. Against the plaster walls hung a pair of sun-bleached lithographs entitled "The Birth of Venus" and "Diana's Bath." The two Freshmen seated themselves at a table. A negro in a stained apron, wiping sweat from his brow, came shuffling to take their orders.

Felix resented the vulgarity of his surroundings. Why was it that the first step in certain new experiences brought disillusionment, dissatisfaction, and disgust?

"What will you have?"

The boy glanced furtively at the lounger by the bar.

"Beer," he said, with a careless air.

He raised his glass, buried his lips in foam, and took a long drink. He had an instant of intense surprise. Setting down his glass empty, he looked round thoughtfully.

"By George! You must be thirsty!"

Felix stared seriously at the other, without replying.

Some students passing by noticed the two emerge from the saloon. Departing arm in arm with his companion, Felix gave them a proud glance.

Neither youth confessed to the other that he had just learned something new.

Felix soon found his friends, the sons of rich parents, jolly, full of spirit, eager to try their wings. They lived in expensive style, drove automobiles breakneck along the country roads, went walking with a swarm of dogs about them, kept polo ponies, had liquor cases in their "studies" and actresses' pictures on their dressing-tables. Their evenings—when other, earnest-faced young men were making play with eye-shades and lexicons in private—they spent round smoky tables, where the crash of Rabelaisian choruses was emphasized by the clinking of pipe-stems on steins. Becoming sophisticated, finally they believed that they had little more to learn of "life." They grew to detest their work; and, with delightful feelings of irresponsibility and freedom, evaded, day after day, the tedious routine of lecture-rooms.

In the June of his fourth year, shortly before examination time, suddenly Felix realized that all

through his college course he had learned nothing
well. Sitting up every night till morning with his
books, he tried to do in two weeks the work of four
years. In the still hours, while he bent beneath the
lamp, all his past heedlessness—its charms grown
stale—recurred to him, amazed him, filled him with
remorse. Then recollecting himself, scanning his
text-books afresh, he was aghast at his inability to
grasp the meaning of whole chapters. He was
thrown into a panic. He went to his examination
hopeless. The examiners refused him a degree.

"Well, I've learned my lesson," Felix said to himself. He made resolutions. He came back the following fall, did all his last year's work again, and
finally was graduated among the young men whom,
in Sophomore year, he had "hazed."

One evening they sang their last song together,
sitting on the grass beneath tall elms, the shadowy
foliage of which was splashed here and there with
the soft light of Chinese lanterns. A silver loving-
cup went round; each, as he received it, stood up
and drank from it, while the rest sang to him. Tears
ran down their faces.

It was all finished. Felix went back to his rooms
and found them stripped: the walls bare, the pictures
in piles, the chairs full of ornaments and souvenirs,
in the midst of the litter a servant packing trunks.
What desolation! Returning to the campus, he wandered off to find some friends, dragging his feet, his
eyes wet. He had never felt so before. It seemed
to him that he was full of grief and experience.

Presently he found roaming about another sad young man—a poor student who had worked his way through college, who had never found time to make friends or to hunt pleasure, who had spent his four years in a small room with a bed, a wash-stand, a table, a coal-scuttle, a lamp, and a pile of second-hand books. In a café, where there was a dejected gathering of his friends, Felix presented himself with his arm across this young man's shoulder. He felt that to be a fine gesture; he was touched by the thought: "Sorrow, shared in common, levels all barriers."

Felix was sent round the world. He saw strange seas and lands. On shipboard he awoke, sometimes, to find blowing through the open port-holes air as extraordinarily flavored as if enveloping another world. He perceived across water for the first time, yet with the inexplicable thrill of an old traveller returning after many years, minarets, pagodas, a Chinese junk, spider-like Malay catamarans. He became enamoured of strange perfumes, antipodal music, women so fantastically charming that they seemed unreal.

In those surroundings precious thoughts came to him, lingered just long enough to enchant him, and then were crowded out of his brain by more. He longed to save them all, to perpetuate them, to move others with them. Beside old ruins—amid the desolate alleyways of Pompeii, in the red trenches of buried Carthage, before the colossi on the Nile at that fleeting moment when the setting sun, touching the desert hills, turns green—he was tormented because his ecstasies were inexpressible. Closing his eyes, he felt the past renewed about him. Pompeii was alive again, full of white togas and bright shawls: the ivory spokes of chariots flashed in the lanes; the gladiators showed their huge bodies and brutal heads along the promenades; delicate, black-haired women, with ear-rings dangling to their shoulders, went undulating under scarlet parasols; and at the street corners little, thin Greek girls blew plaintive tunes on flutes. He saw the tall pitch-covered palaces of Carthage risen afresh: the streets were full of camels, wild soldiers, and women in black robes with painted eyes; the images of gods, moving in procession, glittered above the heads of the barbaric crowd. The monuments beside the Nile were new and unscarred again, and in and out between the pillars of the temples stole the lean Egyptian priests, with flowers in their hands, the last of the sunlight flashing on their brown, shaven heads. Ah, to have such thoughts—which Felix considered very fine—and to be unable to disseminate them, to create with them in countless minds amazement, admiration, and respect! At last, on shipboard, he began struggling with pen and paper. But nothing looked the same on paper!

He was away a year, and came home "greatly broadened." He had received his education. What should now be done with him?

Sheridan Piers, rousing himself to interest, pondered this problem with Felix. They talked of a career in finance: it would be easy for the young man to obtain, through friends, an excellent position in Wall Street, with every chance of quick advancement. They discussed the advantages of law and of the diplomatic service.

"You see, you should do something, Felix," the old man said vaguely, winking his washed-out eyes in his perplexity. "Most everybody does. I haven't; but then they say that I'm 'peculiar.' And you know you don't take much after me."

They were, in fact, so far apart in temperament, that they had never possessed in common an important interest or understood each other. Sheridan Piers's uncongeniality and sadness chilled the boy and had their effect inevitably on the home. The house was characteristic of the man who lived shut up in it: a place furnished, with faded richness, in an unæsthetic fashion obsolete for two decades, filled with the souvenirs of a departing generation, exhaling the odors of old things, dim, chilly, full of echoes, lonely. Felix had seen so many bright and joyous regions that he was unable to have affection for his home or a desire to inhabit it.

"Perhaps," he said, "I'd do well in the diplomatic service." And he pictured himself in some foreign capital: at brilliant garden parties, balls, and state dinners, surrounded by beautiful and gracious women, courtly soldiers in fine uniforms, grave diplomatists expert in repartee and cynicism—in a world out of story-books, where everything was exhilarating, gay, sumptuous, remote from gloom.

They decided that he was to "take his time and

think it over." Felix, while doing so, enjoyed himself—laughed, played, spent money, fell in love, got
over that, glanced every day at some lesson of the
sort not taught in books. Sheridan Piers, for his
part, went on dreaming, regretting, thinking of his
wife. Beginning to grow feeble, he imagined that
he had all sorts of ailments. He complained of ver-
tigo, tremors, and roaring in the ears. He thought,
now and then, that he heard a voice calling him by
name. He commenced to read the Bible.

One day Joseph, an old servant who had been
with the family for thirty years, brought to his master
a little, rusty, tin box, which he had found while
rummaging an attic room. Sheridan Piers pried the
box open. It contained a heap of tarnished trinkets,
faded ribbons, dilapidated dance favors, newspaper
clippings, a sheaf of yellow letters. It was a collec-
tion of his wife's mementos.

A mist rose before the old man's eyes; at first he
could not bring himself to touch those objects which,
long ago, she had used, cherished, and packed away
with her own hands. After a while he drew from
the box a coral necklace and a crumbling flower.
Upon the brown leaf splashed a tear. Once she had
held that blossom in her fingers; that necklace had
been clasped about her throat. He remembered it,
and how she had looked while wearing it. His
memory of her was of a beautiful young woman,
fresh, radiant, redolent with a delicious sweetness.

Trembling with emotion, he began to read the
letters.

He did not know the handwriting. Each letter was signed simply with a "P." All were dated "Paris," where he and his wife had lived for several winters, where, at the death of his father in America, he had been forced to leave her for a few months. He remembered that year perfectly; it was the year of Felix's birth.

But whom were these letters from?

He read some sentences. Written in French, they were exquisitely worded. They spoke of love. He realized that he was reading the love-letters of some other man, addressed to her.

He stared before him, without breathing, his face disfigured by apprehension. For a minute his hands trembled so that he could not continue reading.

Presently, rousing himself to action, he arranged all the letters in order, according to their dates. The correspondence had extended over a period of two years!

He commenced with the first letter. Cold all over, he read deliberately page after page. He was terrified by the elegance, the charm of each succeeding period. He had a sensation of faintness at seeing here expressed for her, with passionate fluency, such thoughts as even he had never had.

The letters began with protestations, entreaties, accusations of "cruelty." But soon the anxious note in them gave place to an accent of assurance. Each page brought him nearer to the discovery he dreaded. Should he go on?

Soon he was reading of passed notes, kisses behind

curtains and in carriages, subtle machinations and deceits, finally clandestine meetings. After all the years, her feminine reluctance to destroy those sentimental treasures, her woman's yearning to keep by her all her dearest trophies had betrayed her.

He came to the letters that had been written while he was away. A terrible suspicion seized him.

Suffocating, he got up to raise a window. Suddenly he fell flat upon the floor, as if struck down with a club. Old Joseph found him there, lying amid the scattered letters.

To Sheridan Piers's bedside came quickly two dignified physicians. With the impassive countenances of those who see, every day, tortured bodies struggling between life and death, attentively they watched the patient. Lying on his back, unconscious, with half-opened eyes, slowly puffing out his cheeks, he expelled his breath. They raised his eyelids, listened to the beating of his heart, felt his arteries with their long, flexible fingers, tapped his knee-caps, lifted one by one his arms and legs and let them fall. They put their heads together and decided that he had suffered a stroke of apoplexy.

"Well, Doctor, what would you say?"

"A hemorrhage of the interior capsule, Doctor, but not a fatal one. We have this time merely a paralysis of the left arm, extending to and including the pectoralis major. We can, I think, at a conservative estimate, give him a month for a partial recovery. We shall have then considerable debility, feebleness of the affected parts, and perhaps—remembering the patient's well-known past oddity of conduct—an increased eccentricity. As for the second shock, when it comes, he may survive it. But of course a third would finish him."

They did everything necessary and departed.

When he recovered the use of his body, every one in the house observed that he was greatly changed. He would not see Felix; he spoke to none save Joseph; he sat alone in his room, huddled before the fireplace, staring at the flames. Every day he became more debilitated. The foundations of his existence had been struck from beneath him; he was crumbling to pieces.

He could not keep his hands off the letters. He reread them, crushed them, tore them, hurled them from him. Then, gathering them up, he smoothed them out and pieced them carefully together. Poring over them, with bated breath, he thought of his betrayal by the woman who had been for him a divinity, imagined the secrets of her life, pictured to himself all that she had lived through without his knowledge —with another. It was as if it had just happened, for he had just discovered it.

He perused the clippings that he had found with the letters. They revealed the history of the man; all his public activity was reported in them. Of everything he had done in those days she had treasured these accounts. How she must have loved him —this stranger!

At last, in a frenzy of hatred, he hurled the tin box and its contents into the fire. The letters and the clippings burst into flames; the trinkets glowed and melted among the coals; the tin box crackled and twisted on a bed of ashes. When all was consumed, how he desired to have it back again!

Sometimes he called out her name, over and over, in reproach, till old Joseph came running to him. Then he was apt to believe that she was living, that they were in Paris, that she was planning with her lover to deceive him. "Where are they to-night, Joseph? You must hunt for them. Let me tell you: you'll find them at a ball, in an alcove, behind some palms; or in the back of a box at the opera; or, if you hide on a street corner, you'll see them coming home in a closed carriage with the horses walking. You're to go up to the carriage window and whisper: 'Mr. Piers wants to speak to you.' That'll surprise them; don't you believe so? You know they think I'm very stupid."

Finally he got the idea that Felix was involved in their deceit and that he must outwit the three of them. How could he do it? He sat plotting by the hour, looking cautiously about him. He hit upon a plan.

He sent for a young broker who had been involved in some "shady" business in the past and of whom persons of integrity knew nothing edifying. Sheridan Piers received this man with a calm and plausible demeanor. He had attained the cunning of the demented.

"You see, Mr. Noon, I'm afraid I haven't long to live, and before I die I want to make considerable changes in the disposition of my property. If you undertake my affair, you'll find it a large one. But I shall have my work done very quietly. No gossiping. There are some, you know, who think a man has no right to do what he wants with his own money."

The broker, looking down, smiled deprecatingly.

Sheridan Piers sold all his outlying real estate. He disposed of all his stocks. He borrowed, quietly, as much money as would equal the value of his house, his stable, and their contents. Little by little, withdrawing his deposits from the banks, he accumulated his whole fortune in his house without any one knowing that he had it there. One evening he had a hot fire kindled in his room. He locked himself in and paid no attention when the whole household besought him to come out.

At midnight Felix sent for a physician.

They broke into the room. They found the old man standing, with a blank face, beside the fireplace, which was choked with ashes. He could not recognize anybody, and took his physician for the man who, twenty-five years before, had wronged him. At this hallucination he had another "stroke."

He died in a few hours. Before the end, to Felix, who bent over him, he whispered significantly:

"You're to look to them hereafter, d'you understand?"

He had destroyed his fortune, leaving nothing.

Felix, in distraction, rushed off to the family's lawyer.

When that gentleman appreciated the disaster, at once he took thought for his reputation. Malicious persons would say that he was to blame for not having long since deprived his client of power to transact his business. Looking at Felix thoughtfully, he asked the miserable young man:

"Who knows about this destruction of the property besides you?"

"Joseph."

"Ah, we can depend on him! Now, of course, it must go no farther—it's too shocking. We can't make the family name notorious with such an extraordinary tale. I'm your father's executor, and in his last will everything is left to you. You and I will appear to go over the estate together. We shall find that it was 'greatly overestimated'—you understand me? That will do for the present. A year from now there will be no public interest. That's the way to fix it!"

The lawyer, though not troubled ordinarily by conscience, felt some responsibility in this affair. He was just then on the point of setting out for a vacation in the woods. It occurred to him that it would be a generous act to take Felix along with him. Before he went he saw the house and its contents sold, to pay the debts that Sheridan Piers had contracted. When he and the boy set out, Felix had nothing left but fifteen hundred dollars, his balance at the bank.

In a fishing camp at the edge of a great forest, where the clear air was sweet with the odor of spruce-trees, where loons laughed in mid-lake and deer came down to drink and the cool nights were made beautiful by northern lights, finally the boy conquered his dismay. Plied with encouragement and good advice, he became almost philosophical. At twenty-five the greatest sorrows are not poignant for long, the greatest losses soon cease to seem irreparable. Youth, instead of repining, looks always forward. Felix turned his eyes toward the future.

He had decided what he was going to do. It seemed to him now that all through his life every inclination and predilection of his had been urging him toward one vocation. With feelings of calmness and of assurance, as if he had solved at last the meaning of all his spiritual cravings and emotions, he contemplated his career. He intended to become "a famous writer."

Late in the evening, when, on the luminous waters of the lake, islands and peninsulas seemed like mysterious, long shadows suspended in mid-air, Felix, looking with awe into the spangled sky, felt in himself illimitable possibilities. The solitude, the hush, the swimming vagueness of the lake, the solemnity of the bright heavens ennobled him. It was as if a strange soul, finer than his own, possessed him. For the moment, so ethereal were all his sensations that no heights seemed unattainable. Exalted by superb aspirations, he dreamed of the future, which appeared before him like a bright mist, glittering resplendently.

CHAPTER II

IT was toward the end of June when Felix got back to New York.

He found the place greatly changed. The streets that he had known from childhood all appeared strange to him; the faces of the people seemed selfish and unfriendly; his own city wore a cold, hostile aspect.

He felt at once great need of sympathy. The bluff encouragement, the slap on the back that he might expect from his friend the lawyer, and from other men, would be of no use to him. He pictured to himself the solace of a gentle woman's comprehension: the soft hand resting on his hair, the eyes so quick to fill with tears, the tender heart so ready to share sorrow. He might, he thought, unload much of his sadness upon some fond woman.

At his club—to which he went at once, with the intention of staying there till he contrived some definite scheme of living—he found waiting for him a letter. It was from a widow of sixty, a Mrs. Ferrol, who had gone to school with his mother and who had always been his friend.

Writing from her summer home in the country, she told Felix that she wanted him to come and visit her. "I can think of no better place than this for you to spend the next month or two; you need, just now, what we have here. The country is beautiful; the sun shines every day; and you will find here two women who are very fond of you."

She alluded to her daughter Nina, twenty-three years old, whom Felix had known all his life, and for whom he had, whenever he thought of her, the affection of a good brother.

He was touched by the letter. It offered him what he had just been longing for. He thought of how he would appear before them, changed by misfortune, rather a pathetic figure, and of how they would indulge him, divert him, humor with a thousand little tender wiles his gloominess. Two gentle women to console him, in beautiful surroundings!

He telegraphed to them that he was coming, and the same afternoon set out.

The Ferrol farm was in Westchester County. Felix rode for an hour on the railway; and Nina, bareheaded and tanned, met him at the station with a cart.

She was a brown-haired girl with a plump, vigorous shape. Her skin was fine; her cheeks were pink; her blue eyes were wide open, showing a good deal of the whites, which gave them an alert, frank expression. Her upper lip was lifted to a little point. She looked competent and self-reliant.

"Dear old boy!" she exclaimed in a full voice.

"This is very kind of you, Nina."

"Is it? Jump in. I want to show you this horse."

She drove swiftly through the village and out into
a country road.   The hills on either side were emer-
ald green.   The soft, blue sky was flecked with little,
brilliant clouds.   A breeze, perfumed with verdure
and wild flowers, blew in their faces.

Giving him a quick glance, she remarked:

"You're looking fairly well."

He sighed. Apparently she did not hear. She said:
"I'll let him out here."

The horse leaped forward.   Between his collar and
her hands the taut reins quivered.   The wind
whistled past.   Her loose hair, coming undone, blew
round her forehead and out behind her neck.   Her
face was calm; she wore a look of satisfaction.

In the fields farmers straightened themselves and
stared.   A boy on a plough-seat held himself motionless, his whip half raised.   All along the road, behind
the cart, a fog of saffron-colored dust hung trembling
in the air.

Ahead, on the top of a hill, appeared the house surrounded by tall trees, with terraces before it covered
with the white, purple, pink, and yellow bloom of
hardy shrubs.   Above tiers of flowering spiræa, lilacs,
azaleas, and jasmine bushes rose a long, solid-
looking building of three stories, flat-roofed, of red
brick trimmed with white stone in the Georgian
style.   Beyond it, to the right, showed through trees
the top of a windmill and the roofs of stables and
farm buildings.   A sound of many dogs barking
suddenly came down the breeze.

As the cart climbed the hill, in the mellow sunshine

of late afternoon the terraces displayed hues almost unnaturally gorgeous, the trees seemed powdered thick with ruddy gold-dust, the brick walls of the house were rose-colored; from the windows flashed a blinding, flame-like radiance. Above, the fleecy clouds, all motionless, were turning pink. And Felix saw, standing between the stone pillars of the doorway, shading her eyes with one hand, Nina's mother.

He thought: "It's almost like coming home." In fact, he reflected, it was better, for he had never come home to two kind women.

On the hill-top Felix began a tranquil, indolent existence. He told himself he was there taking leave of leisure, and he wished to enjoy that farewell lingeringly. Every morning when he awoke, leaning from his window he looked forth lazily, replete with placid satisfaction.

The house stood high. Below it, on all sides stretched out undulating vistas, vivid in sunlight, bluish in great spots beneath eclipsing clouds, fading at middle distance into a haze of old-gold summits and vague valleys touched with shades of golden green. Through that region, winding roads lay like yellow threads cast down at random; among the hills church spires of distant hamlets stuck up like needle points; and on the horizon sparkled the water of Long Island Sound, as tenuous and keen as a thin edge of steel.

The air of a new day drifted through the long, open windows of the breakfast-room. On the table the silver and the glassware glittered in the clear light;

a blue flame flickered underneath the coffee-pot; the flagrant red and yellow of nasturtiums in a crystal bowl epitomized, for Felix, the vigorous beauty of the morning. Seated at breakfast between the mother and the daughter, he had sensations of domesticity that softened him.

When, after breakfast, he made the rounds of the farm with Nina, the whole world seemed so freshly washed, so pure, that all his thoughts were simple, guileless, and immaculate. He felt full of kindly, innocent impulses. Looking about him—at the sunlight on the hills, the sky, the birds in flight—he thought, with a thrill of exaltation: "How beautiful the world is!" He appreciated everything. He shared with Nina all her enthusiasms.

In the stables, which smelled of clean straw and ammonia, he caught her affection for the horses, her pride in their fineness, her anxiety when any one of them fell ill. In the barn-yard he counted eggs with her; they drove a brood of fledglings to and fro, to see them scamper; they laughed together at the haughty airs of old roosters. In the kennels, where white bull-terriers came rushing forth with yelps and whines of welcome, he was pleased at the fondness that so many dumb things showed for him. Nina gave him a five months' old puppy, whose parents had both won ribbons at "bench shows." Felix named the dog Pat, and taught him to fetch, lie down, go home, and heel. The little, shambling beast followed his new master everywhere, howled outside closed windows, scratched the sills, brought in dead birds that he had found in the fields, frisked through the flowers, hid bones among the roses, had to be cuffed every hour.

In the garden enclosed by trellises, its plats defined by narrow gravel paths, Felix lounged on a bench with a book while Nina tended rows of blossoms. The rose-stems drooped with the weight of full-blown petals, on the smooth surfaces of which lay little drops —like tears, as Felix thought, on satiny cheeks. The daisies made him think of simplicity—of young girls in white dresses. Mignonette exhaled a dainty, languorous redolence; he imagined, while smelling it, moonlit balconies covered with pale flowers to which dark chamber windows opened. But the forced tuberoses, with their excessive, almost corporeal sweetness, suggested, to his amazement, the intoxication of a long embrace. He looked at Nina. She was stooping, with scissors and a wicker basket, before the flower borders. Her back was toward him. The thin stuff of her dull-blue dress was stretched across her shoulders; about her, on the gravel, her full skirt belled out. Felix, watching her, was lost in curiosity. Had she, too, sometime believed herself in love? What sentimental experiences did she remember? These questions Felix found peculiarly engrossing.

She had a fine figure, but feared that she was growing stout. To avoid that she had got made an India-rubber coat, skin-tight, which she put on underneath her clothes when she went riding. She weighed herself every morning, examined her shape in mirrors

with anxiety, and was in the habit of asking Felix over
her shoulder, while smoothing down her skirt about
her hips:

"Do you think I've taken any off to-day?"

Every day they rode abroad through the country
lanes, searching out unfrequented ways where sumac
bushes hung in wild tangles over the edges of the
gullies and the road-bed was soft for galloping.

She rode astride, in a gray skirt and a white waist,
with stained gloves on her hands, bareheaded, ruddy,
alert.

"Come on, Felix!"

They went at full speed to a swift thudding of
hoofs and a patter of flying pebbles. Protruding
twigs tore at their shoulders; they lowered their
heads sharply to escape branches of outgrowing saplings; knee to knee in the narrow road, each strove to
pass the other. They forgot everything but the rushing of the wind, the cadence of the gallop, the spasmodic plunges of the beasts beneath them. At sharp
corners, seized suddenly with apprehension when it
was too late to pull up, they shouted frantically:

"Look out ahead!"

Sometimes, after a long ride, they would walk their
horses all the way home. They talked of themselves,
of their ideas, perhaps of their impressions got from
the books which they had read the night before, of
what they liked and disliked, of the things that
affected them the most. And their conversations
would be interrupted, now and then, by such exclamations as: "Has that occurred to you, too?" "You

feel that way also?" "Imagine your having thought of that!" "Then you can understand me when I say . . ." Finishing their discussions, riding on in silence, they would feel a peculiar contentment, tinctured with surprise, at being able to express their thoughts so clearly to each other.

Where old stone boundary walls beside the road were masked with honeysuckle they heard the wild bees droning. Where, at the entrances of little woods, the tree tops came together overhead, passing into spaces of cool shadows, they smelled moist moss and loam, and listened, with upturned faces, to the unexpected, capricious melody of birds. Occasionally, while climbing their own hill, they were surprised to discover high in the fading blue the pallid outline of the moon, almost invisible. They turned, on the ascent, to gaze back at the purple shadows lying in the valleys, the obscuration of the east, the first lamplight twinkling in some cottage window. For them there was a subtle charm in coming safely home at nightfall.

One evening when, tired, happy, full of tranquillity, they reached the summit of the hill, they saw standing before the house an automobile. A visitor had arrived! They found him sitting with Mrs. Ferrol in the dusky library. He rose—a tall, thin shape— and took a step forward. A quiet voice said:

"Nina?"

She gave a start.

It was an old admirer of Nina's who had been travelling in Europe for his health. Landing unexpectedly that morning in New York, he had just got back to his father's summer home, which lay some fifteen miles away across the hills.

His name was Denis Droyt. He was a sedate young man, rather old for his age, of steady habits, always full of that serene assurance which comes from contemplation of such assets as a secure place in good society and an impregnable fortune. When in New York, he occupied a position in his father's bank. By matrons he was called a "very sensible young man"; young girls, with vague expressions, admitted that "one must respect him," and brothers described him to marriageable sisters as a "good risk."

In the library the lamps were lighted: the new-comer was revealed. His narrow skull was becoming prematurely bald on top; the scalp showed slightly through short yellow hair as downy as a baby's. He had small gray eyes, an aquiline nose, a long chin. His features were expressionless. Pale and thin, he seemed far from robust, though he assured his friends that he had entirely recovered from the nervousness on account of which he had been travelling.

He was sitting in what Nina reminded him was "his old chair." Mrs. Ferrol, while making him a cup of tea, remembered that he liked two lumps of sugar. Nina, getting him cigarettes, asked him if he still smoked that kind. Felix sat staring at him with a feeling of resentment. The fellow certainly looked very much at home!

Nina and her mother expressed delight at seeing him. So he was going to live for a while in the country—right across the way, if one considered automobiles! They would be neighbors again. How pleasant, especially for Felix, who "must be getting tired of women." The eyes of the two young men met; and Denis Droyt murmured a sympathetic phrase regarding Felix's bereavement.

"A friend of ours wrote me about it, and said you had come out here. By a lucky chance I happened to get the letter just before I left the other side."

He stayed for dinner. Sitting in the place that Felix usually occupied, he entertained the ladies with stories of his journeyings. Warmed by their flattering attention and enthusiasm, little by little he expanded in his manner; he blossomed into the traditional voyager from afar, the spinner of tales, the weaver of enchantments. To Felix he seemed like that "universal witness" who is always on hand when anything sensational occurs. Had they read in the papers a certain bit of foreign news? He was there; he had the right of it. At the German yacht races he had seen a royal sloop in collision; he had watched a mob burn the betting booths at Longchamps; he had happened to be on hand when a poor, ruined gambler at Monte Carlo jumped from a bridge and dashed himself to pieces on the rocks.

"Weren't you horrified?" ejaculated Nina, gazing at him fascinated. Looking very cool and brave, he answered:

"Why, not at all. Perhaps it was the moon, the strange scenery, and everything that made it seem quite like a play."

Felix could hardly repress a gesture of irritation. What tales he could have related—of China, of India, of Arabia! He felt a great contempt for people who retail with gusto the same old stories that every excursionist has told. He said, indifferently:

"Some one kills himself at Monte Carlo every day."

In the morning, when he awoke, Felix asked himself at once: "What unpleasant thing has happened?" And he remembered Denis Droyt. Why the devil had he turned up here? Now he would be hanging round all the time: everything would be different. The farm already seemed less homelike.

In fact, that was the beginning of a new order of living on the hill.

Every day, if Droyt did not appear in the morning, at least he telephoned to make plans for the afternoon. Sometimes a note from him awaited Nina at the breakfast-table. A groom rode over from his house with fruit grown under glass, and orchids. He sent her a Virginia hunter to try—one could not enter the stable without seeing the beast's bony head sticking over the top of a box-stall. Candy from Droyt always lay on the library table. And every morning, when she awoke in her white bed, Nina's eyes fell on a writing set of silver that he had bought for her in Paris. When he was absent, by a thousand such artifices he recalled constantly to her the thought of him. His intentions were obvious to every one. Immediately on his home-coming he had plunged into courtship with tremendous energy.

As for Nina, her eyes grew brighter, her demeanor more alert; she even looked at Felix with a sort of suppressed curiosity and eagerness—she was, as one might say, "on edge." It seemed that in person she expanded delicately, took on beauty, became radiant with swifter blood. She was like a rose unfolding. Felix, perceiving the change in her, said to himself at last, in amazement: "She is in love with him!"

At once he felt like an outsider, an intruder. That night, after dinner, he told Nina he was going back to town.

They were standing together at an open French window in the library, looking across the terraces and out into the darkness. She had on a low-neck dress, sky blue in color, fastened over her shoulders with two narrow bands of blue velvet. Her hair was wound round her head in thick braids, like a fillet. She wore a turquoise necklace and some finger rings. Droyt was expected for the evening; in fact, Nina and Felix, while standing at the window, were listening for the sound of his automobile.

For a moment she made no reply to Felix's announcement. She drummed with her fingers on the wood-work; then she said:

"Let's walk outside."

They went out on the terrace. Turning the corner of the house, they were enveloped in the shadows.

The world seemed swimming in obscurity; the stars, as if all withdrawn to the very limits of the firmament, were hardly visible. From the damp earth rose a delicious exhalation—that cool, sweet breath of night in summer which rouses in the heart tremulous emotions too delicate for comprehension; a longing for unknown ecstasies, desires that one can give no name to.

She slipped her arm through his, "in order not to stumble"; leaning against him gently, she kept pace with him. As they strolled slowly through the darkness, stopping now and then to look round them, the warmth of her bare shoulder penetrated the thin cloth of his sleeve, and from her hair and skin emanated an odor of powder and sachet. This intimate fragrance, this contact in the gloom, caused him to think: "If I were only walking so with some one whom I loved—who loved me!" What profit would he not find, then, in this beautiful night, mute, veiled, mysterious, made for lovers! He felt lonely, neglected, isolated. A profound melancholy descended upon him.

She, for her part, appeared changed: her natural exuberance was subdued, all her habitual vigor had melted into tender weakness—she had become clinging, meek, entirely feminine. It seemed that everything which she perceived to-night was fraught for her with romantic meaning. She could turn no phrase, about the stars, the obscurity, the enfolding hush, without a sentimental intonation. Looking at the sky, she quoted, with a sigh:

> " There we heard the breath among the grasses . . .
> Well contented with the spacious starlight,
> The cool wind's touch, and the deep blue distance,
> Till the dawn came in with golden sandals. "

"She is thinking of him," he thought. And perceiving something indelicate in that revealment, he was half angry with her. He imagined that, leaning against him with closed eyes, she was trying to make herself believe he was the other. He said, shortly:

"I don't know much about sandals for this sort of wear, but if you stand round in the grass in those blue slippers you'll get your feet wet."

She withdrew her arm. Returning to the path, they found themselves before the trellises which formed the boundaries of the garden. They entered there; she wanted to sit down among the flowers. Felix wiped a bench dry with his handkerchief. Leaning back on it, side by side, they smelled the tuberoses. She remarked, dreamily:

"How sweet they are!"

Again their heavy fragrance, rising about him, made Felix think of the intoxication of a long embrace. He lighted a cigarette, and the aroma of wet blossoms was adulterated with tobacco smoke.

The burning tip of the cigarette cast over Nina a vague glow. Her necklace, all its gold settings twinkling, gave her an unusual air of dainty artificiality. Her blue dress, with its smooth silk shimmering, made her look unnaturally slender, sleek, and elegant. And the arrangement of her hair—which to-night was dressed with exceptional fastidiousness—seemed to complete the enrichment of her whole appearance. As he looked at her, Felix felt a growing astonishment and a new respect for her. She was almost like a beautiful stranger whom he saw now for the first time. He was amazed that he had never before realized her worth. He was like a person who, every day through a lifetime, has passed by some familiar object without noticing its charm, and who may be roused to appreciation only by a combination of extraordinary influences.

She had said something, but he had not heard her; and she was forced to repeat:

"Felix, I tell you I want your advice."

"Ah. Very well."

"Shall I marry Denis?"

He was silent. At last he retorted:

"Why should you ask me that?"

"Because I'm not in love with him."

He was amazed—then, of a sudden, elated. He exclaimed, in a hearty tone:

"Well, then, don't marry him!"

"But I must marry some one."

"Marry a man you're in love with."

She drew a long breath, clasped her hands in her lap, and asked:

"Will you marry me?"

With his cigarette half-way to his mouth, he sat as if thunderstruck. She continued, in a voice that trembled slightly:

"I know how that must sound. But I don't care. I won't let you go back to town without hearing it. I wish you could have said it. But you didn't; so I have to.

"You're not in love with me, but at least I know you're fond of me. I'd be satisfied with that. I'd be happy if I could be sure of having, all my life, just your sort of affection, full of sympathy.

"We know each other so well that I believe we'd never have to fear any disillusionment. Just as you know all my faults now, I know all yours; but I know all your virtues and possibilities as well. I think I know your possibilities better than you do yourself. I'm so afraid, sometimes, that you won't realize them fully. To think what you could do and might miss doing! I want to see you famous some day—a great man, honored and respected everywhere for what you've done. Oh, my dear, if I could be with you then, and know that I had helped you! No one would ever be able to say to me that a woman can do nothing."

And as she expressed that thought her eyes shone through the gloom with the intense desire of an aspiring nature to break the chains of a subjective sex, to take part in great performances—to be in some degree responsible for them.

He was dazed; he could not believe it. She loved him; she wanted to marry him; she offered herself to him! She, in whom just this evening he had discovered a personal seductiveness, was pleading to become his wife! And in imagining the worth of all she tendered him in proffering herself, he was unable to avoid thinking also of the fortune that went with her.

He saw himself, in a future transformed and enriched, living without apprehension, assured of everything. Some day the farm would be his, and the

house in town, and a fine income—a larger income
than he would have possessed if he had not lost his
inheritance. Nothing was impossible. They would
live at home in any way they pleased; tiring of that,
they would travel; no corner of the earth would be
too remote for them; he even thought of a great
yacht sailing into every sea. A part of each year
they might spend abroad, occupying in gay capitals their own hotel, the sort of hotel he knew of—a
historic mansion full of splendid memories, built of
gray stone carved like lace-work, with gables and
tourelles and noble chimneys, and a great entrance
doorway where a servant, in white stockings and a
laced coat, leaned against the jamb. Or they might
have a villa somewhere beside the blue sea, but no
ordinary villa. He had seen one, rose-colored, like
a little castle, smothered in orange-trees and ilex-
trees, enclosed in labyrinthine gardens; he thought
that he could work there. For, relieved of all anxiety, how he would work! Every one would marvel
at him—a rich man gaining so brilliant a name,
rising so high, when he might have done nothing but
enjoy himself. People passing by his house would
look up at the windows. They would point him out
in public places where, modestly ignoring the attention he excited, he would shine, despite himself, with
the combined lustre of genius and of wealth. He sat
motionless, dazzled by his thoughts.

But suddenly his dreams disintegrated. An apprehension seized him; was he, indeed, only dreaming? He dropped his cigarette, which had gone out.

He peered through the darkness at Nina. She seemed so nearly impalpable that, reaching out his hand, he touched her arm.

"Is it so hard to decide?"

She spoke as timidly as if she were offering him nothing.

"How much she must care for me!"

The thought touched him to the heart. He promised himself that he would do everything for her. For all that she would bring to him he would repay her by making her proud of him.

When he kissed her he had a soft shock of surprise; the novelty of that embrace set him to trembling. In the shadows, among the tuberoses, she had suddenly become desirable to him for many reasons. He had no difficulty in repeating, over and over, with an accent of passion:

"I love you! I love you!"

"Oh, do you, Felix?" And, putting her head upon his shoulder, she sobbed as if broken-hearted in her gratitude.

It was the clatter of Denis Droyt's automobile that recalled them to reality. Returning to the house they met the visitor before the door.

When Nina informed him that she was going to marry Felix he turned pale. A ghastly smile of politeness appeared upon his face. He shook hands with both of them, re-entered his automobile, and departed. He had not uttered a word.

"Poor Denis!" exclaimed Nina. Felix made no reply; he was occupied with something more important than commiseration.   What was Mrs. Ferrol going to say?

They found Mrs. Ferrol in the library.   Dressed in black, she was sitting beside a shaded reading-lamp, which illumined with a soft glow her small, pale face and her gray hair, arranged in precise waves upon her temples.   Putting down her book, she looked at the two young people with a gentle smile.   She said:

"I was hoping so.   I'm very glad, my dears.   Ah, if your mother were here now, Felix!"

His eyes filled with tears.   How everything came to him all of a sudden: good fortune, love, and the affection of a mother!   What had he ever done to deserve such kindness and benevolence?

"How can I thank you?" he stammered.

"By making Nina happy," she replied, and dried her eyes.

That night Felix could not sleep.   He rose from his bed, went to the window, and gazed out.   The world, he thought, had never looked so beautiful.

The moon had risen, the color of the heavens had changed—no longer black, it was that serious, noble blue which lies in the depths of sapphires.   Across the sky were spread long, trailing clouds, scarf-like, and sewn with pallid stars.   In that radiance the garden underneath the windows was revealed, its gravel pathways gleaming white, its flower beds furnished with unnatural, vague hues.   The tall trees roundabout seemed to be wrapped in silver veils; beyond them the hill-tops were repeated like the majestic, moonlit billows of some ocean of enchantment, until they were lost, on the horizon, in the shimmering waters of the sound. All things appeared strange, unstable, mystic—as if drawing, down the moonbeams, beauty from some lovelier world. Flowers blossom in sunshine, hearts in moonlight. It was the hour for transports of the soul.

The limpid rays shone down into his eyes; the breeze, approaching from afar to a pervasive sighing sound, caressed his body. It seemed to him that Nature touched him with tender, reassuring hands. A great peace filled his heart: he had never known a like emotion—that all was well with him; that a supreme power, the same which held the stars in place, had taken care and would thereafter, if he chose, take care of him. Looking up at the heavens, he was possessed with the confidence of such as, gazing in the night toward those vast, ordered spaces, come to imagine clearly a divine benevolence in whose existence and persistence they can trust.

Presently he felt tears rolling down his cheeks. How good, how valuable life was; how dazzling its promises; how sure, at that moment, its triumphant consummation! He would have liked to formulate a prayer of gratitude.

But, since the impulses of youth are rarely devotional, the desire for prayer, when it comes at last, finds one awkward—as if one were struggling to speak in a strange tongue.

Finally, however, he achieved, at least:

"I'll pay it back!"

And he pictured his lifetime nobly spent in that requital.

CHAPTER III

As soon as his engagement to Nina was made public, Felix felt that he could bear no more idleness; he wanted to prove at once, to every one, that he was worthy of his good fortune. So he said good-by to Nina and her mother, full of ambition and optimism, like a young knight about to plunge forth into the unknown to find the Holy Grail. He was going back to the city, to begin, to make his way, to become famous.

As for the two women, looking at his bright eyes and inspirited countenance, observing the new assurance of his presence, they considered fame as good as in his grasp. For them, in that moment, he was the young adventurer of all the ages, the hero setting out from among idolizing women to win the world.

Nina drove him to the railway station. She shed a few tears on the way, but when, as the train was beginning to glide forward, Felix leaned out through the open window of the car, her upturned, earnest eyes shone clearly.

"You'll telephone to me every morning, Felix?"

"Every morning; and write, too. Good-by, dear."

"Not good-by, Felix!"

"No, no; that's right. Not good-by."

The train rushed toward New York.

The fields, blond with ripening grain, flowed past. Acres of cabbages appeared, dull green, their long rows, swiftly changing in perspective, suggestive of rotating spokes in some vast wheel. Strips of woodland burst out upon the landscape, closed in against the track, tired the eye with a fluttering repetition of tree trunks, then vanished suddenly, exposing open country. Rail fences straggled by as if alive; a herd of dark-red cows were grazing in a pasture which appeared to be revolving slowly under them; a dust-colored man was tramping toward a dilapidated barn that had the look of moving forward at him. A town presented itself in an instant, then melted into a blur of brick sheds. The earth fell away; the train rattled over trestles; far below one glimpsed a peaceful stream, undulating among willow-trees, upon its banks a group of naked little boys who, while they stood up and waved their arms, were whisked out of sight. Into large meadows came sailing lines of boarding covered with gaudy advertisements. The sky-line faded from soft green to drab; smoke obscured the horizon, and beneath it spires, towers, chimneys, and high walls showed themselves above a confusion of vague roofs. The fields melted; houses were clustered everywhere; one saw a row of dwellings all made from the same pattern—then a dozen rows, and paved streets with lamp-posts. The buildings were transformed from wood to brick; flat-houses fled by close beside the train; between them white mists, of drying undergarments, flashed for a second. The interiors of shabby homes were revealed as if in a blaze of lightning, and one remembered, when far past, the woman above her stove, the children at a table, the man in a red undershirt, the tousled bed. Factories loomed up; behind their windows men were moving to and fro amid machinery; girls were sitting in long rows, their hands all fluttering; steam was escaping over the roofs; drays were crowding the streets. The successive vistas, compressed, confused, bewildering because of the variety of activities they revealed, seemed reduced, finally, to one long blur in monotone epitomizing work.

While the train sped forward into New York, Felix felt closing round him an atmosphere surcharged with energy. He was affected by it. He felt so strong, so capable, so sure of himself, that already he could see the great city offering him homage.

He went at once to the office of the lawyer who had taken him into the woods. Entering a "sky-scraper" in Broad Street, he ascended in an elevator to the thirteenth floor. In an antechamber, carpeted with green Wilton, a youth disappeared with his card behind a door, on the ground-glass panel of which was painted: "Mr. Wickit." The door burst open, disclosing a room full of mahogany office furniture, law-books bound in yellow leather, black tin boxes; out strode Felix's friend, lean, gray-haired, sharp-featured, smiling, both hands extended.

"My dear boy, my congratulations." And when they were in the private office Mr. Wickit added, with a knowing and admiring expression: "To think that I'd lost patience with you for wasting time out there!"

They sat down for a chat. Felix resented Mr. Wickit's attitude; from it one would have thought that they enjoyed a secret understanding. The lawyer apparently believed that Felix had deliberately gone out fortune-hunting and brought down a fine prize. And Felix, with a sinking sensation at his heart, reflected: "Just now it would be impossible to convince him, or any one else, otherwise. How maliciously unfair people are!" He was filled with righteous indignation at that thought. He said, somewhat stiffly:

"I came to ask you for some advice before setting in to work."

"Certainly," returned the lawyer, smoothing his face into an expression of concern. "You're more determined than ever now, I suppose; you don't intend to occupy an equivocal position, eh? Of course not. That does you credit; but I knew it would occur to you. Well, what did you think of doing?"

"I'm going to write."

"You persist in that idea?"

Mr. Wickit looked serious. Finally he said:

"Recently I met Oliver Corquill, the novelist. I talked to him about you and the intentions you had when we were in the woods. He told me some things you ought to know before you rush into that profession. We'll lunch with him to-day, if you're at liberty."

"At liberty—to meet Oliver Corquill?"

To make that acquaintance Felix would have been at liberty if he had contracted a conflicting engagement even with Nina.

Oliver Corquill, still spoken of as a young man, was one of those fortunate writers who are able to produce, every year or so, a novel of the sort called, in publishers' parlance, a "best seller." So accurately had he gauged the appetite of the reading public, that for the mental refreshment he provided there was a continual demand. And so adroitly did he conceal beneath the surface in his tales an admirable art, that professional critics united in acclaiming him. In consequence he enjoyed both fame and fortune.

Felix and Mr. Wickit, dashing uptown in an electric hansom, met him in a club-house near Fifth Avenue. The novelist was a quiet-looking man at whom Felix ordinarily would not have glanced twice. His smooth-shaven face was prosaic and illegible; his clothes were unobtrusive; his hair was very short; his whole aspect suggested that he had just stepped out of a business office. Nevertheless, for Felix everything about him possessed a peculiar distinction. The young man thought the face of the celebrity remarkable, was impressed by his manner, wondered what romance was connected with the scarab pin in his cravat, noticed that his collar had pointed tips instead of round, and, when Corquill opened his mouth, listened with feelings of respect and modesty. He could not help looking round the club restaurant to see if others observed the company that he was in.

At the table, Mr. Wickit, with a genial grin, said:
"This is the young man, Mr. Corquill, who wants
to be a writer. I wish you'd discourage him for me."

"I almost wish I could," answered Corquill, gazing
at Felix with a kindly smile that changed his face as
if a mellow light had suddenly been thrown upon it.
Then, in reply to the look that expressed Felix's
amazement, he explained:

"I say that because I'm afraid you'd go into this
business with the popular idea of it.

"Nearly every one with a good education and
some imagination has thought that he could scratch
off at least a story. Very many persons are seduced
by this belief into contemplating a career in literature.
Men who have failed in other professions, lonely
ladies, young girls brimming over with indefinite
cravings, young men who desire to entrance every
one with the thoughts that seem to them entrancing,
all say to themselves: 'At least, I can write a book.'
How do they set about it? They sit down at a desk,
prepare some paper, take up a pen, and begin."

"Of course," thought Felix.

Corquill continued, with increasing animation:

"They have begun with the popular idea: that
literature is, of all the arts, the one in which any
novice can surpass at once. Does a young girl, after
walking through the Metropolitan Gallery, go home
and set up a great canvas, expecting to paint a
picture in the style of Rosa Bonheur? Does a young
man, on finishing an inspection of the Elgin Marbles,
rush off and buy a block of stone, convinced that he

can carve a Theseus in the manner of Phidias? I think not. But the tyro, who sits down at his desk and says: 'Now I shall write a book,' expects to astound every one immediately with his genius.

"What is the result with him? Confusion, irritation, anguish at his impotence—he's lucky if he doesn't think of suicide. Ah, my dear young man, what agonies and incoherent, vain hopes are wrapped up in the first manuscripts of these poor people! It's true that now and then such things get printed; but just as we have enough chromos in the world already, and enough *papier-maché* statuary, so we have already enough books made by the misguided souls who are not writing, but merely practising at writing.

"Now, if a young man came to me and said: 'I want to become a writer,' I should reply to him: 'I presuppose that you have thoughts worth recounting, so I pass that point by. But are you very patient? Are you very industrious? Can you bear disappointments, discouragements, defeats? Have you an inflexible determination? Then, if you are so equipped, this is what I should advise you to do: Study every day text-books of literature and the works of great writers. Shut yourself in; write; tear up; write; tear up; keep nothing—everything you do is worthless. Get a position on the best newspaper in the country—say, *The Sphere*—and when you have had a million words of yours printed in its columns, then write your first book, bring it to me, and I'll tell you whether you will ever amount to anything.' "

Felix sat silent.

Oliver Corquill, watching him, concluded with a frank laugh:

"This discourse is intended for a serious young man with high ideals."

Felix drew a long breath.

"Thank you," he said, in a low voice.

The novelist, with a polite gesture, promptly banished the animation from his face, resumed his illegible expression, and went on eating without another word.

After luncheon, when Felix and Mr. Wickit, in the lobby of the club-house, had said good-by to Corquill, the lawyer asked his young friend:

"Are you still determined?"

"Perhaps more so. Now I'm going down to the editor of *The Sphere* to ask him for a job. If he'll let me, I'll begin to-morrow morning." As he said that, Felix could not help feeling proud of himself.

Mr. Wickit, after a moment's thought, shrugged his shoulders. With a quizzical expression he returned:

"After all, what's the difference? In a year's time— By the way, is this engagement of yours and Miss Ferrol's going to be a long one? If I remember, you have less than fifteen hundred dollars in the bank?"

Mr. Wickit closed his eyes, tapped his teeth, then sat down at a writing-desk near by. In a moment he held out to Felix a freshly blotted check. It was for one thousand dollars.

"Pay it back later." And the lawyer, smiling

shrewdly at the boy, looked, with his lean, yellow face wrinkled round the mouth, somewhat like a benevolent old bandit.

Felix was overwhelmed. "How I've misjudged him," he thought remorsefully. He was unable to express his thanks to Mr. Wickit—all of whose cynical insinuations were excused instantly—in whom Felix, at this princely generosity, could perceive only the most praiseworthy qualities. A thousand dollars! That sum, which a few months before would not have seemed at all remarkable to Felix, appeared now like a little fortune. When he set out for the office of *The Sphere*, from time to time he patted the wallet in his breast pocket, to assure himself that it was safe. When he touched it he was fortified; that contact with money imparted even to his body an exceptional vigor; and he approached his destination with the independent bearing of a man who, instead of asking favors anxiously, demands them.

The Sphere, a daily newspaper noted for its literary brilliancy, was published in a little, old building of discolored brick, which, shabby and insignificant amid modern "sky-scrapers," faced westward on the City Hall Park. Delivery wagons and trucks laden with great rolls of paper blocked the street before it; about its doors swarmed newsboys; and on the narrow pavement pedestrians hurried by, jostling, in two interminable streams.

Felix entered the office on the ground-floor, where, behind a long counter opposite the door, young men were folding newspapers.

"Where can I find the editor?"

"Two flights!" The youth whom Felix questioned jerked his head toward a wooden staircase on the left.

From the second story, where he saw nothing but rough partitions and closed doors, Felix mounted by a flight of spiral iron steps that ran up through a gloomy shaft. He smelled dust, steam, hot metal. A persistent, heavy rumbling seemed to make the whole building tremble. Suddenly, close beside him, downward dropped a freight elevator laden with men in grimy undershirts. He was next startled by the shrill scream of a circular saw, and, looking below, through the interstices of the staircase he perceived, as if at the bottom of a well, a confusion of machinery, fires, caldrons of molten metal, half-naked figures glistening with sweat. People began to climb behind him; he pressed on. A boy with a handful of papers, clattering down the steps, collided with him. Three men, descending, waited impatiently for him to pass. Finally, he emerged into a large room floored with iron plates. Youths in leather aprons were rolling ponderous, table-like objects back and forth or running about with steaming mats of felt. Beyond these a swarm of men were engaged in various peculiar performances. To the left, some, with armfuls of metal spools, were walking between lines of small, racketing machines. To the right, others, wearing eye-shades, were standing before type-cases. Ahead, some distance off, among a huddle of desks, in a fog of tobacco smoke, reporters in their shirt-sleeves were writing, calling out to one another, waving above their heads large sheets of paper, which boys snatched from their hands and scurried off with.

Felix, approaching the reporters' desks, stared about him blankly. Nothing was as he had expected. He was bewildered by the strangeness of everything he saw, and the confusion. With a momentary sensation of timidity, he wondered if, in coming there, he had not made a mistake. He felt that he was doing something exceedingly fantastic.

He attracted the attention of a young man who seemed to be unoccupied. This person had his shirt-sleeves rolled up, wore on the back of his head a black felt hat, and was puffing at a disreputable-looking corn-cob pipe.

"I'd like to see the editor," ventured Felix.

"You'd better wait; an edition is going to press now."

"In the afternoon?" Felix exclaimed.

"Ah, I think you've made a mistake. This is *The Evening Sphere* office. *The Morning Sphere* is on the floor below. The two staffs are quite independent of each other."

"What's the difference between them?"

"They publish at midnight; we publish four times during the day. Their hours are from noon till almost any time; ours are from eight in the morning until four."

"Indeed," said Felix, with a more nearly satisfied expression. "Then this is the editor I'm after!"

He found the editor of *The Evening Sphere* in a

box-like compartment somewhat larger than a cupboard, at a disordered desk, knee-deep in crumpled papers, in his shirt-sleeves, smoking a cigar. The journalist was small and delicate, with a gentle face and a cautious manner.

"Mr. Piers?"

"Yes, sir."

"Take a seat if you can."

When Felix had explained his wishes—which he did a little as a church-goer repeats a creed the worth of which he is beginning to doubt—at once the editor looked sad and tired. The newspaper's staff was complete; besides, there was a long "waiting list"; the managers even thought of getting rid of a reporter or two—they had so many; and so on. Felix, rising, without feeling much downcast, prepared to take prompt leave.

"Wait a minute. I've not finished," the editor said, staring at him.

Beginners were a speculation, pure and simple. After careful training they might be of some use—again, they might not. At any rate, Felix was to understand, they were not worth much to a newspaper. "A beginner," gently remarked the editor, "would surely not be worth more than fifteen dollars a week." And he glanced speculatively at Felix, who happened to be wearing a suit of dark-gray English flannel, silk shirt and stockings, chamois-skin gloves, and a fine pearl in his cravat.

Felix, for his part, had conflicting thoughts. While fifteen dollars a week did not at once seem to him small earnings, since he had never earned a penny, he felt an impulse to appear indifferent on that point. He took out a cigarette, in order to exhibit as if casually his gold cigarette-case; he even wished that in some apparently accidental way he could manage to display the thousand-dollar check.

The editor inquired, abruptly:

"Mr. Piers, are you doing this on a bet or for a whim?"

"I'm doing it because I want to learn to write good English."

"That's your object? Well, I will give you fifteen dollars a week. Can you begin at once?"

"Why, thank you, yes."

"Go outside, sir, and sit down."

Felix was a reporter. It did not occur to him to be elated or surprised at the ease with which he had secured that position. With a wry smile, he asked himself: "What will Nina say—and everybody else?"

That was the beginning, for Felix, of a new epoch. He found himself one of those young men who hurry forth throughout the city at the first hint of unusual happenings, who pry into everything sensational, who are present at all curious episodes, all tragedies, and all disasters. Doors opened at his knock, and, half-unwillingly, yet fascinated, he peered in at the secret lives of strangers. He contemplated degradation; he intruded on anguish; in awe he looked down at the mysterious masks of suicides and murdered men. He made the old remark of all beginners in that business who are sensitive: he had discovered the "Human Comedy"—the comedy of human hearts, absurd, grotesque, repulsive, terrible.

In these first days, while hurrying back to the newspaper office, Felix would see, as if they were before him still, the eyes of the abandoned wife; the waxen face of the girl searching for her lover in the Morgue; the little children in the squalid flat peeping into the parlor at the coffin; the dead man sprawling on the ground, his rival's weapon lying near him. Thrilled by his bit of "Human Comedy," Felix would write in a fine frenzy, then hover near the copy-readers while they slashed at his pages with blue pencils; finally, with a feeling of suffocation, snatch the warm newspapers and scan them for his story—the story he had made, that fifty thousand eyes would see, but which, in its deflated form, he could hardly recognize as his. "They've cut the best part out!" Still, no blue pencil could undo the great fact—that he was in print. When, riding uptown in the trolley-car from work, he saw men glancing at a certain column in *The Evening Sphere*, his heart went out to those readers: they were his brothers; he had an almost uncontrollable desire to seize their arms, to make them look at him, to say to them: "I wrote that!" He cut out everything that he got printed and, at night, pasted all his clippings in a scrap-book.

Answering an advertisement in the newspapers, he rented an apartment, furnished, on a top floor in Thirty-second Street. He had there a studio

with a skylight, a bedroom, and a bath. The place
—which belonged to a young artist with weak lungs,
exiled in the Adirondack Mountains—was full of
imitation "antique" furniture and trivial curiosities.
Rejected paintings lined the walls; a model's throne
stood in one corner; a wooden mannikin leaned
against the mantel-piece in the feeble attitude of a
drunken man; and all the useless paraphernalia of
an "artistic" studio was strewn about. The stomach
of a terra-cotta statuette was scratched with matches;
the top of a tabouret was marked with rings made
by wet glasses; the chair-arms had been burned by
cigarettes. Felix, with ingenuous admiration for this
Bohemian environment, considered himself lucky in
obtaining such a scene for his performances.

At night he worked there faithfully, studying literature, thinking always of Corquill and the heights
which that celebrity inhabited. Such was his enthusiasm and determination that he took pleasure
in seeing little of his old friends—in taking the pose
of a recluse for art's sake. When lonely he repeated: "All great men live in themselves while they
are cultivating fame."

Every morning, before he left the studio, he telephoned to Nina.

"Good-morning, dear."

"Good-morning, sweetheart. Ten minutes late
day!"

"Really? How are you this morning?"

"Very well; and how are you?"

Then there would be a pause—what shou

next? Could it be possible that he had exhausted every topic interesting at long distance?

He spent his Sundays on the farm. Nina always met him at the station. When they reached the first stretch of deserted road he kissed her. It was always at the same spot; and always in just the same way she held in the spirited horse, and leaned down toward him from her higher seat, her breast pressing against his shoulder, her long eyelashes lowered on her cheeks, her soft lips slightly pouting. And she always wore the same perfume, simple, clean-smelling. In time, Felix ceased to notice it.

It was autumn. The countryside was touched with that beauty, slightly melancholy, which nature has in its final, all but languishing, exuberance. Spring, with its soft breezes capable of thrilling hearts with strange delights, was now a memory; and the presentiment of fall was almost like a presentiment of loss. Where was that first ethereal elation—that novelty of love among the budding flowers? In autumn the foliage on the hills, the blossoming of which one greeted with delight, has grown familiar.

All Felix's first amazement at his good fortune had given way to complacency. Nina's love, Mrs. Ferrol's affection, the luxurious home in which, every week, he took his place he came to regard finally as a matter of course. When, on Monday morning, he returned to the newspaper office, from the anxious, struggling reporters he was distinguished by such an air of independence as comes with a conviction of security.   He was assured of everything.   What had he to fear from any one?

One day, when he was passing on some errand into the vestibule of the Supreme Court House, he came face to face with a tall, earnest-looking young man in a brown cutaway coat, who exclaimed joyously:

"Felix Piers!   What are you doing here?"

This young man's name was Gregory Tamborlayne.   He was a lawyer who had been taken into a rich firm that safeguarded various large corporations in the courts.   He was an old friend of Felix's, but for some time, separated by divergent interests, they had seen nothing of each other.

They had an enthusiastic reunion.   Each related his experiences.

Tamborlayne had been married for two years; his wedding had taken place while Felix was going round the world.   His wife, after a summer spent in Europe, had just returned to him.   Felix must meet her; he must dine with them—in fact, why not that night?

Why not, indeed?   The lonely evenings in the studio were becoming slightly irksome.

At eight o'clock that night Felix presented himself at Tamborlayne's house in East Seventy-ninth Street.

The drawing-room in which he found himself was rose-colored.   Into the walls were set tall panels of rose-colored silk covered with a design of little garlands.   On the waxed parquetry stood chairs

and sofas fashioned in the style of Louis XVI,
their rose-colored upholstery embroidered with
slight, curving sprays of flowers, their light wood-
work embossed, fluted, and gilded. Opposite the
doorway was a fireplace of white marble with a pink
silk fire screen, in a gilt frame, before it. On the
mantel-piece stood a round clock supported by six
marble columns. This ornament was flanked by
large urns of French china, like the furniture suggestive of the eighteenth century, with an oval panel
in the front of each on which was painted a "Mar-
quise," with bold eyes and demure mouth, after the
manner of Watteau. A mirror, extending from the
mantel to the ceiling, reflected the massive, globular
pendants of a crystal chandelier. At the rear of the
apartment there glimmered in the gloom a beautiful
harp and a grand-piano, in the same style as the
furniture—gilded and of chaste outline. The whole
room, as if reflecting the intimate personality of some
individual, suggested daintiness, fragility, discretion
—a discretion that seemed almost to veil an inclination toward delicately sensuous extravagances.

There was a light step in the hall. Here, undoubtedly, was Tamborlayne's wife. Felix, who had never
met her, thought: "Now we shall see what he's done
for himself!"

At that moment she appeared in the doorway.

She was nearly as tall as Felix, slender, pale, with
black hair. Felix did not think her good-looking,
but he could not help admitting that she had elegance
and was exquisitely dressed.

She wore a low-neck, trailing gown of black lace laid on silver tissue, which accentuated the smallness of her waist and the slightness of her hips. As she advanced with softly rustling skirts, her hair very dark, her skin very white, her eyes intently fixed on his, it seemed to Felix as if something extraordinary was approaching him. Then she smiled slowly.

"How do you do, Felix?—as Gregory always says."

His feeling of strangeness vanished; they were friends at once.

Her voice was low and calm, her gestures all were leisurely and graceful; everything about her expressed tranquillity and self-confidence. Felix admired her behavior, the arrangement of her hair, her neck, in which, despite her slimness, were no hollows. Her clear, smooth skin contained a smothered lustre. She was, he thought, an excellent example of what, sometimes, he chose to call, with the manner of a connoisseur, "the hot-house type"—a type in which he took small interest. He had often said emphatically to other young men: "I can't bear thin, dead-white women."

Tamborlayne came in with a hearty greeting. Putting an arm round Felix's neck, he said to his wife, whom he called "Eileen":

"Now that I've found him again I'm going to hang on to him. What a pity that people lose track of each other so easily in New York! Here I've missed three years at least of this old fellow's friendship. Well, we'll make up for it now—eh, Felix? We'll revive old times. D'you remember the schooldays?—the scrapes we used to get into? We'll go over it all after dinner."

The young lawyer, somewhat serious ordinarily, looked as eager and cheerful as if, in coming across Felix, he had done himself a valuable service.

The dinner-table was decorated with white roses and pearl-colored candle-shades. The silver, of which there was a large quantity, made a brilliant show. There was Venetian glassware beside the place-plates, which were covered with gold etched in an intricate Persian design. Two English-looking man-servants waited on the table.

Felix remembered that the Tamborlayne family had a good deal of money. And he pictured to himself how, when he was married, he would entertain his friends no less agreeably. "Just wait!" he said to himself.

It was a pleasant dinner. The wine that Felix drank aroused his eloquence and he described wittily, with a pretence of whimsical astonishment, his exploits in the newspaper office. His becoming a reporter appeared like a mad prank. Tamborlayne, laughing enthusiastically, looked like a boy on a holiday; but she, gazing steadily at Felix while he talked, flattered him more by her slow, comprehending smile.

Soon after dinner Tamborlayne took Felix off to his "den," on the top floor of the house. There, smoking pipes, laughing, talking of old times, they managed between them to empty a decanter of Scotch whiskey. When, finally, Felix rose. it was midnight.

While he was passing through the second floor on his way downstairs with Tamborlayne, she came out of a brightly illuminated, yellow room to say good-night to him.   He was vaguely surprised that she had not yet gone to bed.

"Nearly every afternoon I'm in by five o'clock," she said, in a pleasant, matter-of-fact tone; then added: "And Gregory is usually home by six."

When she gave him her cool hand he noticed at once that she had taken off her rings.

And as he left the house he imagined her in a yellow boudoir, before the mirror of a dressing-table covered with silver brushes, vials, and jars, drawing her bracelets from her arms, putting on some clinging robe of silk, and letting down her thick, black hair.

CHAPTER IV

FALL had come to the city. The restricted landscapes of the public squares assumed that graybrown, naked aspect which, at twilight, when windows brighten in tall buildings roundabout, suggests to the beholder sombre reveries. The evening air grew chilly; pedestrians moved homeward briskly beneath foggy street lights, and on Fifth Avenue, as dusk, like a dun veil of gossamer, was slowly settling over everything, an endless procession of fine carriages restored to the thoroughfare a patrician quality that it had lacked all summer. The winter season—the time of dinners, balls, and operas—was approaching.

Nina and her mother had returned to town. They lived, when in New York, on lower Fifth Avenue, just north of Washington Square, in one of those old brick houses of massive, plain exterior, with Ionic pillars of marble and a fanlight at the arched entrance, that preserve unobtrusively, in the midst of a city which is being constantly rebuilt, the pure beauty of colonial dwellings.

The place was an heirloom of the Ferrols that had been proudly kept for generations in its pristine state. Mrs. Ferrol, from being at first but mildly interested in this tradition of her late husband's family, had come finally to regard the house as a sort of ancestral monument and herself as its curator.

The walls were covered with faded silk or with "landscape paper." From the ceilings were suspended slender chandeliers on which dangled fringe upon fringe of long glass prisms. Beside the doorways, branching candelabra were affixed to oval, gilded frames of misty mirrors. The furniture was all from the period of Heppelwhite. And above marble mantel-pieces, as mellow as if filled with oil, hung large likenesses of simpering ladies and sedate gentlemen, in quaint dress and uniform, with obsolete-looking faces. Throughout the house, in short, the same "antique" effect prevailed. The expensive modern dwellings of the Ferrols' friends, situated further uptown, seemed almost like architectural parvenus when compared with this place, the chaste, faded fineness of which was like that of an honorable old aristocrat.

This formal environment was not, however, of the sort in which young men are most pleased to spend their time. Felix, who dined nearly every evening at the Ferrol house, began to think, on recovering from his first enthusiasm, that comfort had there been somewhat unreasonably sacrificed to the hobby of the family. It was almost impossible to take lazy attitudes on the Heppelwhite furniture: the sofas were too narrow, the chair-backs too straight. And in nearly every room there was a portrait of some stiff old gentleman who seemed to follow all one's actions with the forbidding eyes of an arbiter of etiquette. Felix at last found these surroundings irksome; and he resented secretly the "ancestor-worship" that he held responsible for his discomfort.

Perhaps, while sitting in the drawing-room with Nina after dinner, he would murmur solemnly: "This is the chair that George Washington had to sit in as a punishment for chopping down the cherry-tree"; or: "This sofa was used in the Spanish Inquisition. The question was put to the unhappy prisoner; if he refused to answer, he was stretched at full length upon this instrument." He had names for all the ancestors portrayed there, which he told Nina in private: one, whose face was nearly covered with black whiskers, was "The Man in the Iron Mask"; another, in Continental uniform, stout and rosy, was "The Little Lost Dauphin"; and a figure in a large wig, which had almost disappeared beneath a brownish murk, Felix called "Adam, the Founder." One evening, when he had been spending a couple of hours with some friends in a hotel café, he stopped on his way to the dining-room before this portrait, which he saluted, while asking whether "the dinosaurs were still breaking into the garden and getting at the fig-trees."

Nina, taking him aside after dinner, reproached him with having had "a little too much to drink."

They were drawn into an argument, in which Felix found himself asserting that one must be agreeable with one's friends, while Nina, growing impatient, declared that she had no sympathy with such a point of view. She liked to think of Felix as different from other young men. "For her part, she was not like those girls who pretend to admire dissipation."

"Dissipation!"

Felix said something hotly about feminine exaggeration. They were both exasperated. They looked at each other indignantly. It was their first quarrel.

Presently, without kissing her good-by, he left her standing motionless in the centre of the drawing-room. He did not intend to slam the front door; and when it came shut behind him with a bang, for an instant he was frightened. Departing in a dull rage, he knew that he was at fault; and he was on that account all the more angry with her. The next afternoon, when he returned, she came to him quickly, put her arms round him, and sobbed on his shoulder. It was she who appeared mutely to implore forgiveness. His self-respect was restored. Subsequently, he felt more assurance than before.

Nina and Felix, who had agreed not to be married until spring, spent many hours planning how they should live together. But every week their schemes were altered as new ideas came to them; and finally, of all the pleasant modes of life at their disposal, they were uncertain which to choose. Their future, in which as yet they could discern distinctly no details, they contemplated with trustful satisfaction.

All days were sunny now for Felix; it seemed as if the current of good fortune, once having begun to flow in his direction, was growing ever fuller. When he went about, those who before had given him but

vague bows greeted him with kind smiles, stopped
him on the pavement for a moment's cordial conversation, called him to the steps of carriages in order
to shake hands with him. The women of that circle
in which Mrs. Ferrol lived now turned toward him,
whenever he encountered them, eyes full of friendly
interest; and Felix—who but a few months since had
felt himself in danger of slipping gradually from the
gentle world to which he had been born—understood
that in this feminine attention, concerted and deliberate, lay the assurance of his social future.

As for Mrs. Ferrol, no one could have been more
amiable. She sent useful articles to the studio. She
remembered Felix's birthday and, that night, had
on the dinner-table a frosted cake with candles.
Once, for a week, she dropped mysterious hints, and
then, when he arrived one evening, the front door
was opened by a bent, white-haired, withered old
fellow in sober livery, who quavered:

"Master Felix!"

It was Joseph, Sheridan Piers's old retainer! After
the disaster, Mr. Wickit had got him a good position;
but he had been restless—"those strangers didn't
understand his ways"— and at last Mrs. Ferrol,
learning of his discontent, had taken him into her
service. When he saw his young master again, tears
filled his reddened eyes; he patted Felix on the arm
and hovered round him with long, rattling sniffs.
He had seen the boy grow up from childhood, had
made him his first wooden whistle, had taught him
how to fold newspapers into cocked hats. They

were both touched by that meeting; for Felix, at sight of the old man, remembered, with a flood of longing, the lost home.

He sat down beside the faithful fellow on the hall bench.

"And so you're a-goin' to marry Miss Nina? Look at that, now! I remember her no higher than this, drivin' her little basket cart in the park, as smart as ye please. An' d'ye still keep up your ridin', Master Felix? Faith, I'd love to see ye on a horse again. Remember, 'twas ould Joseph put ye on your first pony."

"And I've got the riding-whip you gave me once, Joseph."

"No, ye don't mean it! You're foolin' an ould man!"

"I'll bring it here next time I go riding with Miss Nina."

And next day, when Felix did so, Joseph cried out in his gratitude:

"Ah, God bless ye, now. To think ye kep' it all this while!"

In Central Park, where Nina and Felix often rode toward nightfall, moist, gray snow, riddled with drippings from the trees, mantled the undulating ground to the edges of the bridle-path, on which the earth-colored slush was fetlock-deep, and covered with small pools each the shape of a horse's hoof. Twilight enfolded the cold landscape; mists lay like long scarfs amid the black brushwood of the hollows, and through the naked tree tops shone yellow lights, re-

mote and faint. Horsemen went splashing by like
mounted ghosts, each face a pallid blank. Where
the bridle-path ran under bridges, one saw, leaning
over the parapets above, indistinct, solitary figures,
motionless, mysterious. An inexpressible loneliness
enveloped everything, and even thrust itself between
the two young riders. Saddened by their bleak surroundings, they remembered with regret the summer-
time, their gallops through green lanes—the hot sunshine, the sweet, soft breeze, the sounds of birds and
bees, and farmers calling in the fields. They were
unable to reproduce the pleasure of those delicious
days.

In the evening, sometimes they went to a dinner
or a theatre party or the opera. In the darkened
opera-house there glittered vaguely overhead five
golden balconies, each full of shadowy spectators
who, in the topmost gallery, rising in tiers to a height
that one observed with dizziness, looked like innumerable tiny caryatids supporting the vast golden
roof. Before the lower edge of the bright proscenium
appeared the agitated head and arms of the conductor; and from below him rose the music of the
orchestra—a pervasive, ceaseless harmony blending
with the occasional utterances of the singers; a harmony now delicate and winsome, now swelling, at
the union of all instruments, to extraordinary maj-
esty. And, on the stage, the lovers, as if exalted
by the sensuous music that played round them, were
swept through their sublimated tragedy, wherein, for
Felix, love had that remote grandeur with which, in

his young dreams, he had invested it. Wistfulness
stole over him, as if he were contemplating some
unattainable splendor. Then the curtain fell; the
lights sprang up; people began to talk and move
about; he saw the conductor blowing his nose; and
Nina's familiar face recalled him to reality.

Now and then, from the opera or the play, they
went to a dance—in those days they were always
invited out together; or perhaps Felix was always
invited then on her account. In large, brilliantly
illuminated ballrooms, embellished with gilding, festooned with hot-house flowers, the music, with an
arpeggio of muted strings, glided into the languorous
melodies of waltzes. Here and there upon the polished floor appeared in motion two joined figures,
one in black, one pale and shining. The dancers
grew more numerous; the floor was filled with them;
the colors of the women's dresses formed a gorgeous
haze. One felt upon the face, in little gusts, warm
air laden with perfume. One caught glimpses mo-
mentarily of beautiful women whirling by with half-
closed eyes, of smooth bosoms powdered white, of
bare, dimpled backs, of the nape of a neck with a
loosened curl trembling on it. The strains of the
violins, the rustling of swirling skirts, and the sound
of countless shoe-soles turning on wax united in an
intoxicating rhythm. The music ceased; the dancers, with the staring expressions of persons emerging
from a dream, walked slowly toward the gilded
chairs arranged in rows along the walls. Some men
made off toward the smoking-room, their long, black

legs and coat-tails giving them a grotesque, bird-like appearance as they departed. More remained, standing in groups, with bent shoulders, before women who, sitting with their luminous trains spread out beside them, smiled vivaciously over their fluttering fans. Around the edges of the ballroom extended a row of black backs, like a broken hedge; and through the intervals between these could be seen snowy shoulders, diamonds, roses, twinkling dresses. A babble of voices, like the sound of little waves breaking on a beach, rose to the frescoed cupids floating in panels on the ceiling.

Such scenes fresh in mind, Felix returned in the morning to the shabby newspaper office with somewhat the sensations of a man who leads a double life. He felt that he was superior to that place; he longed to finish his apprenticeship there.

But he discovered presently that his hours of evening study were being slighted for diversions. When, in the small hours of the morning, he returned to the studio from some entertainment, he was troubled by the sight of his neglected writing-table. Then he had a touch of fear at the thought that he was accomplishing nothing of importance. He was filled again with virtuous and serious inclinations; and all those careless, laughing people in whose company he had amused himself seemed like so many wastrels. He had no patience with them! He told Nina energetically that he was going, thereafter, to work every night; she would have to do without his company at such times. To his surprise, she was greatly

pleased. She looked as if her mind had been relieved of some apprehension.

Every evening, then, he shut himself in the studio.
The clock ticked; the fire crackled; and on the divan
the white bull-terrier puppy that Nina had given
Felix sniffed in his sleep and twitched his legs.
Felix stared at the little beast, at the pictures on the
walls, at all the trivial bric-a-brac. With a sigh,
reluctantly he resumed his reading. "It was not all
beer and skittles, this studying literature!" The
sleet lashed the skylight; the wind howled round the
cornices. Felix helped himself to a drink of whiskey.

At his occupation of the studio he had found on a
buffet an array of dusty glasses and dry bottles. He
had promptly bought a stock of cigars, liquors, and
seltzer water for the regalement of visitors. These
decorations, he thought, added to the room a cosey
and hospitable touch. Moreover, he found the buffet
a convenience. He used to "take something" in the
evening if he was in low spirits, or before going to
bed, or in the morning, if he felt lethargic. After
some trouble he had, like most of his young
friends, at last got so that he could finish a drink
of whiskey without a grimace.

When his book wearied him he would walk round
the room, hands in pockets, always stopping before
a little, rickety bookcase to stare with an air of dissatisfaction at the volumes on the shelves. He had
read them all, worse luck! But one night he found,
behind the rest, another novel, covered with dust.
It was a historical romance of the middle ages that

he had never read. What a relief! He bore the
novel quickly to his writing-table, sent his text-books
whirling out of the way, and read of knights, monks,
damsels, and troubadours till two o'clock in the
morning. It was a good story—but how much better
he could have done it! Well, then, why not better
it? Remembering Oliver Corquill's admonitions, he
snapped his fingers scornfully. The next night he
prepared excitedly to write a short story dealing with
the middle ages.

He could see, as if they stood before him, those old
fellows in their scalloped coats and armor, those
ladies with head-dresses, towering like steeples, the
quaint, mediæval faces, the eccentric actions of a
people long since done with. Certainly, no one had
ever perceived such things so clearly! Sure of himself, he knew how he would make every point effec-
tive. The phrases took place in his brain as the
crystals of a kaleidoscope slide swiftly into symmetrical designs. He was astonished at his capability.
He believed himself to be inspired.

As he wrote, his delight increased, his pride rose.
He threw down the pen, sprang up, and strode about,
smiling, happy, confident. He talked to the dog,
who, alert on the divan, watched him with cocked
ears and open jaws. "Hey, Pat, we've begun!
We're on the way! We're going to be famous! Salute, you little devil; salute the illustrious author!"
Pat, springing to the floor, bounded round his master
with sharp yelps of joy. Felix took a drink, lighted
a cigarette, and again attacked his work.

He sent the manuscript to an important monthly magazine. One morning, standing by the hall door in his pajamas, he tore open an envelope; a check fell out; it was for two hundred dollars. The story had been accepted.

Despite his previous confidence, for a moment he was stupefied. Then he tingled with exultation. Fame lay before him! That morning, in the street, passers-by turned to look again at his radiant face.

The story was published with handsome illustrations. Nina read it five times. Mr. Wickit, telephoning to Felix, expressed astonishment and congratulated him effusively. Gregory Tamborlayne, putting both hands on Felix's shoulders, said, with a smile that made him good-looking:

"Old boy, you don't know how glad I am!"

Of all Felix's friends, Tamborlayne had become the closest. He took an intense interest in Felix's progress, talked flatteringly of him everywhere, predicted for him a fine future, told people that "there was a young man who was going to write the great American novel." They were seen everywhere together, arm in arm, swinging their canes, smiling, chatting with animation. They confided to each other their affairs, and Felix became, for the Tamborlaynes, a "friend of the family."

At the close of winter afternoons, when the streets grew gloomy and lights, surrounded by foggy nimbuses, made deep reflections on the wet pavements, Felix liked to enter the Tamborlaynes' house, warm, fragrant with flowers, illumined by the glow of lamps

in shades of favrile glass. In the library, lined with
Japanese leather, full of glistening books and comfortable furniture, he sat, in the attitude of a man entirely at ease, beside the tea-table with Eileen Tamborlayne, while waiting for her husband to come
home.

He took pleasure in talking to her about himself
—"she was so sympathetic." She said little; but
sitting in a deep chair, with a cigarette between her
slender fingers, she looked at him intently, all the
while he was speaking, with the serious gaze of a
person who is listening to something of importance.
When he chose to be humorous, immediately her
quiet, appreciative smile appeared to flatter him.
When, after refreshing himself with the Scotch and
soda that he preferred to tea, he unveiled a little the
longings of his heart, so difficult to describe in speech,
in some way she made him feel just by the expression
of her face that she understood him perfectly. How
rare—that ability for exact comprehension! He told
himself that she was an unusually intelligent woman.

When he had become thoroughly familiar with
her appearance it no longer occurred to him that
she was "too slender" and "too pale," that her
fingers were too long, that her feet, in thin house
slippers were so narrow as to have seemed to him
at first almost abnormal.

Sometimes, in answer to his confidences, she made
little confessions of her own. She, too, had found
this or that to be the case; and with an air almost
meek, as if she considered her affairs of small in-

terest, she would cite as an example some past experience of hers. In that way he got to know something of her life.

She had lived in Washington until her marriage;
Gregory had met her there. She spoke of her former
home in the capital; it was on such and such a street.
Her father had been a well-known lawyer—had
Felix ever heard of him? Felix thought he had.
She had gone to school at a certain convent. When
only seventeen, she had nearly married a young man
who had subsequently turned out badly. And so on.
Felix listened attentively to these disclosures; but
afterward, while reflecting on them, he discovered
invariably, with vague surprise, that he knew no
more of her real self than he had known before.
One afternoon, however, she admitted with a sigh:

"But, you see, I'm twenty-nine years old!"

Felix would not have suspected it. He was then
twenty-six. From that moment she obtained, by
reason of her superior age, a subtile prestige.

In the midst of their conversations Gregory would
come in rubbing his cold hands, beaming.

"Well, here we are again! What's the good word
to-day, Felix?"

And, bending over his wife, he would give her a
long kiss. Then, throwing himself into a big chair,
with a tender look at her he would say:

"How good this is! D'you know, Felix, I rather
like this old girl."

In fact, he was still madly infatuated with her. He
could not keep away from her; he patted her hand,

or put his arm round her, or drew her into a corner
to kiss her. When he contemplated her his eyes
brightened, his serious, plain face wore a look of
devotion. She received his caresses gracefully, with
a pretty humility, keeping her eyes cast down for a
moment after he had embraced her.

While Felix was generously permitted to be the
witness of these tender passages, Gregory was less
demonstrative when other guests were present.

Occasionally Felix met at the Tamborlaynes'
house a thin, stoop-shouldered young man, with a
weak, "clever" face, eyes that were pale and watery,
lank, black hair precisely brushed, finger nails cut to
a point, and dainty manners. This young man's
name was Mortimer Fray. In lieu of any serious
occupation, he was an amateur of all the arts—a
dilettante. Smoking one cigarette after the other,
wearing all the while that expression which is called
"soulful," he talked volubly, in an excessively re-
fined voice, of painting, sculpture, literature, music,
and the drama. His conversation was ornamented
with such terms as "atmosphere," "nuance," "chi-
aroscuro," "tonal quality," "the unities," "French
feeling." Gregory thought him "an interesting chap,
though a bit effeminate."

He had been introduced to the Tamborlaynes
at an exhibition of paintings. In a moment's conversation he had recommended to Eileen Tamborlayne a new book. A few days later he had telephoned to ask if he might call and learn her opinion
of the author. He brought with him a portfolio of

etchings, which Mrs. Tamborlayne admired. Fray thereupon immediately bestowed them on her. He remarked the music on the piano. Mrs. Tamborlayne was the musician? How pleasant! For his part he played the violin a little. One afternoon he appeared with the instrument—perhaps they might run over a piece or two? He forgot to take his violin away with him—it had been covered with sheet music—and he had to return for it next day. After that there was no telling when he was going to drop in.

One day he appeared at the Tamborlaynes' house, bursting with pride. He had just made the acquaintance of Paul Pavin, a famous French portrait-painter, who was then in New York executing some commissions. Fray had managed to lunch with this personage, had walked up Fifth Avenue with him, discussing art at every step, and on arriving at the Velasquez Building, in which Pavin occupied a studio, had received an invitation to call "some day." Beside himself with satisfaction, he began practising on Eileen Tamborlayne and Felix with a host of artistic aphorisms, each beginning with:

"Paul Pavin said to me."

When he had left the house Eileen Tamborlayne looked vexed. Staring at Felix absent-mindedly, she exclaimed:

"I wonder if Pavin would let him see——"

"See what?" asked Felix, in surprise.

Finally, with a smile, she said:

"I'll tell you something, if you'll promise to keep it to yourself." And she confessed that she was secretly having her portrait painted by this Pavin, as a surprise for Gregory.

Felix was amazed and delighted. How pleased Gregory would be!

"Tell me about it," he besought her, eager to take part in this amiable deception. How had she come to think of it? How had she gone about it?

It was very simple. During the summer she had met Pavin in Paris. He had been enthusiastic; he had said at once that she was a woman of whom he could paint a fine portrait. It was evident that this suggestion, implanted in her mind, had grown to a strong desire; in her thoughts she had undoubtedly perceived her likeness, done by this celebrated artist, hanging in an art gallery on exhibition, surrounded by admiring critics, talked of everywhere. On Pavin's arrival in New York at once she had given him his commission. She had a sitting nearly every afternoon. The portrait was beginning to take its final shape.

"If only I could see it!" ejaculated Felix.

Well, why not, since he was in the secret now? It was arranged that he should call for her the next afternoon at Pavin's studio, to meet the artist and look at the picture.

When he presented himself the spacious studio was already dusky; at the far end of it a "north light" formed a great square, luminously gray, against which some heavy furniture appeared in silhouette with blurred outlines. But just as Felix entered lights burst forth.

The bare, high walls were covered with faded burlap that had once been gilded. Worn Turkish rugs lay underfoot. There were some divans, upholstered with gray cloth, and a dusty grand-piano in one corner. Here and there were heavy chairs of carved wood. An easel, bearing a large canvas, was turned to the wall. Other canvases were piled up between two doors, at which hung curtains of gray velveteen. There were no ornaments; everything was practical; this studio was a workshop.

Felix saw Eileen standing by the "north light," wearing her hat and fur coat, pulling on her long gloves. A tall, broad-shouldered man advanced with out-stretched hand.

The Frenchman was about fifty years old, still blond, ruddy, with a great yellow beard trimmed square across the bottom. His eyes were shrewd and humorous. His hands were the heavy, working hands inherited from peasant ancestors; for he was not a Parisian born, but a native of the farm country of Touraine. In his youth, urged by those whispering voices which call some souls from the dullest, most unpromising surroundings into electric regions where fame may be met, he had set out for Paris. There he had lived in a garret, struggling, starving, watching a poor sweetheart die for lack of proper care, contemplating suicide, cursing the city that was cruel to him. Finally, in a frenzy of determination, he had plunged through all obstacles—he had got fame by the throat. Nowadays he was wealthy, renowned, and welcomed everywhere—this son of a

Touraine farmer who, as a boy, had tramped cow pastures in wooden shoes and, as a student, had devoured stale bread on benches in the public parks.

Felix took the artist's hand respectfully. He was charmed at once by the Frenchman's cordiality, his precise English, his graceful manners learned through long contact with fashionable people, his way of implying constantly: "You and I, as men of the world, can understand." Felix's satisfaction knew no bounds till they went to inspect the portrait.

The portrait was life-sized. Eileen Tamborlayne was pictured standing in a black ball dress covered with black spangles and with jet. Enveloped in shadows, with her back half turned, she was looking over her shoulder at the observer, while parting with one hand some indistinct curtains in the background. Her slimness and pallor seemed to have been exaggerated by the artist; her lithe grace was nearly caricatured. The face, which still appeared in flat, unfinished tones, wore a look which Felix thought unnatural. He considered the portrait exceedingly bizarre. He was sure that Gregory would not like it.

But, reflecting that he might betray ignorance by any adverse criticism, he said nothing, when he and she left the studio, except that the picture was "very odd—quite striking." With a pleased expression, she agreed with him.

The thought of sharing the secret of the portrait fascinated Felix. Whenever he passed the Velasquez Building he looked up at the windows intelligently. One afternoon, unable to withstand his curiosity, he returned to Pavin's studio. She was there, and had just finished her pose. While smoking and talking with the artist, he heard her, behind the gray curtains, in another room, changing her dress. Silk rustled; silver clicked against silver; presently she emerged ready for the street, with a tranquil, demure air and a business-like word to Pavin regarding her next visit. Felix could not help finding in the whole affair something adventurous and daring. He wondered whether Gregory, if he had known, would have appreciated all this exertion for his sake.

Half assured of a welcome by the Frenchman's cordiality, Felix began timidly to visit Pavin. The artist was pleased; he seemed to have taken a fancy to the boy. He said:

"When the light holds good, I work; the door is locked. When the light goes, I have an hour to lie about and smoke. Come then. I like you, Monsieur Félix. You have something that attracts me. You refresh me. I remember the time when I, too, was young. I have a souvenir. Of myself? Of some one else? Who knows? But I seem to see Paris thirty years ago, the Paris that is gone, that we oldish fellows sigh for. Come always at dusk. I shall enjoy it."

Felix was overwhelmed with pleasure at this condescension. His manner was more dignified for days; he could call himself the friend of a great artist!

Sitting together in the twilight, they talked, as if almost of an age, of Paris, of beautiful things every-

where, of life, and finally, as was inevitable, of women.
Of women Paul Pavin had his own ideas.

"They have their place, a charming place—yes;
but it is not in art. They are a distraction. And
what is a distraction? A detriment—not so? Suppose I am alone in life? I work with all my brains
and energies. Suppose a woman enters and becomes indispensable? All is confusion. When there
is a woman, of what are you thinking? Your work?
Not possible. Your work is her rival, her enemy.
So, she is my enemy. When my work is done, yes,
then perhaps I meet the enemy; but I recognize her
for what she is; I am on guard; she makes no wound;
she does not occupy my castle."

"But," Felix ventured, thinking of Nina, "I have
always thought that the inspiration of one good woman, the companionship of a lifetime——"

"One for a lifetime? Believe me, *mon ami*, as
I have found it, human beings are not like that!"

Felix was impressed. But sometimes, when there
was a light knock on the door, he could not help
exclaiming, with a laugh:

"The enemy!"

For women came frequently, late in the afternoon,
to Pavin's studio.

They were all attractive and well dressed, their
hats laden with trailing feathers, soft furs wrapped
round their necks, the fingers of their tight gloves
swollen with rings. They brought in with them
faint odors of perfume, dropped their gold purses
anywhere, and seated themselves in the carved chairs

with exaggerated primness. They all seemed to
regard Pavin with respect, and to consider it a privi-
lege that they were permitted to visit him.

Of these casual visitors, Felix remembered two
particularly. One, called Miss Sinjon, was a slight,
red-haired girl, with a square chin, rather prominent
cheek-bones, and a translucent skin. The other,
named Miss Llanelly, was tall, red-cheeked, with a
vivid appearance of healthiness. These two always
came together. Felix gathered from their conversation that they were, from time to time, "on the
stage." He had never heard of them before; but
their faces seemed familiar to him.

Pavin treated all these fair guests with the good-
natured tolerance of an old bachelor on whom a lot
of spoiled children are imposing. But there was one
visitor—who, as it happened, never met the rest—
for whom there was invariably a hearty greeting, a
chair proffered instantly, a bustling hunt for the
coffee-pot. This visitor was Mme. Regne Lodbrok,
a noted dramatic soprano, engaged for the winter
season at the Metropolitan Opera House.

She was a beautiful Scandinavian, about forty-five
years old, with pale-yellow hair and a majestic figure.
Gay, abrupt, frank, she had the good spirits and the
direct manners of a big boy. When she laughed, she
threw back her head and opened her large mouth,
disclosing all her fine teeth. As Felix said to himself, she "filled a chair comfortably." Sitting beside
the lamp, drinking cup after cup of coffee, she talked
to Pavin as one man talks to another. They had

known each other for years in Europe; each respected the other; they were good friends.

She liked Felix at once. Whenever, on entering, she saw him there, she called out to him, in a jolly voice: "Hello!" Sometimes, instead of shaking hands with him, she pinched his cheek. Once she called him " *liebchen* "—then laughed heartily at his embarrassment. She had a wholesome, motherly way of smiling at him, which made him feel very young. He admired her, and was proud of knowing her. This contact with artistic celebrities made him feel important.

One afternoon Mme. Lodbrok was sitting at the piano with her fur hat on and her gloves rolled over her wrists. She was about to hurry off to an early dinner; that night she was going to sing *Venus* in "Tannhäuser." As her strong fingers touched the piano keys at random, she gazed round the studio. Her eyes fell on the easel.

"Tell me, Pavin, that portrait of the pale lady; when will it be finished?"

Pavin rolled the easel out from the wall.

"It was finished yesterday."

They all stared at the picture—Pavin thoughtfully, Mme. Lodbrok intently, Felix with secret disappointment.

He had been right, he thought: it was nearly odd enough to suggest caricature. Yet the pose was exceedingly graceful; the very attenuation of the figure did no more than emphasize Eileen Tamborlayne's peculiar, lithe elegance; and the general effect, as the white skin and shimmering jet showed through swimming shadows, was of richness and distinction. After all, it was the face with which Felix found himself dissatisfied; for he seemed to see there her habitual expression of placidity and meekness subtly caricatured.

Mme. Lodbrok exclaimed emphatically:

"It is wonderful! How did you ever catch it?"

And, after a pause:

"What did she say, this lady, when it was finished?"

"Well," answered Pavin, with a smile, "she said yes, that it was beautiful, but that she was afraid her husband, who was not artistic, would tell her: 'I do not know this woman.'"

Mme. Lodbrok, while staring at the portrait, was playing softly, on the treble keys, the Venusberg music. She opened her mouth, closed it—then, with a shrug, remarked:

"So? Well, then, that much the worse for him!"

And in the ensuing silence slowly striking three chords, she sang in a rich, vibrant voice, which filled the room, the first utterance of Wagner's *Venus:*

" *Geliebter, sag', wo weilt dein Sinn.*" . .

CHAPTER V

ONE afternoon, at dusk, Felix met Eileen Tamborlayne on Fifth Avenue. She had been shopping; she was tired and thirsty; and she wanted a cup of tea. They entered a hotel near by, and in a tea-room full of potted plants, where one was likely to meet anybody, sat down at a table.

It was the first time since his engagement that Felix had appeared in a public place with any woman except Nina. Ill at ease, he kept looking at the doorway, where new-comers were continually appearing. He expected every moment to see Nina standing there and staring at him.

He was exasperated at the leisurely manner in which Eileen Tamborlayne sipped her tea and nibbled cakes. When she had finished, he thought she would never get her gloves buttoned and her veil arranged. She mislaid her purse; they looked for it everywhere; the waiter moved several fern pots and crawled under the table on his hands and knees. At last she found the purse in her muff. Felix rose quickly, with a sensation of intense relief. But where was her package; she was sure she had brought in a little package. Felix was sure she had not. The waiter agreed with him. Finally, she started toward the door.

In the doorway Felix came face to face with Miss Llanelly, the tall, red-cheeked girl he had met in Pavin's studio. As soon as Eileen Tamborlayne was past her, Miss Llanelly smiled and nodded.

This, also, irritated Felix. He thought: "If Nina were with me, she would do just the same!" And suddenly he was afraid of her, and of all the other women he had met and chatted with in Pavin's studio—and not only of them, but of Eileen Tamborlayne as well, whom, through some instinctive reticence which he could not explain, he had never spoken of to Nina. His eyes were opened; he had been treading on dangerous ground; he had been risking a great deal for nothing. What incomprehensible rashness had he not been guilty of!

A sudden apprehension is an excellent incentive to good resolutions of a sweeping character. He resolved not to go back to the Tamborlaynes' house or to Pavin's studio; he determined to avoid Eileen Tamborlayne thereafter; and as for the Miss Llanellys, whenever they got in his way he would look straight through them! He had obtained all at once, through trepidation, some high ideas of the obligations of an engaged young man.

When he set out that evening for the Ferrol house, he had a refreshing sensation of honesty, as if, at his resolution, all his past faults had been obliterated. When, on entering the old-fashioned drawing-room, he saw Nina waiting for him, he was touched with remorse at the sight of her clear, trustful eyes, and he embraced her with a tenderness so unusual that she was surprised. His quiet evening with her delighted him. He had no thoughts but sincere and simple ones—no wish but to repay her for her constant faith in him. Then, rediscovering her beauty, he recovered a good deal of his old ardor. As he was leaving her, she put her arms round his neck, gazed up at him with shining eyes, and whispered:

"What a dear boy you are to-night!"

The next day Felix began to devote all his leisure hours to Nina. They rode in the park; they took long walks, with Felix's puppy trotting at their heels; they strolled through streets full of furniture shops, looking into the show windows at draperies of crimson damask and brocade, at carved Italian chests, at tall chairs fashioned like the thrones of cardinals, at tables the heavy legs of which were carved with posturing cupids, at four-post bedsteads, with woodwork fluted and gilded in an antique style, large enough to conceal a family behind their curtains. They planned the decoration of a dwelling of their own. Alert, with ruddy cheeks, they returned to the Ferrol house for dinner. Old Joseph, opening the door for them, was wreathed in smiles.

Felix now found a novel pleasure in perfecting his behavior. He seemed to have experienced an intensification of conscience; and, somewhat like a convert to religion who, in his burst of zeal, will be content with nothing less than asceticism, Felix, day by day the more enamoured of his pose of rectitude, was always hunting for fine resolutions to make. He even drank nothing, for a while, but a bottle of light beer

with his luncheon; for a week he kept down his allow-
ance of tobacco to "three smokes a day." In such
mortifications he discovered a subtle voluptuousness:
when his appetites presented themselves to him he
enjoyed anticipation. As he reflected that there was
nothing in his conduct with which anybody could find
fault, feelings of calmness and superiority pervaded
him. While walking through the streets he gazed
on passers-by with the gentle tolerance of an exem-
plary character.

He worked hard. At the newspaper office his
salary had been raised to twenty-five dollars a week;
at home he had begun to write a novel.

After perusing several books of Tolstoy's, he had
decided to write a Russian story in the "realistic
style." Having been in Russia, he was sure of his
ability to concoct the "atmosphere." He had visions
of tall, bearded gentlemen with close-clipped hair, in
uniform, smoking cigarettes; of pale ladies with pendent ear-rings, sitting in overheated rooms; of frowsy
peasants in boots and quilted coats; of mobs, cos-
sacks, three-horse troikas driven breakneck through
snow, lonely steppes all white in moonlight—a string
of political prisoners tramping in the middle distance.
He had begun to write with energy, inscribing at the
top of the first page, with a flourish, "Chapter I,"
and immediately introducing his hero with the words:

"Tchernaieff drew rein and listened. He thought
he had heard, coming across the snow-covered
steppes, a faint cry of distress."

Unfortunately, while composing this tale he read,

by way of recreation, some novels of Alexandre Dumas. When he had scribbled thirty thousand words Felix discovered, on glancing over a "Critical Study of French Authors," that he had been writing, not in the realistic style, but in the romantic! Immediately he tore up his work and began again. But the realistic style was elusive, as he was then perusing, for amusement, a story of Nero by Sienkiewicz. The Russian steppes began to seem to Felix artificial, like scenery in a theatre; and whenever he contemplated his Slavonic hero, he had difficulty in not picturing him in a *toga virilis*. Perhaps, after all, he would have done better with a tale of Rome! And he remembered his thrills of imagination in the Forum, the Roman museums, and Pompeii. He saw the ancient streets, narrow, precipitous, dirty, and, moving through them, the triumph of some returning general—the brown crowd leaning out from roofs and windows, the soldiers marching in brass and leather, the golden eagles, the rising incense smoke, the dropping flowers, and, against a background of innumerable helmets, all glittering, as if in one of those radiant mists which enveloped—so one reads —the presences of pagan deities, the conqueror in his chariot, robed, crowned with laurel, his face covered with vermilion, splendid and terrible, like a god showing himself to men. The harsh trumpet blasts, the rumbling "Alala!" of the Roman legionaries, filled Felix's ears.

Late one afternoon, while sitting at his writing-table, staring disconsolately at the manuscript in which he had lost interest, he heard a murmur of voices in the hall, a rustle of skirts, then a knock on the door. The puppy rushed forward, barking frantically. It was Eileen Tamborlayne with two woman friends whom Felix did not know.

They had been passing through Thirty-second Street; Eileen Tamborlayne had remembered his address, and, seeing the studio windows illuminated, she had brought the others upstairs "for a lark." Smiling as if she had last seen Felix the day before, she explained:

"There were so many of us, we thought our visit could hardly be improper."

In fact, the three women seemed to fill the studio. One sat on the divan, another on the model throne; Eileen took his chair before the writing-table. Their elaborate hats and dresses, their glossy furs and shining purses, enriched the room. When they all jumped up together to examine some object, their skirts swished about their slim figures, their perfumes sweetened the air, the feathers on their hats commingled; and Felix, despite his vexation, could not help feeling a certain complacency. He noticed that neither of Eileen's companions was as attractive as she.

They thought the place "delightful—so Bohemian!" They petted the dog, laughed at the mannikin, stared at the skylight, the buffet, the bedroom door. They wanted to know if they were intruding; they implored Felix to be frank; was he expecting any one? He was not expecting any one.

He brought out the teapot and telephoned for some cakes.

As they were leaving, Eileen said to Felix, gently:

"We miss you uptown at tea-time nowadays."

"I'm working very hard."

"So Gregory tells me. But you need some recreation. You'd better drop in now and then and save me from Mortimer."

"Fray, you mean? He's there often?"

She made a grimace of weariness.

"And the portrait?"

"It came home last night—Gregory's birthday."

"And Monsieur Pavin?"

"He was asking after you."

As the women descended the stairs with backward glances and laughter, Felix, leaning over the balustrade, smiled politely. When they were out of the house he slammed the studio door.

"Good riddance!" he ejaculated, with every external evidence of satisfaction—because that, he felt, was what he ought to say. But he did not deceive himself. He sat down thoughtfully.

So she had not forgotten him; she had missed him all these afternoons! Indeed, she had liked him well enough to hunt him up. He recalled the hours he had spent in the Tamborlaynes' dim library; he remembered the silences, broken only now and then by speech, as he sat with her at the tea-table, waiting for Gregory to come home and sometimes wishing that he might be late. And he was sad, feeling that something unique amid the experiences of life had receded from him, or as if he were walking slowly, with backward looks, away from an undiscovered country upon whose borders he had hovered, nearly tentatively, for a little while.

"Ah, it's just as well I left off going there. In the end, I might have made myself unhappy—who knows?" He said this without surprise, or any condemnation of himself. For there had stolen over him such sweet melancholy as, while softening the heart, renders the mind defenceless before all wandering thoughts. Sitting in the chair that she had occupied, he looked about him at the room, which seemed in some way changed; and the faint perfume that lingered in the air was somewhat like a seductive, incorporeal inhabitant.

The clock struck; it was time to dress for dinner. He rose, went to a mirror, and contemplated his reflection. He discovered on his face an expression of profound ennui. "How monotonous life is! . . ."

She returned, in a few days, alone.

She made no excuse for her intrusion. Dropping her furs beside his manuscript, she sat down in his chair with the declaration:

"I've been standing in a dressmaker's shop all day. I'm just worn out! Can you let me make some tea and give me a cigarette?"

She looked so tired, pale, and meek that Felix felt his uneasiness slipping from him. He found himself making solicitous remarks. With a shrug, she answered, in the tone of a martyr:

"A woman has to wear clothes."

As usual, she was dressed in black. Everything about her was exquisite; and the precise undulations of her thick, black hair, together with the large pearls which she wore in the full lobes of her ears, seemed to be trying to counteract, with an effect of dainty sophistication, her habitual demureness. Felix thought that she was better looking than formerly.

She talked of Gregory: he did not seem well; he was becoming nervous and despondent. "They're working him too hard. A young man in a big law firm never has a moment's rest, it seems. And as for you, I think you're overdoing it, too." She glanced at his writing-table with an expression of dissatisfaction.

Then, after a pause, she asked:

"Did you mind my bringing those two women up here? You wouldn't if you knew what they said afterward. I wonder if I ought to tell you?"

She pretended to think better of it, insisting that their remarks would make him vain. He urged her to go on. At last, laughing, she said:

"They thought you were the sort of young man that a woman could fall desperately in love with."

"What nonsense!" he exclaimed, much flattered, nevertheless. And his reserve slowly melted in the glow of gratification that stole over him.

Presently they found themselves talking quite as formerly; the familiar silences of those other evenings sealed each fragment of discussion with the mark of intimacy. The window-panes grew black; the lamplight made amber patches on the glass; and in the

quiet, she sat motionless, with eyes pensively downcast, her pale face and slender figure forming within
the wings of the deep, crimson chair a charming
picture of repose. Upon the skylight rain began to
patter; and at that sound Felix, in the warm, cosey
room, had a sudden pang, half sad and half delightful. His voice took on, for one moment, a fuller and
more tender intonation which surprised him. Her
lowered eyelashes fluttered; a faint color stole across
her cheeks; her whole person seemed to stir, though
almost imperceptibly, as a flower stirs at the slightest
breath of a caressing breeze.

They had begun by talking about Gregory. But
finally, progressing in their conversation through the
subjects of marriage and of married life, they found
themselves discussing love.

"Why is it," she was saying, "that love is almost
always described to us in such flattering terms, as if it
were a state of perfect happiness? For my part, I
think there is little happiness in it, if happiness is the
same thing as contentment. In love we are forever
longing for something that can never be attained.
We reach out for what we desire, we seem to seize it,
for a moment we think we have it safe; but we find
that we haven't—that it has escaped us."

Felix, scarcely understanding her, expostulated
gently:

"But how can any one say that, who is as happily
married as you are?"

"Am I?" she returned, raising her eyes to his.
He made a gesture of astonishment.

"I could hardly imagine a more nearly ideal home than yours. Gregory is devoted to you absolutely."

"Oh, yes," she assented indifferently, and added, with a little bitterness: "His devotion is complete, and consequently it is always the same. It would never occur to him to be impatient with me—to show jealousy or anger or brutality. In his treatment of me he is perfect. Perfection! Is there anything so monotonous?"

Leaning back, she closed her eyes wearily. Her pale eyelids looked transparent.

"If he would only fly into a rage at me some day! If he would only hate me for an hour! I have even said, if he would only strike me! Then I would know that he, too, had somewhere in him violent, irresponsible impulses—that he was no better than I."

Felix uttered, sharply, an incredulous laugh. Amazed, secretly agitated, he stared at her face, which he had come to think of as a living symbol of tranquillity.

"Violent, irresponsible impulses in you? I have never seen you moved by anything," he said.

Her eyes opened. Looking at him intently, she retorted, in an even voice:

"And yet, merely at the chance touch of another man, I have felt weak all over."

Silence fell, a silence more dangerous than speech, in which Felix sat incapable of motion or of utterance, like one of those neurotic unfortunates before whom in a flash a suicidal thought presents itself, and who become immediately like birds fluttering before a serpent, fascinated by the very peril contained in their imaginings.

The clock struck; it was half-past six.

"I shall be late," she said quietly. And after a while she rose.

He helped her to put on her coat.

"Tuck in my sleeves."

Her eyelashes dropped; she bit her lower lip. Then at last she gazed straight at him with humid, misty eyes, her mouth relaxed in a weak, tremulous smile.

He took her in his arms. She turned her face away. He kissed her ear, her hot cheek, her eyelid wet with a tear, her lips. At once she became limp and clung to him. And all the while, as if in a dream, he kept repeating to himself: "This is terrible! This is terrible!"

He was caught. From that evening, amid his most poignant desires for recovery, he felt in the bottom of his heart a subtle sense of hypocrisy. Like a man who, while passionately reiterating a desire to be rid of some habit which is ruining him, cannot help remembering the enticements of that habit, so Felix, crying out to himself, "If only I could return to where I was before!" found himself in the same moment thinking, with rapt attention, of that from which he told himself he wanted to be free. He seemed to see, opening before his eyes, such a region as was revealed at a talismanic utterance to those adventurers of the Arabian Nights: a strange region unutterably alluring, wrapped in rich shadows and in tinted mists through which glittered heaped-up treasures, guarded by motionless, armed images that might, and might not, stir into life at the foot-fall of the explorer.

Sometimes, in a sudden access of strength, he bound himself with resolutions, and for an hour or two—perhaps a day—felt safe. But then, when he unlocked the studio door, he found lying on the floor a note from her; or the bell of his telephone commenced to ring; or he heard a foot-fall on the stairs. At these sights and sounds, invariably he was startled. As for his condition when she herself appeared, it came to pass, at length, that she could not cross the threshold of the studio without his good resolutions beginning to slip from him.

Now she would enter with wide eyes and parted lips, perfectly pale, with the look, almost tragic, of a person before whom all obstacles are ineffective. Again she would arrive melting, tremulous, ready to burst into tears, half incoherent, swearing that this was the last time she would ever see him. Whatever guise she came in was sufficient; he could not resist her; she dominated him. He was filled with an amazement always fresh at the sight of this elegant woman—so tranquil, so cold, apparently so unapproachable, before the world—exhibiting just for him these uncontrolled emotions.

The studio became a place of memories—one of those spots impregnated with the essential personality of an absent one, into which it is impossible to penetrate without succumbing to a flood of reminiscent reveries. When he entered in the twilight the very air of the room recalled her to him; and when he turned up the lights all the objects about him were, at first glance, nothing but souvenirs of her. In the crimson chair he seemed to see her sitting, head pressed against the wing, a strand of her thick hair caught and spread out against the rough-woven fabric. On the old couch by the window—where she reclined occasionally, while he sat beside her on the ottoman—shadows contrived now and then amid the tumbled cushions the vague simulacrum of a slender figure clothed in black. Even the ticking of the clock reminded him of her exclamations of dismay and petulance, when it was time to go. She called the clock "our enemy," and, like an adroit enemy, it always caught her unawares. "Six-thirty? Good Heavens, it was only a moment ago that I came in that door!" She noted the passage of those hours with the qualms of a miser who is forced to spend his gold.

When she was departing, all his contrition would return to him at her stereotyped cry: "How can I go back?" For, perceiving from the first how much, at such times, he took his frailty to heart, she, too, was lavish with evidences of remorse. Accurately her self-reproach kept pace with his, so that he believed she paid, in after-thoughts, as heavily as he. Together they marvelled gloomily at their condition; they said to each other: "If only we had never met! It must have been fate!" Between them they managed to weave, in time, that fabric of excuse with which persons in their position try to veil their fault; some influence more powerful than their wills had done this; they were not responsible—rather, they were to be pitied.

There were days when he felt that he could bear no more duplicity. He confessed his inability to leave her, but declared that he should no longer face the trustful eyes of those he was deceiving. Excited to a state in which nothing seemed extravagant, he cried:

"We can go away, anywhere, to the end of the world! They will never forgive us; we shall always be hated; but what difference does it make? We shall have each other!"

And in thinking of a life in some remote country with this woman whom now he could not do without, the familiar city receded to the horizon of his consciousness—became impalpable, like a mirage—and in the faces of Nina and of Gregory, as they appeared before him in diminished form, he could not recognize the features.

But at such outbursts invariably her eyes widened, a look of reserve and caution flickered in her face, and, without stirring, she seemed in some way to retreat from him. Then, comfortingly, nearly as if talking to a child, she whispered:

"Calm yourself. Have patience. Wait."

She was far-seeing.

He became accomplished in evasions, skilful in lies, which accumulated till his whole existence was enmeshed in falsehood. Deception seemed to him, after all, an art learned very easily; and he went on mastering it with increasing confidence, sometimes lost in astonishment at the facility with which he hoodwinked every one.

As he acquired dexterity in imposition, he lost the extreme caution which had guided him at first. At length, quite confidently he took risks that one time would have turned him cold with fear. One after-noon Gregory entered the studio not five minutes after Eileen had left it. Smiling, contented, pleased at having half an hour with Felix, he sat down in a chair whereon the cushion still retained an impression of her head. In the Tamborlaynes' house, where Felix had resumed his visits, the thickness of a single curtain was screen enough for a quick embrace. Gregory's momentary absence from the room fur-nished the opportunity for a murmured word, a pressure of the hand, a hurried kiss. In fact, he had only to turn his back and a swift glance flashed between the two. But Gregory Tamborlayne per-ceived nothing; one would have thought that he was blind and deaf and, maybe, dull-witted also. For not even when he had almost surprised them in each other's arms did he notice that phenomenon which affects fine sensibilities so often: a "void in the air," so to speak, at the sudden suspension of two guilty impulses.

Gregory, whenever he came near Eileen, continued to make Felix the witness of his affectionate demon-strations. With askance eyes, Felix would watch him bend over her and kiss her. "Poor fellow!"

he thought. He was sorry for Gregory. And this pity made him, at times, assume involuntarily such gentleness that Gregory was drawn toward him the more. They managed to maintain that intimate ac' cord which had begun in honest friendship; and it came to pass, at last, that Felix could spend an hour in Gregory's company enjoyably—without remorse. "What a situation!" Sometimes it seemed to him that he was existing in a grotesque dream.

But, never easy for long, he had moments of acute apprehension. Now and then an innocent remark, like a chance shot finding a fatal billet, drove into his heart a terrible fear of discovery. When he saw a mere friend, Felix was apt to scrutinize him carefully. If he was unusually nervous on a day when he met Gregory, he had one breathless moment till the "poor fellow's" face brightened with kindliness. And almost always when he greeted Nina he watched her intently for an instant—then felt a general relaxation as he told himself: "She knows nothing."

And what was to be the end of it? He did not know. He drifted from the swift current into the rapids and through the rapids toward the cataract.

One afternoon he met on the street Gregory and Mortimer Fray. They were going to an auction of old Japanese prints concerning which Fray was enthusiastic. The names "Hiroshige," "Outomaru," "Kiyonaga," "Hokusai" bubbled from the young dilettante's lips; he went into raptures over "a beautiful demonstration of the Chinese feeling of a

Yamato picture—a mountain and some fir-trees"; joining thumb and second finger, he made a dainty gesture in the air as he described "six 'joro' of the Ukio-ye school." He could not have been more glib if he had just finished reading a treatise on Japanese art. He had his check-book in his pocket; he expected to bring away some bargains.

"I'll show you what I get, Piers—that is, if you're interested in such things."

"Very much," said Felix. He had so thoroughly acquired the habit of deception that he would have avowed instantly an intense interest in something he had never heard of; and undoubtedly he would have found some way to prove his affirmation.

"You'd better come along," urged Gregory, affectionately linking arms with Felix.

"I have some work to do."

"Always the industrious apprentice! How does the book get on?"

"Very slowly."

"The best work always does," remarked Fray, with a flattering smile.

Felix, believing that he saw on the dilettante's face the shadow of a sneer, wondered "what the man could have against him." Perhaps, he considered, it was partly his own fault: he had instinctively disliked Fray from the first.

While walking home he thought of his work, which they had recalled to his mind. He reflected dismally that he had not been able to write an original sentence in a month.

"What am I coming to? What is going to happen to me?"

Pedestrians passed him with indifferent glances. He began to look absent-mindedly at the faces of these strangers. After a while it seemed to him that they all wore the same expression—an expression of sanity and health. And suddenly he felt like one who, nursing within him some consuming, hidden malady, walks bashfully among independent, strong men—his superiors.

It was toward the end of March. The winds were keen, but flavored with an essence vivifying, fresh, and new—an exhalation of the moistened earth, borne to the stony city from afar, presaging spring. Memory returned to Felix. He thought of that other spring amid the roses, of the sun-steeped countryside, of his old sensations of simplicity and innocence. How far away, those days! He had been happy then. And he realized that he had not been happy since.

Contentment, self-respect, honesty, everything worth keeping, he had thrown away. Crime after crime against the hearts of others and against his own heart he had committed; and for what? The image of Eileen appeared before him; he contemplated it with heavy eyes, all his curiosity appeased, all his cupidity dispelled. Nearly every sentimental feeling grows feeble some day, and the more violent emotions are worn out the sooner. The enchantment that had held him helpless was dissolving.

And hope began to stir. Each year, he thought, the land grows cold and dark; the winds are blighting; all the tender, growing things are frozen and die, till one who did not know would say, "This is the end." But a day comes when the earth stirs beneath its shrivelled surface, when a breath of new life plays about it—when sap starts in the trees and buds appear and grasses thrust through the soil. Presently the hillsides bloom again, bright-feathered birds come warbling, flowers nod everywhere, warm sunshine floods the ravishing vistas, and the world is reborn.

While Felix walked a fine rain fell. But in the midst of the drizzle there was a sudden illumination, somewhat as if a great gas-jet had been lighted overhead. Looking up at the leaden clouds, he saw them breaking. Behind them appeared a white film, moving, suffused with brilliancy. Then, through this parting veil, down streamed the sunlight, transfiguring everything, glinting in mid-air upon the falling rain-drops, brightening the streets, the house fronts, the faces of the people. It seemed to Felix that this radiance flowed into his heart—that something impalpable had released itself from his body and was mounting upward through the golden mist. His eyes quivered. Gazing a-sky, he walked with parted lips.

When, finally, he reached the studio, he found her waiting for him. She was sitting in the crimson chair, facing the door, expectant. Without moving she said, coldly:

"How late you are!"

"I've been walking miles."

"Alone?"

"Yes."

"And I here!"

"Yes."

He did not approach her. She stared at him uneasily.

"What's the matter with you to-day?"

"I'm about to say good-by to you."

She rose, went hurriedly to him, and seized him by the shoulders.

"Felix!"

"That's quite useless, I assure you."

"Felix, Felix, look at me!"

"I'm looking at you."

She drew a long, quivering breath. Tightening her hold on him, she cried, hysterically:

"And you mean to tell me—you can look at me and tell me—that it's all over?"

She hid her face against his breast.

The latch clicked. Gregory and Fray were standing in the open doorway.

Fray was in front, with a portfolio under his arm; it was he who had opened the door quickly, without knocking. On his weak face appeared a bitter and malignant smile, containing no surprise. Making a slight bow, he turned, pushed past Gregory, and descended the staircase. Gregory entered the room with the vacant countenance of a somnambulist.

She went, with dragging feet, to the crimson chair, sat down, and turned away her face. Perfectly pale, her husband gazed at her alone. His mouth trembled; tears appeared in his eyes and rolled down his twitching cheeks.

At last, in a low voice, he said:

"Come."

And as she did not move, after clearing his throat he repeated, softly:

"Come, Eileen."

She rose. With fixed eyes, her gloved hands pressed against her temples, swiftly she passed out of the room. Gregory followed her. He closed the door behind him carefully.

For twenty-four hours Felix remained shut up in the studio, smoking, pacing the floor, lying in bed tormented by oppressive dreams, waking with a start to tell himself: "Yes, it has happened at last!" He had so often, in painful moments of imagination, pictured to himself just this catastrophe that at its occurrence he felt no great shock of surprise. "But what have they said to each other? What are they doing now? What will their future be? I have ruined two lives!" Still, he found these thoughts negligible; his sympathy and self-reproach were numb as he speculated on his own future.

At first it seemed to him that every one must know, and hour after hour he waited for Nina's renunciation of him. But he began to reason: "Why should she know? Those two would never reveal it; whatever Gregory does will be done very quietly. But Fray was there! And yet, why should Fray betray us all?"

Then he thought it very strange that Nina had not

telephoned to ascertain if he was ill. It was the first
time she had neglected him so long; her silence terrified him. "That's it; she knows everything!"
But, again, who would tell her?

At last, unable to bear uncertainty any longer, he
set out, toward evening, for the Ferrol house.

The streets were clean and bright; the sun was
setting; the upper stories of the white stone "sky-
scrapers" glowed with an orange-colored light against
a sky deep blue, in which the little clouds, by means
of their transparency and tender contour, called to
mind thoughts of spring.   On lower Fifth Avenue
people were walking buoyantly, with cheerful faces;
working girls, passing by in groups, emitted shrill
laughter; two young men, with overcoats thrown
open, strode along swinging their canes and smiling
genially. So, many an afternoon, he had walked
with Gregory!

Carriages passed at a brisk trot, the horses throwing out daintily their slender legs. The boyish
driver of a dray, wearing an apron of burlap, a
round badge stuck in the side of his cloth cap,
imitated, with puckered lips, the trilling of a bird.
Ah, the countryside; the lilac bushes; the path
through the woods, its coolness delicious after the
hot sunshine; the cadenzas of the birds amid
the glossy leaves! Spring was coming again, bearing all its fresh and pure charms—but not for him.

He neared the Ferrol house.   A carriage stopped
before the door; he saw that it was Mrs. Ferrol's
brougham.   His courage turned to water; he stood

still; he was about to make his escape. But Mrs. Ferrol stepped out of the carriage, turned, and saw him. Automatically he approached, suffocated by the beating of his heart, with everything dancing up and down before his eyes, like a man walking toward the scaffold. He removed his hat and tried to smile.

Her small, white face, with its thin features and precise frame of gray hair, seemed to him curiously unfamiliar. Looking at him steadily, she said:

"You were coming to my house? My house is not open to you, sir."

And she went in, through the old-fashioned doorway.

Returning to the studio, he found a note from Nina. It contained the words:

"I shall never lay eyes on you again."

Two weeks later, he read in the newspaper that Nina and her mother had embarked for Europe.

PART TWO

MARIE

CHAPTER VI

As the weeks passed, and, even in the stone-bound city, the promises of April, vaguely sweet, were reiterated with more emphasis by May, Felix, of evenings brooding in the studio, realized how much he had owed to Nina's love, and—while losing that— how much else he had lost. Every door leading into the rich and pleasant regions which, but a little while before, he had thought to frequent for life, was closed against him now. His isolation seemed perfect.

After reflection, there remained with him invariably a dull amazement—it had been he, erstwhile full of good impulses and honest aspirations, that had so used those who cared most for him! Such amazement always ended with the exclamation:

"I was mad!"

And of this, at least, he was sure: since, in his cold retrospection, that period, its allure now incomprehensible, its pleasures proved empty, appeared before him all hazy and turbulent, with details confused as if each episode had been but half appreciated at the time of its occurrence—like something that happens in a delirium, and the remembrance of which is but a jumble of feverish extravagances.

So he would fall to wondering what power outside himself, what evil genius, had driven him headlong to disaster—or, as he said, to ruin.

"That's it," he would repeat, "I've ruined my life!" Thereupon, he would consider the prospect of his changed future with feelings of loneliness and helplessness so profound, that a great lassitude would steal through his body, and he would sit with eyes fixed, with chin sunk on breast, with limbs heavy as if wrapped in lead, incapable of putting forth sufficient strength to raise his hand.

Indeed, this lassitude from dejection did not entirely leave him at any hour. In the morning, he awoke weary, downcast even before he had his wits about him. While getting out of bed, he remembered with disgust the office of *The Evening Sphere*. Sometimes, half-clothed, unable to make up his mind to finish dressing, he would stand for a long while behind the window curtains, thinking of nothing, gazing out on the brightest sunshine gloomily, his whole being permeated with a vague bitterness toward everything. Then, people hurrying by reminded him that he must get to work.

His work in the newspaper office, from which all the charm of strange adventure had departed, he approached with a heavy heart; necessity had transformed a pastime into drudgery.

Every morning, on entering *The Sphere* building, he breathed in the odors of fresh newspapers and linoleum with an enervating sensation of ennui. Climbing the spiral staircase, emerging into the office of *The*

Evening Sphere, to be enveloped invariably by the same pandemonium, he felt as if he were slipping into one of those confused dreams full of interminable, distasteful labors.

Round him machines clattered, steam hissed, iron clanged. At a shout and a rumble, he dodged men who, in their undershirts, with black smears across their faces, rolled form-tables at full speed over the metal-covered floor. Near-sighted proof-readers, pattering about with hands full of paper, bumped into him. At every step, he was jostled by "copy boys," young fellows in inky aprons carrying galleys of type, impatient foremen, bewildered visitors, reporters scampering out for news. Then, escaping all these, approaching a fog of pipe smoke, he stopped in an attitude of resignation amid the reporters' desks. These, dilapidated and dusty, covered with old newspapers, shreds of tobacco, mucilage pots, and dirty plates left from breakfasts brought in to the "early shift," surrounded the square desk of the city editor, and were themselves hemmed in by telegraphers' tables, all the instruments clicking, by typesetters' cases over which, as if over barricades, appeared the bald heads of old men, and by pneumatic tubes and hoists for manuscript, running to the typographers' room on the floor above, and always rattling and banging.

Here, when he had a few minutes' leisure, Felix would sit oblivious to the uproar round him, staring out at the little blossoming park and the City Hall, but seeing nothing, his mind, in a sort of stupor, always groping toward recollections that induced remorse, melancholy, and bodily languor. "Yes, yes, I've ruined my life," he would repeat to himself. All his thoughts were repinings for the past; he could see no future.

Perhaps, when he had come back to the newspaper office fresh from looking down at the calm, inscrutable features of some suicide, he would wonder:

"Was he as bad as I? Is he better off now?"

But then, with a great gush of self-pity:

"If I were in his place, who would be sorry?"

It seemed to his nature an indispensable concomitant to such an act, that one should be sure beforehand of some one's being sorry, of some one's remembering with at least a little tenderness.

As for Felix, he had no one! Tears would fill his eyes, till he had to screen his face with his hand, while the park, the tall buildings round about, and the bright sky, all swam together into a sparkling mist. He believed there was not anywhere such loneliness as his. Occasionally, he had an intense longing to journey to his mother's grave, and there, throwing himself down, embracing the moist mound, cover the budding flowers with his tears, while crying out:

"You loved me, I am sure! You would understand!"

But his mother's grave was in the cemetery of Père-Lachaise, in Paris, where, at the last, she had begged to be buried, in order that "she might remain in the place she had cared most for."

He dreamed of other lands, remote and wild, not furnished with conventionalities, where, possibly, with no one knowing anything about him, he might begin his life all over, and make a fortune and a name for himself. But where, and how? Those visions of his were of the haziest: he saw nothing but hot landscapes filled with sunbeams, vivid flowers, and palms, through which he drifted at random, and which faded, all at once, like a mirage.

Once day he read in a "society journal" that Denis Droyt was in Europe. Though he felt immediately a chill, this news did not surprise him. "It's his chance," Felix admitted. He imagined that serene, indefatigable young man following Nina everywhere, persistently exhibiting before her all the admirable qualities that he had lacked, dissipating her disgust for men, rousing in her gradually a new trust, and, finally, winning her. They would be married, and all the delightful plans that Nina and Felix had once made they would carry out—the voyages afar, the sojourns in beautiful and tranquil places, the rose-colored, random adventures of the fortunate. So it was Droyt, after all, who was going to possess her! Yet Felix grieved more over the loss of what went with her than over losing her.

Had he ever really loved her? What, after all, was love? Felix had an idea that it was something superb and transfiguring, a divine flaming of the heart, a soaring to a higher plane of sense—else all the world's great lovers were impostors. Would he ever experience that exaltation? Or would he die having known no nearer approach to it than his frail, pallid affection for Nina, or his febrile and unhappy madness for Eileen?

The Tamborlaynes were gone from New York; their house in East Seventy-ninth Street was closed and boarded tight. Where were they? Had they separated? How would they patch out their shattered lives?

And where was Mortimer Fray?

When there floated before him a vision of the young dilettante's face, sharp and clever, with its lurking smile half ingratiating and half spiteful, Felix felt a hot thrill at the pit of his stomach; his hands clenched, he had a spasmodic desire for violence. If only he could meet the wretch face to face!

But Felix never met him, and knew nothing of his friends or haunts. It occurred to him, though, that Paul Pavin might know; and that, at any rate, here was one person who, thoroughly "continental," with experiences of wide latitude, and social opinions of unusual generosity, should be the same to him as ever. But the artist had left America for France; his studio was possessed by a stranger, and he was not expected to return to New York until mid-winter.

So that chance of friendship was denied Felix.

His evenings he spent in the most aimless ways. He lounged in his rooms, his puppy, subdued and silent, gazing at him mournfully. When he could bear the ticking of the clock no longer, he went out and wandered through the city, looking at the lights, the moving crowds, the brilliant hurly-burly of amusement districts, as if from a great distance. His despondency attracted to his notice all sorts of depressing sights; a profound pessimism made him see in everything the saddest, the meanest, and the most contemptible elements; his comments were all sneers, he meditated on the fatuity and baseness of humanity.

Wickit, the lawyer, sent him three typewritten notes asking him to call. Each note Felix tore up with a savage laugh.

"So he's finally heard about it, has he? And now he wants his thousand dollars back in his pocket!"

One night, as he was returning home, a bent, familiar figure issued upon the pavement from his doorway; it was Joseph! Felix, concealing himself in a shadow, watched the aged servant shuffle away. The young man was disturbed by obscure forebodings.

"Now why should that old devil be sneaking round after me?" He could see nothing but a menace even in Joseph's visit. Why not? "All the world was against him."

He was more and more attracted by the relief from monotony and mental tension that alcohol effects. In intoxication he found a means by which he could, for the hour, become, as it were, another being, indifferent to misfortune, as much superior to regrets as to anxieties, contemptuous of Fate, replete with grandiose, chimerical intentions that he was going to translate into deeds "beginning to-morrow." During the day, he looked forward to the evening, when such temperamental transformation would be possible.

Since shame, and fear of rebuffs, now kept him from showing himself at his club—from which, indeed, owing to his neglect to pay his dues, he had been suspended—he frequented the gay hotel cafés along Broadway. There, sitting at a small table with a glass of whiskey and soda before him, he became a familiar figure. The cashiers, crouching on high stools behind their little grilles, bowed to him as he entered; the bartenders smirked at him patronizingly; the waiters, hovering about him with napkins rolled up under their left arms, assumed the easy and confidential manners which such servants exhibit toward old customers. He came to have a sort of affection for these places, because at his appearance, smiles greeted him. He liked always to sit at the same table. Now and then, he held long, serious conversations with his waiter—banal discussions full of trivialities, but which, since he was drinking while engaging in them, seemed to him at the moment of great interest and importance.

Then, often, in the midst of this recreation he realized the puerility of it, the pitiable quality of his satisfaction, the difference between the present and the past.

Occasionally, Felix did what he had never thought of doing in the time of his prosperity: he spent the evening with some associate from the newspaper office. To one, a reporter called "Johnny" Livy, Felix was particularly agreeable, perhaps because it was Livy who had given him his first information the day he had sought employment of *The Evening Sphere*.

This reporter was a lean, nervous, anxious-looking young man who did everything in jerks, with yellow stains on his fingers, and distinguished by a "Bohemian" nonchalance of dress. Between fitful bursts of self-assertion, he exhibited unconsciously all sorts of apprehensions—fear of his inability, of his employer, of the future, of everything. A precocious hypochondriac, he was fascinated by medical journals. While dining, he could not help asserting that oysters caused typhoid fever, soup indigestion, meat skin diseases, tomatoes rheumatism, cheese cancer, and so on, not failing to ask the waiter apprehensively: "Is this water filtered?" At other times, announcing that he was, at heart, a Christian Scientist, that nothing save fear harmed any one, he devoured course after course voraciously, with a defiant manner.

Felix, starving for companionship, dragged this young man, with his broken collar and shiny right elbow, into Broadway restaurants, which the reporter entered rubbing his chin, and where he appeared ill at ease till he had tossed off a couple of cocktails. When they had finished disparaging their superiors in the office, they discussed journalism, and, finally, literature. As Felix, slightly intoxicated, became eloquent, uttered great names, talked of "schools" and "movements," dived into history and emerged scattering quotations, a cloud passed over the face of his companion, who sat listening with an air of reluctance. Truth is, this young reporter's wings were too feeble for him to accompany Felix in those flights. Besides, always noting a thousand minute differences between his and Felix's clothing, person, voice, manner, and instincts, he was unable to meet friendliness half-way. Removed from the democratic air of the newspaper office, each discerned the social and constitutional differences in the other. Their evenings together ended. So passed that hope of friendship.

For a time Felix patronized the theatre assiduously. But to the tragedies enacted on the stage he compared his own tragedy, and in the gayety of the comedies he found something false and depressing. Then, as June ended, one by one the theatres closed, till there were left running only a few musical reviews. When he had endured the illogical uproar of each of these half a dozen times, he gave up play-going in disgust.

He took long walks with his puppy Pat, nursing his melancholy through empty streets and amid the deep shadows of the park. Looking up at the stars, he pondered the insignificance of individuals and their travail, the occult object of life, the riddle of the beyond, the possibility of there being something supreme.

His sense of loneliness did not diminish when he tried to imagine the propinquity of a God. He could not convince himself that anything, human or supernatural, had a care for him.

He read Nietzsche and Hegel, Marcus Aurelius and Renan, Loyola and Luther. So many great minds in conflict! Which to believe, when all seemed scuffling together crying, "No, no, God is like this! Not so, this only is man's proper attitude! Nay, here alone is peace!" Rumpling the leaves of "New Thought" volumes, he essayed to find therein some credible gospel. His eyes alone perused the pages. Those bland, charitable authors, with all the mannerisms of congenital saints, were just then so far removed from him in texture of the soul that he could not understand the tongue in which they wrote.

In the bookshops he saw on all sides placards advertising Oliver Corquill's latest novel, "The Rainbow." Felix read this book with amazement. Its pervasive optimism persuaded the young man that Corquill's was, after all, a surface intellect, without deep experience, of the sort that takes everything for granted. As he reached "Finis," his idol fell to pieces. The book was actually calculated to enamour one of life!

Felix, for his part, dreamed of writing a great novel crushing in its bitterness and cruel truth, that should reveal life "as it was"—a mad mask of stupidities and agonies.

So, sitting down at his work-table, he lighted a cigar, took up his pen, and waited for the thrill of inspiration.

But soon, in the silence, his thoughts turned inward. And he would remain for a long while in one attitude, dreaming of a different sort of life, eating out his heart for the responsive touch of another's hand, for the brightening of another's eye, for one vocal intonation of affection.

Such evenings often ended in hard drinking. And now, through the stupor so induced, the melancholy note still faintly struck, like the distant, lugubrious tolling of a bell, seeming to make the sound: "Alone . . . Alone. . . ."

There were times when he sprang up, crying aloud, in an incredulous voice:

"Somewhere people are happy!"

Then, with the thought, "Happiness! In God's name, where is it to be found?" he would rush out into the darkness and roam everywhere.

One such evening, early in September, when he had tramped the streets till footsore, as midnight struck Felix found himself before a large hotel in Times Square. Seeing men and women descending from automobiles and entering there, he believed that he, too, was hungry; he thought that he would enjoy something dainty to eat and a pint bottle of champagne. He entered the hotel restaurant.

This apartment, illuminated from its lofty roof of glass with a green radiance imitating moonlight, was fashioned to resemble the approach of an Italian garden—buff stone terraces, with staircases, balustrades, and urns containing scarlet flowers, rising at the rear against a background of scenery painted with a nocturnal landscape full of poplars, and embellished by an artificial moon. The white tables in the body of the restaurant, scattered under trellises, were nearly all occupied; a monotonous ripple of conversation was punctuated occasionally by a thin clash of silverware; before the terraces a fountain tinkled;

beneath the moon, violins and flutes were uttering waltz music.

Many persons looked attentively at Felix. Suddenly he saw, some distance off, at a table beside a stone pillar, a familiar face—then another. Miss Llanelly and Miss Sinjon, whom he had met in Paul Pavin's studio, were staring at him. A man, seated with them, presented a broad back.

The head waiter attempted to lead Felix past their table. Miss Llanelly put out her hand.

"You in town?" she exclaimed, with a rich, Irish smile, her ingenuous astonishment at once subtly flattering him. Her skin contained contrasts of red and white no less dazzling than ever; she fluttered her eyelashes, which were long and heavy, in a coquettish manner. Her large figure, full below the shoulders, at the hips adroitly constricted to a resemblance of slimness, was encased in a tight dress of taffy-colored Tussur silk. A wide-brimmed hat, tilted off her forehead, let some "willow" plumes trail half-way down her back.

Felix eagerly shook hands with both young women. A glow of pleasure stole through him; unwilling to pass on immediately, he uttered some remarks at random—he complained of the hot weather, regretted the invigorating days of winter, and began to recall Pavin. Miss Llanelly interrupted, quickly:

"But pardon me! Mr. Piers—Mr. Noon."

The man with them got upon his feet.

This was a burly fellow, clad in blue flannel, with a superb Persian opal, cut like a scarab, in his cravat.

Prematurely gray at the temples, his heavy, dark cheeks smooth-shaven, his expression at once shrewd and self-indulgent, he seemed to belong to that class of young New York men which spends the day feverishly clutching at money in order to pass the night gayly letting go of it. He was withdrawing his large, soft hand from Felix's when, at a sudden thought, he inquired abruptly:

"What Mr. Piers, may I ask?"

And as Felix answered, a flush slowly invaded the dusky countenance of this stranger.

"You're all alone? What a pity!" said Miss Llanelly. By dint of looking fixedly at Mr. Noon, she caused that gentleman to mumble:

"Why not join us? We're just beginning."

"Fine!" cried Miss Llanelly, vigorously. "We've ordered all kinds of things." Her lips, a vivid red, puckered greedily; she had, she announced, "one grand appetite."

Felix glanced at Miss Sinjon. She continued silent, calmly and disinterestedly regarding him with her green eyes, the lids of which seemed somewhat reddened. He felt himself blushing; he hesitated, then sat down stiffly. He was not used to indifference from women.

This one was less obtrusively attired than her friend, in linen dress and hat of russet—a hue harmonizing with her hair of reddish-brown, and lending to her translucent skin, touched round the eyes with the faintest possible coloring, a delicate warmth. Her irises, clear as the brooch of green beryls that she wore, lost effect because of the lightness of her eyelashes; her cheek-bones, without actually protruding, still seemed prominent; her white chin was square to a degree unusual in young women. She was eclipsed, as it were, by her handsome and exuberant companion. Her self-possession, however, was perfect.

When Felix ventured, with an accent of regret, that it was a long while since he had seen her, observing him serenely she answered, in a quiet voice:

"Do you count the times you have looked at me without bowing?"

Her reply was like an unexpected blow in the face.

"I? Never!" he ejaculated.

But in the most indifferent tones she recalled that behavior of his exactly to his mind; it had occurred in midwinter—once at Twenty-third Street and Broadway, again before a hotel in Fifth Avenue. Greatly embarrassed, he stammered that there was some mistake, that he had not recognized her. A sarcastic smile barely touched her lips; and her perspicacious gaze, as if penetrating to the depths of his brain, seemed to assure him: "I am not easily taken in." Then, at last releasing him from that look, leaning back and scrutinizing the whole restaurant, she uttered:

"I don't seem to see any one I know here to-night, do you?"

Felix was first dumfounded, then angered. What impertinence! From her manner one might think she deserved everything due to a person in the most impregnable position in society! As a matter of fact, however, what was her exact position?

Miss Llanelly, after an awkard pause plunging into distracted conversation, speedily informed him.

That evening a musical extravaganza, called "The Lost Venus," had commenced at the Trocadero Theatre; Miss Sinjon and Miss Llanelly were engaged in it. According to the latter, the "first-night" had gone with such a dash, and even the newspaper critics had been so well pleased, that the piece was bound to remain in New York all winter. The music was "the kind you like to whistle"; there was a "square laugh in every line"; the manner of production was superb; no expense had been spared; it was "in Montmorrissy's best style." "And you know his shows, Mr. Piers. You missed it? Isn't that miserable! Well, you must rush to it to-morrow night, for sure; Marie and I are on at a quarter to nine, with the *Six Daughters* of the *Duc des Champs-Elysées.* Such swell gowns! Where is that waiter?" And to Noon, in a voice of authority: "Billy, Mr. Piers's glass is empty." She pronounced Felix's name as if it were something unusual.

The waiter arrived with another quart of champagne. He removed the oyster-plates and served minced crabs *à la cardinal.*

The encircling babble of voices was penetrated by several deep 'cello tones, then by a sweet violin phrase, scarcely audible, and the rhythmic rippling of flute notes.

"Anitra's Dance!" exclaimed Felix, forgetting all else, wishing only that he could hear distinctly.

"From the Peer Gynt suite, by Grieg," assented Mr. Noon, in a rich bass voice, profoundly nodding. He gulped down another glass of champagne; then, turning his moist eyes on Felix, apparently apropos of nothing he declared:

"The Philistine element in life is not the failure to understand art." He frowned in perplexity. Suddenly he added, with an air of heavy satisfaction:

"Oscar Wilde said that. Now, Oscar Wilde——"

Miss Llanelly broke in:

"If you're fond of real good music, Mr. Piers, that's another reason why you must hear 'The Lost Venus' right away."

"I am fond of all good things," said Felix. "Or perhaps I should say, of all beautiful things, all sense-stirring things—of everything that can lift one emotionally out of monotony." He had no sooner finished speaking than moisture filled his eyes, so deeply did his whole being thrill at that profession— as if, with a few words, he had made by accident a revelation exquisitely true, as if he had never so clearly interpreted for himself the supreme instinct of the soul within him.

The emotional stimuli in life, the divine exaltations that, transfiguring the nature, at the same time transform the world—how he longed to experience all of them to the full! To enjoy, and in enjoying to forget, when there was so much to forget, and—it seemed after all—so much to enjoy! Wine in the blood, throbbing music, odors of flowers and perfumes, visions of red lips and humid eyes, combined to evoke indeterminate and lovely promises—earnests of such oblivion, of such effacement of the commonplace and sad, as may have come in premonition to those worn mariners out of the drear and vacant sea, trembling even to sniff the fumes of Circe's cup. Ah, to be young in every fibre, to search out and seize the treasures that the world should hold for youth! And before his mind's eye the horizon of existence seemed to widen, to recede immeasurably; fogs blew away; sunlight poured down; he saw, far off, a myriad transports prepared. The joy of the discoverer of a new paradise flowed through him; he quivered from anticipation of great happiness; he recognized his youth and its potentialities as a god might recognize his divinity. And what, indeed, was contact with divinity if not this exaltation? He would have liked to raise his glass and cry to the whole world:

"I give you the senses, in enrapturing which we soar free from all chains toward the sublime!"

The music palpitated in more ravishing tones; the soft green scene took on a dreamlike aspect; the faces of the women were invested with all sorts of beauties hitherto unsuspected. Miss Llanelly's cheeks and mouth called up the thought of full-blown roses; but in the pale face of Marie Sinjon Felix discovered a delicate allure, such as exists in a bizarre, exotic flower. His heart beat heavily. A mist passed before his eyes.

"Why do you dislike me?" he whispered in her ear.

"I do not dislike you," she replied, looking at him calmly.

He thought, "She means she neither dislikes me nor likes me." And while Noon, leaning forward with cigar smoke curling round his massive face, was telling a long anecdote which threatened to conclude equivocally, Felix watched intently the unusual squareness and the whiteness of her chin.

The music ended; the musicians, packing away their instruments, departed. In corners of the restaurant attendants were putting out lights and piling up chairs. A few feet away, a waiter stood contemplating Mr. Noon reproachfully.

"What time is it?"

"Two o'clock!"

"You don't mean it!"

As they issued from the hotel, they saw, all along Broadway, an army of dirty laborers strung out beside the car tracks, tearing up the street by the light of gasoline torches, which roared overhead while shooting forth horizontally blinding yellow flames. A tepid breeze wavered through the unwashed town, bearing with it odors of gasoline fumes, soft asphalt, and sewer gas. Shredded rubbish glided along the pavement. Even the black sky looked dusty.

Mr. Noon, choosing an electric cab from the line drawn up in front of the hotel, opened the low door. Miss Llanelly jumped in.

"Shall we give you a lift home, dear?" she inquired sweetly of Miss Sinjon.

"You know that it's only a step, for me."

"If you will allow me," proposed Felix.

Miss Llanelly sank back on the cushions with a bright smile.

"Good-night, then," she called, gayly. "Good-night, Mr. Piers! So glad! To-morrow evening, remember!"

Mr. Noon ponderously waved his hand. The cab disappeared. Felix and Miss Sinjon remained together on the sidewalk. He signalled the nearest chauffeur.

"But it's only a step."

"Never mind."

They entered the vehicle; she gave an address in Forty-eighth Street. They were whirled northward through the stale night air.

Street lights one after another shone upon her face; her eyes were fixed ahead, her lips composed; even while in contact with him how far removed she was, apparently, in thought!

"What are you thinking of?" he asked her, gently.

"I am thinking of this abominable city."

"Let us escape it for a little while." And as she made no reply, he called to the chauffeur:

"Drive through the park."

The automobile passed Forty-eighth Street, rushed on along the empty thoroughfare, and, finally, plunged in amid the trees.

Sweet and pure air blew round them, soft as a tender breath upon the cheek, redolent of dewy blades and leaves. Beyond the roadway the bushes rose in blue-black masses; then, here and there, a solitary gas-light was surrounded by a wide aureole of foliage, the raw green of which was like no hue in nature. As they penetrated the odorous recesses of the park, their progress was, for Felix, like an abandonment of the known universe, a passage into absolute phantasma, promising who knew what rapturous revelations?

Two funnels of light appeared far ahead, approached swiftly, dazzled, and flashed past. In the deep tonneau of that automobile, a man and a woman, arms round each other, were united in a kiss.

Farther on, they met a hansom cab, flitting through shadows, drawn by an old, ambling horse. Their lanterns illumined for an instant two figures close together. And Felix imagined all the dim roadways of that place, all the secret by-paths, all the perfumed, silent coverts, thus peopled, full of love. When he kissed her, the quality of her submission seemed to tell him that she had expected this conclusion from the first, and did not care one way or the other.

Soon, turning her green eyes full on him, she said, with a stiff smile:

"You see, one doesn't escape the city by coming into the park."

CHAPTER VII

FELIX made haste to attend "The Lost Venus" at the Trocadero Theatre. There, sitting in the first row, he saw, amid the grouping and melting of tableaux on the brilliant stage, Marie Sinjon, all her charms enhanced, wearing in the first act an extravagant hat and dress the color of autumnal leaves, and in the second act a spangled, low-neck gown of black and green, with a train extraordinarily long, and a tiara of paste brilliants.

When he remembered his evening with her, his heart beat heavily: the glamour of the footlights informed that intimacy with a new value. At last, she looked down and recognized him. It was he who blushed.

She, like her friend Miss Llanelly, was a "show girl"— one of those actresses whose rôles consisted in little more than standing round and looking handsome, who were distinguished from their harder-working sisters of the chorus by their beauty, their costly costumes, their simulation of an elegant languor, their air of conferring a favor on audiences merely by their mute appearance. Stories remembered of a few of them concerning jewels, automobiles, journeys to Europe, winnings in Wall Street, and suits for breach of promise, invested them all with a perverse dignity.

In the sphere which they inhabited, if anywhere, thought Felix, was to be found gayety and distraction. The young man was grateful to the chance that had offered, at a moment of profound depression, this opportunity. He lost no time in returning to West Forty-eighth Street, where, on the ninth floor of an apartment hotel, Marie Sinjon occupied two small rooms—the "parlor," lined with crimson cartridge-paper, crowded with frail cherry furniture, band-boxes, and theatrical trunks, looking out over the back yards.

She received him in negligée with unconcern. Their discussion of "The Lost Venus" was interrupted by a woman hairdresser: Marie Sinjon, in a wadded kimono of gray silk, sat down before a cheval-glass and, without any coquetry, submitted to this person's ministrations.

The hairdresser, squat and shapeless, her lips discreetly clamped upon a bristle of hairpins, kept shooting at Felix, by means of the mirror, stealthy glances out of her small, black eyes, which were set in a face of indeterminable age. Finally, she mumbled, in an innocent tone:

"Didn't you wish to pay to-day?"

A faint flush stained Marie Sinjon's cheek-bones. She answered, rather sharply:

"You know I always pay on Saturday."

The hairdresser raised her eyebrows, shrugged her shoulders, and compressed her lips the more, as if she had been rebuffed while offering to do her customer a service. Packing her brushes and curling-irons into a black satchel, she cast a last look at the young woman's head—a monument of tawny curls and undulations. Then, with another stare at Felix, she took herself off.

He understood that little comedy. "This girl is at least not mercenary," he considered. And, in his self-satisfaction at having made so shrewd a judgment, he invited her to dinner.

But, with a sudden gleam of eye, she shook her head.

"Some other time."

Then, seeing that he was really disappointed, she became curious.

"Why do you ask me that? I thought——"

"What?"

She looked at him in a nearly spiteful way, then flashed forth:

"You might meet some one, perhaps!"

Moving to the window, she turned her back on him. Dusk had fallen upon a rainy day; through a thin mist, the back yards and rear walls of the houses opposite appeared unutterably shabby, gloomy, and forlorn. She continued gazing on this scene.

He joined her. He was flattered by her speech, which seemed to him almost born of jealousy; he was delighted by the atmosphere of intimacy that she had evoked so swiftly, all without intention, he believed. The prospect of entering forthwith into a sentimental part exhilarated him. He was quite careless what he said so long as it was tender. His voice fell instinctively into the most melting tones.

"How you have misjudged me! As if I could feel that way toward you! It would mean that I did not understand you, that I did not recognize you instantly for what you are—utterly different, a nature superior to all this, misplaced just for the moment—"

He hesitated; should he have employed more delicacy? But she, to his amazement, laying her arm across the window-sash, leaning her forehead on her hand, began to sob.

"Life is so unfair!" she gasped.

In stifled accents, she stammered an incoherent synopsis of her sorrows—the isolation of her heart amid the wastes into which fate had forced her, the meanness of every one's intentions toward her, the struggle against continual disgrace, the cruelty of the world's judgment, the injustice of protected women: in fine, she exposed a whole gallery of pathetic views of life. Why she was telling all this to him, she said, she did not know. Perhaps it was because something in his face promised that comprehension, that sort of friendship, she had sometimes dreamed of.

"What am I saying!" she cried suddenly, showing him her green eyes full of what seemed consternation, and her translucent cheeks smeared with tears. "I am crazy, to talk this way! What is there about you—you had better go quickly, and not come back. That's it, go, go!" Her voice had hysterical intonations. She tried to push him from her. Her arm, protruding white as marble from the sleeve of her kimono, was peculiarly strong.

But he, at first bewildered by this outburst, was in a moment greatly touched. He saw her just as she had portrayed herself in the paroxysm of self-pity that one gentle word of his had caused. Poor little girl, so lonely, so helpless, and so put upon! In compassion, his frivolity of purpose disappeared.

He took her hand, which was neither cold nor hot, but cool; he put his arm round her shoulder with the gesture of a brother. In a low voice—all the while thinking that he was acting rather finely—he spoke of the impermanency of misfortune to the brave, of "a divine something that takes care of all of us in the end." Many a scrap of comforting philosophy he murmured that he had read but, in respect of his own case, had been unable to believe. He exhorted her to hope for better times, for truer friends, and, as one of these, he offered himself, with a sweet courtesy, "for so long as she should need him." She grew calmer, drew a quivering breath or two, used his handkerchief, and softly thanked him. And he, who had come with the most selfish of designs, was vaguely conscious that he had stayed to incur, just how he did not know, some subtle kind of obligation.

This obligation, without trying to analyze it, he accepted carelessly, while marching home that evening in the highest spirits. His heart was expanded by delectable anticipations: he was going to escape solitude, to know excitement, to have companions of some sort.

Night after night he attended the Trocadero Theatre, sitting always in the first row, on the right-hand side of the auditorium, near the drums. It was not long before he had all the music and lines of "The Lost Venus" by heart. He knew each cue for the entrance of the "show girls"; and when they appeared—six in number, undulating in their beautiful dresses, gazing out over the orchestra almost arrogantly—he would wait without moving until Marie Sinjon, coming to a stop near by, should recognize him. Finally, losing all interest in the performance when she was not on the stage, Felix would watch the drummer.

This fellow had a broad, ugly face, ornamented with dyed "mutton-chop" whiskers that merged into his mustache, splotched across the nose from alcoholic poisoning, and farther distinguished by the watery eyes and tremulous, lugubrious mouth of one of those neurasthenic persons always ready to burst into tears. He beat his drum as a virtuoso plays the piano, with the most exquisite attention to the score and the conductor's baton, rolling up his eyes and throwing his head about in an artistic ecstasy. His behavior diverted Felix, who wondered what sort of life the man led outside the playhouse.

Felix became known by sight to the chorus girls and the comedians, to the ushers and the ticket sellers, and even to the owner of the play, Montmorrissy, a short, obese, debilitated-looking individual with a large nose and a black mustache, who sometimes, in evening dress, stood in the lobby of the theatre, smoking a cigar, exhibiting his diamond rings, and chatting with acquaintances. Those em-

ployed about the place commenced to nod to Felix
and, perhaps, to smile behind his back. The keeper
of the stage entrance—an old ruffian with a growl
for every one—so far unbent as to accept his messages and tips.

He grew used to waiting in the shadows of West
Thirty-sixth Street, by a dingy door from which, soon
after eleven o'clock at night, issued the chorus girls,
their faces pale from fatigue and scrubbing with cold
cream, their clothing and demeanor in acute con-
trast to their dainty costumes and sprightly manners
on the stage. He saw, in the gloom of that side
street, the reverse, as it were, of the theatrical medal
—the butterflies of the footlights changed into drab,
serious working people. The dancers were reduced
to the appearance of shop-girls; the comedians
emerged from their false noses and ridiculous wigs
as aging, harassed-looking men; the tenor—just now
how fascinating, devil-may-care a rascal, in his azure
uniform of the Hussars!—was pounced upon by a
resolute wife and hustled home; the very prima
donna—queen of a glittering kingdom, half an hour
since—appeared fresh from wiping off her girlish-
ness and animation with her rouge, to wrangle,
maybe, with some shabby pedler of lace under-
wear who, bill in hand, had managed to waylay her.
It seemed that of all the company there was but one
set which did not lose, on contact with the open air,
whatever distinction the lights of the proscenium
had shed. This group was made up of the "show
girls."

Frequently, late in the afternoon, when Felix was calling on Marie Sinjon, these young women ran in for half an hour's gossip. For him, there was fascination in that intercourse through which, all the while, ran a faint undertone of obliquity. Yet sometimes, while sitting in the little crimson parlor, where the shades were drawn against the dusk, where the saturnine hairdresser Miriam was silently at work, where two or three girls, as well off for fine feathers as so many peacocks, were chattering "shop-talk" at once, Felix would feel a mental confusion, an enervation of will power, a moral suffocation that at the same time shamed and thrilled him—as if his manhood were being smothered in so much flagrant femininity.

When these visitors had gone, Marie Sinjon would usually give him in some way to understand that they distressed her by their conversation, that she wished they would not come to see her. "But in the profession," she would say, "it's a bad thing to make enemies. One has to own to nearly every sort of friend!"

There was one "show girl" whom Felix found different from the rest. This was a gentle-faced, quiet girl named Miss Qewan. Her soft voice, with its intimation of self-restraint, her modest conduct, and her charitable views caused Felix to wonder why Marie Sinjon had not recognized in her a kindred soul and chosen her for an intimate instead of Miss Llanelly.

The latter, exuberantly blooming, bursting with rude vitality and high spirits, reminded Felix of a splendid peasant whose metropolitan veneer is no disguise. She was one of those daughters of the people who, amid the meanest surroundings, had expanded into a majestic and disquieting beauty, her vivid allure becoming finally too superb for its environment, and making escape from the monotonous and drudging life of her own kind too easy. With a great appetite for fine clothes, rich food, scenes of excitement, and the homage of men, she had "risen," as she would have said, from some shabby home that now, no doubt, she could scarcely see in its exact proportions, while looking back through all the vicissitudes that must have intervened.

It was "Nora Llanelly's good heart," Felix was informed, that had first attracted Marie to her.

"A kind heart! I thought myself so lucky in finding such a thing that I was glad to take everything else with it. You don't know, perhaps, how rare good hearts are, in some situations, and how terribly one can long for them."

"Poor little girl, as if I didn't!" Whereupon he assured Marie that he understood her, in that case as in all others, perfectly.

And yet, he reflected, how inaccurate an impression of her he had got at first!

On that first night, ill at ease before her cold scrutiny, angry at her deliberate rudeness, baffled, finally, by her indifferent surrender to his kisses, he had believed her to be everything that she, by all her subsequent utterances and actions, had convinced him she was struggling not to become. For no sooner had he shown her his impressible disposition than she had seemed, in a burst of trustfulness, determined to reveal to him, at least, her true self. Little by little, with touching confidences murmured in the dusk, with long clear looks disclosing untold yearnings, with low sighs at the thought of other sorts of lives, she wove about herself a fine, transfiguring fabric— a veil tinged with the wan hues of moral beauty smothered by mischance, a veil through which, as the glamour of it thickened, she appeared to the young man ever the more remote, in instincts, from those round her, ever a rarer and more estimable personality, ever worthier of pity, of comforting services, and of respect.

Many a time, indeed, he told her how much he respected her. "For did he not know the golden heart within her, that had been forced to suffer so much, yet still retained, as if by a miracle, its first fresh beauty, longing for the heights it ought to occupy by right, and—if there was justice in the universe—was going to gain some day?"

"You are good," she would reply, gently laying her cool hand on his. "How you help me: how you give me hope! What if I had never met you?"

And, wrapped in a secret reverie, she would gaze at him for a long while, her green eyes seeming not only to take in all his visible features, but also to explore his nature to its depths.

He was, no doubt, more valuable to her than he suspected, with his good looks, with his air of good breeding, with his conversation from which there was always something to be learned, and with that suggestion, which he continually disseminated, of aristocratic antecedents and good fortune. There are some persons of whom it is thought instantly: "He cannot possibly be ill-born, or poor, or uncertain of his future." It is toward such individuals, with their indescribable, yet convincing, promise of great things to come, that those turn their eyes who have everything to gain, and who can gain nothing save through attachment to another.

Marie, by spinning pretty tales about her girlhood—wherein she appeared a quaint, delightful little innocent—encouraged Felix to talk about himself,—to tell her something of his life, his work, and his ambitions.

Quite naturally he contrived for her a history of himself half true, half false: he related all that was flattering in his career—anecdotes of his family, his luxurious early years, his travels, the wealthy friends one would have thought his boon companions still; he avoided mentioning his loss of fortune and his social downfall. "His work in the newspaper office—an uncongenial apprenticeship, perhaps—was going to be of great value to him some day: he would not regret it." Like many another of a disposition easily affected, he was apt to enter into a rôle so thoroughly that, for the moment, it took on the aspect of reality. So, often, while uttering some such rhodomontade about his journalistic business, for an instant he would see himself again in his old guise—a hero, making great sacrifices for the sake of literature.

With so much ability for self-delusion, it was not strange that he should manage to delude another. Crossing their wits, they played a well-matched game of fence, he as dexterous in feint of reminiscences as she, and, no doubt, giving her just as much accurate information as she returned. All these lunges and parries may have ended by somewhat dazzling the eyes of both. For just as he failed to perceive that in her story there were hiatuses to spare between her "life at home" and her present situation, so, probably, she did not see that none of his fashionable adventures were in actual progress.

The part which his pride had urged upon him proved an expensive one to play.

Fall passed, and winter came: the languishing and sombre nuances of these seasons, erstwhile fraught with explicit charm, were this year but vaguely felt by Felix. He who had been wont to draw keen pleasure from innumerable tenuous sources, found his old interests all turning stale, his old visions losing their beauty, then suffering eclipse. Finally, he threw overboard everything except his idol of the moment, Pleasure. So, without ballast, like an antique voyager lured on by siren songs, he steered a plunging course into uncharted, mist-filled seas, where, on all sides, through vapors crawling sinuously along the hollows of wine-colored waves, appeared white, glistening shapes, leaning forward with fair arms outstretched, and uttering cries of provocation.

At such a pass, there is no rationalizing force so

swift in effect as an awakening to poverty. One
afternoon, while sitting alone in a café, Felix made
some reckonings, laboriously, with growing consternation. He stared at the result in horror. He was
at the end of his resources, and in debt.

Dismally looking up, at last, from his empty glass,
he saw, approaching amid the café tables, Mr. Noon,
in a fawn-colored overcoat the lapel of which was
decorated with a white carnation.

The new-comer and Felix, because of their sentimental projects, were continually being thrown together. On scores of evenings spent in each other's
company, they had enjoyed to the full that disinte-
gration of reserve which alcohol induces. It was on
the rambling discussions of those hours, the involuntary confessions, the maudlin protestations of esteem,
that their friendship had been built.

Recognizing the young man, Noon smiled, rumbled
a facetious greeting, sat down, and smote the bell on
the table a hearty blow. But he stopped in the
midst of a remark to stare at Felix's face.

"What's wrong?" he asked.

Then, glancing down, he saw, on the table, two or
three envelopes with figures scribbled over them.
Felix made haste to pick these up.

"I feel a little blue this afternoon," he answered.
"It may be the weather." And he looked out of
the window at the dusk, powdered with snow-flakes,
which was bringing to an end a cheerless day.

Noon gulped his highball, lighted a long cigar,
inhaled the smoke, and rolled his eyes toward the

gilded ceiling, all the while wearing furtively an expression of discomfort. Twice he opened his mouth to speak, and twice checked himself with a forced cough.

Felix, meanwhile, regarded him enviously. For from the hands of this burly fellow, this sybarite and Wall Street speculator who burned the candle night and day, there perpetually rained money. Up and down Broadway, wherever lights shone brilliantly by night, he was referred to as "a prince." At first-nights in the theatres, at midnight supper parties in the restaurants, at "stag" dinners where actors and their managers congregated with a hilarious swarm of artists, hotel proprietors, playwrights and politicians, he was a familiar figure. Men greeted him jovially; women stared at him. With his dark eyes, gray temples, heavy jowl, big shoulders, and resplendent clothes, he was what girls of Miss Llanelly's way of thinking called "a handsome dog."

Amid his amusements, he had an air of ponderous vigor, of somewhat taurine formidableness. With his devotion to elaborate menus, strong cigars, and potent alcoholic drinks, he revealed on all occasions his unbridled and unappeasable appetency. But whenever he had drunk a good deal, there rose from the depths of this heavy roisterer's nature—just as strange, unsuspected objects rise sometimes from the bottom of a stirred up pool—an æstheticism curiously delicate, a pleasure in sensuous, brilliant, and decadent forms of art. He delighted in the erotic dissonance of the "Salome" of Strauss; he knew by

book the "Fleurs du Mal" of Baudelaire; he was en-
raptured by the "Sataniques" of the etcher Rops.
Invariably, genius, if, instead of soaring, it clung to
earth, found the way straight to his heart. All gifted
men who had conspicuous vices fascinated him—
"they were so human."

He had evidently grown fond of Felix. On relinquishing his first attitude toward the young man—
which, in a less stalwart person, would have seemed
like disquiet—he had assumed an eager amity, a
kindliness beyond his wont, nearly such solicitude as
that by which one may strive to neutralize a hidden
remorse. If he had one day unwittingly done Felix
an injury in secret, he could not more pains-takingly
have tried to make amends.

When his gaze had thoroughly explored the gilded
ceiling of the café, Noon uttered, in an artificial
voice:

"Have you seen the ticker to-day? It was fierce
downtown. I'm nearly used up, what with the customers and my own little affairs—we stock-brokers,
you know, Mr. Author, wouldn't make much if we
depended on our commissions. But wait till to-
morrow; there's going to be a massacre. I've got a
tomahawk up my sleeve, myself. It's the chance of
the year, for a man who has some spare cash."

Then, as if at a chance thought:

"Why, look here, Piers! I could put it in your way,
if you happened to have a fair balance at the bank!"

A bitter laugh escaped Felix. Then, recollecting
himself, with averted eyes he answered:

"That's kind of you. But the fact is, I'm already over my quarterly income. The old wretch who handles the estate won't ever advance a penny."

"Ah, what a shame! And such an opportunity. Hold on, I'll tell you what!"

And, slapping a check-book upon the table, Noon scribbled a check, in Felix's favor, for ten thousand dollars.

"To-morrow morning put this check into your bank. Then send me immediately, by messenger, another, made out to my firm, for the same amount. I'll put it through my office as an order from you, for a certain stock, never mind which, on margin. Your bother ends there; the rest is up to me. No risk to you, d'you see, and you're on hand when the melon is cut."

"But why," faltered Felix, with dry lips, "should you do this for me?"

"Nonsense!" growled Noon, while banging the table bell.

Five days later, Felix received, from the brokerage firm of which Noon was a member, a check for three thousand two hundred and eighty-three dollars and fifty cents.

In his wild outburst of thankfulness, Felix swore that he had learned his lesson, that he would impose no more upon the providence which, with awesome regularity, was manifest in his dark hours. Here was the chance for a fresh start; these talents, falling out of the blue into his lap, how faithfully he would husband and augment them! Old dreams grew bright; optimism and a sense of power returned to him. He felt able to perform Herculean feats of strength, to work with the titanic energy and fecundity of another Balzac, to achieve fame at a bound, to become, while still in his twenties, a colossal figure —a literary Napoleon. Ah, what a career he was now free to enter on!

And all this thanks to Noon!

Before Felix's incoherent thanks, the speculator seemed to flinch a little. Then, fixing the other with his eyes, he answered, while making a secretive gesture:

"We'll forget it now. It was just between you and me, you understand."

"As you say." Felix drew a long breath of relief. So Marie need not know how close he had come to a smash-up!

His elation demanded outlet; his prosperity tempted him into extravagances. It was Christmas week; he would give in his studio a Christmas eve party of the gayest sort. A graceful excuse would be a recent triumph of Marie's. On the withdrawal of an actress of small importance from "The Lost Venus," she had, by the greatest luck, obtained a part in which she spoke a dozen lines.

Felix turned his rooms upside down, bought new hangings, consulted the caterer whose employees had waited on him at balls in other days, ordered flowers and holly, ran in and out of jewelry shops in search of supper gifts, then, standing under the skylight, with his dog barking round him, viewed the arrival of many hampers. For this business he had plenty of time. He had resigned from *The Evening Sphere.* He was too much occupied by great plans, now, to "think of writing murder stories."

He invited a dozen guests, glowing with pleasure at the thought of having again so many friends. Had he forgotten any? On Christmas eve, at dusk, while passing the Metropolitan Opera House, he saw stretched across the billboards Mme. Regne Lodbrok's name.

Paul Pavin! Surely he had returned by this time? Felix hurried to the portrait-painter's old studio.

"Yes, he had returned; he was even in the building, on the top floor west."

It was the Frenchman's hour for relaxation. He was at home, alone, stretched out on one of the faded couches like a huge Viking, ruddy as ever, his spreading, golden beard aglimmer.

He rose slowly to his feet, with a bewildered look.

"Who is it?" he cried, in French. Then he lowered his eyebrows and, with a great laugh, strode forward.

"*Mon Dieu*, it is that Félix! What a strange thing! For a moment, while you stood in the shadows, I thought I don't know what. At least, the present seemed to melt away. But what you reminded me of, I cannot just put the finger on. How curious!"

He scrutinized Felix in perplexity. Soon he shrugged his shoulders, smiled, and clapped his heavy hands upon the other's arms.

"Why did you disappear, answer me that, sir! It was unkind of you: those smoky twilights were beginning to make me young again. But there, I forgive you. You come back in a good hour. Noël rings you in."

What a kind heart was here! thought Felix.

They sat down together. Without asking a single disconcerting question, Pavin talked about his own life of the last six months. He had been in Paris, Vienna, and St. Petersburg; he was going soon to Washington to portray the President; he had done several pictures, and had sold one to the French government. Near his chair, there was a large canvas, on an easel, turned to the wall.

Felix remembered the portrait of Eileen Tamborlayne, her sittings in Pavin's studio, the evenings when he had called there for her, to find her, sometimes, scarcely ready to set out with him, though daylight had long since faded.

Now, able to view that whole epoch in perspective, he interpreted with startling clearness many minute circumstances lost on him before.

"How soft I was!"

He looked at Pavin intently, full of conjectures, but without resentment. One could not, at this late day, hold such feelings toward a splendid celebrity who permitted an obscure young man to call him friend. Felix carried away the Frenchman's promise to "look in round midnight" as if it were a priceless boon. His supper-party was going to be distinguished as well as gay.

Returning home, he found everything in readiness. The florist had gone; the caterer's men had made their preparations; the caretaker was sweeping the hallway.

The studio had been stripped of nearly all its furniture. The four walls were banked to the skylight with box-trees and holly-bushes. All the glossy foliage was powdered with fine tinsel. The circular table, with twelve chairs ranged round it, laden with china and wine-glasses, nearly hidden by masses of mistletoe and deep-red roses, seemed laid in the hollow of some little glen where snow had just fallen.

Felix turned on all the lights. Producing some chopped ice from a waiter, he mixed himself a couple of cocktails. Then he lighted a cigarette, picked up *The Evening Sphere* and, with a sigh of satisfaction, sat down beside the refulgent table, to kill time.

On the second page of the newspaper he read:

"Paris, December 24. Mrs. James Corrochie Ferrol, of New York, died suddenly to-day, at the Hotel Ritz, of heart failure. . . ."

Felix sat motionless, intent on this catastrophe. He imagined the scene which was doubtless being enacted at the moment, thousands of miles away: in an alcove heavy with shadows, the daughter sitting beside the body of the mother, while, throughout the French city, church bells were uttering Christmas chimes.

But he was unable to feel the poignancy of that picture. He groped in his heart for the appropriate emotions. He could not find them. They had been obliterated?

CHAPTER VIII

HALF of Felix's guests, with a nonchalance engendered of long dinners and hours spent in cafés, brought with them to the supper-party their companions of the earlier evening. In the studio, amid a confusion of large coiffures and close-trimmed heads, appeared on all sides unfamiliar faces. "Show girls," radiant in light-colored dresses, coolly introduced strange young men who apologized unsteadily for intruding. Some one dragged in the tenor of "The Lost Venus," who had managed to give his wife the slip at the stage door. Noon produced no less a personage than Montmorrissy, the theatrical manager; and, as if this were not enough, Pavin arrived with another unexpected celebrity—Oliver Corquill, the novelist. These two had been dining at the same house on Fifth Avenue, and Corquill, remembering Felix perfectly, had consented—out of curiosity, perhaps—to "look in for a moment."

Felix soon perceived that the writer's eye was on him constantly. If he had played the complaisant host well enough before, forthwith he surpassed himself. He gave confidence to dismayed waiters, made persons whom he had never seen before laugh outright at the whimsical good nature of his greetings, and drank a cocktail with nearly every group of new arrivals. Twenty-one persons wedged themselves round the table, to which a dozen had been invited, in such good fellowship that several young women agreed to share their plates with total strangers. For a time it was thought that Montmorrissy would have to take Marie's quiet friend, Miss Qewan, on his knee.

With the appearance of the champagne, the assembly, for the most part already stimulated, became hilarious—as if the mere sight of those large bottles wrapped in napkins were exhilarating. The continuous vocal din, pierced by shrill laughter, Felix presently imagined to be like the babble of some loose, pagan ritual of antiquity; and in the solemn countenances of the waiters, moving to and fro above the beaming faces of the guests, the young man found, to his diversion, something sacerdotal, as if there were ministering here a bizarre priesthood of the vine.

"So, surely, the creatures of Dionysos in secret glens," he thought. "Why, for that matter, does not time turn back to-night: have we not here the most charming mænads, and as many ægipans, and no doubt a satyr or two—the whole rout—besides the proper woodland setting? Beat, drums; blow, pipes; we'll swing the leopard skins again! What is it blotches the recesses of the forest with red fires? The god's afoot; the green eyes of his lynxes come flickering through bracken; the torchlight wavers nearer over the convolutions of great branches— louder the corybantes' drums; frenzy bursts round about: the world's aflame, and writhing in a fanatical ecstasy. Join in! Who knows the ancient cry? Evoë! Saboï!" And, shivering with delight at the pictures of primeval orgies which those words evoked, he repeated, under his breath:

"Evoë! Saboï!"

"Felix, what are you muttering?" exclaimed Marie, who, in a new dress of old-rose silk, her tawny hair bound with a fillet of black velvet, sat beside him.

He raised his head. As he gazed round at his friends, with the sensations of one returning from afar, loneliness chilled his heart. Three times a waiter had to whisper to him that "a party wished to see him in the hallway."

At the end of the hallway, Felix found a sad-faced little woman, plainly dressed, standing in a diffident attitude, and staring at him with large, lustrous eyes.

She was evidently taken aback by this apparition of a fine, flushed young man in evening dress, with valuable pearls in the embroidered bosom of his shirt, and a gold fob glittering on his hip. Protesting timidly that "he was not the gentleman she had expected to see," she inquired for the consumptive artist from whom Felix had rented the studio.

"But he has not lived in New York for over a year!" the young man informed her.

Her small, pale face, the face of a woman of thirty, slowly expressed weariness and despair.

"Thank you very much, sir," she said, listlessly— then turned toward the staircase.

Through the half-open doorway of the studio came voices of women raised in a waltz-song from "The Lost Venus." Half-way down the first flight of steps, the stranger paused to listen, her white face upturned and seeming to float mysteriously midst the shadows of the staircase well, wherein her sombrely clothed shape was blotted out. Presently, at the outer corners of her lustrous eyes appeared two tears, ready to roll down her cheeks.

Felix, distressed, leaned over the balustrade.

"You are in trouble. Surely I can help you in some way? At least, let me try to find your friend's address."

She shook her head, and the two tears slid quickly, glistening, down her face. Then, like a child that knows whom to confide in:

"He was my husband's friend. I thought perhaps he could tell me where my husband is. He's left me again, this month past, on one of his lovely sprees. But I thought Christmas eve might bring him home, or that I might find him!"

Leaning against the rail, hiding her face, she sobbed:

"Oh, if I hadn't come here to-night, and heard people having a good time!"

Suddenly, the stranger flashed at Felix a horror-stricken look, cried, in an agitated voice: "What can you think of me!" and ran down the stairs.

"Stop!" he called after her. He started in pursuit. But he had not reached the second floor, when he heard the street door slam.

As he re-entered the studio, every one stopped talking to look at him. Marie's green eyes seemed to plunge into his brain.

When he had recounted his experience to her, she whispered, in a voice trembling with anger:

"I should think, my dear, that you could manage a little more cleverly—at least so that twenty people couldn't have the laugh on me!"

He protested in bewilderment. As two or three girls were, indeed, watching them with sweet, malicious smiles, Marie turned to Noon, who sat the other side of her.

The speculator, his massive face shining, had reached the æsthetic stage of his intoxication. With half-shut eyes, he was muttering:

"The most subtle epicureanism consists in chaste pursuits in the midst of frenzy." And, amid the uproar of advanced revelry, he began to intone, in his bull's voice, an old Latin hymn in which the first syllable of every line resembled a note of the musical scale. At a remark of Marie's, he was good enough to leave off shouting. And presently Felix, to his amazement, heard the two discussing—she as intelligently, it appeared, as Noon—the principles of the Gregorian chant.

Good heavens, the curious scraps of knowledge that every little while he was discovering in her! For the hundredth time, he pictured for himself a scene that many an indefinite "confession" of hers had helped him to construct: an old, placid homestead somewhere, in which, part of a gentle family

circle—how pitiful, the loss of it—she had been cultivated for far different ends.

Nora Llanelly, on his other hand, leaning against
his shoulder, was laughing softly at what had just
amazed him. Her exuberant form was laced into
a light-green dress; her cheeks were bright with
pulsing blood; her lips glowed vividly; her eyes
shone with unusual brilliancy. She was a disturb-
ing beauty at close quarters.

But she seemed moved by no feeling save generous
admiration for Marie, who was meeting Noon's jargon
so nearly on an equal footing.

"Listen to her," whispered Nora, somewhat unsteadily. "Isn't she the wonderful kid? Would you
ever think she started life as she did—faith, as both of
us did? We grew up in the same block, you know."

"You and she! I thought you had known each
other only a little while!"

"That's a good one!" She laughed in his face.
"Why, I've known her all my life."

Carried away, Felix thought, by something analo-
gous to the pride of a "self-made man" recounting
circumstances of his humble origin, she began, gig-
gling, to relate what she called "comical" reminiscences of her early youth, in which Marie had a
part. And there rose before the young man views
of mean city streets on summer nights, lined with
flat-houses all open windows and rusty fire-escapes,
swarming with slattern figures lightly clad—views
midst which two immature girls of the people, untidy
in cheap clothes, thin from malnutrition, but full of

the feverish energy of curiosity, moved seeking their first taste of puerile romance, mischief, consternation, deception, and distorted ambition.

A bolt from the blue—that disclosure!

When, in the smoky studio, revelry had reached its height and failed from sheer exhaustion; when the blue glimmer of the Christmas dawn, creeping through the skylight, had sent all the jaded roisterers dragging off to rest; when, for Felix, a heavy sleep had given place to all the aches and nauseas of resuscitation, there contested for the young man's notice, with his bodily pain, an agonizing query. This girl of faint flushes and translucent tissues, this creature of obscure, ingratiating charms, so adroit in simulation of refinement—where had she acquired the qualities that made her seem superior to her surroundings? In what long-attended schools, from what deeply interested teachers, at whose patient, fondling hands? He had now, for the first time, visions of predecessors more cultivated, brilliant, and amiable, than he. Such thoughts were scarcely to be borne.

All the while, she must have been laughing at him for his gullibility. To the devil with such deceit!

Ah, but the long, perfumed hours!

It needed no more than this to show him how closely the coils of tender habit had enwrapped him. In that play which he had begun, for diversion's sake, with tongue in cheek, he could now pull a tragic enough grimace. Forthwith, he began to suffer all the anguishes inevitable in a passion fashioned on such a pattern and of such materials.

The first explosion immediately followed their next meeting; it was she, with an angry reference to his "mysterious" visitor of the supper-party, who unwittingly fired the train.

"I can guess who it was, too! I should have thought, if words mean anything, you would have given that up."

"I don't understand you."

"Ah," she retorted, "you think I haven't heard! About you and a woman with black hair—oh, a very fashionable-looking woman—whom you used to be seen with everywhere. Deny it if you can!"

"That belongs to the past," he answered, wincing. Then, in a gust of rage:

"And your past! Have I ever taunted you with it?" And his volley of recriminations, brutally accurate, thanks to Nora Llanelly, made her give back as if he had showered her with so many blows.

She sank upon the couch, and buried her face amid the pillows. Finally, there came to his ears, between sobs, in muffled tones, her self-justification:

"What wonder if a loving woman should strive to appear worthier than she was? And the more recent past—how she hated it, how she had hoped to forget it now! But no: women were never forgiven, even when, in their own souls, they felt themselves clarified by love. Fond, foolish, pitiable dreams of one who had never loved before! She had thought to find in him a unique nobility, a nature rising above the heartless judgment of the world!"

Thus, in effect, her plaint. Attacked at his most

vulnerable points, seized, at sight of so much agitation, with an overpowering physical excitement, he threw himself down beside the couch, and took her in his arms. That was a bitter-sweet, incoherent quarter of an hour, wherein sobs gradually ceased, and tears were kissed away, and one, at least, groping with his senses instead of with his logic, had no clear understanding how all had been ostensibly made right once more. In such exhaustion as ensues from self-abandonment, they drew themselves slowly back toward sanity by feeble and pathetic discourse. She faltered:

"If you only knew the dreams I've had! To escape all this, and all that's past, with you—never to see it, or think of it, again! A place far away in the country, so quiet, so peaceful, where I could be happy with you, where you could do those great things you are planning, and have dogs, and horses, and old friends round you."

This tableau abruptly gave him pause: it was arranged decidedly in an atmosphere of domesticity. A host of wistful ambiguities which she had uttered in the past seemed now made plain.

Still, with her arms round him and her breath upon his cheek, he could not see, in the vague portents that were gathering, sufficient incongruity to alarm him. All sorts of extravagance, if contemplated from a sentimental view-point, presently grow reasonable.

From that scene Felix emerged, to his subsequent surprise, as poor in information as before: Marie, it appeared, while admitting everything he had taxed her with, had neglected to offer further particulars. Moreover, he had promised "never to bring up the hateful past again."

What, then, had he accomplished? He had been the means of breaking the friendship between Marie and Nora Llanelly, who, after a violent quarrel, had parted company "forever."

This was the easier since Nora—who had first met Noon while rehearsing for "The Lost Venus"— began the year by informing every one, while waving plump hands which glittered with some new rings, that she was "tired of acting." She abandoned the stage. Undecided whether to make a little journey of recuperation to Monte Carlo or to Bermuda, she favored Monte Carlo, since Paris, with its dressmakers, was, she understood, on the way. However, she remained in New York, never far from the racket of theatres and night restaurants, and regularly every fair Sunday afternoon appeared on the East Drive in Central Park, reclining in a hired victoria, elaborately dressed, brilliant of complexion, but very prim in mien, and with an unhappy eye on the coachman when his hat was cocked too far over his ear.

Marie could presently afford to smile at Nora in her elegant leisure.

Since other of her unconfessed ambitions were not easy of immediate fulfilment, Marie, who appeared to favor the maxim that inaction equalled retrogression, set all her energies to the feat of climbing the theatrical ladder.

One night in February, favored by that cool audacity which Felix had observed in her at the first, without warning she played her trifling rôle at the Trocadero Theatre in mimicry of a well-known tragic actress. The audience, at once relishing the malicious travesty, stirred in amusement, burst into laughter, and, as she trailed her skirts toward the wings, sent after her a clatter of applause. In the second act, when, from the auditorium, a general chuckle greeted her reappearance, her effrontery was pardoned by Montmorrissy. Within a week, that shrewd personage was himself drilling her in an amplified version of her part; in March he permitted her to try her voice in an eccentric trio; and in April he promised her the soubrette's rôle in his forthcoming summer review, "The Silly Season." By his confession, he was nearly as much astonished at Marie's performance as was Felix.

The latter, from wavering between pride and an intuitive uneasiness, ended by wishing that she had never "made her hit."

Everything about Marie was now in process of change.

She moved from West Forty-eighth Street to a larger hotel on Lincoln Square, where, in three rooms, she supplemented the furniture with a hired piano, some "Turkish" chairs, a davenport, and fresh portières of pale-green velours. Her door was opened by a small, lax-mouthed mulatto woman, Mattie by name, whom she had taken as maid.

Amid her altering surroundings, Marie herself sometimes presented to Felix, when he chanced on

her unexpectedly, a new presence. Her figure—in
dresses of the prevailing, so-called "Empire," style—
attained so extraordinary a slimness that it resembled
the attenuated models in fashion journals. One
could not now, however, any more than formerly,
find a detail in her appearance that was in bad taste.
"Refinement" was evidently more than ever the
shibboleth with her; and she did not even neglect to
note every week, while poring over the "society"
photographs in *The Sunday Era*, how the coiffures of
rich women of distinction were arranged. Her own
hair appeared to have turned a darker auburn; her
eyebrows and lashes, which, on account of their light
hue, had made her eyes too pale, no longer seemed
at fault.

Perhaps it was for this reason that her charms
gained emphasis. She was more often stared at on
the street. Men followed her about.

Then, too, in restaurants, at every other table
there now seemed to be some old friend that had
found his memory, moved by that amiability felt
toward persons who, by their successes, make even
mere acquaintance with them valuable. Felix was
disgusted and angered by the polite grins of strange
men who saluted her. Into many of these faces he
looked with sickening conjectures.

Her time was now much occupied. She had rehearsals to attend, appointments to keep at costumer's and shoemaker's; her dresses required
interminable fittings; the stupidity of wig-makers
necessitated unexpected absences from home; Mont-

morrissy "wanted to see her about her new part."
Felix's afternoon hour with Marie had frequently to
be abandoned.

The young man accepted everything in silence,
with a heavy heart. She seemed, as she became
more valuable in all ways, to be slipping gradually
from him.

Sometimes Marie, showering his gloomy face with
kisses, would beseech him to be reasonable. One
evening, coming home in the twilight to find him
waiting at a front window, she inquired, out of
patience:

"Where is Mattie? Why do you stare at me that
way? No doubt you think I've been enjoying myself, rehearsing the same song fifty times in a dirty
hall! Is it my fault if I'm always busy now?"
Then her eyes softened; she embraced him, and
murmured:

"Some day, perhaps, it won't be so?"

He had told her long since, when driven into a
corner by her gentle inquiries, that "his family estate
was to be turned over to him when he was thirty."

Unresponsive to her caress, he demanded, suddenly:

"Who brought you home in the hansom?"

While slowly lifting her large hat off her curls, she
mumbled indifferently, through a sheaf of hat-pins:

"Billy Noon. I met him on the street; he was
kind enough to give me a lift."

"Your quarrel with Nora doesn't include him,
then?"

"Why should it?"

As always when irritated, Felix had recourse to a cigarette. Marie also took one from his gold case. She was trying to inure herself to smoking, since it had become so fashionable an accomplishment.

"Noon isn't well," she remarked. "You've seen him lately? He's got a nervous habit of twitching back his head."

Felix shrugged his shoulders. Whenever, nowadays, he met the speculator—who invariably had something flattering to say about Marie—it irked him to maintain the warm manner imposed upon him by his debt of gratitude.

"His condition isn't remarkable," Felix answered, shortly. "His father died of locomotor ataxia. Noon had St. Vitus's dance when a boy. He may expect nearly anything before he's through." This thought almost pleased the young man.

"Do you believe that sort of stuff? His trouble is just that he leads too irregular a life. Do you know, dear, I think you might almost take a little warning from him?"

Indeed, during the past half year Felix had been following closely in Noon's footsteps.

His new environment, with all its provocations of opportunity and example, was constituted as if for the very purpose of unbalancing a nature not able to resist the call of pleasure. Felix, always immoderate in exhilarative pursuits, soon reached a stage where excitement was his common habit. He was finally at a pass where artificial stimulation had become so large a feature of his existence that he was lost without it.

Occasionally, he recalled with surprise times not long past when, though living in all satisfaction, he had not smoked incessantly, or felt at sight of liquors an almost automatic impulse to sample them. Scrutinizing certain men, he would marvel at their unconscious continence. One cigar, one drink—these finished, they seemed to desire no more! With him, one cigar, one drink, were but the incitement.

In return for his debility of mornings, he experienced at night—so long as his potations did not stupefy him—a superb deliverance from all restraint —the sloughing, as it were, of a cumbrous mental envelope. What ravishing emotional expansions did he not then enjoy! What delicate perceptions did he not then attain! How prodigally the world revealed its treasuries of opportunity! How richly life was englamoured with romance!

At those moments, his relations with Marie were clothed in exquisite refinements. Now and then, returning toward morning to his rooms, he sat down at his writing-table—his dog Pat, freshly awakened, yawning against his knee—and poured out to her on paper such gossamer fancies as a troubadour, all spiritual love, might dedicate to some white queen. He could never tease Marie into telling him where she kept his letters.

But perhaps, while wandering home in the small hours, he found his intoxication waning on the way. Then, in empty streets full of the freshness that fills

a city before dawn, he gloomed upon a time when
contact with immaculate nature had engendered no
remorse.

Late one night, his feet brought him before the Ferrol house. Doors and windows were boarded over.
A sign proclaimed the place for sale. From the attic
shone a light; old Joseph was still there, perhaps?

Ah, the sunny days of boyhood, the clarity of early
youth, the countryside, and friends in whose lives
there was no fault!

Was he forgotten? No, surely not forgotten, but
remembered with contempt.

Rage surged through him—rage at himself, at
everything, at Nina. Making a threatening gesture,
he ejaculated:

"I'll show her, yet!"

Some day, in contemplating his fame she would be
forced, to his revenge, into unreasoning regret!

He had continually a conviction of great years to
ensue. A nebular theory of his—wherein he found
no small excuse for present laxity—was that there
would rise, at last, from the ferment of his emotional
and physical excesses, an invaluable essence of experience. "A great artist," he had read somewhere,
in effect, "must himself have known everything that
he transcribes." Felix—who had also read Schopenhauer—considered that he showed at least one instinct of genius in this aspiration: to express, finally,
not what he had accumulated in his brain of the experiences of others, but the countless conceptions of
that unique personality he felt himself, in all deep

moments, to be. To add to the world's recorded knowledge of humanity something unprecedented, and not only to the world of his time, but also— working with an art so sound as to defy the years— to the world of some remote posterity! Undying fame! He thrilled at the thought of thus conquering ordinary human limitations, of not perishing at death, of stamping an almost ineradicable signet of his brain upon the sphere he lived in.

With such motives developing, he gathered energy to work, despite the violence of his pastimes, at a furious rate. Indeed, for the moment the very, excessive stimulation of his nerves assisted him to performances of unnatural merit. The same means that released him, nightly, from the commonplace in thought, freed him, daily, from all natural mental inhibitions.

It came to pass that his brain was stagnant when he was not agitating it with tobacco or alcohol. He worked best, he asserted, with a pipe in his mouth and a decanter near at hand.

His short stories found ready market with the magazines; a novel, the very motive of which he contemplated with exultation, was roughly taking shape. Editors began to write to him in flattering and inquiring terms. Oliver Corquill, meeting Felix on the street, was quick with compliments. He declared that the young man had surprised him.

But the novelist still had a good deal of advice to offer. He concluded a technical dissertation by saying, in a kindly voice:

"If you will pardon me, Piers, I think that at present you are too much an actor, not enough of a spectator, to appreciate the drama accurately."

"But," protested Felix, with a blush, remembering his aphorism, "can one describe without having felt?"

"I will say this, at least," Corquill replied. "One cannot describe clearly what he is experiencing. In the midst of stress, one sees everything with partial eyes. Judgment, such as is necessary for intelligent work of our kind, contains no emotional prejudices. He records life precisely who views it from without, just as it is an alien historian, not a soldier in the heat of battle, who records the true complexion of a war. So it is that you will not begin to attain your ends till you detach yourself from the hurly-burly of experience. The difficulty is, in many cases, finally to detach oneself. To take a violent example: sometimes the soldier is so seriously crippled on the field that he never comes to write his memoirs."

Paul Pavin, too, preached his sermon, and more emphatically.

"It is well to be young, my Félix, and to learn life; but, *mon Dieu*, even youth, if it is to develop into something, should contain a grain of moderation. You go too far: one of these days you will find yourself beyond your depth, and the swim back too long. Put down that whiskey and soda; you are not drinking it because you are thirsty. Suppose, now, I painted portraits with my stomach full of champagne? Or with my head full of some woman?

Art is its own stimulus, and foreign stimulation has wrecked it many a time. Mme. Lodbrok is going to look in here presently: I will get her to tell you a story."

The singer, having supplemented her season's work in opera with a profitable concert tour through the Middle West, was about to sail for Europe. Indeed, she came that afternoon to Pavin's studio to say good-by. As majestic of port, fair, and good-humored as ever, she greeted Felix heartily, and, in passing to her deep chair beside the copper coffee-pot, could not forego the pleasure of pinching his cheek.

"What is there about him, Pavin, to make me do that? He will go far, I think—this boy!"

"I have just been telling him that he will go too far, unless he takes care," returned the artist, as flatly as if Felix were not present. "I am reminded of a certain old history that we both know too well. *Chère amie*, are you willing to relate it?"

Mme. Lodbrok set down her coffee-cup. Her face clouded.

"You wish me to tell him about Buron?"

For a while she looked out, through the great "north light," at the tender sky. High in the blue lay motionless a few transparent little clouds, all trailing shreds, slowly reddening in the sunshine of the late afternoon. It was early May. A light breeze, drifting through open sections of the "north light," dispelled the tobacco smoke and scattered faint, fresh odors.

Mme. Lodbrok woke.

"Thirty years! Figure to yourself, Paul, that it is thirty years!"

Then, to Felix:

"Did you ever hear of Pierre Buron?"

He shook his head.

"Well, that is natural. 'My vision reaches too far ahead,' he used to say. 'It is not my own period, even in my own country, that will appreciate me.' But when you speak of the three little, thin books of Pierre Buron to the very few in Paris who know, they will answer—'There is the quintessence of literature. It will rise again.'

"He was handsomer than you, *liebchen*, and with such eyes!"

Pavin, nodding his big beard, interjected:

"I used to pass him on the street, when I was a poverty-stricken young devil of a student. Eh, how those eyes of his held me! Without knowing him, I loved him. Then, one day, in the Luxembourg Gardens, he sat down beside me. From that time, he permitted me to be his friend."

"Yes," assented Mme. Lodbrok, "he had a great charm for men, and, faith, a charm for women! For my part, I considered him a god. I was eighteen, fresh from Sweden, a student in the Conservatory, when he married me.

"What prospects! He had youth, elegance, the prestige of an old family, a sufficient fortune, and talents that put his head among the clouds. He was a person absolutely different, enjoying a—what is that phrase—'divine release from the common ways of men.'

"When his first book appeared, the marvellous life that was expected of him!

"Then he took to drink, deliberately, as he took to all dissipations, in order to feel every human thrill. What a curiosity about life he had! Before it was appeased, he found himself caught.

"We know how much more quickly a delicate mechanism is ruined than a coarse one. Bit by bit, all that beautiful fabric of genius was strained to pieces. In time everything admirable in his nature was destroyed. His brilliancy, his good name, and his fortune gone, he sank, through all sorts of shameful vicissitudes, from sight. And there remained only those three little books, that had been thought the forerunners of how splendid a career!"

After a long pause Felix, clearing his throat, asked, timidly:

"He is still alive, then?"

Mme. Lodbrok produced a handkerchief, and blew her nose. She replied:

"If he were dead, I am certain, I should feel it. Yes, poor creature, surely, somewhere or other, he is still dragging round his chains."

CHAPTER IX

FELIX considered the philosophy of Paul Pavin.

That Frenchman, worldly-wise, cynical, irreverent, assuredly no social moralist in either theory or practice, still had his deity, in naming which he became grave on the instant, and to preserve the perfect image of which he would undoubtedly have turned ruthless as a fanatic—throttling habits at the moment of their first encroachment, bludgeoning friendships proved cumbrous, and stabbing hearts grown overfond.

Such devotion to art the young man found magnificent. In viewing that career, it was as if he were gazing on a great cliff of coral rock, dashed by the waves, yet never shaken, amid all lashing tempests teeming with a creative energy that built the summit, year by year, to proportions ever nobler.

The echoes of Pavin's admonition continued to strike on his ears—clear, sane notes piercing a confusion of futile sounds. Not Mme. Lodbrok's story —since he could not, in vigor, feel prescience of disaster any more than of death—but Pavin's words, "Art is its own stimulus," decided him to try, at least, another way of living.

Felix swore off drinking, then limited himself, as once before, to three cigars a day, and finally, feeling a spiritual exhilaration as he contemplated absolute sobriety, made so many good resolutions that, if he had proved able to fulfil them all, his life would have been scarcely less hedged about with decorous restrictions than an anchorite's.

Then came a morning distinguished by sensations of superiority, when he seemed to be looking down from a great height on a misguided humankind—a swarm of groundlings scrambling about, their noses to the earth, in silly, unprofitable, and perverse pursuits.

He quickly found opportunity to make all his friends aware, as if by chance, that "he was not drinking any more," that "he smoked very little now," and so on. He insisted on discussing dissipation, which, he asserted, "had never yet been good for any one, and was particularly bad for those who worked with their brains." In short, he declaimed in public, rather than considered in private, his half-formed reasonings.

But his tone of voice was so authoritative, and his continent demeanor so imposing, that he gave his auditors an impression of strength. Maybe it was the memory of old resolves, old struggles, old relapses, rousing a secret envy in the region of the conscience, that so clouded the faces of those listening friends of Felix's. Marie herself, since he seemed to have taken her advice, had a thoughtful manner—as of one who has found, unexpectedly, a strange element to cope with.

And now, declared Felix, for work in earnest!

But his work did not proceed.

The stimulus that had driven him for months withdrawn, that "stimulus of art," which was to replace it, failed to appear. For art itself had a depreciated aspect now, and all the conceptions pertaining to it lost their lustre. Just as one emerging from a dream full of agreeable illusions is saddened to find enclosing him again a dreary and monotonous reality, so Felix, all his induced enthusiasms waning, looked mournfully on an altered world, wherein only prosaic features were obtruded.

He sat by the hour at his writing-table, listless, at gaze, thinking not of literature, but of abjured pleasures. All that he had regarded as unprofitable, in his burst of zeal, took on again insidiously, in this retrospection, its allurements. The arguments which he had thrown into the faces of his friends were logical no longer.

What a fool he had been, to run about publishing his fine intentions! Already he was furtively arranging the excuses he might offer, should he reappear clothed in his old habits.

It was the first of June—a mild, sun-drenched afternoon made for all sorts of joyous dilatations. The air that blew through Felix's open windows in West Thirty-second Street was a draught as intoxicating as champagne.

Drab thoughts, long faces, forbidding gestures, continence that shrivelled the heart—what had they to do with youth in Spring? They belonged to age, sitting cold and cramped beside the empty hearth, shaking its old head dismally, hypocritically, over what it could enjoy no longer.

Pavin himself—a nice pattern for a preacher, even now! And in his youth? Little likelihood that he had put on so much as a shred of crape till curiosity had been jigged to death!

"That for his fine maxims!" cried Felix, snapping his fingers at the writing-table. "Not a line scratched off—that's what they're worth! He works best who acts like 'a man of this world'; I can see that, clearly!" Old ways lay bathed in roseate light; just the determination to speed back to them made him himself again. The dog, Pat, bounded round his master, barking.

So ended that experiment.

Pavin, at least, was not a witness of Felix's relapse. The portrait-painter, his commissions finished, gave up his studio in the Velasquez Building and embarked for France. He left with Felix the information that he had recently renewed acquaintance, in some fashionable gathering, with "a Mr. Fray," who, on inheriting a fortune from a distant relative, had managed with a thousand ingenuities and urbanities to work his way up, through various social strata, into the most admirable company. Indeed, he was even then all but engaged to be married to a girl of distinguished family.

Felix's hatred of the young dilettante was fanned to a more furious flame than ever. That miserable shallow-pate, all self-conceit, duplicity, and spite— that weak Judas, with his eyes of a sick kitten!

Again Felix longed to get his hands on Mortimer Fray's thin neck.

He over whose very shoulders, as it seemed, the fellow had wriggled into wealth and place, saw himself hardly better off for money than for social status.

Convinced by Noon's benevolence that luck would extricate him in the nick of time from any quandary, he had been extravagant as ever. In six months, to be sure, he had banked eighteen hundred dollars, earned from the magazines; but who could live agreeably, along Broadway, at that rate?

Noon, on the other hand, having served in the beginning to set the pace, was now able to accelerate it.

The speculator, sensing financial reverses near their origin, as a seafarer senses remotely-gathering storms, played the game of stocks so shrewdly that his occasional large losses were far exceeded by his profits. A born gambler, confident of the ultimate success of his luck, judgment, and audacity, he no more revealed despondency at a disastrous day than triumph at a rich coup. A ponderous air of mastery was developing in him at the expense of genial traits. His smiles were less amiable, his features in repose more grim. His very dissipations—though exceeding in prodigality all previous limits—now had in them, Felix thought, something reserved and calculating.

Whenever Noon met the young man, he complained of "those two girls, with their silly quarrel, ending so much good sport." Surely, he hinted, it was Marie's fault; for Nora had never in her easy-going life been known to nurse a grudge. At last, after jerking his head involuntarily half a dozen times, Noon would rumble:

"Felix, why don't you reason with Marie?"

But Felix's ideas in respect of that had changed. He saw enough of the speculator as it was. Besides, his instinct no longer recognized in Noon, for all the latter's slaps on the back, whispered anecdotes, and grins, the eager friendliness of other days.

The reconciliation was, however, effected without Felix's aid.

Marie, with compunction for an excuse, donned her newest hat and dress, and went to call on Nora. Noon, opportunely strolling in toward dinner-time, found the two young women together. They had "made up"; everything was to be just as formerly! The three, driving to Marie's rooms, burst in upon Felix, laughing, bustling, demanding that he snatch his hat and come to dinner. His gloom, acquired from waiting long alone, was not much abated by that tableau.

So it was that those four found themselves again in close association. But for all Nora Llanelly's charms, it was now Marie's personality that prevailed. The beauty of the one had been eclipsed, in the last few months, by the other's various developing talents.

No one could well have mistaken Nora's origin, what with her loud laughter, elementary vocabulary, ready amazement, and ignorance of everything not duplicated in the life of Broadway. But even Felix had been imposed on by Marie's conversation and behavior.

And these she was continually improving.

In public, nothing escaped her: from the slightest interplay of manners in which cultivated persons took part she got instruction. Moreover, no lesson had to be repeated to her.

Then, in private, whenever Felix touched on a topic unfamiliar to her, without betraying lack of knowledge, she succeeded in enlightening herself. Frequently Felix learned, from her reference to some minor usage of polite society, from an opinion recently relieved of bourgeois quality, or just from the corrected pronunciation of a word, that he had taught her something.

Her discourse, always confined to well-learned topics, appreciating common subjects from a superior view-point, was delivered in a voice free from any plebeian accent, well modulated, never loud. It was her habit to drink but one glass of champagne: so, unlike many of her woman friends, she had no lapses from good taste, made no false moves, revealed no ignorance. She was at pains to show, in all situations, that she could "do the right thing." Although she needed no foil now, it was when Nora was with her that she shone most brilliantly.

"That girl," Felix was assured by Noon, "is going to get there."

Indeed, she was already "getting there" in several ways. Toward the middle of July, she had a notable success in her profession.

"The Silly Season," Montmorrissy's new summer review, was produced on the roof of the Trocadero Theatre. There, beneath the stars, amid clustered lamps, palms, grottoes tinkling with cascades, painted precipices overhung with growing flowers, an audience in summer dress waxed hilarious while gaping up at the bright little stage.

It was a burlesque of the chief happenings of the year: in it the affairs of crowned heads, politicians, actresses, and a host of persons locally notorious or celebrated, were extravagantly travestied.

From the first moment the action struck a furious gait. Scene melted into scene: horse-play was swallowed up in exaggerated sentiment, which, in turn, was annihilated by a broad joke. The stage was one instant full of marching amazons, next empty save for the tenor and the prima donna gyrating in a swift dance, then, in a flash, filled for no particular reason with small girls in the extremity of dishabille, who fell to kicking in a way that bade fair to disjoint them. Comedians, all plaids and grease-paint, bounced through the rout with howls in the dialect of the "Tenderloin." "Show girls" came strolling forth in costumes that amazed the audience. A dancer, whose further appearance the police were expected to prohibit, exercised herself till her powder disappeared beneath a flood of perspiration. Lights rose and died—as the scenery dissolved and took new form—on scurrying choruses that glistened half bare skin, half spangles; sunshine, moonlight, and all the rich rays of the spectrum, played on the painted eyes of singers scattering know-ing winks, on broad hands passing over whitened shoulders, on comely faces placid at the embraces of buffoons as inhuman-looking, in their "make-up," as gorillas.

With the progress of that spectacle, in which there appeared to be no place for any rational thought, a sort of vertiginous enthusiasm was communicated to the audience. Applause grew wild; laughter be-came hysterical; men's eyes expressed their natures; women forgot to look askance; in nearly all faces there was something rakish.

But Felix sat gazing at the stage without a smile.

He saw Marie, slim as a wood-sprite, wrapped apparently in nothing but a rose-colored scarf be-strewn with golden flowers. The corsage of this costume was immoderately low in front and wholly lacking behind; the skirts clung to the young woman as if wet; the fringes, a foot in length, swung from her knees.

She had complained of this attire, of certain lines in her part, of the general effect that she would have to produce. Her ideas, it appeared, had been all for a rôle in which one could preserve some vestiges of propriety. She had even gone so far as to tell Felix, after the dress rehearsal, that "she had a good mind to walk out." Yet once on the stage, nothing could have been more nearly perfect than her serenity. She also knew, no doubt, that she had never looked so prepossessing.

Her wig, elaborately puffed, set with three golden bands, was auburn of the darkest shade. Amid that emphatic aureole her face gleamed like a cameo, all its decisive lines of cheek and chin but adding to the clear-cut beauty of the whole. Her eyes, never previously fine, were strangely elongated and languishing; her lips, by nature thin, had gained, from some new trick with carmine paint, a voluptuous contour plausible even at close quarters. To add final accent to her air of delicate artificiality, pendent ear-rings of coral, carved, like threaded rose-buds, were permitted to graze her shoulders.

She uttered a song with seemingly capricious changes from *parlando* to clear musical tones; she filled a dance, in waltz time, with a hundred unexpected, dainty gestures. Made perfect in every note and posture by innumerable rehearsals, exhibiting with a sure touch all Montmorrissy's devices as her own, she surprised friends and roused the admiration of strangers.

Men searched the programme for her identity, bandied her name about, stared at her with critical and impudent expressions. And it seemed to Felix that all those glances rested on her with a material contact. He was like one who sees some belonging, of the most intimate associations, exposed, handled, and appraised by cynical auctioneers.

That night, he began to hate Marie's environment.

But nowadays it seemed as if the only air he could breathe was that of the theatre. It filled Broadway, permeated all the resorts in which he passed his time, penetrated Marie's apartment, where there seemed to cling to the very hangings something of the close, cosmetic-laden atmosphere of dressing-rooms.

There the flatly scandalous note was struck by Mattie, the lax-mouthed mulatto maid—who now costumed Marie at the theatre and was hand in glove with all the other servants—and by Miriam, the saturnine hairdresser. From this functionary's black satchel, worn shiny on her questionable rounds, seemed to issue with the curling-irons and the brushes, as if from a Pandora's box, all sorts of greasy calumnies. The hairdresser was, perhaps, as much an unexpurgated gazette as a constructor of coiffures.

There, also, were aired by visiting young women attired in their best, the politics of the stage—the machinations for advancement, the combinations made by spite against popularity, the disparagements of talent. Felix grew weary listening to tales of the jealousies of actresses, the vanities of actors, the despotism of Montmorrissy—to such phrases as, "She didn't get a hand to-night," "He queered her turn with a lot of comic business on the side," "That couple ought to be playing the tank towns," "He always manages somehow to sneak upstage and steal the scene," "She's had her two weeks' notice from Monty." Little Felix cared that the ugly drummer, whose behavior had once diverted him, was discharged for habitual drunkenness, or that the young tenor—whose name was Mackeron

—had finally got his wife to divorce him. But Miss Qewan, Marie's gentle friend, was for some obscure reason dismissed from the company without warning. Marie expressed her indignation to Felix.

"All those weeks of rehearsing without pay, and part of her own wardrobe to buy! Did that matter to Monty?" And, with a fixed stare, Marie vehemently exclaimed:

"The beast!"

She hastened to add that every one said the same; for Miss Qewan, "as good a girl as ever stepped," was trying to bring up an eight-year-old sister.

Felix thought less than ever of Marie's instructor.

Whenever he met the manager, he found it hard to look politely into that flaccid countenance, cunning, self-sufficient, quizzical and reserved by flashes. For some reason, Felix always seemed to afford Montmorrissy amusement. Possibly it was the young man's ingenuousness, not yet altogether destroyed by the buffets of experience, that entertained the other.

Then, too, it irked Felix more and more to be agreeable in Noon's company.

Every day he had to watch the speculator cut a fine figure with his inexhaustible wallet. That burly, deep-voiced fellow, shaved to the blood, odorous of toilet-water, always "dressed to kill," flashing a great ruby and diamond finger-ring every time he raised his hand, was surely the most blatant, vulgar creature drawing breath. Felix was disgusted with his stories of successful gambling, his disregard of money, his reckless proposals, his "cock-sure," masterful demeanor—in fine, with each act of his beyond emulation.

It was Noon who took the lead in all excursions—who telephoned for the table in the restaurant, ordered the automobile, harangued the head waiter, accepted the courses with a nod, mixed the salad-dressing, sent word to the chef, so that "the rascal should know whom he was cooking for." Familiar with the city to its farthest outskirts, famous in all places of amusement for his generosity, he was, as Marie argued, "a comfortable person to have along."

Perhaps he conducted them through the night to some road-house, surrounded by shrubbery, its broad porch, full of dinner tables, encircling it with a shining zone, violin tones issuing from its open windows to mingle with the songs of crickets and katydids. There the proprietor skipped down the steps to greet him; waiters recalled his name and hovered round him to suggest his favorite dishes; orchestra leaders bowed while beating time; servility and eagerness filled every face. His departure was like the exit of a grand duke incognito.

The two young women confessed, just by the flashing of their eyes, at such parade of respect, how inspiriting they, at least, found Noon's companionship.

Every fair Sunday now saw them speeding far afield in his red automobile.

On country roads, they were caressed by the sweet, tepid breezes of midsummer. Homesteads nestling amid apple-trees, with sheds, bee-hives, the dairyhouse, the rustic pump, scattered round about, evoked from Marie and Nora exclamations of delight. They had to pause where lines of willows leaned toward a brook, where glassy ponds reflected sky and clouds, where water-grass was stirred by zephyrs into ripples. Nora wanted to take off her shoes and stockings and go in wading, to uproot lily-pads, to find a nest with fledglings in it, to ask some farmer for a drink of fresh, warm milk. She displayed, in those rural regions, the artlessness and excitement of a city urchin on his first country outing. She scrambled through underbrush regardless of lace petticoats—then reappeared with dishevelled tresses, with flushed face moist, her skirts studded with burrs, her arms laden with coarse, yellow daisies. Marie was content to pick a couple of wild rose blossoms by the roadside, with which she decorated the lapels of Noon's and Felix's coats. Sometimes, espying on an eminence a charming bit of landscape, she would press the young man's arm, and murmur:

"Our house ought to be built in such a place?"

She had grown frank in that respect.

At dusk, from the pavilions of casinos by the sea, they watched remote lights steal across the water over a maze of wavering reflections. Stars filled the heavens in great patches, like a glittering spawn. With ejaculations of triumph, they discovered the Great Dipper, the Bear, the ruddy twinkle of the planet Mars. Then a realization of the immensity of space, of the illimitable field of worlds, of the earth's insignificance, subdued them. They sat

silent, looking over the water with wistful, vacuous
expressions.

In the cool depths of midnight returning at full
speed, they were lulled to lethargy by the reiteration
of long, narrow vistas, leafy, streaming, leaping from
blackness into brilliancy at the flash of their acetylene lamps.   Then, midst the obscurity aloft, there
grew before their tired eyes a tremulous, far-stretch-
ing radiance—the city's nimbus.   Finally, they
reached the littered streets, roused themselves at the
noises of humanity, and, a little sad, penetrated
the constricted places they called home.

Through the open windows of Marie's parlor
entered the nocturnal racket of Lincoln Square.
Brakes and gongs of trolley-cars, automobile horns,
horses' hoofs, shrill voices, filled the street with
echoes of that clarity which seems peculiar to Sunday.
Hot, malodorous exhalations rose from the pavement, which was covered with broad, sticky-looking
stains.

Felix, his various elations worn away, his head
throbbing painfully, stood by the window.   Remembering the savor of the sea, the perfume of meadows,
the wafted smells, at nightfall, of invisible wet earth
and flowers, he suffered as if from a spiritual retrogression.   Thus he was invariably drawn back by
destiny—from the serene, pure reaches of the woods
and fields to sickly turmoil, from something that
approached contentment of the heart to feverish
desires in gratifying which there was more pain than
pleasure!

Was he, indeed, himself in this great, stone-bound prison of a city, or did he but step in time with countless others? Was it his own will that drove him through the vortex, or the mingled impulses of a million other minds? How to be one's own master, how to stand isolate in spirit, unshaken by any impact—the cliff with summit high above the surge? Perhaps, far away, buried in the fastnesses of forests, or on a mountain side above the clouds, one might, like those Brahmin mystics who sit on the peaks before the Himalayas, find oneself? He recalled a passage from a Persian poem: "There is safety in solitude." And for a moment he glimpsed the wisdom that belongs to age: he wondered if happiness, so violently sought, did not consist in peace.

"For heaven's sake, Felix, what are you dreaming about!"

With a start, he turned from the window.

A shaded lamp, of yellow porcelain, made the centre table bright, but left the walls in shadow. The lower portions alone of the green portières were revealed distinctly; the claw-like feet of chairs showed little patches of light; the pattern of the rug was emphasized: an intricate design of flowers, yellow, green, and blue. Beyond an open door appeared, in a dim sleeping-room, a dressing-table. The mirror, tilted forward, reflected jars of cold-cream, flasks of essence, powder-boxes, crumpled handkerchiefs, hat-pins, and combs of tortoise-shell.

And the odors of benzoine and "*peau d'Espagne*," emanating from that inner chamber, drove out of

Felix's brain the last souvenirs of unsophisticated country air.

Those rooms were now the centre-point of his existence: to them his thoughts continually turned; thither his feet were always leading him; therein were forged for him chains of irresolution, pliancy, and subservience, which he dragged everywhere, to the exhaustion of his individuality.

He trod the path that led to her with an invariable agitation. This nervous disturbance, less pleasurable than discomfortable, increased as he entered the hotel, mounted in the elevator to her floor, and pressed the bell-button at her threshold.

The door swung open; Mattie, the maid, with lowered eyes, mumbled: "Good evening, Mr. Felix"—then shrank into the shadows. Felix traversed the short private hallway, knocked on the parlor door, parted the green velours curtains, saw her again.

Maybe she was sitting by the window, in a loose gown, reading attentively the story of some such enterprising person as Mme. du Barry. Without laying down her book, calmly smiling, she stretched her neck slightly for his kiss. At such moments, her self-possession dissatisfied him.

"My dear boy, don't you see that my hair is dressed for the evening? Did you stop to give the photographer a blowing-up, and to get the sheet music I wanted? I'll wager you forgot those Russian cigarettes!"

He did errands for her, was at her beck and call,

deferred to her in all things, suited his hours to her convenience, made every sacrifice to please her. In short, with his innumerable concessions he crushed from his consciousness all sense of freedom. She dominated him completely.

Yet he had none of his old illusions in regard to her. He made no more fine speeches concerning "her misfortunes," "the injustice of fate," "a day when she would attain the place that she deserved." Nor was she now at pains to play that part.

It was no longer necessary.

Amid his present surroundings—wherein the market-place of the affections largely throve on traffic in damaged goods—Felix soon found it reasonable to cherish what was not apparently excelled about him. In Rome, as it were, he did after the fashion of the Romans; and, without much surprise at the deterioration of his sentiments, he learned that he could expend no less extravagant an ardor on the tawny, speckled lily at hand than if it were the rare, white flower of his early dreams.

But he had to pay, in consequence, the penalty of jealousy.

The enigma of Marie's past tormented him: he tried to solve it by all sorts of devices. He became adept in leading a conversation deviously to perilous ground, where Marie might, by some slip, reveal a little of her secret. He grew shrewd in deciphering the looks, gestures, silences, which followed his innuendoes, in comparing present with past utterances, in putting two and two together. His mind was a repository for scraps of information dropped by her at random, from which he hoped to piece out some day a coherent history of her career.

He wondered if he might not have learned a good deal about her from Pavin, in whose studio he had met her. But this seemed unlikely: the Frenchman had never shown enough interest in her to discuss her willingly. At any rate, Felix might question women unfriendly to her; then, too, Nora Llanelly was "such a fool it would not be hard to pump her"; while Mattie, who had "worked for Miss Sinjon before," could probably be bribed.

Nevertheless, he neglected these opportunities, less from shame than from a conviction that Marie would find him out.

Occasionally, he seemed on the point of learning something definite. She had said so-and-so; at a remark of his she had looked thus; at a certain query she had shown agitation, had risen from one chair to take another farther from him, while exclaiming angrily, "You promised me once that you would let all that sort of thing alone!" Such actions surely meant that he was on the right track.

She had undoubtedly known some one with such and such qualities, with an appearance of this and that sort. A certain man in her life, for instance, had been an inordinate consumer of cigarettes, fastidious in his apparel, of excellent manners, well-read, fond of the arts, indeed, a dilettante and a collector—yes, a collector of fine prints! To such details did Felix's ingenuity assist him.

The conjecture of one day became next morning a certainty: nothing was too extravagant for belief after it had aged a night. Now and then, when intoxicated, Felix looked at Marie craftily, with half-shut eyelids, thinking: "I know a great deal more about you than you imagine." In his opinion, it was a kind of struggle between them.

But for what guerdon?

From his machinations Felix got nothing but unhappiness. No sooner had he discovered in her past, as he believed, some new detail to her detriment, than he was pierced with anguish. While lying awake at night—when his ingenuity seemed at its best—a fresh conviction, flashing forth at the plausible union of half a dozen surmises, frightened him as much as if a cold hand had reached out of the darkness and clutched him by the throat.

"Yes, yes, whoever that fellow was, she must have been in love with him! At least, he had surely been in love with her!" And Felix's relations with her could be nothing but a repetition—who knew but an inferior repetition! No doubt he was suffering all the while by comparison.

It was not to be expected that the young man's jealousy should fail to invade the present.

Every breath of gossip that reached him bore hint of trust betrayed in the lives round about. He noted the gullibility of infatuated men, the security of secrets known by all save one. He remembered Gregory Tamborlayne.

Thereupon he became preternaturally alert. His

eyes were on Marie whenever she spoke to any one.
He even visited her at unexpected moments. A
cloud of cigarette smoke in her rooms seemed portentous, but it was only "Nora and some other girls
who had just left." An afternoon newspaper of
sedate tendency, lying on the centre table, made his
heart beat fast: she had never bought it; who had
left it there?

"They're always sending up the wrong newspaper
from the office. What's the matter with you? I
never saw such a face! Why, one might think——"

"I was just wondering if you had changed your
brand of news."

"That's not the truth! I can read you like a
book. And let me tell you, people never have such
thoughts unless they give good cause for the same
kind!"

While looking at him steadily, her green eyes
became vacant. Her lips gradually parted in a
smile. Her rapt expression was new to him. After
some moments, she inquired, absent-mindedly:

"What would you do if you found some one?"

For an instant he could not believe his ears. Was
it she who had said such a thing?

At last, his lips quivering, he answered, in a low
voice full of sarcasm:

"Nothing, of course!"

Her eyes seemed to wake, her smile disappeared.
She made haste to slip her arms round him.

"Oh, you poor boy, I'm so sorry! You take everything the wrong way! I was only joking; the idea of

such a thing seemed so ridiculous. If you only knew how foolish you are to have such thoughts!"

But from that day he had a definite apprehension.

He even went so far as to consider what rôle it would be proper for him to take in such a scene. He scanned the ground carefully, like a man about to fight a duel. In the top drawer of her dressing-table, under a pile of handkerchiefs, she kept an extra key to her hall door. Felix abstracted it.

One afternoon, a craftiness developed by numerous cocktails urged him to use this key. Just as he slipped into the private hallway, he heard her clear voice raised beyond the curtains:

"Do you think I keep papers of that sort about me? They're in my safe-deposit box. And rest assured, they'll come out only when you've made up your mind about them."

Felix tore the green portières apart. She turned, perceived him, and, with a gesture that at least seemed deliberate, hung up the telephone receiver. Her eyes did not relinquish his.

"You? How did you get in?"

"The door was unlatched."

"That careless Mattie again!"

"So, you have a safe-deposit box with papers in it? What papers? Who was that telephoning?"

She smiled pityingly, shrugged her shoulders, and turned away, the ruffles of her dove-colored dressing-gown slowly tumbling after her.

"Well, my dear, it was Montmorrissy telephoning,

and 'the papers' are my contract. I should hate to have your disposition!''

She soon took to parrying such attacks with insinuations of her own—then, forcing the fighting, always managed to get in the first thrust. Felix, on the defensive, had to free himself from the most extraordinary accusations. He was compelled to account for every hour of his time—to tell her whom he had met, where he had lunched, what streets he had passed through. She declared that he flirted with every girl in sight; she harped on "that black-haired woman, that old flame of his," whom she "knew all about." Their squabbles invariably ended with the cry:

"I'm sure you're dying to go straight back to your black-haired friend! Very well, run on! I suppose I shall survive it."

She knew, no doubt, that he never dared to leave her presence without patching up their quarrel.

At the coming of autumn, he remembered the September of the previous year.

How bright had seemed the promise of regions then unexplored, to-day attained! Had he not told himself that happiness lay on the horizon? He had covered the ground, had reached the place of his desires, to find the horizon as far away as ever.

Pleasures, it seemed, grew vague at his approach; at his embrace they melted into nothingness, as nymphs—one is told—were wont to do when in archaic woods surprised at twilight. No moment of gratification was as he had pictured it.

When had he been really happy?

One dull October day, he entered Washington Square, sat down upon a bench, looked northward toward Fifth Avenue and the Ferrol house.

Clouds of pulverized plaster enveloped the familiar dwelling. Through that pall loomed dump-carts, scaffolds, laborers in canvas overalls. The upper story was gone; the house was being torn down.

He walked slowly away. Round his feet fluttered withered leaves, such as old men near by, in faded blue, were feebly raking into little heaps.

He saw, on another path, a woman looking at him, hesitating timidly. Her large, lustrous eyes woke memories. Was it she who had interrupted his supper-party on Christmas eve? The woman made up her mind to bow. Yes, it was she. He raised his hat, passed on, and soon forgot her.

Considerably before his usual hour, Felix reached the hotel in Lincoln Square. Passing through the lobby, he entered an elevator—one of two that ran up and down in the same shaft. The cars passed each other in mid-air. Felix caught a glimpse of a thin-shouldered, pale young man in brown, weighing in one hand a bulky packet of letters at which he was gazing with a sneer.

It was Mortimer Fray.

A gush of blood blinded Felix and almost raised him off his feet.

"Stop the car! Take me down again."

He stepped out into the lobby, glared round, gained the street entrance, confronted the carriage-starter. "Yes, a strange gentleman in a brown suit had left, this very moment, in a hansom."

The fellow, his weather-beaten face exhibiting solicitude, made bold to add:

"You don't look well, sir. Begging your pardon, you'd best have a little something for it."

Felix turned away. In the lobby, people were moving quietly to and fro on their sane affairs. They recalled him to himself. What had he thought to do in such a place?

The reaction to common-sense exhausted him. With an effort, he made his way upstairs and appeared before Marie.

She, turning from the window, stared at him aghast.

"What is it? What has happened?"

If he told her anything of Fray, he would be drained forthwith of every secret in his life—the stories of Eileen, of Nina, worst of all, of his ruined prospects. Throwing himself into a chair, he answered:

"Just an old enemy I've run across. What of that? The world is full of enemies."

She approached him slowly, hesitated, then knelt beside him. She looked away. She uttered, as if suffocating:

"Not here, Felix."

His heart was touched.

"No, not here, Marie."

Presently he clasped her close. Something crackled in the bosom of her dress.

"What was that?" he asked, listlessly.

She closed her eyes.

"That? I don't know. It must be my last week's salary."

CHAPTER X

In the bleak transparency of public parks and the early dusk pierced by a thousand lofty window lights, in the quickened activity of amusement districts and the return of elegance to finer thoroughfares, Felix saw only uneventful repetition. At last, even amid excess he had discovered monotony.

Sometimes he was tormented by unconscionable desires.

He dreamed of environments remote in place and time, freed from all the restraints of modern, civilized, or even rational, society, in which abandonment to pleasure had reached transcendence. His mind's eye perceived such pictures as took shape round banquet tables in the Golden House of Nero, where, on a dais rising like an island from a sea of revellers, the imperial purple was smothered beneath rose-petals, ivory-white arms, and gold dust shaken from dishevelled locks. Or else his fancy conjured up the Hanging Gardens of Babylon, in which the dawn, as if stealing over a field where had been waged to the death some appalling combat of the senses, struck through a reek of incense fumes upon an acre of spilled wine, torn garlands, fallen diadems, prone bodies laden with barbaric jewels and gleaming under silvery meshes and nets of threaded pearls.

How tremendous, yet how exquisitely embellished, the debaucheries of those pagan times! Again, and now for a new reason, the young man was rendered melancholy by thought of epochs ended so many centuries too soon. A longing for irrevocable days made his eyes swim with tears.

By persistent excitation of his nerves, Felix had increased his emotional instability till trifling thoughts were able to rouse in him not only ardors, but also irritation, anger, fear, despondency. Since his equilibrium was now so easily upset, any sudden crisis in which he had especial need of calmness was sure to catch him at a disadvantage. Marie, armed cap-à-pie with self-possession, had the best of him in every clash.

Their altercations increased in frequency and violence. For Felix's jealousy grew with Marie's popularity.

As he observed the development of public interest in her, it seemed to him that he was already sharing something of her with a host of others. When he considered those who now made a point of greeting her courteously everywhere—men of affairs, of money, of accomplished deeds—he was consumed with fear: if it came to the worst, what rivalry could he oppose to them? In hours when the green portières had been drawn against the world, his apprehensions wrung from him the cry:

"Swear that you love me and no one else!"

"Foolish, foolish boy! Must I still swear to that? Will you never be sure? Why do you look at me so?"

What was more nearly Sphynx-like than the face of
the beloved, when seen through the film of jealousy?
What was behind those eyes that stared straight into
his, while the lips, barely moving, uttered reassuring
words? Those eyes, were they false? Those lips,
did they lie? How could he be sure of her so close
to him, yet—because speech and visage can hide
everything—so remote?

Frequently, unable to contain himself on feeling
conjecture turning to conviction, he charged her
incoherently with all the infamies of his imagination.
His fury distorted her before his eyes: she, whose
every feature he had but a little while before adored,
took on the appearance of a perfidious enemy. He
could almost have throttled this woman just released
from his arms.

Marie, leaning back, turning up her eyes des-
pairingly, would utter, in shocked accents:

"Good heavens, what a wicked heart he has!
What insanity!"

"I won't afflict you with it any longer!"

"No doubt that's the best thing."

"Good-by!"

But within the hour he had returned, exhausted,
crushed, to save the fragments of his pride mumbling
something about "his promise, made long ago, not
to leave her alone."

Disregarding that rigmarole, turning from him
with a hopeless gesture, she retorted:

"And your insults, that you forget? What have I
done to deserve them?"

"It was my love for you that made me, as you say, insane. Surely you'll forgive me on that account?"

But she held him off with her white arms, the strength of which invariably surprised him. Her resolute face was like the countenance of an outraged divinity.

"You were wrong? You were wicked?"

"Yes, yes! I was wrong. I treated you terribly!"

"More terribly than you suspect. Such words leave scars. Afterward, it's never quite the same."

"Ah," he cried, in acute distress, "don't say that, Marie!"

So each reconciliation left her stronger, him weaker.

It was he who now harped on "a little place, far away, amid trees and roses, just for two." All his instinctive scruples had succumbed to passion; he was ready to pay the price implied for surcease of anxiety. As one lost in the desert gazes toward the flowering mirage, so Felix, in the city, contemplated the thought of some remote, verdant region where the haze of evening, gemmed with infrequent, mellow twinklings, might wrap him gradually in peace. Who knew but that in such a spot two hearts might be renewed—two natures, beneath the solemn spread of stars, together turn to simple and immaculate desires? An end, then, at any rate, to the theatre and its publicity, to Broadway and its provocations— no more thereafter of associates such as Nora Llanelly and Noon!

Marie had come to share at least a part of his antipathy. She was beginning to dislike Nora.

When alone with Felix, she mimicked maliciously her old-time friend's coquettish airs, impetuous table manners, unconscious illiteracy, satisfaction in conspicuous attire. If Nora presented herself in a particularly striking costume, Marie, scrutinizing her every appurtenance in a single glance, would exclaim, "My dear, isn't that the hat you wore in 'The Lost Venus'?" or, "Oh, my dear, you must really put those violets out!" Miss Llanelly received such thrusts in bewilderment. If she chanced to take offence, it was only for a moment; with her, flushes of mortification were succeeded by good-humored smiles as quickly as in children's faces. She appeared to have no place in her broad bosom for rancor; she had even forgiven Marie her professional success. One evening, she informed Felix confidentially that Marie was "getting cranky on account of overwork." The girl should have left "The Silly Season" for a little vacation when cold weather forced the review from the Trocadero roof down into the auditorium.

Marie's disfavor did not as yet extend to Noon. She had discreet smiles for all his anecdotes, intelligent attention for his discursions in æsthetics, keen interest in his reports of speculation. He obtained her ear especially when, leaning well across a table with cigar smoke curling round his jowls, he described to her, between involuntary twitchings of his head, the career she might have on the stage, did theatrical managers but realize her capabilities.

"Any one ought to see what you could do if you had a proper chance. I'm continually talking about it to Montmorrissy."

That personage was planning to produce in midwinter, at the Castle Theatre, a new musical extravaganza called "The Queen of Hearts." This being a side venture, in which he was experimenting with some unknown authors and musical composers, he wanted to fill the stage with inexpensive, if unnoted, actors. One day, Noon burst in upon Marie and Felix, flourishing cane and gloves, his cigar point threatening his eyebrows, his long coat-tails in commotion. He had just left Montmorrissy! The parts in "The Queen of Hearts" were all assigned! The prima donna's rôle was Marie's!

Noon's grin seemed to add for him, "Thanks chiefly to me." Felix wished that the fellow had dropped dead with his tidings in his throat. There, as he watched the light of ambition blaze up in Marie's eyes, his dreams of escape into the countryside disintegrated. He saw himself, in future as in present, the prisoner, the victim, of the city.

And the city, as he now knew it, was already taking heavy tribute of him.

His excesses were depriving him of an accurate conception of propriety, in regard not only to his conduct, but also to his literary efforts.

It befell that a girl friend of Marie's suddenly died. Into the chamber of death, banked with flowers sent by contrite women, came hurrying half a dozen saddened men, all well-to-do, strangers each to each, who, meeting in the fragrant gloom, stared at one another, at first indignantly, then suspiciously, finally sheepishly. The secrets that the fair deceased had kept in life were there revealed.

"What a tale!" thought Felix. "How full of the irony of existence, how human, how beautiful!" He rushed off to the studio, seized pen and paper, and commenced what he believed was going to be the most wonderful short story in the world. But when he had written half a dozen pages, there came to him the query:

"What magazine in this country would print it?"

And gloomily he remembered a great public whose sense of moral proportions he had once shared, but now had nearly lost.

Yet he was long in realizing that the cynicism developed by his mode of living was affecting his work. The ideas, not extraordinary so far as he could see, which now moved him to exercise his talents, proved to be such as editors of magazines regarded with distrust. His stories came back to him; from the envelopes that he tore apart fluttered letters of regret, instead of checks.

By such rebuffs Felix was plunged into despondency. Could he have been mistaken in himself? Were all his dreams of eminence to result in nothing? His energy failed; his writing-table grew dusty; his balance at the bank was near exhaustion.

The studio in West Thirty-second Street became a place of dying aspirations. Through tedious, gray days, when snow in its descent made wavering shrouds about the windows, Felix bade good-by forever, as he thought, to his most precious hopes. Stretched on a divan, he seemed to see passing in the twilight all the pageantry of literary genius's creations. There, in the midst of apparitions still more vague, showed the flame-licked robes of Dante and of Virgil, Don Quixote's basin-helm and cuirass, the little breast of Juliet, Salammbô's jewelled forehead, the ardent eyes of Lucien de Rubempré, whose desire it was "to be famous, to be loved." Felix, who had so vehemently desired love and fame, watched these phantoms—the children of great brains—glide on athwart the shadows, their gaze fixed straight ahead, their pace unhesitating, their ranks already full. No place among them for another; no vigor or wit to force a place! He turned his face to the wall, and, as if life had ended there, surrendered to despair. The white bull-terrier thrust a cold nose against his cheek.

Felix could no longer bear to spend an hour unnecessarily in the studio. While Marie was performing in "The Silly Season," he wandered on Broadway. Under arc lamps, he watched crowds entering theatres. From automobiles stepped young girls, bareheaded, slight, trailing fur-lined cloaks light blue and pink, looking round with the eager eyes of innocence. Felix paused to contemplate them, then roused himself, passed on, and entered a café.

Every night, he sought systematically, and obtained, a counterfeit of satisfaction, a false jauntiness, such insensibility as bordered on oblivion.

Sometimes, he moved in a light-shot mist that, clearing now and then, revealed the supper-table before him, the shirt bosoms of waiters, Marie's white, square chin and wandering eyes, men rising and bowing, women with red lips slightly curled in envy whispering behind their glittering fingers. Between such lucid intervals, Felix had little accurate knowledge of his conduct, which, however, would seem to have contained itself automatically within decorous bounds. Occasionally, his whole recollection of an evening was composed of insignificant vignettes, such as a moment's conversation with a stranger, a dispute—incited by Marie—about a supper-bill, the joke of a cab-driver, the pinched face of a child from whom, just before dawn, he had bought a Sunday newspaper.

Or perhaps he was late in reaching the theatre.

The surly keeper of the stage door, before darkening the hallway and locking up, was taking a last look in a cracked mirror at a wart-like protuberance on the end of his nose. Enraged at being discovered in this vanity, the fellow growled that "she had gone, with Mr. Noon or some one else."

Felix had a sudden faintness, a contraction near the solar plexus, a touch of nausea. He hailed a hansom cab. Hurried from one restaurant to another, he calmed himself with an effort before questioning imperturbable head waiters.

"Miss Sinjon left here half an hour ago with Miss Llanelly and Mr. Noon."

He breathed again.

At times, he pondered his condition well-nigh impersonally. "These frail, pale creatures, indeed! To think how one of them, whom we met one day long ago without any premonition, can become at last a terrible tyrant, from whose tyranny there is no escape!"

In the loneliest recesses of Central Park, surrounded by melting snow, naked underbrush full of evening vapors, gaunt tree-tops fading to a blur against the dusk, Felix asked himself again the purposes of human sojourn. In withered grasses and dead leaves he found an answer sufficiently pessimistic for his mood; it was always from quickly-perishing, apparently vain aspects of Nature that he now drew material wherewith to construct his theories.

Darkness drove back, from distant thickets, the dog, Pat, muddy and scratched, weary after foolish quests, yet with wagging tail and eager tongue displaying his certainty of Felix's caress. The master envied the dumb beast.

He longed for a sympathetic confidant. If Paul Pavin, at whose solicitude he had snapped his fingers, were only near! But the Frenchman was not coming to America that winter.

To Oliver Corquill, whom he met by chance at the entrance of the park, the young man was impelled to relate something of his literary reverses and his dismay. When he had concluded with a wholesale complaint so rambling as to be hardly intelligible even to him, the novelist said, kindly:

"Why not come away with me for a month's shooting in Maine?"

The forest fastnesses! Then, remembering Marie, he answered that he could not afford it. Corquill offered to lend him a couple of hundred dollars.

A thrill passed through Felix's body. He stammered his thanks.

"Then you'll come?"

"Why, the fact is, if your offer held good anyhow, I could work here now, I think."

The light in Corquill's eyes was extinguished.

"As you choose."

That was a narrow escape: the balance at the bank was overdrawn! But what was two hundred dollars? Felix, with the effrontery of desperation, penetrated Broad Street and called on Mr. Wickit.

He was admitted into the office carpeted with green Wilton, full of black tin boxes and volumes bound in yellow leather. The gray-haired lawyer, without rising, pointed to a mahogany chair. His angular, sallow face did not relax; his sharp eyes examined rapidly the visitor's physiognomy and clothing. Felix, once in the presence of this glum-visaged creditor, wondered what madness had impelled him thither. He had difficulty in beginning his preliminary speech, which, as he uttered it, appeared to him absurd.

"Perhaps, by this time, it had been found that there was at least a little money due him? He seemed to remember that Mr. Wickit had written him some sort of note, which he had been prevented from answering by various misfortunes. Could the lawyer have communicated with him on account of good news? Felix sincerely hoped so: a young man did not find money growing on bushes in a big city."

Mr. Wickit, assuming a smile of commiseration, explained:

"My dear sir, there is nothing new in regard to your poor father's estate. The three letters that I wrote to you, over a year ago, were about quite another matter."

Felix, with burning cheeks, plunged into his next manœuvre.

"Then it was about the thousand dollars? You shall have it, at the earliest possible moment. I've not done so well as I expected. Indeed, I'm wonder-ing where my current expenses are to come from. But when I get a start——"

"I understand. However, you can hardly expect me to do anything further in that line?"

Felix, rising, his spirits in his boots, made haste to murmur denial of such a thought. The lawyer's last comment, dryly delivered, was:

"What a pity you threw away your chance with Mrs. Droyt."

"With whom?"

"Mrs. Denis Droyt, of course. Miss Ferrol that was."

Felix, toiling home through the falling snow, had in payment for his pains this new chagrin.

And he, who had practically thrown them into each other's arms, who was responsible for the amal-

gamation of their two fortunes, remained at his wits'
end for money! He even requested a loan of Noon.

The speculator reluctantly produced from his fat
wallet fifty dollars. But on a second occasion, clearing his throat deliberately, looking fixedly at some
distant object, he rumbled:

"I haven't got it on me."

Felix went to a pawnshop on Sixth Avenue.

When within sight of the three gilt balls suspended
over the doorway, he slackened his pace, and began
to look intently into shop windows. Arriving before
the pawnbroker's showcases, he stopped, simulated
interest, put on a whimsical smile—at last, as if seized
with a playful desire for exploration, marched boldly
in. When the dejected-looking customers had all
departed, he produced, with a sensation of shame, a
pair of valuable cuff-links. The niggardly estimate
of the usurer amazed him.

His watch and fob, pearl shirt-buttons, rings,
cravat-pins, and gold cigarette-case, were one by one
relinquished in the little, cluttered shop, where the
air, as it seemed to Felix, was charged with hostility
generated through years of heartless bargaining and
sullen acquiescence. He told Marie that his watch
was being repaired, or that Noon's parade of precious
stones had disgusted him with jewelry.

Marie compressed her lips.

If he could only confess to her his long-continued
fraud, implore forgiveness, patience, temporary fru-
gality, enlist such compassionate support as ought to
issue from true love! But the many cynical concep-

tions engendered by his jealousy had so affected him, that now he was never sure enough of her attachment to put so great a strain upon it. To reveal to her, who had already learned his every temperamental shortcoming, all his material inadequacies as well, would, he felt, have been to strip himself of his last worldly value. Constantly dreading formidable rivalry, he continued his deceit: he went on regretting glibly that "his family estate was not yet in his hands," or that "his quarterly income was used up too soon." While adding invention to invention, he trusted that Providence would shower him in the nick of time, as formerly, with some miraculous windfall.

Once, in the midst of his distraction, he asked himself, was he not greatly like some antique devotee of Moloch, who, before a towering, brazen image of the divinity, hurled into the flames his treasure, his birthright, his very offspring, while adoring, half in terror, half in aberrant ecstasy, the impassive idol which was to pay him for his sacrifice in currency of ruin and blighted hopes?

But from the full measure of his sacrifice Felix could see no way of escape. Before his idol, his heart was burning. Long practice of excess had driven from his mind the contemplative and comparative forms of thought by aid of which the temperate protect themselves. With all the irrationality of the nervous sufferer clinging ever the more desperately to that which threatens his destruction, Felix saw, in a world full of distorted images, nothing so precious as the pellucid skin, the fragrant hair, the red mouth of the beloved.

On her return home tired from a day's rehearsing, she occupied the couch, while Felix, sitting beside her, gazed into her face. Her quivering lashes, her pulsing throat, the almost imperceptible flush that gathered round her cheek-bones, were for him extraordinary manifestations. A mist obscured his sight; in a choked voice he uttered:

"Don't move! How beautiful you are now!"

And, afflicted with faintness, hypnotized, as it were, by her glimmering face, he stammered that she was like a lily drooping from its own sweetness—that the room was filled with an indefinable, perilous emanation of her beauty.

At this flattery, gently she shook her head, then, opening her eyes, gave him a prolonged, humid look. A beam of light gradually bisected the shadows of the ceiling; the door swung open; Mattie, the maid, tiptoed in to light the lamp and arrange her mistress's coiffure. Becoming proficient at this office, she had finally replaced Miriam. The hairdresser had received her discharge with resentment.

Window-shades were drawn; the dressing-table was illumined; odors of heated hair and brilliantine were spread about. While at work, the mulatto, shrugging her shoulders, recounted in scornful tones whatever she had gleaned from other servants concerning the spite of actresses to whom Marie had been preferred. The mistress, with an inscrutable smile, remarked:

"It seems I'm finding out my friends, through 'The Queen of Hearts.'"

Preparations for that extravaganza proceeded rapidly. On Marie's dressing-table, amid the silver and the perfumes, were now always scattered the typewritten pages of her part; her songs, roughly scored by hand, trailed over the piano. She spent hours reiterating musical phrases or repeating lines; she always paused before her mirror to try a gesture or to practise a smile. Sometimes, Felix entered her parlor to find her, with skirts pinned up, posturing before the cheval-glass. Noticing him only by a contraction of her brows, she would, perhaps, press her hands against her breast, and, looking upward with a sweet, wondering expression of innocence, exclaim, in a clear voice:

"Is it a dream? Can there be anything so lovely in the world?"

She was to represent a sort of Cinderella, a foundling discovered, one morning after a terrific storm, before the hut of an old witch in a forest. Brought up a drudge, wearing rags which could not hide her charms, whenever her taskmistress was elsewhere astride a broomstick she hugged the hearth, dreamed of the unknown, contrived games of "make-believe" by aid of a pack of tattered playing-cards. One evening, as she was falling asleep, the strewn cards began to move, to grow, to change into strange, living creatures. They thronged round her: would she come with them? She assented; the hut dissolved, and, in its stead, appeared a dazzling realm called

"Cardland," where rose palaces of pasteboard and minarets of poker chips. But this place, where all should have been gay, was gloomy: years before, a great storm, while blowing down the palaces, had whisked from her cradle and carried off the new-born daughter of the King of Hearts. The King being forced into retirement by his grief, the pack was thenceforth incomplete, and all the games of "Cardland" had to be abandoned. However, on the lost infant there had been hidden beneath swaddling-clothes a heart-shaped birthmark; and presently, on the fair visitor from the forest this birthmark was, in an interesting way, discovered. Forthwith, the King recovered, and the deck again entire, all ended with a ballet in which, amid a rain of golden coins, various combinations of poker and bridge whist were formed by the evolutions of the card folk.

Montmorrissy did not know how his public would receive so innocent a conceit. He was tempted to interpolate, by way of precaution, a few local, "up-to-date," indecorous incidents. Occasionally appearing at rehearsals, he watched the action as narrowly as if it were a conspiracy against his pocketbook.

All day long they rehearsed "The Queen of Hearts" in an old hall on Sixth Avenue, up two flights of stairs, using a loft with discolored walls, a low ceiling stained by leaks, and a bare, splintery floor. Whenever the pianist, hired for the rehearsals, stopped his exertions, one could hear trains rumbling on the elevated railway. At the passage of expresses, violent concussions shook the building; all voices were drowned; the players closed their mouths, dropped their arms, and waited.

Felix wondered how any merit could be evolved from such confusion and incertitude as were there displayed. The diminutive dancing-girls called "ponies," in their blouses and short skirts, the "show girls" with their furs, feathers, and gilt purses, the chorus men in their wasp-waisted coats slashed with diagonal pockets according to a Broadway style, the fat comedian, the slender tenor, the soubrette, and Marie, turned helpless eyes toward the stage manager. This despot seemed to contain all the zeal and intelligence in the assembly. With his coat off, his collar wilted, his bald head shining, he fell back in scrutiny, rushed forward in reproof, with a word corrected erroneous ideas, with a gesture conjured up imagination. He lumbered round the room in ironical imitation of some clumsy "show girl," listened with a sarcastic smile to the enunciation of choruses, snatched individuals from corners where they were practising dance-steps, herded the company together, ordered the whole act begun again. When the ordeal was ended, he declared, to Felix's amazement, that "the thing was taking shape."

As the crowd disintegrated, girls lingered to read, from a bulletin tacked on the door, the names and prices of hotels in Boston. The extravaganza was going to that city for a week before beginning in New York.

Rehearsals were transferred to the Castle Theatre.

On the stage stripped of scenery, with oblong frames of canvas piled against the brick wall at the rear, the performers, used to rehearsing in a hall, had difficulty in manœuvring toward the centre of the footlights. All the concerted pieces were thrown into confusion, and forty young women, huddled together awkwardly, listened with vacuous smiles to the rasping voice of Montmorrissy denouncing them from the obscurity of the auditorium.

As the first-night approached, disquieting rumors flew about. A rival manager, from whose ranks Montmorrissy had wheedled some attractive "show girls," was going to retaliate by stealing the best "business" of "The Queen of Hearts." Moreover, at the last moment the comedian did not seem sufficiently comic, while the young tenor, Mackeron, who was having trouble with his throat, could not bring himself to give up cigarettes. In the wings, a boyish physician, employed to look after the "ponies" when they fainted from their exertions, was always spraying the tenor's larynx with an atomizer.

The dress-rehearsal, with full orchestra, began at midnight on Saturday and continued without interruption till late Sunday afternoon. Marie returned home white as death, with purple streaks beneath her eyes, scarcely able to talk. "No one liked the show. Every one was blue. Monty had never left off growling. So, according to the superstition, it should be a success."

On Monday morning, the company was entrained for Boston.

In the resounding railway station, Felix said good-by to Marie. She had the more easily dissuaded him from accompanying her, as he could not find anywhere funds sufficient for a week's extravagance.

Her last embraces had been perfunctory; her farewell seemed absent-minded. Evidently, her every thought reached toward the future. As the train rolled forth, she was busy reminding Montmorrissy of "her right to the best dressing-room."

Felix walked downtown in dejection.

How empty the city seemed! Seven days of loneliness! And then?

Terror seized him. He was utterly cleaned out, heavily in debt, even threatened by his landlord with eviction. Now, indeed, Marie seemed on the point of slipping from him. Clenching his fists, he repeated, desperately:

"I must have money! I must have money!"

That morning he resumed his writing. But so pressing was his need, and so great his fear of failure, that his labors resulted only in puerilities. He spent those days scribbling feverishly, tearing up pages, groaning at his impotence. Every hour he wondered why Marie had written him but one short note, why he could not reach her by the long-distance telephone, why the most urgent telegrams failed to elicit a response. Perhaps she had broken down from overwork! Should he go to her? Or maybe Montmorrissy was slashing the play to pieces, and she was too busy to think of him? He wrote to the manager and to Mackeron for news.

Late on the night before "The Queen of Hearts" was expected in New York, the door of the studio burst open: Nora Llanelly entered.

She had come in a cab, bareheaded, wearing slippers, with a long blue burnoose thrown over a dressing-gown. Her eyelids were swollen; her nose was red; her whole face was blowsy from some tempestuous grief. She leaned against the door-jamb, dishevelled, wide-eyed, breathless, a large apparition at once imposing and alarming.

Felix's heart stopped beating. He cried out:

"What has happened to her!"

Nora, exposing her full throat, laughed bitterly.

"To her? Nothing! It's to me and you that it's happened!"

He did not understand. Exasperated, she leaned forward and shrilled at him, with breaking voice:

"For God's sake, get next to yourself! And you with a reputation for smartness! Why, I can see it, now, from the beginning—every bit, every bit!" And sinking into a chair, she informed him that Noon, whom she had believed to be in Philadelphia on business, was in Boston. The thing was not even surreptitious; and Miriam, the hairdresser, to whom all scandalous rumors flew like homing pigeons, had just decided that it was "a duty" to enlighten Miss Llanelly.

"And some one I've known all my life—that I done everything for when she was up against it!" While fumbling for a handkerchief, the ex-"show girl" squeezed her inflamed eyelids together in order to keep back the tears. Her face slowly faded from Felix's sight; her voice reached him from afar.

When he had finally got rid of her, he gazed about him in curiosity. He was surprised at the inexplicable oddity of his surroundings. He peered in a mirror, and did not recognize his face.

Through the night, he suffered very little. His brain seemed anæsthetized.

Toward dawn, the aspect of trivial objects, during the night examined many times, began to frighten him. He could not bear to look steadily at anything. Was he losing his mind? He drank whiskey, and, at last, stumbling off to bed, found relief in stupor.

At dusk, he awoke. Mechanically he bathed and dressed himself; blindly he walked out; and presently he found himself at Marie's door. The mulatto maid admitted him, and disappeared. He parted the green portières.

Shadows veiled walls and ceiling; but from the middle of the room, level rays of light reached out and dazzled him. She was there, alone, seated beyond the bright centre-table. The lamp of yellow porcelain gleamed between them.

Rising to her feet, she held herself motionless. The lamplight illumined her slender figure from the hips upward, and the lower part of her face. He saw clearly her parted lips. But her eyes, her brow, her hair, remained indistinct.

She wore a new dress of violet-colored silk, the corsage decked with fringes of jet beads. Behind her, a large hat, to match this costume, lay on the top of the piano. Over all the furniture were scattered garments of white lace, recently unpacked. The warm air was redolent of benzoine and "*peau d'Espagne*."

In that familiar atmosphere, evoking with its fragrance innumerable memories, there stole into his heart a poignant, inappropriate longing. He saw her as if after a separation of years; her every beauty was rediscovered; and her attire, strange to him, seemed to invest her well-remembered person with an additional fascination—with a seductive novelty. He had an impulse, almost uncontrollable, to ignore the past, if only for a moment. But, perceiving in the lobes of her ears two large black pearls, he remained as before, while a great lassitude invaded his limbs.

At last, a sob escaped him, and the words:

"What a wretch you are!"

In low tones, she retorted:

"And what about you? What about your deceits —your stories of money and prospects? Ah, but you got round me! And, like a fool, I believed everything about you that Llanelly and others told me. Little they knew! But I know now, thanks to him. He couldn't keep it in any longer. And he had the right of it. Yes, I find that he was your father's confidential business man. The world's a small place!"

He stared at her with open mouth, incredulous. Harshly, he laughed:

"That rounder?"

Then, as her eyes flashed at him through the shadows, he realized that there was no possibility of further and more shameful weakness on his part. It was, indeed, finished.

An infinite reproach thrilled his utterance:

"You never loved me!"

"No, no; don't go thinking that I have no heart at all. I got very fond of you, Felix. This has been hard for me. But there are things in the world that I've never had, that other women have, that I've always craved, that I must get. And life's short. And I've thrown the last fifteen months away. And now I must begin again nearly where I was when I met you."

Her head sank backward: she seemed to be staring fixedly at something above, visible to her alone. The darkness had invaded her whole face, which took on an unreal, an awesome, look. For Felix, there was in her countenance something terrible. The shadows round her eye-sockets, her mouth, her cheek-bones, were like an insidiously gathering decay. She resembled Venus in dissolution.

He found the door. The latch clicked behind him. He had fled a tomb.

Near street lamps, moisture glittered like suspended folds of gauze. Fog was closing round illuminated shop-windows, to blur and enlarge the radiance thereof. At a distance, before spaces tremulously luminous and all reflected in the wet pavement, pedestrians, indistinct, outlined by yellow aureoles, appeared like ghosts floating across deep pools of light.

Felix turned toward the park.

The trees, in the mist more nebulous than the heavens, were gradually pervaded by a threnody of falling rain. From the earth rose a continuous sibilation, and ripplings which suggested mournful voices.

It was eight o'clock when he emerged from the darkness at Columbus Circle. Within the park gates stood a small pavilion, open on all sides, furnished with benches. Felix, dripping, shivering, worn out, entered this shelter and sank into a seat.

Before him, in the centre of a broad stretch of asphalt, loomed the statue of Columbus on its tall, granite column. Round this monument, outside a ring of green lanterns set out for the regulation of traffic, glided an interminable flood of automobiles. Beyond, rose a semicircle of buildings gay with lights, their roofs crowned with electric signs the party-colored globes of which seemed to give off fumes into the lurid sky. At the right of this semicircle blazed the façade of the Castle Theatre.

An illuminated device two stories high, heart-shaped, blood-red, proclaimed Montmorrissy's extravaganza. Underneath, in a pale sheen blotted from time to time by the silhouettes of automobiles, surged a confusion of umbrellas, silk hats, and women's cloaks. It was the audience assembling for the first-night.

Gradually the crowd penetrated the theatre. The bright vestibule stood empty. A clock dial on the corner of Fifty-ninth Street marked half-past eight. She was on the stage, singing, smiling across the footlights.

The young man, his chin sunk forward on his breast, turned to retrospection. There came to him a remembrance of numberless abasements, losses, sacrifices. What anguish had he not suffered; what inestimable treasures had he not thrown away; to what straits had he not brought himself! Twisting his mouth into a bitter grimace, he pronounced, slowly:

"And all for nothing!"

It was the epitaph of that period.

PART THREE

EMMA

CHAPTER XI

His sentimental convalescence was retarded by chagrin. It was not easy to recover from the thought that he, though all aflame, had never warmed her heart.

He recalled that career of his in gullibility, and imagined the ironical applause that must secretly have greeted it. He came to hate the scenes of his humiliation, each remembrance of which was distorted by a savage prejudice.

There took shape before him a nocturnal thoroughfare, disguising its shabbiness with a glitter of colored lights, where automobiles, bearing women flagrantly perilous yet immeasurably ignoble beneath their finery, drove decency into the gutters, where the pavements disappeared under a surge of neurasthenic men penetrating cafés amid the flicker of bold eyes, where the apertures of the side streets were filled with shadows of a predacious restlessness, while, beneath the aura of the "Tenderloin"—a thin radiance quivering as if set in agitation by innumerable spasms of sick nerves—was disseminated an atmosphere, which all thereabouts were forced to breathe, like some vast, enveloping, enigmatically perverse temptation.

Felix, in revulsion, longed for his old contentment in immaculate and simple things, for the tonic reactions from intentions wholly pure, for such companionship as should be but a commingling of sublime tendernesses. And he seemed to see a billowy landscape, wooded, immersed in sunshine, swallows skimming over lawns at the approach of evening, then, emerging from a fading sky, the round, diaphanous moon.

But in the midst of fine resolutions he realized that none of his experiences could be obliterated—that thenceforth he would have to go through life, however edifying his course, with something of the past disfiguring him.

Meanwhile, he had yet to make the first retrieving step. His pockets were empty; he had pawned all his valuable possessions; there was none left of whom he dared ask assistance. His landlord, despairing of six months' back rent, dispossessed him.

When the hour came for him to leave the studio forever, standing beneath the skylight he gazed round as if to impress upon his memory each trivial object. The worn furniture seemed suddenly replete with sentimental value. A flood of reminiscences engulfed him: he pronounced, slowly and gently, three names, "Nina, Eileen, Marie!" They had all entered there; something of their diverse sweetnesses remained clinging, as it were, to the hangings like faint, mingling perfumes; and all their physical and moral variations were confused, at that blending of many memories into one memory diffuse and limitless, to him more exquisite, mysterious, and fragrant than a garden full of lilies in moonlight. "Good-by, old room!" He felt that he was shutting in there something of himself—an essence which would mingle forever with an impalpable part of them, that they had not been able to take away. "No; what the heart gives, it cannot wholly get back. From love, no one escapes entire. There is no utter rupture, no absolute separation." He issued into Thirty-second Street. Pat, the white bull-terrier, leaped and barked to find himself in the open.

On Washington Square South, Felix found a small hotel, square, flat-roofed, built of green brick, six stories high, the narrow entrance trimmed with exceedingly thin slabs of greenish marble, the office furnished with four chairs and two brass cuspidors, the elevator somewhat larger than a bird-cage. There, on the fifth floor, he obtained, for nine dollars a week, a bedroom and a bath, with windows opening on the square. Beyond a rectilinear expanse of trees—their nakedness disclosing asphalt paths, some wooden shelters, and a circular fountain—past the gray bulk of the Washington Arch—a monument of Roman contour, strong and martial—midway of a row of three-story brick dwellings with white window frames and porticos, appeared the beginning of Fifth Avenue: a vista, stretching northward, where the prim roofs of conservative gentlefolk soon gave place to the "sky-scrapers" of trade, and at the right of which, a mile away, above a crenellation of massive cornices, was thrust into the air a marble tower.

From his bedroom window Felix could see the site of the Ferrol house, where was rising against clouds a black steel framework. In that effacement, he took a mournful satisfaction. He was relieved of one hitherto persistent, mute reproach.

Old scenes seemed fated to enclose him. He was forced back to *The Evening Sphere.*

The vestibule retained its odors of linoleum and printer's ink; the spiral staircase trembled at subterranean rumblings; one end of the fourth floor was foggy with tobacco smoke, where five unwashed windows admitted over a swarm of profiles a diluted light. An edition of *The Evening Sphere* was going to press. Mechanics, bare-armed, tweaked mats of felt from metal slabs; "copy boys" scampered to pneumatic tubes; groups huddled round form-tables; young reporters sat at desks, their foreheads sinking toward their speedy pencils. On all sides rose familiar faces: Johnny Livy was there, waving a page of manuscript and bellowing to be relieved of it. None had time to notice Felix.

But the editor, in his cupboard of an office, his coat off, his knees hidden beneath newspapers, carefully laid down his cigar, and went so far as to extend a slender hand. In his delicate face a sly pleasure seemed to struggle with reserve. He did not refrain from asking:

"The prodigal's return?"

"If you'll have me, sir."

The editor seemed on the point of some complimentary utterance. However, he recovered just in time his customary caution.

"What salary were you getting?"

"Twenty-five dollars."

"So much? Well—all right. Report to the city desk."

In a week, it was as if Felix had never left *The Evening Sphere*. He resumed a hundred old habits of obedience and work. A sense of retrogression wore away; he discovered many amiable qualities in his co-workers, from whom he had once thought himself remote in everything.

He smoked a pipe, drank beer, and often lunched with Livy, the reporter, in a café on Fulton Street, where the bill came to half a dollar. These two found themselves much more congenial than formerly.

The lean, jerky young journalist was at last even tempted to confessions. He aspired to be a city editor, "his finger marking the pulse-beat of New York"; he wanted to marry, to live in a suburban cottage, with a baby carriage on the porch, dogs on the step, and chickens in the yard. But many turned their eyes toward the city editor's desk, and Livy had few opportunities to meet "nice" girls. However, he expounded a theory that one got what he set his mind on. There was only one thing to beware of, namely, liquor. And, while returning officeward with Felix from the café, he would point out some elderly waif, drifting beneath the bulletin-boards of the newspaper offices, gray-headed, ragged, half tipsy, who had once been a "star reporter." Felix felt deep in his breast a thrill of fear.

Innumerable past satiations, remorses, and disgusts, had united finally to effect in him, as he be-

lieved, a permanent repugnance, an utter disillusionment, an epochal upheaval of the conscience. His
old arguments in favor of self-denial had recurred to
him. He even thought himself, at last, in sympathy
with those ascetics whose philosophies had once an-
noyed him. There emerged from the phantasma-
goria of history, as if to tempt his emulation, a sort
of cenobitic pageant of the ages, wherein appeared
the multitudes of the world's exalted souls, wherein
swam together countless faces illumined by renunciation, wherein myriads of hands fluttered to make
every manner of devotional sign, while on all sides
the emblems of abnegatory cults rose and drooped in
time to an air-shaking diapason of resolute voices.

Yet Felix soon gazed on this vision, as he had
gazed on that of the lost pagan frenzies of the flesh,
in a preoccupation intrinsically all sensuousness.
He considered less the renouncers of the world than
what they had renounced; and the pleasures spurned
by them were so gilded over with the romance pertaining to old things as to bear no visible relation
to their modern counterparts. Felix, who now expressed abhorrence of debauchery in his own place
and time, dreamed of cities anathematized by antique
saints, over which Astarte, like the chimera of a
colossal courtesan—her brow diademmed with stars,
her pallor looming under veils of smoky indigo that
filled the night—spread on the evening winds the
aphrodisiacal perfume of her sigh, to pervade all
mortals with her madness. In short, Felix would
have liked just then to be Paphnutius praying in his

cell, but would have wished to think, while praying, of Thaïs dropping her mantle in the Alexandrian theatre.

So it was with backward looks that the young man bade farewell to all his faults.

But presently, there succeeded his first satisfaction feelings of solitude. Tremendous spaces, as in trackless seas, encompassed him; doubts obscured, like leaden clouds, the horizon where he had thought to find his haven: land was not there; he had thrown overboard all the palliatives of an earthly voyage; and, his brain reeling in a hurricane of longings, he anticipated shipwreck for that venture.

"Perhaps his sacrifices had been made too violently?"

At this gust, he capsized.

With robust and reckless independence, he marched into a café. Next morning, he was unable to appear at the newspaper office.

Felix then got the idea that by very gradually reducing his indulgences he could, without discomfort, bring them to the vanishing-point. This system never seemed so plausible as when, alone in some obscure café, a long cigar between his teeth, a glass of whiskey and soda in his hand, he saw his surroundings develop values previously unsuspected. Once more life was ephemerally embellished; aspirations came thronging, and, at the utter dissolution of the commonplace, he seemed to glimpse the magnificent, undecipherable object of all human yearning. Those were rare hours, such as he could not frequently afford.

Little by little, the workaday present obscured the romantic past. At length, he found it impossible to recall distinctly Marie's face. He was conscious of no more than a fair aureole, indefinitely representing perfidy wrapped up in passion, evoking a bitterness inextricable from a lurking sweetness.

Felix was always remembering, however, his indebtedness to Noon, at thought of whom he could summon no certain feeling save of humiliation.

He examined his half-finished novel, begun a year before. It dealt with a girl of lowly origin, pursuing, through a gloomy region of abysses, the *ignis fatuus* of honest love. Felix destroyed that manuscript. "He could have written no more with conviction."

But one evening he met on the street Miss Qewan, who had been discharged from "The Silly Season" by Montmorrissy. Felix's sympathetic inquiries unlocked her lips; she related her struggles frankly.

She had left the stage, to try manicuring, hairdressing, peddling sets of books, and office work. But the manager of a barber's shop and a French hairdresser had both found her lacking in complaisance; then her book-selling had drawn her into equivocal situations, and finally she had engaged to work for a promoter of financial schemes "who got too gay." She thought of accepting employment in a telephone exchange—a great, bustling place where the individual, no doubt, was lost to view.

"But, my dear girl, such wages!"

"Yes," she admitted, "sometimes when I look round, I think I'm foolish. The world, as I come in contact with it, seems to think so, too! But then, it's not just myself."

"I know," said Felix, remembering some tale of an eight-year-old sister.

As she looked up at him, surprised, the bright blood flooded her cheeks.

Formerly pale and slender, she was now well-nigh ethereal, and her face, under dark hair arranged in unobtrusive folds, revealed a luminosity seen at times in countenances of women devoted to religion, or to some other elevated, fixed resolve. Felix, homeward bound, asked himself:

"Suppose it had been one of that sort, instead?"

A breeze wafted through Washington Square an earthy odor that was like a hint of spring. He thought of his solitary evenings, and wondered where she lived.

At night, in his hotel bedroom, he scribbled listlessly and tore up synopses of illogical tales. His literary failures of the past year had deprived him of motive force. It was only when disqualified from work by stimulants that he felt able to write masterpieces.

Smoking incessantly, he paced from wall to wall, sneered at the dingy room, peered at the clock without knowing why he wanted time to pass, halted before the mantel-shelf, where stood his mother's photograph. Sometimes he strove, from a sense of obligation, to discover a filial tenderness for the beautiful young woman, in obsolete attire, whom he had never known.

Lives, pleasures, opportunities, ever touching, passing, vanishing away! But there always remained to him the luxury of self-pity. Now and then, when Felix was staring at his reflection in the mirror, Pat, curled up on a chair, would quickly raise his head.

The white bull-terrier had grown to weigh forty pounds. His lengthy skull tapered to a sharp nose; his deep-set eyes, three-cornered and black-rimmed, lay slantwise under a flat brow; his trimmed ears, lined with pink, stood permanently erect; he had the flexible neck, long, narrow body, slight quarters, and sinewy legs of the agile fighting brute. His brass-bound collar was dented with many a tooth mark.

He had spent hours without number listening behind locked doors for the unique footfall, or enduring morosely, in furnace rooms and basement kitchens, the guardianship of servants. Felix, a remorseful jailer, at least discovered a place where he could dine with Pat underneath the table.

On the north side of Eighth Street, close to Washington Square, an old, white dwelling-house had been converted into an Italian restaurant, called "Benedetto's," where a *table d'hôte* dinner was served for sixty cents. Some brown-stone steps, flanked by a pair of iron lanterns, gave entrance to a narrow corridor. There, to the right, immediately appeared the dining-room, extending through the house—linoleum underfoot, hat-racks and buffets of oak aligned against the brownish walls, and, everywhere, little tables, each covered with a scanty cloth, set close together.

Felix, at the most inconspicuous table, consumed a soup redeemed from tastelessness by grated parmesan, a sliver of fish and four slices of cucumber, spaghetti, a chicken leg, two cubic inches of ice-cream, a fragment of roquefort cheese, and coffee in a small, evidently indestructible cup. Then, through tobacco smoke, he watched the patrons round him, their feet twisted behind chair-legs, their elbows on the table, all arguing with gesticulations. Sometimes, there floated to him such phrases as: "bad color scheme!" "sophomoric treatment!" "miserable drawing!" "no atmosphere!" Benedetto's was a Bohemian resort.

One night, Felix made the acquaintance there of a little man with bright, shallow eyes and eager lips, wearing a low collar and a large black bow, who introduced himself.

"My name is Lute. We live in the same hotel, and, I understand, pursue the same profession. So, naturally, neither of us is to be fettered by absurd conventions. May I sit down? Mercy, what's this —a dog! Will he bite? Good fellow! Guiseppe! The regular *table d'hôte*. Mr. Piers, have you read 'A Sunrise,' Oliver Corquill's latest?"

"Not yet. I must, though, or he'll be asking me if I liked it."

Mr. Lute's eyes opened wide.

"A friend of Oliver Corquill's? How interesting!" And, hitching his chair forward, he beamed on the young man. Felix wondered how he could manage to display also his friendship with Paul Pavin.

"And you, Mr. Piers, may I ask what you are publishing just now?"

"Nothing, at present."

The intruder's face brightened all the more.

"Same with me. Put out nothing that's not perfect, eh? I go very carefully. Would you believe that in the last three months I've released only one thing, a quatrain, appearing in the current number of *The Mauve Monthly*, at the bottom of the ninety-ninth page?"

"You are a poet, then?" asked Felix, raising his second glass of Scotch and soda.

"Specifically, but my muse is catholic. I've written a novel, that I shall revise to my liking some day. I've done a play—it was going to be produced last year—in collaboration. You must know of Miss Nedra Jennings Nuncheon?"

"I haven't the pleasure."

"You surprise me! A remarkable girl! I must introduce you."

Next night, Felix was presented to Miss Nuncheon.

She was tall and thin, with a mop of orange-colored hair the ends of which trailed down. In a blue dress of many folds, the neck cut low, the sleeves covering her knuckles, she seemed to Felix trying to impersonate some lank damosel in a Preraphaelite painting. She spoke impulsively, in the uncertain, reedy voice of a person hysterically inclined, and frequently, with the vehemence of her nods, shook loose a yellow celluloid hairpin.

It appeared that she wrote short stories about "the

smart set," a society existing far off amid the glamour of opera-boxes, conservatories full of orchids, yachts like ocean steamships, mansions with marble stairways, Paris dresses by the gross, and hatfuls of diamonds, where the women were always discovered in boudoirs with a French maid named Fanchette in attendance, receiving bunches of long-stemmed roses from potential corespondents, while the men, all very tall and dark, possessed of interesting pasts, were introduced before fireplaces in sumptuous bachelor apartments, the veins knotted on their temples, and their strong yet aristocratic fingers clutching a photograph or a scented note. Miss Nuncheon enjoyed the admiration of a numerous class of readers.

Nevertheless, she lived in a boarding-house near Washington Square, where she shared apartments with a stout, faded, pretty woman named Mrs. Babbage, who usually accompanied her to Benedetto's. Mrs. Babbage was interested in occult philosophies, and wrote articles for an esoteric magazine. She was so calm as to seem almost somnolent; she only put on a beatific smile when an Italian waiter spilled salad-dressing down her back, and when she lost the blue pebble from her cabalistic finger-ring. According to Mr. Lute, if it were not for Mrs. Babbage's sedative influence, there was no telling what agonies Miss Nuncheon might endure on account of her intense artistic temperament.

Felix soon wearied of the "shop talk" that he heard at Benedetto's. There great names were ignored, or else uneasily disparaged, while New York authors so obscure as to be unknown to Felix were vehemently extolled. Mr. Lute, the symbolic quatrain writer, had not heard of the Parnassians; Miss Nuncheon, always talking of the "psychological novel," did not know who Stendhal was; Mrs. Babbage, who could dash off columns about "the mystic ideals of the East," showed a blank face at references to Neoplatonism. Finding his own company less exasperating, Felix took to dining late, and, in the deserted restaurant, while Pat crunched bones beneath the table, progressed at leisure, without interruption, from cheap red wine to high-balls, to liqueur brandy, to inspiring dreams. The same swarthy waiter always helped him into his overcoat, and, from the corridor, called after him:

"Mind da step, signore!"

Once, when he had just ordered dinner, he saw, at the other end of the room, a pair of eyes, large and luminous under arched black brows, staring at him. Surely that was the woman who, in search of her husband, had interrupted his studio party on Christmas eve, a year and more ago! She bowed to him discreetly.

He rose, and approached her. She bolted a mouthful of food, pressed a napkin to her lips, and got up from her chair. This movement surprised him. He noticed her unfashionable hat, and her neat, black dress, which looked home-made.

"How do you do?"

"Very well, thanks. And you?"

"I, too."

And they stood gazing at each other without smiling.

A small woman, evidently past thirty, she was in danger of becoming stout. Her face was fuller than when Felix had last seen her, and beneath her soft chin had appeared an infinitesimal crease. Her skin was a clear white, her hair, blue-black and simply dressed; her blue eyes, extraordinarily lambent—which, from a distance, Felix had thought black—formed her one beauty. Across her outjutting nose ran a slight scar. She had a little, pale, thin-lipped mouth disclosing, when she spoke, small, glistening teeth. In a soft voice, she said, hesitatingly:

"How strange to meet you here!"

"Oh, I find it amusing, sometimes, this sort of thing, as I suppose you do. Besides, I live near by."

"Why, I thought ——"

"No, up there they began to tear down the buildings round me; it got rather disagreeable, and I left. But you?"

"I live round the corner."

"Is it possible! Then you come here often?"

"For a change. I board. I'm still alone. This time, he never came back."

After a pause, she added, timidly:

"Won't you sit down, Mr.——"

Felix pronounced his name. She was Mrs. Meers. They dined together.

She had short, plump hands, well kept, which she used at table very warily, as if apprehensive of her manners. Indeed, she was obviously ill at ease, scarcely touched her dinner, could not be persuaded to take champagne, answered in monosyllables, and, throughout the meal, seemed in a sort of trance. Felix, divining her sensations, exercised his ingenuity to impress her further. His vanity was touched, at the belief that this little bourgeoise stood in awe of him. It was not often, nowadays, that he enjoyed the pleasures of superiority.

When he had paid the bill, he rallied her, gayly:

"Come, now: what were you thinking of while you sat there all through dinner like a little mouse?"

With head slightly lowered, with lips together, she looked at him as if frightened, and, though she made no movement, seemed to stir throughout.

"I was thinking how strange it was to be dining here with any one." Then, by way of explanation:

"I'm so much alone, you see."

It had been drizzling: the pavements, beaded with rain, showed, under mistily irradiating street lamps, humid footprints. From the juncture of Macdougal Street and Waverley Place, the trees of Washington Square spread out a mass of gray-black shadows underlaid with the horizontal, pearly lustre of wet asphalt paths. Here and there, a yellow shaft of light, enlarged in the damp air, streamed past the tree-trunks, and, beyond upper branches, illuminated window-panes shone peacefully, their mellow squares etched over, as it were, by delicate traceries of twigs. Clouds were disintegrating straight overhead. Into a radiant space came floating a frail, shining crescent.

"Oh, the new moon!" cried Felix's companion, with an accent of emotion. "I must make a wish!" She stood still, her lustrous eyes upturned, her small face solemn from superstition. For the moment, she resembled a young girl.

On Waverley Place, near Sixth Avenue, she halted before a house with old window-shutters and a brown-stone portico crumbling at the pediment. Beside the door, a sign announced "furnished rooms and table board."

"I live here," she confessed.

Felix, homeward bound through Washington Square, felt in himself something of the mysterious release of nature that was taking place about him. "This cool air, moist and sweet, is breathing news of spring!" He gazed up at the stars, lips parted, in unaccountable expectancy.

Within the week, curious to know her story— "which might give him some ideas"—he called on her.

In the boarding-house on Waverley Place there was no parlor: she had to receive him in her room, up two flights of stairs, overlooking the back yards. A folding bed, adorned with a blotched mirror, confronted a white mantel-piece. Some old brocade chairs, the relics of more nearly elegant environments, exhibited their threadbare arms and split edges. Between the windows stood a yellow bureau, bearing pin-cushions, brushes, combs, and scissors, laid out precisely. The room, despite its shabbiness, was neat; a work-basket on a stand provided a domestic touch; and, when Felix entered, she was preparing to hang on the walls a dozen framed photographs that she had washed. He suggested helping her; she, at such condescension, excitedly refused assistance; in his most urbane manner, he insisted. Over this mutual labor, they progressed to laughter. He discovered that she could appreciate his attempts at humor. A smile changed her face surprisingly.

All the photographs were of her. She was portrayed in a lace dress, in a light opera cloak and train, in a large hat with plumes, always, in these costumes which looked at once expensive and provincial, standing stiffly, with immobile face, like a wax figure in a show-window. Felix wondered if vanity had urged her to this exhibition. He ventured:

"What pretty dresses! And how well you look in them!"

"I used to have things," she responded, heaving a deep sigh.

Perhaps, then, these were souvenirs by means of which she kept active a melancholy retrospection?

Lonely, bursting with suppressed complaints, evidently a woman to make a confidant of the first sympathetic-looking person, she needed no temptation to discuss her history. "I feel everything so deeply! And few women have had such troubles as I," she declared, with an air of mournful satisfaction.

Born and brought up in a Connecticut town, from which she had migrated as a bride, she had married, for love, the superintendent of a beef-packing house in Long Island City. According to her, this husband was a fellow inexpressibly handsome and robust, rosy from inhabiting cold-storage vaults, resplendent in his white apron amid his rows of carcasses, and, no doubt, deriving from the exhalations of so much raw flesh a brutal lustihood. He had "a good salary"; they fitted out a cottage in Long Island City that she "would not have exchanged for the best house on Fifth Avenue." There she was happy.

But "Lew" had taken to drink, had neglected her, had proved unfaithful. While referring to her husband's many gallantries, she could not help showing something like admiration. She had possessed, or shared, at least, a Don Juan!

Her parents were dead; her woman friends had failed her; men had not been willing to remain disinterested. With nowhere to turn, she had condoned her husband's various offences. She explained, "Then, too, Mr. Piers, you don't know what the name 'wife' means to a woman."

Lew lost his position and could retain no other, dissipated his savings and whatever money of his wife's he could secure, sold the cottage, changed lodgings every month, haunted race-tracks, disappeared for weeks on drinking bouts, finally vanished. She was now spending the last of her inheritance: when that was gone, what should she do?

"He may come to his senses yet," was Felix's suggestion.

She became greatly agitated.

"That's finished! It took me eight years to wean myself away from him. But now I hate his very name! And I shall never love again—oh, never, never again."

Felix repressed a smile. She was diverting, this little, naïve, earnest woman of a class new to him. He thought, "I could write a novel round her." Indeed, he fell to contemplating such a book—a monotone of misfortunes, beginning obscurely, moving through commonplace adventures that his art would make prodigious, then slowly drawing to an undistinguished, yet exquisitely pathetic, close. So he took to calling on her regularly.

He had his chair, the deepest and most comfortable. She bought a metal ash-tray, which she placed near him, diffidently; the receptacle first used by him—a pasteboard box-lid—was not good enough, it seemed.

She was long in abandoning her timidity before this young man with a distinguished air and a nice command of language, this "gentleman," who gave extravagant supper-parties in a studio, confessed himself hand in glove with celebrities, and every evening might undoubtedly have dazzled the town in the most brilliant company. If only she could have received him "properly"! She lamented the loss of her cottage. What good little dinners she had once contrived for persons unworthy of them, the strawberry shortcake a product of her own hands, the table laden, thanks to Lew, with the choicest meats and game! Her very ingenuousness roused his pity.

She had spent part of her girlhood in a convent. While darning stockings, she related anecdotes:

"I had a little room with a white bed, and a shiny,

shiny floor, and one chair. But no mirror! I never saw myself! When I got home, I sat all day before a mirror, rocking and rocking.

"In recreation hour, we made clothes for tiny little orphans. Sometimes I would be sewing in the grape arbor, and a great bunch of grapes would fall right into my lap. How my mouth watered! But the Sister always said, 'Be firm, Emma!'

"I used to pray at night, 'If only I could die this minute: I'm so good, I would go straight to heaven!'"

These speeches, accompanied by shy, bird-like poses of the head, all ending in a whisper like a little girl's, bestowed on her a dainty charm, and made her seem younger than she was. She confessed to twenty-nine years.

One evening, when he was bidding her good-by, their hands grew cold at contact, their glances clung together. She, with a look of consternation, slowly leaned her weight against the door-jamb.

At once, he recalled the past, and all its miseries. He went downstairs quickly. He swore never to enter there again.

It was spring at last; the windows of his room were open; the breeze blew in. And from the darkness something invisible, impalpable, yet almost personal, something soft, languorous, and immense, related to the stars, to flowers, to evening winds, seemed stealing toward him.

He was frightened. Recoiling, he whispered:

"No more! This time, I want to escape!"

CHAPTER XII

FELIX avoided Benedetto's restaurant, stopped wandering in Washington Square at night, made détours round Waverley Place, even thought of changing his abode. But in a week he asked himself why his apprehension had been so intense. He had, it seemed, been afraid of an obscure little woman no longer youthful, neither pretty nor talented, who should have excited in him only pity and amusement! Had he not learned his lesson, through much suffering, at the hands of those with whom, in point of charms, she was not to be compared?

Sometimes, however, he imagined her sitting in her room, the metal ash-tray empty on her bureau, with her dozen photographs, suggestive of "better days," for company. This picture seemed indirectly to reproach him.

He became angry. Deserted and lonely? So were a hundred thousand other women in the city; he hoped he was not under obligations to them all! "My worst trouble is that I am naturally a sentimental ass!"

Well, he would make an end of that with his other weaknesses. Recalling to mind great historic figures, he told himself that those who hardened their hearts and rode rough-shod over humanity attained the highest eminences. With the intention of emulating such characters, he assumed an air of energy and sternness, was unnaturally curt in all his intercourse, and, in the street, regarded passers-by—to their evident surprise—with a set, inimical face. In this mood, as in all others, he was swept quickly to excess.

These enforcements of vigor proved only so many additional incentives to inebriety. For just as he could no longer feel depression without the desire to relieve it by familiar means, so he could not experience exhilaration without the impulse to appease in like manner a nervous appetency that accompanied it. His recent ideas of abstinence faded in a moral obscuration continually renewed. Nearly every night he reached his bed half stupefied by his potations. At the newspaper office, he welcomed eagerly an "outdoor job," as promising the opportunity to snatch some highballs on the way.

Now and then, when Felix, at a battered desk, was scribbling of defaulters, homicides, and politicians, the editor, on the threshold of his compartment, a newspaper clipping in his hand, gazed at the young man as if absent-mindedly. If he had in prospect a delicate commission, which threatened libel suits, he beckoned Johnny Livy.

This reporter managed to get himself affianced to a modest girl who lived with her parents in a suburb. Immediately, he left off drinking, discarded his black felt hat and corncob pipe, strove to be at once better dressed and more economical, worked desperately to attract the favorable notice of his superiors, had no

small talk that was not about "the cost of living."
Felix, his frequent confidant, disguised commiserat-
ing smiles, like one who sees others striving for such
fruits as have withered at his touch.

But one brilliant afternoon in May, when all the
trees of Washington Square were stippled with a
tender green, there came to him a sadness not to be
dispelled by sunshine; and he paused, in the doorway of his hotel, to look again at a young couple
promenading, slowly and silently, beside the red and
yellow tulip beds, beneath the budding leaves, to the
twittering of mating birds.

When he went upstairs, he found on the door-sill
of his room an envelope addressed in an unknown,
childish hand. It was from Emma Meers.

She had been wondering how she could have
offended him. The thought of losing, by some inad-
vertence, a kind friend—if she might call him so—
with friends so scarce, had nearly "brought her down
ill." "Your calls were something to look foreward
to; they made me feel like I wasent all together
alone. I know it was a great kindness of you to
bother with me, being so busy, and haveing so interesting people to take up your leisure, but if you could
find it conveniant only to drop in sometimes when
you are not engaged, and cheer me up like you used,
is the wish of yours very gratefully" .   .   .

Poor little woman, this letter, with all its errors so
painstakingly engrossed, had been a troublesome task
for her! Her face, timid and beseeching, appeared
before him no less clearly than on those evenings

when they had forgotten in company their loneliness. He wondered how he could have been apprehensive of a personality so submissive, so helpless, so easy— if the utmost befell—to leave behind.

For was there not to be read, between the lines of that laborious script, a meaning more wistful than she dared express; did he not perceive, with an intuition sharpened to discern every sentimental approach, that something was seeking him which he had never yet been able to withstand? He gazed, in fact, toward a new horizon, where hovered the promise of a passion the more piquant for its humble and almost domestic setting. At the revival of his ineradicable curiosity, all his determinations were forgotten.

He returned to Waverley Place.

She rose from a chair; her hand flew to her breast; she stood motionless, staring at him.

"Oh, how you frightened me!"

"I wasn't expected?"

"No. Yes. That is, I hardly hoped. So you got my poor letter?"

"A charming letter."

"Ah, you say that!"

She was within his reach, her small, upturned face assuredly betraying the secret he had expected to discover. But suddenly, remembering their short acquaintance, he became incredulous. What if he were on the verge of a humiliating mistake? He hesitated, lost his chance, and sat down in "his chair." She placed the metal ash-tray at his elbow.

"And what have you been doing, all these three weeks?"

"Working every minute. And you?"

"Trying to forget my troubles."

So they began again. After all his anticipations, such an anticlimax!

Yet whose fault was it, if not his? That evening, while returning home, he denounced his vacillation; he vowed that their next meeting should be different. As always, when once tempted to tamper with his resolutions, he was to be satisfied with nothing less than the annihilation of them.

Such dexterity in love-making as he now possessed was not needed in the slightest. His first change of voice from commonplace to tender agitated her; at his near approach she fixed him with a dewy gaze through which her soul seemed to flow toward him; at his touch, she closed her eyes, swayed forward, inarticulate, and fell into his arms.

He was less elated than vexed; by this point-blank surrender he had been cheated of innumerable tenuous pleasures such as, in his opinion, should have composed their amorous progress. Clumsy haste! His æsthetic sense was outraged, and, in his heart of hearts, he blamed her for his disappointment.

Nevertheless, he could not help being flattered by the confession she gasped out while clinging to him with averted face. She had intended never to love any one again; she had not believed it possible for her to do so; yet from that first night in Benedetto's she had suspected that it was "all up with her."

"But I fought against it! I never meant to love you, either! Oh, why, why, did you make me? Why did you come back? Something terrible will happen to us—a judgment from Heaven! Don't try to comfort me; I know it, I know it! Oh, if the Sisters in the convent heard; if my mother could look down!" She sobbed violently, struggled to escape his arms, collapsed in a sort of swoon, her head thrown back, her large eyes glassy and motionless in their sockets. Presently, from her pallor and immobility, one might have believed her dead, save that tears continually welled up in the outer corners of her eyes, and, unexpectedly, ran down her cheeks. "This woman frightens me," thought Felix. Her outburst took on for him an ominous aspect: without knowing what he feared, he wished himself far away. When he strove to withdraw his hand from hers, she held him fast with unexpected alacrity. He remained still, an uncomfortable prisoner.

Thus, as if with subtle portents, their intimacy was inaugurated.

It soon became necessary for him to visit her every evening, if he was to escape lugubrious sighs, pathetic references to "lonely hours," such parade of melancholy looks as would have been an appropriate reproach for a desertion covering a period of years.

She had not been long in rallying from her first remorse, in denying her scruples, in discovering excuses for her weakness. "Lew had abandoned her, so she was no longer under obligations to him; as that life was finished, she had the right to begin

another. Who knew but that Felix's coming had
been intended as a recompense for so much unhappiness?"

Her idea, unconsciously disclosed, that relations of
a permanent nature were commencing, caused Felix
to open wide his eyes. The devil! Here was a
woman who made up for lack of other qualities with
a fine abundance of impetuosity! "I see that I must
think well of Lew, for I suspect him to be the chap
who is going to save me some day from a warm situation!" Indeed, it occurred to Felix that the wisest
plan would be to disappear at once. But there was
a charm in Emma Meers's society that he could not
deny.

She showed him nothing but gratitude, naïve admiration, and humility. Such behavior gave him an
excellent opinion of himself, and caused him to
assume toward her a manner affectionately condescending.

On summer nights, in her darkened room—when
the warm breeze, swelling the window-curtains of
white scrim, brought across the back yards sounds of
piano-playing, of voices warbling scales, of cats in
combat—Felix, "worn out by a hard day's work,"
reclined in his chair, while Emma knelt beside him
in a pose that she protested was quite comfortable.
A faint light, from other back windows, penetrated
the curtains; her face, pale and indistinct, showed a
beauty so ambiguous as to make him wonder whether
it was she indeed, or some amorous incarnation from
his dreams. Then her shadowy eyes, full of solem-

nity, approached; he felt her breath on his lips; he recognized her.

In intimacy, he soon lost his earliest impression of her looks—just as, by seeing any object every day, we come to forget our first appraisal of it. She seemed younger to him than formerly. Perhaps that was owing to her manner of a little girl, habitual in moments of tenderness?

"Make love to her," she would whisper, childishly.

Caresses sometimes recalled to her other scenes: in the hushed voice that sentimentalists reserve for tales of old romances the charm of which survives all disillusion, she spoke of her honeymoon, of her early married life, of her cottage, where so much sweetness was once imprisoned. That had been a home! Suffering from the suppression of her strong domestic instinct, she longed for a field, however narrow, where she might play the housewife.

Then, unable to deny herself the pleasures of melancholy, she dwelt on her misfortunes. An almost chronic emotionalism caused her to dilate and confuse all stories of past happenings and sensations, so that overstatements of Lew's cruelty got mixed up with extravagant reports concerning his good looks and dissolute accomplishments. Felix made a gesture of annoyance.

"You're fond of him yet, I think!"

"Never! Never! Would I be in love with you?"

After a silence, she mused:

"But I'll tell you this, that since him I've never met any one but you that I could love."

Had she, then, been looking round for some one? If Felix had not come along, would she not, finding isolation of the heart intolerable, have succumbed to another? The young man was not much flattered by this idea. From that night, he exerted himself to convince her that his merits were supereminent; and, on account of the earnestness with which he entered upon this task, he began to lose his pose of superiority.

Reflecting that he could hardly be damaged, now, by any indiscretion, he frequently appeared with her in public. The most frugal excursions seemed to delight her.

They rode by trolley-car to Coney Island, where, in pleasure-grounds full of grotesque buildings made of staff and tinsel, with rococo bridges arching across lagoons and minarets rising on all sides, they sat at table on a balcony above the crowds, Felix drinking highballs, and Emma, in a broad-brimmed sailor hat and a white linen dress too tight for her, laughing at the merrymakers below. She was quick to appreciate humorous incidents, and occasionally astonished Felix with a flash of wit.

"Yes," she cooed, in a tone of infantile complacency, "sometimes she can say funny things. But not often when you're round."

"Why not?"

Emma shook her head, mysteriously.

"'Cause she's afraid."

At dusk, when electric lamps outlining the fantastic edifices all glowed forth, they set out through the crowd toward an open-air restaurant near by, where a band of Tyrolese sang under trees festooned with yellow lanterns.

On the way, the spectacle of countless faces streaming past him gradually bewildered Felix. His eyelids drooped; he caught his toe in something. She tightened her grasp on his arm.

"I beg your pardon! Do you know, I was just wondering what would happen if we met your Lew?"

She compressed her lips; her eyes flashed fire; abruptly, she looked her age. In a high, metallic voice, she replied:

"I'd soon settle him! I'd say, 'Why, what have you to do with me? I was divorced from you months ago in South Dakota, and this is my husband now!'"

While he considered this reply an amusing one, Felix could not help wishing that another had occurred to her.

At dinner, he became more intoxicated. Lanterns among the trees, each lending to an enveloping mass of leaves a hue violently green, appeared to him like fruits in an enchanted garden; the voices of the Tyrolese women, wafted from a distance, barely surviving the continuous rattle of dishes, were like the staccato cries of sirens rising above the plashing of a surf; while Emma's face, at once mature and girlish, expectant and demure, slowly turned beautiful before him. He leaned forward, his temples throbbing, some wild, lover's eloquence rising to his lips. But a phrase in the Tyrolese women's song reminded him of "The Lost Venus," and, as he looked away, he saw a profile that brought his heart into his mouth. Great heavens, how like Nina Ferrol!

"Felix, what is the matter?"

He turned his eyes toward Emma.

"Nothing. But we'll go home, if you don't mind. My dog's back there, shut up in a room, alone. The poor brute, I've had him since he was a puppy, and this is the way I treat him."

And, as they rode cityward, he thought:

"If only I could begin my life all over!"

But one night he took Emma to a theatre, where they watched just such a review as Montmorrissy habitually produced. The lively music, the brilliant stage thronged with smiling girls audaciously attired, the atmosphere of reckless gayety that floated out across the footlights, affected Felix with a species of nostalgia. He recalled many hours that had been fraught with pain, but in which he now discovered the charm that frequently enriches the most unhappy episodes, at retrospection. No, he would not have omitted that portion of his life!

In the crowded lobby of the theatre, Felix came face to face with Oliver Corquill. The young man had an impulse to draw back: he owed this celebrity two hundred dollars.

But the latter, advancing with a smile, grasped Felix by the hand.

"What an elusive fellow you are! I called at your old rooms, to find you vanished."

"I meant to send you word. Don't think I'd forgotten you."

And, uncomfortably conscious of Emma's home-made hat, he introduced the novelist. She received, along with a courtly bow, one of those looks that seem no more than amiable, but which, while covering in a flash the entire person, plunge, as it were, into the heart. Emma promptly conceived an antipathy against Corquill, and could not help complaining of him to Felix before they reached Waverley Place. Excitedly, she burst forth:

"I mistrust him! Besides, he doesn't like me. Oh, I could see it, in spite of his smiles! He'll call on you, now, and talk to you about me. Yes, he'll show you all my faults; he'll persuade you to leave me!"

"What rot!" ejaculated Felix, with the first accent of irritation that she had heard from him.

Stopping short beside a lamp-post, she stared at him with eyes dilated, as much aghast as if he had struck her. And, to his consternation, her lament rang through the silent street:

"You see! You're changed already! Oh, I knew it! I felt it!"

It took him half an hour to make her "listen to reason."

However, as she had predicted, Oliver Corquill lost no time in calling at Felix's hotel.

In his gray flannel suit and dove-colored cravat pierced with a coral pin, he still suggested the business office far more than the study. Apparently without even glancing round the hotel bedroom, he made himself at home, and spoke of Paul Pavin.

The Frenchman had been in Corfu painting a portrait of the German emperor's daughter; thence he
had gone for a jaunt among Scandinavian fjords; he
might come to New York within the year, but meanwhile wished especially to be remembered to Felix.

The young man was moved by the persistent
friendliness of so fine a personage. Corquill continued:

"Yes, I'm sure he feels a sincere regard for you.
But then, beneath all his irreverence, he has a heart
of gold. Also, a past eventful enough to make his
advice worth taking."

Felix was blushing. He blurted out:

"Why not say at once that I'd better profit by it?"

"Well, I know how much more profitable than
good advice experience is. All the same, if you'll
pardon me, one oughtn't to need an annual repetition
of experience. To be frank, while I was glad to hear
that 'The Queen of Hearts' had gone on the road,
I was as sorry as if it hadn't, when I met you in the
theatre the other night."

Felix, his lips trembling from indignation, stammered:

"A rather hasty deduction!"

The novelist, with a gentle smile, shook his head.

"You'd be surprised how many people of all sorts
I know, how much I hear, how frequently insignificant episodes have unseen witnesses, how often a
man believes that he lives in secret when his whole
activity is talked about."

Felix was dumbfounded. At last:

"If I may be so personal, in my turn. what business is this of yours?"

Mr. Corquill was not at all embarrassed.

"My dear boy, I have as much solicitude for talents as you have, probably, for human life. If you saw a foolish fellow putting a rope round his neck, what would you do?"

The other stared before him.

"I think I'd wish him good luck."

The novelist stood up.

"Dine with me to-night."

"I—I have an engagement."

"We'll break it," Corquill announced, and marched Felix off to the restaurant of a quiet hotel on Fifth Avenue.

They seated themselves by an open window in a spacious room panelled with mahogany grown dull from age, where the brass chandeliers were old-fashioned, the thick Turkish carpet faded, the buffets antiquated, the grey-headed waiters of that placid and paternal mien which results from long service in an environment sedately rich. Few persons were dining there: some elderly gentlemen, their hair neatly parted down the back, sat erect at small tables; in a corner was to be seen a family party—the father, the mother, and three little girls in white eating ices with the lax, contented looks of well-bred children. Felix gazed round him with a sensation of shame. Memories of his own childhood came to him, and, sick at heart, he inquired of his companion:

"Why did you choose this place?"

"On a hot night, I like quiet and elbow-room," was the innocent response.

The novelist, who had never before seemed capable of boastfulness, talked of his past successes, the royalties earned from his books, an estate that he had just bought in the country, his dogs, his roses, and his polo-ponies. Felix commented, bitterly:

"Yes, you are to be envied."

The celebrity shrugged his shoulders.

"Oh, when I was your age, I couldn't write such good stuff as you've turned out."

In Corquill's opinion, to attain success one had to expend his entire force in pursuit of the desired object. Only disaster was foreshadowed by Felix's belief that one should experience all he intended to portray. The artist, to describe destruction, did not need to destroy himself. He was informed with an intuitive comprehension of life, developing, as Felix would find out, more fully year by year. As the paleontologist reconstructed from one fossil bone the whole skeleton of a prehistoric animal, so the adept in literature, prepared by long and intense scrutiny of human hearts, found in a phrase caught at random, in a look surprised on a strange face, the clue to a character, to a life. In fine, the great novel resulted from perception, intuition, and logic. And Corquill cited a quotation, to the effect that Balzac— who had avoided nearly every material diversion in order that his mentality might be the clearer—depicted his characters so marvellously as to make one

think he must have been, at some time, a janitor, a
spinster, a swashbuckler, a demirep, a priest. Even
in his youth, that speech of Strindberg's could never
have been applied to him: he had never been the
artist "yearning for the pinnacle of ambition, without being willing to pay the price required of those
who are to reach it."

Felix, to whom the last theory always seemed the
most admirable, was greatly impressed.

That night, the young man assured himself that a
new life should begin for him at once. He had never
so clearly perceived his folly. He marvelled at the
stupidity which had brought him to such a pass. He
would escape all his detriments, Emma included.

This last project, however, required thought.

Meanwhile, for three days he drank nothing, and,
since this mood demanded of him, as usual, the
strictest behavior that could be imagined, did not
smoke so much as a cigarette.

Then, his pleased amazement—that such continence
had been latent, all the while, in him—gave place to
depression. He fell to gazing dismally at strangers
wreathed in tobacco smoke, and at jolly fellows,
glimpsed through the doorways of cafés, pouring
whiskey down their throats with gusto. He considered that he suffered much more from strict behavior
than from reckless.

Thereupon, without any sense of repetition, he
began an old farce.

He decided that he had been wheedled into a state
no less absurd than dolorous. Why should he tor-

ment himself by renouncing pleasures that the world enjoyed? Besides, Corquill's homilies would have been more suitably lavished on a middle-aged man who had frittered away his life. Felix, for his part, was still young enough to feel that he had eternity at his disposal. His exalted determinations in respect of work went by the board; he had no thought for anything save his immediate desires.

But no sooner had he broken his every resolution, than, with satiety, his scruples all returned. Corquill's reproofs again seemed portentous. Fear of the future once more assailed the young man, who remembered suddenly that this was not the first time he had failed in such a struggle.

And there began for him a period of alternating renunciations and relapses. His solitary hours were passed in such shamefaced vacillation as precedes the final weakness, or in such gloomy self-reproach as follows it. So many discomfitures ended by crippling his self-confidence: he came to make fresh resolutions mechanically, without conviction; his struggles grew weaker, and, finally, ended. All his old habits were again in daily practice.

He tried to excuse his frailty by argument. Was the world fashioned for the avowal of life, or the denial of it? Were not morality and right conduct dependent solely on contemporary opinion? Who knew but that asceticism was not more abnormal than licentiousness? If continence reacted on the modern conscience in the form of a spiritual reward, suppose there had been no inheritance of a modern

conscience? The pagans, expansive, appetent, un-
moral, happy in their pursuit of every earthly pleasure, lucky in their ignorance of Christianity and its
renunciations, gained, perhaps, a satisfaction far
more intense than did the saints? Ah, to plunge into
pagan ecstasies, unhampered by the heavy chains of
Christian remorse! But, alas, such possibilities had
been done for almost with the hamadryads; the setting of purple and azure undulations was obliterated;
the very air of the earth was changed in savor since
young men in hyacinth and gold had ceased wandering, at nightfall, free from all disabling compunction,
toward the Bacchic rendezvous, or the grove of
Venus Callipyge. The drab present, aswarm with
elongated, hypocritical faces, blotted out the sheen
of a remote age, sensual and care-free.

So Felix, full of classic cravings, had to content
himself with Washington Square, Coney Island, and
the *table d'hôte* at Benedetto's.

On nights of intense heat, resonant in that neighborhood with an ignoble clatter, when, in the Italian
restaurant, the whirling wooden fans seemed to churn
to a more stifling consistency the vitiated air, he still
heard, occasionally, through a meal of wilted, stale,
and melting food, the literary aphorisms of Mr. Lute,
Miss Nuncheon, and Mrs. Babbage. Their constant
avidity for "shop talk," their excitement in trivial
debate, their relish for revealing superficial knowledge, all that exuberance which has been entitled
"the enthusiasm of the artistic *parvenu*," caused
Felix to curse the luck which made it necessary for

him to listen to "such trash." From sheer spite, masking his sneers with the benignity of an attending physician, he prescribed for Mr. Lute the "History of Criticism," by Saintsbury, for Miss Nuncheon some fifteen volumes of essays by Sainte-Beuve, for Mrs. Babbage all the works of Kant and Spinoza. Truth is, besides indulging in covert ironies, he made the mistake of exhibiting his information and talents; and no doubt his acquaintances, like humble travellers at an inn who find themselves dining with a stranger rigged out in jewels and fine clothes, would soon have preferred, for their greater self-satisfaction, a separate room.

But Mrs. Babbage was producing esoteric pamphlets that sold everywhere for a half dollar a copy; Miss Nuncheon had got a publisher for a book of her short stories about "the smart set"; Mr. Lute had joined the staff of *The Mauve Monthly*, and from the office of that magazine he sent Felix a patronizing letter asking for "a glance at some of his latest efforts." What mortification! While those three were guarding bravely and letting shine their little flames, he, burning with great visions, suffered at the mere sight of his writing-table an extinguishment of all his fire!

His melancholy, his savage pessimism, his increasing irritability, bewildered Emma. Finally, she convinced herself that he had met "some one else."

Her fits of despair came on whenever he kissed her carelessly, avoided a caress, or remained preoccupied at her plea, always uttered in the same childish tones, "Now he must make love to her."

"Yes, yes, it's true: his kisses aren't the same; his thoughts are always wandering; he is often cross with me, now! Ah, I knew this would happen—I was too happy; it's my punishment! There's some other woman, some silly little thing, some actress— that's it, some old friend! Oh, didn't I see them that night, in his studio, through the crack of the door—a lot of gay, cruel-hearted, mercenary creatures? But could they love him as I do? Never! Never! No one could ever love him like me!" She became limp in her chair; her blue-black hair, pressed out against the cushion, accentuated her pallor; her white throat shook with sobs; and, her pupils disappearing beneath her heavy eyelids, she seemed to be fainting. At such moments, her condition was apt to frighten him. He seized her cold hands, called her name, ran for a glass of water or a flask of cologne.

"Emma! Speak to me!"

At length, her pupils still invisible, she whispered:

"My heart! I feel as if it was going to burst." And, in a thin wail:

"Who would care?"

Pity seized him: he cast himself down beside her chair, put his arms round her, mingled with reassuring words a hundred kisses of a convincing warmth. Under this treatment, she revived, clung to him weakly, between long, quivering sighs made demands that stirred his memory.

"Swear that you love me, and no one else!"

He vowed eloquently that she was all the world to him.

But for Felix the novelty of that attachment was already gone: he had found, beneath Emma's innumerable caresses, protestations, and excesses of emotion, the monotony of a passion long since thoroughly explored, lacking, this time, the ornament that wealth and beauty, beauty and notoriety, had lent it formerly. Still, from timorousness, from want of ingenuity, from lassitude of will, he continued with her, in the midst of his most ardent avowals thinking:

"What a fool I was! Now how shall I get rid of her?"

CHAPTER XIII

On a night of early autumn, Felix received a letter and a package, postmarked in Paris, from Pavin. The letter announced that the portrait-painter was going to spend another winter in New York. The package contained an old volume of French prose— the third and last work of Pierre Buron, once Pavin's friend, and Mme. Lodbrok's husband.

Seating himself by his writing-table for the evening, Felix began to read this book.

Passages at once exact and gorgeous, like clusters of strange gems reflecting multi-colored rays, filled the young man with wonder. Very soon he knew that he had in hand one of those masterpieces which can only be "a communion of thought between a magical writer and an ideal reader," since the author, by ignoring the predilections of the many, by regarding solely the sensitiveness of the few, has made to pride the sacrifice of contemporary fame.

One was borne away to regions obscured as if by a perpetual twilight, where men and women, rendered well-nigh indistinguishable by the subtlety of their emotions, appeared to move through ancient groves aglimmer with decaying shrines, monuments to obsolete ardors. These wanderers, wraithlike in the constant dusk, seemed ever to gaze round them with the uncertain gestures of the lost, to pause by crumbling columns, to heave a sigh at finding only ruins, to utter tentatively the first measures of a song composed for an archaic use, to droop on hearing that melody die away without an echo, while setting forth again, to chance, perhaps, on relics underfoot: broken sword-blades, little shattered idols, corroded diadems, rotted treasure, all burdens cast aside, in other ages, by weary predecessors. The whole work, indeed, typified a labyrinth, where solitary figures moved in and out, tossed up their arms, and sobbed, "I have not found it!" The last page left this impression of unsatisfied desire intact; and the thought remained that through an eternity the same gloom would cover the same intricacies, while the same phantoms stumbled on in the same vain search.

It was as if Felix were gazing on a landscape never previously seen in life, with that thought, which makes the scalp tingle, "Have I not always dwelt here?" It seemed to him that his soul for the first time mingled with another, the soul of an unknown, to whom he could have cried, "Surely, in some world you and I have been as one!"

He fell to thinking about Pierre Buron. Did he, like those spectral creatures of his brain, still move through shadows, or had he given up his quest?

Well to have lost one's self in such a labyrinth, if one could leave on its outskirts so beautiful a relic! And Felix was chilled with fear, at the thought that he, when ultimately vanishing, might leave behind him nothing half so precious.

He sprang up, and approached the window. Already the mature foliage of Washington Square was covered with a bluish light.

How quickly the days succeeded one another, and melted into years! He was twenty-nine. Who could foretell the duration of this gift of life?

To die in an hour, to be obliterated, never to be recalled, to have lived in vain!

Cool breezes, bearing from afar a simple fragrance, set to vibrating gently in his heart chords long untouched. Then the dawn, like a golden fluid, descended upon distant towers; and, as the city thrust its innumerable transfigured roofs out of the shadows, there seemed to unroll "the kingdoms of the world, and all the glory of them." Should he not wring therefrom all that he had missed? Looking up at the vivid sky, entranced by that spreading symbol of renewal, he felt in himself the strength, the purity, the splendor, of a new day. From before him the vapors of irresolution shredded quite away, so that he discerned once more, in an immaculate zenith, the radiant pattern of a great life, promising immortal consequences.

That day, he plunged again into work. Every evening, as soon as he could escape from Emma, he hurried home, cleared his writing-table, strove to reduce to black and white the thoughts with which he hoped to earn quickly an enduring fame.

But these thoughts proved to be too large for expression by such terms as he could master. The moment he set pen to paper, he experienced the confusion, the impotence, the despair, of those who dream that splendid edifices can be constructed with a few unseasoned tools.

He recalled the first homily he had ever heard from Corquill, about the preparation of the prospective author. He returned to the study of the technique of writing.

Then he favored successively a score of masters, pursued each theory of exposition a little way, imitated and abandoned every mannerism; in his anxiety to employ all artifices at once, accomplished nothing. In literature, just as in life, he was seduced by every whisper into excursions far afield, till, lost amid strange scenes, in a daze he halted, dejectedly to retrace his steps. At last, glimpsing on all sides vistas that he would have needed a dozen lifetimes to explore thoroughly, he understood the magnitude of his enterprise. For him, there could be no sudden composition of masterpieces; the waiting would be tedious and fraught with travail; only a whole existence devoted to labor could bring him such honors as he had in mind.

Nevertheless, he determined to press on; for he felt that he was made for this attempt or none; and at the thought of turning to some other career, he became dizzy, as if on the point of slipping into a void.

"Is it not curious," he reflected, "that I alone, of a family for generations notoriously unimaginative, should feel this impulse?" Inspecting his mother's photograph, he wondered whether that young face, beautiful, and strange with smothered fire, contained the answer to his question. "Yes," he concluded, "no doubt I owe my sensibilities to her." He poured out a drink of whiskey, lighted his pipe, and set to work again.

The clock ticked off the hours; the pen scratched over the paper; Pat, stretched on the bed-quilt, woke from time to time, feebly wagged his tail, and went to sleep again. Silence crept upon the city. A bell, far off, struck two. Felix rose, and Pat scrambled briskly from the bed. The dog knew well what movement of his master's presaged their nightly promenade together.

They traversed empty thoroughfares, where shadows on either side projected masses apparently material, where converging rows of lights gave off scintillations like small, white-hot ingots, where, midway of each perspective, the sky let down into the street its veils of solemn blue. Felix found the side door of a café ajar. The bartender, who was putting on his hat, consented to remain till his customer had gulped down some highballs.

They turned homeward, the dog pattering ahead, the young man loitering to enjoy his exaltation. While passing the blank front of Benedetto's restaurant, he smiled pityingly at thought of Miss Nuncheon, Mr. Lute, and Mrs. Babbage. While pausing to look down Waverley Place, he shrugged his shoulders at recollection of Emma. Nowadays, with her most passionate speeches ringing in his ears, he was like a man listening to a hard-working but inferior actress in a play heard too often

But Emma, like the tobacco he smoked to excess without awaiting any craving for it, like the liquor he continued to drink just because it remained at hand, had become for him a habit. Well, presently he would leave her, too, behind!

There was still some whiskey in the decanter on his mantel-shelf. He finished it, and went to bed.

In the morning, no matter how great his lethargy, he had to rush downtown to *The Sphere* building.

On rising, he "pulled himself together" with a cocktail, which was brought to his room on a tray, by a bell-boy with dirty thumbs. On descending from the elevated railway station at Chambers Street, he took another drink in a saloon. This stimulus was usually sufficient until lunch-time, even if he was not sent out, meanwhile, to gather news.

But Felix now rarely escaped the newspaper office.

From many such excursions he had returned in a state of mind more suitable for highly imaginative writing than for veracious. At length, the editor, with a smile of mysterious benignity, had assigned Felix to the "copy desk"—a table six feet square in the midst of the office pandemonium—where the young man sat all day, in the company of three mature journalists, correcting, reducing, and entitling the manuscripts of reporters. Felix took pleasure in slashing with a blue pencil the work of Johnny Livy —a married man at last, with two instalments paid on a frame cottage in the Bronx, where he had a fine expanse of vacant lots on every side, a garden, the size of a counterpane, bristling with stakes for peas and lima beans to twine on, a street lamp directly before his porch, and an heir in prospect. Moreover, Livy was now referred to by "copy-boys" as "the star reporter." In fact, his modest dreams were all in process of fulfilment.

He was moved, one day, to acquaint Felix with the reason for this. It was very simple: he had become a Christian Scientist.

"An elementary soul," thought Felix, his lip curling. "A mind without metaphysical sense, without ability for introspection and observance, for great doubts or great sins. A man who can deny that pain and ruin exist, who always sees the world as does a child on a clear day. What immense regions of experience are closed to him! Better to suffer, than to be half alive, like that!" And, as Livy marched jauntily from the office on a fresh hunt for news, Felix returned to his copy-reading, which he detested.

He missed the excitement of the chase throughout the city, the swiftly alternating contact with comedy and tragedy, the variety of excessive scenes unveiled to the reporter, who enjoyed continually the nervous gratification felt by those witnessing, in safety, a rescue of life, a ruinous conflagration, the death of a criminal, the room where a murder had just been committed. The editor, with whose professional phlegm a constitutional kindliness often struggled for expression, had deprived Felix of two "stimulants" instead of one.

As a result, every afternoon, when the last edition of *The Evening Sphere* had gone to press, his pent-up appetite for excitement demanded satisfaction. After lingering in cafés on the way uptown, he reached Washington Square with the feeling of defenceless-ness—as if at the weakening of delicate protective qualities—which invariably prefaced his inebriety.

Once, when in such a state, he approached his hotel to see, before the entrance, a familiar-looking figure in blue serge. It was Corquill, who had called for the purpose of asking Felix out to dinner.

This invitation irritated the young man: it seemed to him that the novelist, trading, perhaps, on the two-hundred-dollar loan, was subjecting him to a sort of espionage. Planting himself firmly on his heels, he enunciated, carefully:

"Many thanks. But it's impossible this evening."

The celebrity, at that rebuff, only nodded gravely.

"Well, then, some other time."

As Corquill turned away, Felix, ashamed of himself, suggested that they walk a short distance up Fifth Avenue together. They set out northward through Washington Square.

In the light of the sunset, beneath masses of autumnal leafage, some vagabonds, occupying wooden benches, rested unshaven chins on soiled shirt-bosoms, or let large, red hands hang down in front of threadbare knees. One fellow, small and frail, his broken shoes stretched out, his beard up-tilted, a felt hat covering his face, gave vent to a suc-cession of rattling snores.

"The reward of his desires," was Corquill's comment.

Felix, in low, unsteady tones, retorted:

"Perhaps he, too, in the only way he knows, is a seeker after the ideal."

A poor way, according to Corquill, if his business were the reproduction of his findings. But, for that matter, it was the same in any work: temperance and achievement went hand in hand, as did excess and failure. All tales of genius accentuated by drugs and drink were absurd. To Poe, De Quincey, Coleridge, even Baudelaire and Verlaine, common sense had given, at last, the credit for their achievements. It was in the sober hour that a man produced work acceptable to others.

But Felix was staring at a distant clock with an air of stupefaction.

"Is it possible! An hour later than I thought! Will you pardon me?"

And he took himself off, consumed with chagrin and rage.

So he had come to the pass where his friends believed they had to bombard him, at every meeting, with remonstrances! That settled it; he would show them, now, one and all!

When in his sober senses, he discovered that each good determination was weakened by the memory of countless similar pledges, made only to be broken. The piled-up failures of his will had become a crushing incubus, under which he struggled ever the more feebly.

But late at night, when his desires were satiated, when he was flushed with self-confidence, he made vows apparently so easy of accomplishment that he went to bed convinced that the morrow would usher in a different sort of life. In the morning, waking to find his cravings once more active, he relapsed, with scarcely a thought of his midnight resolutions.

Nevertheless, a cancerous remorse robbed every aberrant act of pleasure. At the bottom of each draught lay bitter dregs.

Therefore, his hours were punctuated with little struggles and defeats. When he had smoked till he felt premonitions of nausea, when he had drunk till mental clarity was slipping from him, he threw away his tobacco, or emptied his decanter down the waste-pipe. This necessitated his buying more cigars and whiskey—an expensive process for a young man living on twenty-five dollars a week.

Such conflicts gradually filled his life, engrossed his thoughts, nearly drove from his consciousness all appreciation of the outer world. In the newspaper office, his work was insufficient; at home, his writing came to a standstill. This paralysis of energy increased his wretchedness.

If only he could escape the neighborhood of his temptations! Oh, for some Arcadian spot far beyond the zone of provocation, some remote, unsullied isle, where, in a tropic silence, in a solitude that was not loneliness, one might live caressed by pure winds and pellucid waves, thrilled by the savor of the sea and the aroma of flowers, the heart expanding to perfection beneath friendly stars! But such regions existed only in imagination, or in another world than his. The prisoner of his environment, he could not escape one of its detriments—not even Emma.

As for her, maybe she accepted his weakness—despite her belief that it rendered him susceptible to "every pretty face"—as something which made association with him possible. Resting her small, soft hands on his shoulders in an almost insidious caress, she would murmur:

"Why do you torment yourself by fighting against your nature? If you changed, you would be some one else—not yourself. No, no; she wants him as he is!"

Watching her gloomily, Felix asked:

"Did you give that advice to your husband?"

When she had comprehended this question, she replied, in haste:

"It was different with him. I should have known what was going to happen: the weakness was in his family. But with you, it's just that you're young. All young men are so; and, when they're like you, they get over it naturally, as you will."

"How do you know that I'll get over it?"

She crept closer, and gazed at him in adoration.

"Ah, because of something about you, I don't know what, that makes me sure! Just to look at you one can tell you've got great things before you. It shines in your eyes; it makes me feel small, and frightened, and jealous. Sometimes, I say to myself, 'How I wish he didn't have it!' But all the while, I know that on account of it I worship you." And, clinging to him, she began to tremble, and to sob:

"You'll never leave me? You'll never leave me?"

Then, suddenly, her fingers sank into his shoulders; her lips parted on her teeth; in her white face her eyes blazed as if through a tragic mask. Wildly, she declared:

"If you did, it would mean that all my suspicions were true, that there were others! All right; take warning; it would be your last act on earth! Should I care what I did, then?"

Doubtless they became frightened simultaneously; for she threw herself on his neck, besought pardon, protested, in broken accents, that "she didn't mean it." Felix sent forth a silent prayer for Lew's return.

If he but knew the fellow's whereabouts! "There must be some way of forcing a man to live with an inoffensive wife." But Lew had vanished, as it seemed, forever, in that maze of barrooms which Felix now penetrated nightly.

"His work" was his excuse to leave Emma early in the evening. From Waverley Place he set out with the words, which no longer deluded him, "For the last time."

Leaning against a bar, in the company of garrulous strangers, he passed, sometimes, from an ostensible stimulation of brain and body to a reactionary torpor, and, on rare occasions of protracted drinking, to an extinguishment of all conscious faculties. In this plight, he rambled blindly at large, engaged in unknown adventures, next morning woke in his bed without remembrance of arriving home. But wherever he went, Pat was at his heels, peering upward with the bewildered look of a dog that misses intuitively in his master the intelligence which guides their intercourse.

Once Felix came to his senses bolt upright in an alley thick with lamp-posts, where fire-escapes dangled in mid-air, and, in the shabby doorways of invisible houses, black visages seemed hovering without bodies underneath. Negroes were pressing round him; his ears buzzed with whispers of a sinister intonation; a hand began to feel his pockets.

He jerked himself loose, and swung his fists at random. The snarl of a dog was followed by a scream of pain.

Felix struggled desperately to regain his vision. The scene cleared; he saw a swarm of aboriginal faces closing in. But another howl resounded.

"Kill the dog! Don't shoot toward the cobbles! Get a club!"

A husky voice, at Felix's elbow, bellowed, in reply:

"That'll do, now! Any more out of the bunch of yez, and I'll call the reserves to break every head in the block."

And, in the ensuing hush, a fat Irishman, wearing a sack suit and a derby hat, escorted Felix from the alley.

They walked, as Felix thought, for miles. They rode in a trolley-car, where a conductor protested against admitting the bull-terrier till Felix's protector drew from his trousers pocket, along with a handful of small change, a nickel badge. Presently,

trees surrounded them: they were in Washington
Square. And Felix reached his room in the hotel
before realizing that he had not once observed the
features of the detective, or obtained his name, or
thanked him for his services.

Next day, the young man was smitten with horror
and disgust. But was this horror salutary, would
this disgust be permanent? He feared that there
was no strength for good left in him. Yet were not
some men able to draw strength from God?

That night, he went to church.

It was a breathless evening in September—an
evening of mysterious streets, of blue stars, of purple
skies into which the upper stories of tall buildings
melted, so that high-set, golden window lights suggested the casements of an imminent heaven. On
Fifth Avenue, at Fiftieth Street, there rose above a
gray bulk the twin spires of the Roman Catholic
cathedral.

Within, all was vague, cool, and subtly scented
with stale incense fumes: one breathed a redolence
like the exhalation from a tomb where something
imperial and ancient lies embalmed in fragrant
spices.

Lengthwise of the cathedral, on either side of the
centre aisle, six massive columns, pale below, growing dusky in mid-air, towered to an indistinct region
of groined arches. Behind each colonnade, under
sombrous expanses of stained glass, appeared some
lateral chapels, unilluminated, furnished with effigies
or pictures. But far ahead, beyond the perspective

of the columns, beyond parallel pew-backs seemingly as innumerable as the ripples of the sea, beyond pulpit, chancel rail, and rising steps, a refulgence, as of a sun, dispelled the shadows, and, in its core, the white reredos, rich with sculptured ornament, floated upward from behind the sparkling altar.

Felix entered the last pew, sat down, and gazed at the remote splendor of the sanctuary. Here, surely, one should be able to feel the presence of a deity. Should he pray? In what words, with what assurance of an auditor?

Men, after all, had evolved with their own hands the grandeur of this place—had raised the altar, had composed the reredos, had lighted the candles, had produced the whole effect. Æsthetically, it was satisfying; but who knew if a god was satisfied to call this his especial abode?

Something within him answered, "God is wherever hearts are laid bare in supplication."

"Why, then he must be here."

A few heads showed above the pew backs; to the right, before the nearest lateral chapel, a woman was kneeling; occasionally a worshipper entered from the street, dipped finger in a marble basin, crossed himself, bowed toward the altar, noiselessly glided down the aisle.

Lowered faces, timid attitudes, and sinking knees; the life-long repetition of historic gestures of humility; awe and fear unshaken by the eternal silence. Not the part of these to cry out, "Whence, why, and whither?" or to send forth the plaint, "How do I

know that there are ears to listen?" For them, the
path worn broad by myriads of feet; but for Felix,
the labyrinth.

He rose, and turned his back on the altar. The
woman kneeling before the chapel attracted his attention. He approached her. It was Miss Qewan.
Her eyes remained fixed on a statuette of the Virgin;
the beads of a rosary slipped through her fingers;
her lips were moving.

"Well for her," thought Felix, and went away.

Yet, if there was no omnipresent Ideal, whence this
universal instinct for self-betterment? Every hour,
it struggled for foothold in his heart, warred with
his frailty, and suffered agonies at defeat. Like the
Mahomet of Victor Hugo, Felix could have said, "I
am the vile field of sublime combats."

His conscience, from so much friction, became
raw: he reached that state of nervousness, border-
ing on hysteria, which is full of morbid scruples concerning even the slightest misdemeanors. His every
act appeared despicable to him; and in this moral
revulsion was included the thought of his behavior
toward Emma. Without even the excuse of love, he
had involved that pliant, defenceless creature in his
transgressions!

Emma, however, still ignorant of his nocturnal
drinking-bouts, aware only of an intemperance which,
in comparison with Lew's, seemed moderate, could
not have understood Felix's low spirits. She ascribed
them, no doubt, when her suspicions of his disloyalty
were not active, to that incomprehensible attribute,

an "artistic temperament." She had picked up somewhere the idea that genius was to be measured by eccentricity; in consequence, the more peculiar Felix's behavior, the surer Emma felt that he was developing into a prodigy. In fact, her belief in his talents and prospects was so firm, that when speaking of his future she became excited, as if in thought she were sharing the fame and fortune she predicted for him. Then her face clouded, and she remained staring at him with lips aquiver, beseechingly. Sometimes, she would end a long silence with an outburst of sobs, in which expressions of fear for her own future were mingled with wishes that she had never seen him. "It had been her undoing."

Such statements completed, so to speak, the laceration of his conscience. Seized with a pity as demoralizing as love, he strove to comfort Emma by adding his compunction to hers, by mingling with her tears his own, by stammering that he was, indeed, a villain.

At this cue, she was quick to enter on a new part. She began systematically to weave herself into his remorses.

She recalled her childhood, her convent days, her maidenhood, with a wealth of anecdotes, touching in their simplicity, to show how devoutly and innocently she had begun, how admirable had been her fitting for an edifying life. She recurred to her years of matrimony, throughout which—one gathered— she had remained submissive to misfortune, faithful to her unfaithful husband, confident in her darkest hours of the near presence of God. "But now! It's all changed: I can never go back to the convent; I can never find heart to enter a church, or make confession, or pray to the Virgin! Oh, do you know you've brought me to a terrible pass?"

These lamentations, appearing logical enough to his distracted mind, were of a quality to give the screw its last turn. He had, it seemed, deprived her wantonly of the very spiritual support that he was groping for. Thenceforth, it was Felix who besought indulgence, and Emma who condescended to lenity. He discovered that a tortured conscience could engender a sense of obligation no less strong than if produced by passion.

How should he expiate this offence? By leaving her? Too late! Besides, even if he could have gathered sufficient power of will to do so, she would undoubtedly have pursued him, with who knew what consequences. He had for one moment seen her face, habitually weak and tender, transformed by the insane rage of jealousy. There was another woman concealed in her, of whom he was afraid: when he scrutinized her lowered eyelashes, lax mouth, and listless hands, he was like a voyager gazing on a placid flood, with the realization that beneath its calm lie hidden the elements of fatal storms.

His sick nerves no longer had resiliency enough for any contest; he suffered at once from lassitude, contrition, mental incoherency, and foreboding. Again he asked himself helplessly the old question, "What will the outcome be?" Nothing had been heard of

Lew for nearly a year: every day the chance of his return seemed slighter.

Emma talked of applying for a divorce. No court in the State could well refuse her a favorable decree; and then at least she would be legally at liberty. "Suppose," she asked Felix, sighing, "you had met me when we were younger, and I was free?"

It chanced, one night, when she was seated in her chair, sewing, that he discovered on the bureau a scrap of paper, scribbled over in her handwriting with the name, "Emma Piers." She started, made as if to rise, and put out a detaining hand. Then she subsided; a wave of red swept across her cheeks; and, while stitching rapidly, she ventured:

"Have you ever noticed how like our two names are?"

But their eyes met, and neither was deceived when he returned, in a strange voice:

"Why yes, it's almost a coincidence. What are you working at so hard?"

"Something of yours."

She darned his stockings, mended his shirts, tightened loose buttons on his coats. Articles of his apparel were always lying near her work-basket; his books decorated her mantel-shelf; his cigars were in her bureau drawer. He had to confess that her room had come to seem more homelike to him than his own.

Then, too, she now took care of the bull-terrier while Felix was downtown at work: it was from her doorway that Pat sprang upon his master, every evening, in ecstatic welcome. But Emma's domination did not yet include the dog.

"Look at him, Felix! When you're here, he won't come if I call, he won't even glance at me. And all I do for him: all the petting he gets when we're alone, all the chicken-bones! A grateful animal, I must say! You bad dog, come here, sir! Felix, send him to me."

"Pat, go to your mistress."

At that last word, her eyes glowed, and she smothered the reluctant brute with kisses.

One night in October, Felix entered to find her huddled in a chair, her arms hanging limply toward the carpet, her face swollen from weeping, her mouth a thin, crooked line telling of poignant grief suppressed. He stood still, oblivious to Pat's onslaught —sickened by a premonition of calamity.

"Something has happened? What is it?"

Fixing him with a look of unutterable woe, she held out a telegram.

"Read that," she gasped.

He could not have grown fainter if the telegram had been his death-warrant. It was from the superintendent of a public hospital in Chicago, and announced "the decease of Lewis Meers, from serous meningitis."

After a while, his lips formed the words:

"It seems to affect you deeply."

Indignantly, she cried out:

"Oh, have I a heart of stone? Can I forget the

past—all the happy days when I was in love for the first time? Yes, yes, he made me happy once! And now, he's dead; he'll never come back; he'll be buried way off there—my own husband, who took me home from the altar!"

She rose, galvanized, as it were, by a new thought. She approached Felix, and wound her arms deliberately about him. Her head sank back and from beneath her dishevelled hair two blinding flames leaped forth. In a breathless voice, she uttered what, to his whirling senses, was no mere statement, but a command:

"Now I have no one in the world but you!"

In this form, then, his expiation descended on him?

The same week, they were married.

CHAPTER XIV

ONE driven by violent passions upon a field of honor, and there brought low, grows sane enough in his extremity to utter from the heart, "So all my great dreams are wrecked by the hallucinations of an hour!" Thus Felix, seeing on Emma's finger the new wedding ring.

It was as if she had resumed before his eyes all the faults he had discerned in her at their first acquaintance. Her physical and mental deficiencies, her social and educational shortcomings, in fine, her every imperfection, reinvested her, like a depreciating dowry, to reduce to a chap-fallen state that young man who, his life long, had sighed so windily for a perfect sentimental union. And to this relationship, of which he had already wearied, he was bound, it seemed, till death. "Well, the catastrophe was of a piece with his whole career. Fate was in it—the workings of an unknown power malevolently disposed."

As for Emma, a few words read by a stranger from a prayer-book, a circlet of gold to wear, an engrossed certificate to cherish, and she was as happy as if assured of ten thousand cloudless days. Now for the home of her pent-up desires, wherein her joy might come to its full flower!

After rummaging half the city without any evidence of fatigue, she informed Felix excitedly that the ideal place was found. For thirty-five dollars a month one could rent four rooms and a bath in a flat-house on Second Avenue below Fourteenth Street.

"Second Avenue!" he ejaculated, in dismay.

"But, my darling, you don't know the district. A beautiful, broad street with trolley-cars, old-fashioned, brown-stone boarding-houses opposite, with high steps, and trees in real front yards, scarcely a shop in sight, and Stuyvesant Square only two short blocks to the north. I admit the rooms aren't big; but then, think of the price for such a genteel location!"

"Genteel, with the Bowery practically beginning one block westward?"

But he should be able to hide his declension well in such a spot?

The flat was on the third floor of a yellow brick building with two fire-escapes suspended from top to bottom of the façade. In the entry, one observed a double row of metal letter-boxes, name-plates, and bell-buttons. The front door was opened from the various apartments by means of an automatic latch. Darkness enshrouded the steep staircases; at each landing appeared four doors with frosted glass panels upon which, as one passed, were stamped occasionally, in silhouette, sharp, female profiles with frowsy hair, in listening attitudes. Entering the flat, one stood in a "parlor," its area about twelve feet by ten, its walls papered in a pattern of flamboyant poppies, its mantel-piece, an exceptional specimen of jig-saw work, painted white and then daubed with arabesques of gilt. This nook gave upon the bedchamber, still smaller, and ventilated by an air-shaft. Thence one had access, through the bathroom, to the dining-room, of the same size as the parlor, though not so well off for decorations. The kitchen ended the suite, with a gas stove, a wash-tub, a cupboard, and a sink, encroaching on the floor space.

Emma, however, was enthusiastic, and, as Felix put on the air of a man who no longer cares what happens, they rented the flat.

She got out of storage the relics of her former matrimonial venture. Some Brussels carpet, by dint of dexterous patching, was made to cover the floors. A marble-topped table and three chairs of Flemish oak—the chair-backs ornamented with hand-painted dogs' heads—furnished the parlor. A brass bedstead and a bureau filled the sleeping-chamber, while the dining-room was rendered nearly impracticable by a plethora of walnut chairs. Besides these articles, Emma had saved not only her best china-ware, table linen, and blankets, but also some knick-knacks that caused Felix to marvel at the effrontery of their manufacturers. All the same, one had Emma to thank—and, indeed, Lew as well—for a considerable saving of expense.

She unearthed a crayon portrait of the defunct benefactor; and Felix inspected, in silence, the likeness of a robust-looking fellow with staring eyes and a

romantic mustache. He thought his predecessor
ridiculous.

By tacit agreement, the crayon portrait was shoved
behind the bureau. When the mirror had been
slightly tilted, Felix was sometimes startled to see
Lew's eyes peering at him through the crack.

Emma, with these souvenirs round her, was moved
frequently to reverie. She recalled, with solemn face,
the day when she had selected the Brussels carpet,
when her late mother-in-law had presented her with
the steel engraving of "Queen Victoria and the Prince
Consort," when her first husband, while still a bride-
groom, had brought home the bisque statuette of an
infant crawling on all fours—a gift intended to appease her dissatisfaction at not yet having a baby of
her own. Through empty years, she had come to
regard this image with a melancholy tenderness: it
embellished the parlor mantel-piece, and the dusting
of it was a ceremony.

They employed no servant: Emma declared she
would not willingly have had one anyway, just then.
She was free again to bustle in a kitchen of her own,
there to concoct, every afternoon, dainties for some
one she loved. Felix was apt to find her at the
bread-board, her plump forearms covered with flour,
a checkered apron drawn tight across her breast, her
face made girlish by a smile at once mysterious and
doting.

"Guess what I've got for my boy's dinner to-night!"

"Poor little Emma," thought Felix, and, despite
her apparent conviction that here a demigod was

stooping, he insisted on learning how to dry the dinner dishes. Straightening herself before the dish-pan, she would say, with dewy eyes:

"Some time, we'll look back at these first days and laugh."

But how could she fit herself for companionship with him in that apotheosis? She tried furtively to understand his books, to improve her chirography and spelling, to learn the French language from a primer bought at the corner news-stand.

Felix, however, made small progress toward fame and affluence. His "inspirations"—rarer than ever in this unæsthetic spot—were smothered, as it were, at their incipience by kitchen vapors. Soaring fancies descended with a crash at the rattle of dishes and the clacking of dumb-waiter ropes; the pen slipped from his fingers; he sat contemplating the gilded mantel-piece and the hand-painted chair-backs with a sensation of being lost far from his own. Frequently, he was oppressed by such despair as one feels in a nightmare the motive of which is some vast, irremediable misfortune. Finally, his irritability, at the slightest gusts of disagreeable occurrences blazed into rage; and the brunt of all his outbursts had to be borne by Emma. He considered, indeed, that she was responsible "for everything."

He chafed at her grammatical errors, her bourgeois tastes, her interminable tales of Lew, her trite caresses. He rediscovered the little horizontal scar across her nose; and the sound of her small teeth crunching celery exasperated him. The dozen photographs of her, all hanging against the parlor walls, seemed to multiply, to an extent almost unbearable, her personality.

Sometimes, he came home half tipsy, could not endure the thought of spending an entire evening in the flat, escaped the house on false errands, returned toward midnight, dizzy and sullen. Her amazement at discovering the full extent of his indulgences increased his choler. Violent scenes ensued.

"Oh, that I should have all this to go through again! When you come home so, my old life rushes back to me, and I could almost die!"

"If I don't suit you, why were you so keen on catching me?"

"Ah, to reproach me with my love! But did I ever suspect that you were going to remind me so much of the other?"

"The other! That's all I hear. A devilish pity he kicked the bucket!"

She rolled up her large eyes, fell back against the wall, clapped both hands to her bosom.

"My heart! It'll break some day—yes, and you'll be glad."

Perhaps, at such a moment, he looked curiously at her face, small and white, dazed by the calamity of their quarrel; and, in a return to rationality, he understood that it was no stranger, but his own wife, whom he was harrying. His immediate remorse drew poignancy not alone from her wild eyes and tragic pose, but from every trivial appurtenance to that scene as well—her home-made dress, her rough-

ened finger-tips, the garish parlor ornaments, her
treasures, epitomizing all too pathetically the limitations of her nature, her past, and her indubitable
destiny. He heard her voice wailing, "Whenever I
love you most, whenever I give myself to you utterly,
then I'm about to suffer the worst. Last night I
loved you insanely, more than God; and I think
He's punishing me for it now."

"Emma, Emma, let me hear you say that you forgive me."

"Oh, I must; for I have only you!"

Kind words and kisses were, in fact, so potent an
anodyne for her despair that, after such episodes,
she could fall asleep with phrases of endearment, rendered half incoherent by drowsiness, lingering on her
lips.

In the morning, he woke to see, in the gloom of the
bedroom, her thick braids of black hair spread upon
the pillow, her eyelids nearly lost in shadows, and all
her maturity smoothed out by sleep or softened by
the dusk. Then, at his prolonged scrutiny, her eyes
opened; and her first, vague impulse was to detain
him.

In the evening, after dinner, they sat by the window, looking out on Second Avenue. Winter had
reached the city: in the small, oblong yards of boarding-houses across the street, some trees thrust forth
bare limbs, etiolated by the pale lavender glimmer of
an arc lamp. Their shadows covered the brown-
stone walls with a semblance of great, intersecting
fissures. Occasionally, on the illuminated window-

shades, there moved prefigurations monstrous and indefinite.

After the middle of December, one could glimpse, beyond the corner of Fourteenth Street, many persons moving to and fro before bright shop-windows.

In Christmas week, Felix remembered that his credit was still unimpaired in a jewelry shop on Fifth Avenue. There he selected, and had charged to his account, a gold bracelet set with small turquoises. But when, on Christmas morning, he slipped this trinket upon Emma's wrist, she, with an excited laugh, produced a diamond finger-ring worth at least two hundred dollars. She had spent on this gift a fourth of her remaining patrimony.

Covering his frowns with her hands, she explained, anxiously:

"I wanted so much to get you a fur-lined overcoat, but I was afraid you wouldn't care for anything but sable."

All the tastes that she ascribed to him were of the most "aristocratic" sort. Though he had grown too cautious intentionally to acquaint this jealous creature with many details of his past, she was convinced that Felix, "in sowing his wild oats," had squandered a rich inheritance. That was the reason why he now avoided all the fashionable and brilliant friends he must have had? So much the better for her!

At their Christmas dinner, holly decked the table, cider brimmed the goblets, jellies trembled in bowls, nuts, raisins, and candies ran over on the cloth, and the turkey, flanked by tall clumps of celery, with a

small American flag stuck in its "wishbone," was, as
Emma said, "a whopper." While they were dining,
sleet lashed the panes, and the wind moaned in the
air-shaft. Emma shivered with delight.

"Just you and I, safe inside! Do you remember,
it was on a Christmas eve we met?"

He was thinking of that night, but, at the same time,
of another woman, green-eyed, with auburn hair.

Ah, the laughter and the lights, the odors of perfumes and champagne, the roses not so ruddy as the
lips above them, the glances that united in an imma-
terial embrace! He fell to wondering whom she
was deluding, this Christmas night.

Chance brought him, soon afterward, a partial
satisfaction of that curiosity.

He had begun to patronize a saloon conveniently
situated on Fourteenth Street, near Third Avenue.
Midway of a row of catchpenny arcades, pawn-shops,
and ten-cent concert-halls, two show-windows—displaying against wooden screens some dusty "mag-
nums"—shut in a swinging door with cut-glass
panels. Inside, sawdust covered the floor. To the
left, from front to rear of a long room, extended the
bar, backed by mirrors against which pyramids of
glasses rose just high enough to prevent an inebriated
patron from glimpsing his reflection. To the right,
were aligned a cashier's desk, a cigar-stand, and a
buffet, the last covered with dishes of salt herring,
pickles, sliced Italian sausage, pretzels, and other
generators of thirst. From the ceiling hung down
at intervals chandeliers wrapped round with tin-foil;

and on the walls were lithographs portraying race-horses and pugilists. At the back, a partition concealed a small, unventilated retreat, reached from the pavement by a narrow corridor, where feminine customers were served.

Felix was at first ashamed of himself whenever he entered there. In time, however, he got over such fastidiousness.

One afternoon, the cut-glass panels swung inward with a crash; two unprepossessing figures were seen struggling on the threshold; and a short fellow, half out of his overcoat, plunged headlong into the saloon. Rising from the sawdust, he swayed forward against the bar, at the same time shouting thickly over his shoulder:

"I'll have all I want whenever I want it, and don't you never take it on yourself to interfere with my amusements, Mr. Mackeron!"

Felix turned to the individual thus addressed. It was the tenor of "The Lost Venus."

This young actor, formerly the admiration of "matinée girls," had grown sallow and emaciated. Moreover, the physiognomy that, on the stage of the Trocadero Theatre, had expressed many evanescent emotions, was now almost vacuous, while the man's pupils, even in the reduced light of the saloon, remained at pin-point size.

Mackeron had no sooner shaken hands with Felix than he began eagerly to relate his troubles.

On account of his cigarette-smoking, his singing voice had temporarily "gone back on him." Montmorrissy had refused him work, and "a conspiracy of all the prominent theatrical managers in New York" had kept him off the boards. Of late, he had been employed in a moving-picture manufactory where, before a kinetoscopic camera, he took part in short, serio-comic pantomimes. But the proprietor of this establishment—"a pitiful ass"—had declared that Mackeron, "an artist noted throughout the country for the mobility of his mask," could no longer inject into his face a sufficient evidence of feeling. "I tell you, Piers, the whole profession hates me for my successes, and is out to down me. One man can't fight them all. What I shall do, heaven only knows. Do you happen to have five dollars to spare till early to-morrow morning?"

"I'm sorry, no."

Mackeron's pin-point eyes grew duller.

"No offence taken," he muttered, his glance running over Felix's clothes. And, after a moment's hesitation:

"I suppose you know about Marie Sinjon's new part?"

Felix set down his highball. To hear, after so long a silence, that well-remembered name, made his heart beat fast.

Montmorrissy had provided her with a new extravaganza called "Poor Pierrette," of which an elaborate production was soon going to have its first-night at the Trocadero Theatre.

So she was in town!

"Yes, and Noon too, by George, better off than ever!"

Felix wondered whether he ought not to take umbrage at that speech. But the other continued:

"You remember Noon's nervous trouble—the way he used to twitch his head? Not so long ago, I watched him through—I saw him in a restaurant, dining, and at first I thought he wasn't going to be able to feed himself!"

Felix closed his eyes, the better to enjoy this picture. Then, to prevent himself from smiling, he inquired, hastily:

"And Nora Llanelly?"

"There was a decent sort of girl! I don't know. She's vanished."

Further conversation was prevented by the saloonkeeper, who demanded that Mackeron remove "his friend." They turned to look at the short drunkard in the sawdust-covered overcoat, who, clinging to the bar, was weeping because he had been refused more whiskey. In his broad face, splotched across the nose from alcoholic poisoning, his large lugubrious mouth, his dyed "mutton-chop" whiskers and mustache, his inflamed, vacant eyes running over with tears, Felix discovered something half familiar. Was not this the ex-drummer of the orchestra at the Trocadero Theatre? Mackeron assented.

"No friend of mine, you understand. But his wife's a good soul, and home to her he's going!"

So the actor dragged the musician forth into the street.

The saloonkeeper's comment was:

"There's the sort that gives this business a bad name."

He was a middle-aged Irishman, the speaker, serious-looking, sandy-haired, smooth-shaven, displaying over his left cheek-bone a deep cicatrice, where an unruly customer had once struck him with "brass knuckles." In his boyhood, a barefoot immigrant from "the old country" dumped into the slums, he had quickly learned to endure all privations, to return blows, to run from policemen, to avoid liquor, and to doff his cap to priests. Ward politicians had soon found in him, at election time, a youth at once shrewd, devoted, and eager for profitable combat at the polls. From the captaincy of voters he had worked his way, through various kindred offices, to a position of influence in Tammany Hall, the headquarters of the Democratic political machine in New York. Now, at forty-nine, he was the proprietor of many ballots in his district, the owner of a lucrative business which he considered no less reputable than any merchant's, a widower with two small children, a total abstainer, and an occasional worshipper at mass. His chief desire was to rear his daughters in "good style"; and he had casually inquired of Felix, to whom he made himself agreeable, "if they'd be apt to think much of pedigrees in them young ladies' finishing schools uptown?" All the same, Mr. Quilty's remote ancestors had, it seemed, "worn crowns in Ireland."

Despite this, he thought nothing of taking off his coat, when trade was brisk, and serving drinks across the bar.

Then the lights of the foil-wrapped chandeliers

struck through a blue zone of tobacco smoke upon a phalanx of tilted derby hats. The customers, crowded one against another, with difficulty accomplished the large gestures called for by their unnatural exuberance; but, on the other hand, their proximity made easier those unpremeditated confidences, those secret promises of favor, those touching avowals of regard, which signalize such moments. On all sides, mouths opened to emit unbridled laughter, or snapped shut in counterfeit decision; eyes winked and looked unutterable wisdom; faces were wreathed in rapturous grins, contracted inordinately with cunning, relaxed in doleful reverie. Late at night, some imbibed, apparently, elixirs of transfiguring properties: old men grew young in mien and impulse, young men decrepit in attitude and spirit, while the timid turned fierce, and the turbulent propitiable.

In these scenes, Felix now regularly took his place.

Presently, it was as if, from rubbing against so many shabby costumes, an indefinite suggestion of shabbiness had been transferred to him. One day, he realized that cab-drivers, as he passed them on the street, no longer solicited his patronage.

He could not spare the money to renew his clothing, which, after long service, seemed suddenly impaired at every point. Indeed, Johnny Livy, whose Bohemian habiliments had once made his company in Broadway restaurants a questionable satisfaction, was now generally as well-dressed as Felix. The latter did not hesitate to ask the "star

reporter" for loans, or to approach, on the same
business, friends in the newspaper office whom he
caught wearing optimistic smiles. At last, on seeing
such expressions fade away the moment he grew
confidential, Felix plucked up courage, marched into
the editorial cubbyhole, and demanded an increase
of salary. The editor regretted to inform him that
his work, instead of gaining value, had depreciated.

"With us, you see, efficiency is what counts—
never sentimental inclination, though sometimes we
would like to make that do so. But here, unfortunately, we are all parts of a machine. When a part
fails——"

The journalist gazed into space, slowly shook his
fragile-looking head, and turned to his desk. Felix
went home with a heavy heart.

The money that he gave Emma every Saturday
for housekeeping expenses represented for him· just
so many cigars and highballs missed; as the week
drew to a close, and his empty pockets necessitated
abstinence, he could not help blaming her for his
consequent discomfort. At such times, a sullen animosity invaded him. The dinners which she had
racked her brain to make at once tempting and inexpensive, he ate with lowered brow, in silence; while
she was trying to interest him in cheerful topics, he
was pondering schemes for the replenishment of his
wallet. "What a pity that all his jewelry was in
pawn! His books, then? He could not bear to
part with one of them. Of his clothing, there was
not a suit worth a decent price." Such was his

desperation, that he examined all the forks and spoons for sterling marks. Then, with a start, he recoiled from his intention, as much aghast as a somnambulist waking to find himself on the threshold of a crime.

Nevertheless, he often appraised the diamond finger-ring—his Christmas present from Emma. But, of course, she would remark its absence from his hand.

"Just so: it was she who balked him, in some way, at every point!"

And, when the struggle against his craving, or the desire to indulge it, had stretched his nerves to a tension almost intolerable, any trivial annoyance caused him to turn on Emma in a fury. His voice high and unsteady, he would exclaim:

"Will you be so good as to stop that endless humming? My God, I should like a little peace, now and then, in my own house!"

The light died in her large eyes; her face seemed to wither; and her pale lips barely formed the words:

"Don't you swear at me, Felix!"

At such temerity, a red mist obscured his sight.

"One of these days you'll drive me crazy. Then look out!"

She sucked in her lips, while her eyes, never leaving his, slowly overflowed. And a thin wail rang out:

"Yes, strike me! It's nothing new. There's the mark for you: the scar across my nose that Lew put there!"

His heart, so to speak, turned over.

"Oh, Emma! Oh, my poor little girl! Never in the world, from me!"

"You say that now. But you're getting more and more like him. It's a rep'tition, yes, a dreadful rep'tition, and this is my life!"

Still, when a similar quarrel had prostrated her, when a physician had been summoned to relieve her headache and the palpitations of her heart, Felix had only to kneel beside the bed, cover her cheek with kisses, and lay some flowers in her languid hands.

"Violets, from my bad boy! Ah, now I want to get well this minute, and wear them somewhere."

Reconciled, they walked out, on frosty nights, over pavements slippery with ice, past ridges of dirty snow extending alongside the curbs, toward other parts of town than theirs. Thoroughfares vivid with the electric signs of "dime museums" and saloons gave place to the dim upsweep of office buildings; soon a vista with unobstructed altitudes appeared, where sombre zones of interwoven branches hovered over stretches of unsullied snow; then blocks of fashionable shops displayed monotonously their blind window-panes and iron shutters; and, eventually, where unessential trade gave way to its sustainers, one was surrounded by massive dwelling-houses with gables, tourelles and marble vestibules, their shadowy prospect broken, maybe, at a distance, by a church spire outlined with stars, or by the refulgence of a towerlike hotel ablaze from

portico to cornices with lights. Closed automobiles continually glided past: the twin lamps rushed
forward; the rectangular window framed pale
dresses and shirt-bosoms; the varnished panels
flashed by; the red tail-light dwindled like a dying
coal. Emma stared at that flood of equipages bearing away, to unknown pleasures, the people of an
alien world. She wanted to halt before a house
when some woman, cloaked and bareheaded, ran up
the steps, while a footman in white silk stockings
held open the door. Through the large windows
of restaurants she perceived, by the light of candles
glowing under beaded shades, bare arms, white
cravats, orchids, jewels, raised champagne glasses.
Then, all at once, she confessed that she was tired.
They turned homeward. The mansions were left
behind, the shops ended at the little park, the office
buildings gave place to Union Square and Fourteenth
Street, Second Avenue opened out, and the fire-
escapes of the flathouse came into view. Among
the hand-painted chairs, they removed their wraps
in silence.

Once they went to the Metropolitan Opera House,
where they sat in the topmost gallery, close to the
gilded rafters and the large cupids of the fresco.
Below, hung four other galleries, the attire of their
occupants gaining festive quality at each descent,
till, in the two lowest tiers, fitted out with boxes,
shimmering décolleté dresses, decked with strands of
pearls or sewn with diamonds, clung to the narrow
hips of women smaller, apparently, than marion-

ettes. The house grew dark. Before the audience, in a broad trench where screened electric globes shed rays on many music-racks, the bows of violins lay all aslant, the flutes and horns were raised, two drummers cautiously felt the membranes of their kettle-drums. The baton fell; a sonorous harmony swept upward.

"Venusberg's" foliage was disclosed; *Tannhäuser* sat repining by the couch of *Venus*—she in a shining girdle and transparent robes. To notes vertiginously passional, bacchantes entered; cries burst forth; white limbs were tossed about in reckless measures. But weariness seized upon the dancers: they fell back into a gathering mist, and disappeared. Then the mellow voice of Venus stole forth, to fill the auditorium:

"*Geliebter, sag', wo weilt dein Sinn?*"

"Where stray thy thoughts?" To the past, to a time when, in an artist's dusky studio, those same tones quivered on the air, to youth tentative and yet still uncompromised, to an epoch of boundless promise, to the clear, trustful eyes of a young girl.

Emma, having consulted the programme, whispered:

"That is Mme. Regne Lodbrok."

"Yes, I ought to know. I used to be a friend of hers."

His wife leaned forward to devour with her eyes the radiant figure on the stage. She did not smile again that evening.

Her jealousy returned, and in a form so tempestuous that she could not help disclosing all the ramifications of her fears. "What chance had she"—in effect—"to hold for long a young man who had lived amid the allurements of a sumptuous environment, who had been at home in the boudoirs of famous singers and in the dressing-rooms of actresses, who, besides, must have left back there, in the region of opera-boxes, closed automobiles, and ball-rooms, some elegant, cultivated, beautiful young woman? Indeed, perhaps he had not broken all of those old ties? Why was it that he disappeared for hours, to return morose and quarrelsome, without excuses for his absence? Was she to discover, some day, that even in faithlessness he resembled Lew?"

In the morning, she consulted a paper-covered, dog-eared volume entitled, "Napoleon's Dream-Book"; at night, she "told her fortune" with a pack of playing-cards. As she laid upon the marble-topped table card after card, Emma muttered, "Trouble in the house, disagreeable feelings, an absence, a light woman between him and me." She looked at Felix strangely.

"No matter how I shuffle the deck, there's always a light woman between him and me!"

When, by pretence of the most tender sympathy, she had inveigled him into relating anecdotes of his more prosperous years, suddenly her dark eyes struck fire, and she cried:

"How carefully you avoid the love-affairs! That shows me all the plainer: if you had finished with them, you wouldn't be so wary. But I don't need

your confessions; I'm sure without them! Don't
I feel it here, in my breast—an awful sinking, that
comes on sometimes when you're out, and I'm alone?
Ah, don't think a woman can't tell!"

"My dear Emma, this is perfectly absurd."

Baffled by his smile, she glared at him. Then
approaching her face to his, gritting her teeth, and
rapidly shaking her head,

"Felix, I could kill you!"

To hide his uneasiness, he snatched up hat and
overcoat.

"I'll walk about in the open till you come to your
senses."

She screamed after him:

"Yes, leave your wife! That's all us wives are
for!"

And she collapsed into a chair, with eyeballs fixed,
and twitching hands. The deuce! One could not
leave his wife in that predicament!

He helped her to bed. There she lay motionless,
groaning. "She was choking, her brain felt queer,
her heart was running away." Then her teeth
commenced to chatter. Felix brought whiskey, which
she pushed aside; he wrapped her in blankets; he
ran to a neighboring apothecary's for a headache
remedy. She swallowed one powder, and fell asleep.

He slipped out with his dog, into the cold. "What
a life! How long would it continue so? Till
death?" He stopped in the street, struck his palms
together, and ejaculated, "It can't go on! I was
not born for this. Presently, I shall awake."

Pedestrians halted, some distance off, to watch him. Felix entered a saloon.

Now and then, when his hand touched the swinging doors, he hesitated, drew back, escaped. From victories no greater, he derived extravagant hopes.

But still there came to him at every contemplation of gayety the same longing, at every sight of physical beauty the ineradicable trepidation, at every approach to centres of prodigality and license the thought, "Alas, I am missing that!" The ghosts of old temptations. returned to haunt him; and one, in the twilight of a February day, took corporeal shape.

On a residential street, a slender woman, wearing a long coat of black, smooth fur and a black "Russian toque," drew near to Felix. They were on the point of passing each other without recognition. But the bull-terrier was fawning round her skirts.

"Eileen!"

"You!"

And they both trembled.

The rim of her black fur toque pressed down on all sides the precise undulations of her coiffure; from the full lobes of her ears jet pendants dangled; a frill of white lace clung round her chin. That unobtrusive exquisiteness of dress, that clear pallor and facial delicacy of the "hot-house type" of beauty, that very subtle hint of secret ardors, in Eileen Tamborlayne remained unimpaired. Even the familiar composure almost instantly flowed back into her face: she cast a glance up and down the dusky street; her eyes cleared of apprehension; her lips parted in a mournful smile.

"My poor Felix, to think we should have this painful meeting!"

Her speech, and her quick recovery of equanimity, mortified the young man. With a bitter laugh, he returned:

"Painful, I take it, because of the catastrophe that it recalls?"

Giving him a reproachful look, she started to walk on, though in such a way that he committed no obtrusion by keeping pace with her. He controlled his agitation. He tried to speak indifferently.

"Is it odd that I should feel some curiosity? For three years I've been in ignorance of your whereabouts and fortunes. That seems a long time, perhaps? And yet, I'm still interested in what I was partially to blame for." He hesitated, then blurted out:

"Gregory?"

"He's fairly well. Travelling seems to suit him best. We seldom get back to New York, these days."

"You and he are together!"

She made no immediate reply. At length, with a sigh, she allowed the enigmatic phrase to escape her:

"Sometimes qualities that irk us serve us best in the end."

When he had considered this carefully, Felix ventured:

"Does he ever speak of me?"

"Ah, my dear, that's different!"

He understood everything. She, in some ingenious way, had avoided practically all the consequences; he, while scarcely so guilty, was blamed by Gregory Tamborlayne for everything. He sneered:

"In our case, the usual retributions seem to have been reversed. I'm the one, apparently, who has lost everything of importance."

She looked at him askance.

"Have you been so unfortunate?"

He shrugged his shoulders.

"I hadn't your talents. You see, I was an amateur."

Eileen stood still. Her eyes became humid, her lips parted, and her face expressed perfectly the resignation of a meek woman misunderstood. She faltered:

"We had best part here."

Besides, a lamp-lighter was illuminating the street; and two strangers were approaching. She made haste with her farewell.

"You think harshly of me. You ascribe nothing to fatality, to your unconsciously exerted influence on others, to your own impulses. You don't remember tenderly, as I often do, a season of delicious terrors, of sweet miseries. You forget that we loved each other."

Her chin rose; a well-known, tremulous smile appeared; she seemed to be swaying toward him. A tremor passed through his body. He seized her hand.

"I remember it all!" he uttered, in choked accents. Intense satisfaction shone in her eyes.

"I want you never to forget it! Be careful: people are coming; our moment is over. But we cheated fate of one more thrill, didn't we?"

Without lowering his hand, Felix watched her depart. And not till she had disappeared did he remember his humiliating discoveries concerning her, or realize that Eileen, moved by the dominant impulse of her nature, had again played upon his sensibility. He was forced to confess:

"I don't seem able to hold my own in any situation."

It was on the following day that these words were more unhappily verified.

The last edition of *The Evening Sphere* had gone to press, when the editor called Felix into the private office. "It was not a prosperous year; the proprietor of the newspaper had ordered a general retrenchment; a number of employés would have to be laid off for the time being." In short, after much circumlocution, Felix was told that his services were no longer needed. "But, my dear fellow, you must be sure to leave me your address. I have great hopes of sending for you, when we feel wealthier, and you have refreshed yourself with a vacation." The editor smiled gently. "You must begin soon to live up to my expectations of you," was his valedictory.

The flat was redolent of hot lard. In the kitchen, Emma, wearing her checkered apron, was cooking dinner. She regarded Felix with astonishment and pleasure.

"Home so early?"

"I've lost my job."

She displayed a frightened smile

"That's not a pretty joke, sweetheart."

"It's the truth. I've been discharged."

Emma turned to the gas stove, with quivering chin. He wondered why his news affected her so deeply. From her accounts, this was not by any means the first time she had heard those words.

CHAPTER XV

THE day after his dismissal from *The Evening Sphere*, Felix remembered that he had never yet derived material benefit from the good-will of Paul Pavin. Forthwith, he hastened to the Velasquez Building. In the lobby, a clerk informed him:

"Monsieur Pavin has his old studio for the winter; but just now he is on a visit in Westchester County. However, he is expected back within the week."

"I'll call again."

But it seemed an age before Felix parted the velveteen curtains, saw a burly pair of shoulders rise against the fading "north light," and felt his arms grasped by two strong hands.

"Rascal! I have been in your city seven weeks."

Felix began apologies which Pavin cut short.

"No, I am wrong. We oldish fellows sometimes ask too much. In all ways, my faith! Yes, on a gray day we discover that age must bait its hook." And he turned on the lights before Felix had recovered from his blushes.

They sat down for an "old-fashioned talk," which proved to be a gay monologue by the Frenchman concerning adventures, in Corfu, Brittany, and Norway, that could hardly have befallen a decrepit man. But when Felix refilled his glass with whiskey and soda, Pavin's mind seemed to wander. At last, he said, abruptly:

"My friend, you are not looking well. Have you been ill?"

Felix ceased to smile. His answer was:

"Bad luck seems to have been my principal ailment!"

The artist smoothed his thick, blond beard reflectively.

"No fatal malady, that, for youth. I say it who know. Mine was, for a while, an open-air hospital: trees overhead, iron chairs for beds, a light diet of bread, with cheese on feast-days, and much walking in thin-soled shoes as part of the discipline. My best tonic was observance of the cured."

"Your disease had no complications."

"And you think that in consequence I have no ability to prescribe for your especial case. But why does a physician, who flounders through all sorts of storms without mishap, say to some one, 'I warn you to keep your feet dry'? Because, while not susceptible to colds himself, he knows that for certain others there is only one way to avoid a dangerous illness. A man must shun the elements that don't agree with him."

"Exactly. That's the plan of this world. All the immunity for one, and all the susceptibility for another! And again, after every act that is not formal, the same unfairness in assignment of emotions. For you, doubtless, impenitence; but for me, remorse."

There, according to Pavin, Felix had discredited his own grievance. Life—as the Frenchman saw it—was made up of the happiness and the unhappiness that followed different sorts of conduct. The result depended on the degree to which the individual's higher senses had been developed. An undeveloped nature would not suffer from the worst acts any great contrition; but a nature with fine moral judgment would get, at each divergence from its ideal of conduct, an unhappy reaction. "I for my part," Pavin confessed, "have lived without many scruples and, consequently, with few unhappy reactions. In that speech, however, I admit a deficiency, a coarseness of spiritual fibre, a lack of what you have. I possess the 'quality' necessary for good painting, but you own a finer quality—the capacity for delicate remorse. A cerebral man is tormented with countless scruples incomprehensible to the peasant. Thus, with his very pains, he buys access to rare fields of consciousness, in the far reaches of which move the mystics, the delineators of subtle agonies, those who have gained their 'victories over the invisible.' You have read a book by one of these. But as for him, between his remorses and his will, the latter was the more delicate."

Then, looking at Felix with half-shut eyes, he concluded, in the tone of one surprised by a chance thought:

"We must make your resemblance to him end short of that."

Felix took this opportunity to relate how Buron's

book had changed his literary designs, how its perusal
had been followed by the most exalted aspirations,
how, for his resultant labors, he had slighted daily
tasks, to the depletion of his funds, and the refusal
of his further journalistic services. "Then, close ap-
plication to work had impaired his health; next, while
suffering from nervous instability, he had even been
drawn into an unfortunate marriage; finally, his accumulated troubles had bound him to a habit such as
one did not easily escape." In fact, one might have
thought that all Felix's woes had begun with Pavin's
gift of a volume of French prose. But, during this
plaint, the portrait-painter seemed almost inattentive.

"I have bored you with my troubles," said Felix,
stiffly.

"No, I heard everything you said, and with great
regret, though all the time I was thinking of Buron.
Do you know, a curious thing has happened, in that
connection." And he explained that Mme. Lodbrok had seen recently, on Broadway, an ex-dancer,
half French and half Algerian, once the talk of
Paris, but now grown ugly, fat, and shabby, who,
many years before, had disappeared with Pierre
Buron. This woman, while the opera-singer's cab
was turning round, had vanished in the crowd.
"What a pity," Pavin commented. "Perhaps she
could have furnished some illuminating reminiscences—of his death, or the location of his grave?"

Felix made no reply, being more concerned with
the thought that his elaborate preliminaries to a
request for money had been wasted.

But this was not the case. When the young man rose to go, Pavin pressed into his hand a roll of banknotes, with the speech:

"You need two remedies for your bad luck: one, a temporary loan—if you will permit me—the other, a journey with a friend. In two weeks, I am off for Havre. Come and see me to-morrow; we will conspire against all obstacles. Mind the tall box in the vestibule."

There was, indeed, wedged behind the door, a flat wooden case some six feet high, with express labels pasted on it. Felix, uttering an unsteady laugh, inquired:

"A fresh masterpiece for the Luxembourg Gallery?"

"Unfortunately, no. A portrait I have been doing in the country."

Round the turn of the corridor, he snatched from his pocket the roll of banknotes. It amounted to a hundred and fifteen dollars. He went downtown as if walking on air.

Besides, Pavin's last words kept ringing in his ears. "A journey!"

An escape! Another land! The beginning of a new life! It had come, then, at last—the golden opportunity. And, without troubling himself about the details of that transition, he was whirled away into the jewelled haze of Paris boulevards at nightfall, into the districts of cafés made famous by their patrons, where celebrities of all sorts congregated on plush-covered settees with their backs against a wainscoting of mirrors, into the region of studios where, when the "working light" was gone, geniuses, of whom posterity was destined to be proud, foregathered to display their nimble wit, their cynicism, their exceptional fervors. Then the sphere of Continental drawing-rooms opened to his gaze: he recognized his youthfulness, believed again in his charm and talents, saw himself ultimately made free, through his accomplishments, of the society of elegant "blue-stockings," statesmen, diplomatists, and princesses. A cloud of unknown faces gathered on the margins of his dreams. He perceived, as it were, marble stairways lined with bowing servants, expanses of glistening parquetry over which rose-colored dresses floated, wide doorways filled with palms that masked musicians, conservatories where beautiful women, additionally distinguished by their love-affairs with the illustrious, leaned toward him amid masses of exotic flowers. Or else, he glimpsed lagoons in moonlight and a gondola gliding past the steps of an old palace, carved balconies hanging over an enchanted sea, a villa blushing, in sunset, amid trees that rose against an amber-colored sky, to burst, high overhead, into autumnal opulence, as does the foliage in a design by Fragonard. Those were all scenes of plenty, love, and fame, of unprecedented adventures, of intermingling exaltations and languors, replete with the delights that fortune may secure for the character at once voluptuous and intellectual. And why should those visions not assume material shapes? Did not the whole world, after all, lie stretched out before youth made aware of its potentialities?

Still, Emma's face seemed to float constantly before him. He was enraged by the persistence of that apparition; and, as he had reached Fourteenth Street, to drown his scruples he entered Quilty's saloon.

But the floor covered with sawdust, the foil-wrapped chandeliers, the bar slopped over with beer, roused his disgust. He wondered how he could have spent so many hours in such a place.

Nevertheless, he remained at the bar, drinking highballs, grumbling to himself at the quality of the whiskey, condescending, finally, with an inscrutable smile, to answer Quilty and an habitué of the resort, named Pandle—a rather obtrusively attired, dried-up, pessimistic-looking fellow apparently of unlimited leisure, who wore an auburn wig, and, since he was totally bereft of hair, affected two streaks of brown cosmetic in imitation of eyebrows. "What associates!" thought Felix. "What a den!" From that environment he could not, in contemplation, extricate the flat, or even Emma. All would have to be left behind.

"As for her, did she expect to fasten herself for life to a man of his endowments? If he gave her the slip, she would not be a whit worse off than when he met her. It was the destiny of some to suffer in whatever situations they contrived. And did not the conqueror invariably have to drive his chariot to victory over prostrate bodies?"

On his way home, however, he modified his arrogance. Dissimulation was imperative.

Emma, who had been pressing her cheek against the window-pane, came forward with haggard eyes.

"Your dinner's spoiled hours ago. Where have you been?"

"Collecting an old debt," he answered, and threw fifty dollars upon the table. When she embraced him, her face radiant with relief and thankfulness, Felix grew sick at heart. Could he do this deed?

Notwithstanding such thoughts, next day he went back to the Velasquez Building. "Monsieur Pavin was out."

"Ah!"

He had given vent to an ejaculation of relief. It was a reaction.

And a new struggle began.

He haunted the flat, followed Emma from one room to another, watched her at household tasks—striving to stamp upon his mind, so that he might not for one moment forget, the picture of her docile servitude. Sometimes, remaining perfectly still, he tried to imagine the place as it would be without him. Empty rooms, a vacant chair, the lonely bed, silence. But could he not hear, in imagination, her sobs, and the footfalls of furniture-movers? Her gaze rose to meet his; a look of wonder and inquiry trembled in her face; his eyes fell. He had the sensation of a man who, as his intended victim unexpectedly turns round, conceals a knife behind his back.

It occurred to him that if he could feel a modicum of passion for her, his designs would never be accomplished. So he urged himself to unprecedented exhibitions of tenderness: he made love to her, talked nonsense, kissed her eyelids, chin, and blue-black hair. In his anxiety to reproduce old ardors, he imitated all the blandishments that he had lavished on the others. He cried aloud, "I love you!" his heart crying, meanwhile, "If only I could be content to do so!" For when his lips met hers, he dreamed of princesses; and when he closed his eyes, he pondered "all that might be," but for his conscience. He felt at the same time resentment toward Emma and an intense desire to be satisfied with her. He wished that he might be able willingly to sacrifice himself for her, and that she might then somehow set him free.

To this sentimental pretence of Felix's she made immediate response. Her large eyes once more grew lambent, her doting smiles returned, she regained her girlish airs. "It was like old times," or else, "He had never been so nice." When he was going out, she clung round his neck, or lured him back for another kiss. She could not let him leave her for an hour without participation in the most tender scene. On other occasions, her eyes changing color in an instant, her amorous whispers ending in a catch, she barred his exit till he had sworn to his most trifling intention. He was going, usually, "to negotiate with certain publishers about a prospective book."

After he had left the house, her words lingered in his ears, her dilated eyes seemed still to shine before him, and passing women who bore a vague resemblance to her intruded on each guilty thought of his.

Every day, he went half-way to Pavin's studio, halted, and turned back. And it was as if he were relinquishing, in that retreat, a kingdom full of treasure.

He came to the conclusion that before he could find a plausible excuse for leaving her, she would have to be drawn into a violent quarrel. "Insults cannot be forgotten; contempt in one will counteract pity in the other; the irrevocable phrase, let slip in anger, may prove to be the passport to liberty." But his attempts in that respect were all rendered half-hearted by his self-reproach. Besides, who could push an altercation with a woman dissolved in tears?

Fool that he had been, to forget her transformation in jealousy! He had only to blurt out an allusion to some imaginary woman, create a false impression, excite Emma till she threatened him ferociously, or, still better, attacked him. In the letter left behind him, this sentence would appear, "From what has just occurred, you, too, can measure not only the unhappiness, but also the danger, of our companionship."

Thirteen days had passed since Pavin's proposal, when Felix, ready for anything, appeared again at the Velasquez Building.

"Monsieur Pavin? Why, sir, he sailed yesterday for Europe."

Gone, before the appointed day, without a word!

The mirage vanished; the desert stretched to the horizon its monotonous and barren undulations.

He settled down to write short stories "such as magazine editors want." Humbly he rummaged current periodicals for models. On some of those pages, Miss Nuncheon displayed her theories about "the smart set," and in every number of *The Mauve Monthly* Mr. Lute voiced no less glibly in sonnets than in quatrains some enigmatical and pallid yearnings. Felix, for all his sneers, could not string together half a dozen satisfactory paragraphs.

He went downtown to hunt a job among the newspaper offices. The first refusal disheartened him. As he was leaving that vicinity, Johnny Livy passed, whistling, almost stout in a new plaid ulster.

Felix finished Pavin's loan, and sold his old pawn-tickets. Emma was using her patrimony. Bill-collectors called daily.

Every night, he stayed late at Quilty's bar. Frequently, in the morning he had no recollection of coming home. On rising, he was good for nothing till he had swallowed a drink of brandy.

It was his "one refuge," that state of inebriety, in which all his regrets and anxieties melted quite away; in which a conviction of absolute well-being came to him; in which, as he advanced to an obliteration of all objective consciousness, veil after veil was lifted from his subjective mind, until, like a mystic seemingly on the verge of discovering the undiscoverable, he was stirred, so to speak, by revelations, vaguely splendid, concerning a government whose province was the illimitable field of stars. His soul, taking flight, reached spaces where the mundane and temporal was lost in the celestial and eternal, where the human sojourn became trivial, where the air trembled with a harmony of promises to be fulfilled in perpetuity. It was, indeed, at such moments that his spirit, escaping from the flesh, soared to its only presumption of a God. But at his every return to sobriety the sense of truth departed from those phantasms, the veils descended, as if his ethereal part, having mingled with infinitude, had to be deprived of its discoveries at re-entry into the body. Moreover, there were no terms whereby he could have described intelligibly his fragmentary reminiscences.

Yet he now found those periods the only desirable ones in life. Without any more self-condemnation, he clung to his habit, because indulgence of it made him oblivious to its consequences.

His constant intemperance, his relapse—since Pavin's departure—into his former sullenness, his failure to renew by any remunerative deed Emma's faith in him, evidently forced his wife, at last, to the conclusion that the future held more clouds than sunshine. She no longer had the courage to talk of celebrity and wealth to come. Her attitudes of adoration ceased before the reiterated spectacle of a man made unsteady and fatuous by drink. And, in her apprehensions, every day expressed with greater freedom were mixed up reproaches about "poverty," bald comparisons of Felix's debauchery to Lew's, dire predictions, wails of self-pity, and accusations that he was deliberately going downhill "because he and some girl uptown had fallen out."

Nightly he had to hear her, in a voice monotonously shrill, rehearse her wrongs. The list of his offences was apparently limitless: he wondered, occasionally, if she kept a memorandum-book in which to note the most trifling reprehensible act of his. Even Pat, who crept to his master's side while these diatribes were in progress, drooped his head and yawned. When she had finished, Felix was apt to say:

"After all, your precious Lew was a sensible man, who knew what he was about."

Once, she retorted:

"No doubt you'd like to be rid of me, too! Or even see me die!"

He made no response. But he sent at her, from beneath his lowered eyelids, a furtive look of hatred.

Emma, though apparently engaged in dusting the bisque statuette of an infant, was watching Felix in the mirror above the mantel-shelf. She planted herself before him, with arms akimbo.

"You'll never get off so easy!"

But, unexpectedly, a look of hopelessness appeared upon her face. Her eyes rolled in their sockets. Her mouth was slowly distorted, as are children's mouths just before a fit of grief. She left the room, and threw herself face-downward upon the bed. Her lamentations filled the house. Finally, she was prostrated, without sufficient strength to reach for the headache powders in the bureau drawer.

One evening, Felix was leaving the flathouse when a mail-carrier, in his gray uniform and with his bag of tan sole-leather slung over one shoulder, slipped into the metal letter-box an envelope of unusual appearance. It was from France—from Paul Pavin. A sneer curled the young man's lip; he thrust the missive unopened into his pocket.

"So he recalled the fact that there was a little something to explain?"

When, in Quilty's saloon, he had fortified himself with a drink of whiskey, Felix tore open the envelope. The words caught his eye:

"I first wrote to you in care of *The Evening Sphere*. Then, as there was no time to lose, I telephoned to the editor for your address. I sent a note, by special delivery, to your house, and, at the last moment, another, by messenger. Both were evidently accepted. . . ."

It was Emma who had intercepted them! Then she knew everything? But that was impossible. All the same, there was no other explanation. His hands shook so violently that the note-paper rattled.

"This fills my score against her!"

And he prepared for his arraignment of her by getting thoroughly drunk. Toward nine o'clock, he forgot that he had a wife.

Presently, he became aware that some one was talking to him. Directly before his face, an incomplete countenance was resolved out of a mist: he recognized Quilty by the scar across his cheek-bone.

"A lady in the back room wants a word with you."

"A lady?"

With a vacant laugh, Felix entered the compartment at the rear of the saloon.

Some women, of a foreign appearance, their hats ornamented with draggled plumes, their large, flat hand-bags laid on bare table-tops among half-empty glasses, sat here and there in the relaxed attitudes of tired pedestrians. All were staring, with expressions of antagonism, at a tense figure posted, bolt upright, by the corridor door. It was Emma.

"You! In this place!"

Without replying, her face colorless, her eyes enormous, her lips compressed as if to keep in a cry, she pounced upon him and dragged him, through the corridor, into the street.

There, he struggled to release himself. But she, panting, clung to him with both hands.

"What are you trying to do!"

"You're coming home with me."

"I, after the way you've just humiliated me?"

"Humiliated you! Oh! Oh!"

He jerked himself loose, and reeled against the wall. But immediately, she fastened on him again. He was as much taken aback by her strength as by her courage. She seemed strange to him.

"Will you come home?"

"No!"

"But you will! You will, do you hear? You don't know me yet! I'll follow you everywhere! I'll cry out to every one how you treat me!"

Under the electric signs, a ring of faces swiftly took shape round them. Before the saloon doorway appeared Mr. Pandle, jauntily bewigged, his imitation eyebrows raised. And, all the while, Emma's voice, pitched in a strident key, proclaimed that she was Felix's wife, upbraided him for his neglect of her, paraded before the throng of spectators the secrets of his life. In short, there gushed from her lips pell-mell, like a torrent from a broken dam, all her accumulated grievances.

But she stopped short, and stared, aghast, at the hand with which he was distractedly straightening his cravat.

"The diamond ring! My ring!"

As a matter of fact, he had pawned it that very evening.

Propelled by shame, he thrust the spectators aside, and set out rapidly toward Second Avenue. She ran after him, again seized upon his arm, and, suiting her steps to his long strides, let him feel the full weight of her unavoidable person. From time to time, she uttered an incoherent gasp of menace.

The parlor of the flat enclosed him. His counter-action began:

"I might have expected it. Inborn vulgarity can't be concealed for long!"

Wait, did he not have a better attack than that

"up his sleeve"? Ah, Pavin's letter! Snatching it from his pocket, he shook it under her nose.

"Kindly explain what became of the three messages from my friend? Thanks to this one, which you weren't able to intercept, I know everything."

"Then you need no explanations."

"What," he shouted, "you confess to taking them?"

"And if I did? I felt in my bones that something was going on. Then those letters, written in French —so much caution! Oh, a woman can tell! Why, they seemed to burn my fingers! Yes, I kept them! And if they spoiled any of your wicked tricks, I'm doubly glad!"

He experienced, simultaneously with a hot thrill in the solar plexus, the necessity of destroying something. He was on the point of springing at her, when the bisque infant, crawling on the mantelshelf, attracted his attention. He whirled the ornament above his head, then dashed it into a thousand pieces at her feet.

A scream reverberated. She precipitated herself upon the fragments of that symbol.

"Oh, you devil! I hate you! I hate you!"

"That is what I have been waiting to hear you say," he answered. And, with his dog, he went out, expecting never to return.

Thanks to the diamond ring, he had more than a hundred dollars in his pocket. At Union Square, he threw himself into a public automobile, with the command, "Drive up Broadway." Soon the glitter

ing fronts of theatres and night restaurants were
streaming past him.

With Pat at his heels, he entered cafés decorated
in gilt and scarlet, where marble columns ended in
Corinthian capitals, and, behind expanses of mahogany, were displayed mural decorations of historic and allegorical import. The round tables
with carved legs, the waiters in their long aprons,
the men in evening dress who crowded through the
doorways during the intermissions of theatrical
performances going on near by, were, for Felix, like
fragments in a vision of the past. He wondered if he
was going to be confronted by Noon. But after he
had made the rounds of half a dozen cafés, he gave
up trying to distinguish the faces of his neighbors.

An incessant restlessness urged him from one spot
to another. No sooner had he comprehended a
group of strangers admiring the bull-terrier, than
he was elsewhere, conversing with a bartender who,
to his extreme self-complacency, remembered his
name. "But I must go." "Without finishing your
drink?" "That's so!" He gulped down his highball with the air of one who has committed an
almost unpardonable offence.

What was this place? A gloomy side street, a
baroque façade, a familiar doorway. It was the
stage entrance of the Trocadero Theatre.

Inside, the doorkeeper, before darkening the vestibule, was taking a last look at his features in a
cracked mirror. He turned round. The protuberance on his nose had grown to the size of a walnut.

"Well, what do you want!"

"Miss Sinjon?" Felix inquired, mechanically.

"She left here half an hour ago."

He had a spasm of alarm. Where was she? He hailed a hansom cab: then, with his foot on the cab step, he paused.

"Why, for the moment time had turned back, on its course, a year and more!"

He stumbled off toward Broadway, pursued by the sarcasms of the cab-driver.

And the lights, enlarged, melting together, forming on all sides an uninterrupted radiance, engulfed him, like a shining sea. He was borne hither and thither by chance contacts. Doors yawned before him: he drifted into places where electric globes rotated overhead, and the floors seemed furnished with inequalities. He rested his elbows on tables that he did not see, gazed at the necks of champagne bottles, received on his back the slaps of invisible persons, and in his ears the monotonous assurance that he was "a good fellow." Strains of music stole upon his senses; he burst into tears. He had an altercation with a man concerning the bull-terrier; when he tried to catch his opponent by the throat, a score of intermediaries suddenly swarmed round him. On a lonely street corner, he discovered that he had lost his overcoat. He walked straight ahead, but the same buildings appeared to follow him everywhere. Their foundations were shadowy, their upper stories were gray. It was the dawn.

Late that afternoon, an excruciating headache

roused Felix from a troubled sleep. He was lying, fully dressed, on the counterpane in a wretched hotel bedroom. Pat, perched on the edge of a washstand, was whining at the dry faucets.

Felix, however, knew better than to slake his own thirst with water. Dragging himself to the telephone, he ordered brandy, and victuals for the dog. On paying the waiter, he found that he had three dollars left.

But nausea seized him. He lay down quickly, and strove to collect his thoughts. What had happened?

At full recollection of the previous night's events, remorse completed his distress. He shrank back as if from the tacit condemnation of a multitude of unseen witnesses.

What if her despair had resulted in a dangerous illness? What if she had done herself some harm? Such thoughts brought him to his feet.

While trying to arrange his clothes, he was forced to pause, from time to time, with both hands on the bedpost, until his qualms had passed. His linen was soiled, his trousers were wrinkled, his shoes were covered with mud; but he had to go out thus disordered, unshaven, with drawn and yellowish visage.

It was already evening. Flurries of snow appeared above a confusion of glistening umbrellas.

The pavement, wet and black, seemed so nearly liquid that he hesitated to set one foot before the other. He kept close to the walls for fear that

passing trolley-cars "might run up on the sidewalk."
He took fright midway of street crossings, dodged
at a sound of hoofs, and, with perspiration rolling
down his cheeks, wished at the same instant to run
forward and to lie down. He got into a cab, but
the jolting of that vehicle over car tracks was intolerable. He pressed on afoot. The street lights
danced before him; and the roofs of tall buildings,
indistinct above a whirl of snowflakes, seemed to be
gradually toppling forward.

At Union Square, he hesitated. What was he
going to find at home? When he proceeded, it was
by a devious way, so that he might avoid as long
as possible a fulfillment of his premonitions.

Finally, he traversed Thirteenth Street. Between
Third and Second Avenues, where some shabby-
genteel lodging-houses displayed, behind the falling
snow, their crumbling stonework and cast-iron balconies made frail by rust, two women were conversing on a doorstep. One was a bareheaded, un-
symmetrical creature arrayed in a wrapper, with an
aureole of dishevelled hair. The other was Miss
Qewan.

Felix, in the attitude of a malefactor threatened with
detection, slipped past the ex-chorus girl unseen.

Second Avenue opened out before him. Yes, the
flathouse stood there still, unchanged in any part.
Almost reassured, he crossed the street.

At the head of the staircase, a white-robed figure
was awaiting him. Emma stretched out her hands.
He caught her to his breast.

"Oh, you've come back!"

And, for that magnanimity, she forgave him every-thing.

In the parlor, she sank into a chair: he knelt beside her. They gazed at each other with the blank looks of persons who have passed through a prolonged mutual agony. He observed all the ravages of grief in her white face. In a night, she had aged ten years.

Clad in a dressing-sack and a petticoat, she had remained, since dawn, at the front windows.

"And you, too, have been punished," she faltered, passing her fingers timidly through his hair. "But I? Oh, how cruel you were! How you've made me suffer!" Letting her head fall back, staring, wide-eyed and open-mouthed, at the ceiling, she recalled that suffering of hers—she described, with painful exactitude, her every pang.

Sobs issued from his throat.

"May I be struck dead if I ever speak an unkind word to you again! A new life begins for us to-night. Will you believe that, Emma?"

"Yes, yes; I'll try to believe you now."

But, of a sudden, she grew faint, and pressed her palms against her brow. "Her headache was more than she could bear."

"Have you taken anything for it?"

"It did no good. But get me a powder, any-way."

He put her to bed. Lying on her back, she moved her head from side to side. When a half hour had elapsed, she asked, in querulous, thin tones, for another headache powder. This she took, and, presently, was still. Felix, stretched beside her, fell asleep.

He was awakened by the clink of a glass tumbler.

"Emma?"

"I can't stand this pain."

"You mustn't take so much of that stuff. It's a dangerous depressant."

"I know."

Again he drifted into slumber.

But some one was calling him from a great distance. He sat up in bed, just as the clock struck two.

"Felix! Felix!"

It was Emma's voice, hardly audible.

He sprang up, lighted the gas, and bent over her. Her head was thrown back; her face and mouth had a bluish tinge; her skin was glazed with moisture. From between her parted lips came short, quick gasps.

"I feel so queer, so weak—my heart——"

Felix groped her pulse, which was small, soft, and nearly imperceptible. Her eyes—the pupils extraordinarily dilated—rolling very slowly toward him, denoted terror.

"Do something! Help me!"

He ran into the dining-room, returned with a bottle of brandy, held half a glassful to her lips. But the liquor ran down her chin, as she turned away her face, moaning, "Not that!"

He rushed into the public hallway, shouted, got no response. He dashed to a front window. The cold air blew into the parlor.

Second Avenue was white with snow; the atmosphere, however, was clear; and a pale lavender diffusion from the arc lamps on their tall metal poles was more serene and pure than moonlight. A man in a thin jacket was standing on the opposite corner.

"Get me a doctor, quick!"

The fellow looked up, hesitated, then set off, at full speed, toward Fourteenth Street. Felix returned to Emma.

The bluish hue had deepened in her face; her lips were violet-colored; the eyes, never before so large and black-looking, stared straight upward. Every moment, her head left the pillow, and her mouth, at the same time reaching out for air, imitated the spasmodic respiratory efforts of a fish drawn from its element.

Through the crack below the tilted mirror of the bureau, Lew watched this struggle.

Felix gathered her into his arms. So much to ask pardon for, so much to expiate, and no words producible except the hoarse protest:

"No! No! No!"

A look of recognition flickered into her eyes. With difficulty she achieved the speech:

"I've been a good wife—the sisters—a priest——"

She tried to gain back the breath that she had lost. She grew limp; the pupils disappeared beneath her lashes; after each gasp her mouth remained the longer open. But the almost inapprehensible utterance stole forth:

"You'll go back, now" . . . .

Later, in a murmur so tenuous that it seemed less like a vocal expression than a thought intuitively understood:

"You'll be famous. . . . You'll love other women" . . . .

Her mouth did not close again. He touched her wrist, and could not feel a pulse.

And he was invaded by a vast incredulity.

Two days after, on the thirtieth of March, she was buried in a Brooklyn cemetery. The last of her patrimony paid for a plot of ground—of minimum size—for the undertaker's services, and for the mass, that she would have desired, in a Roman Catholic church near by.

From the church door, the hearse was followed by one carriage, containing Felix and Pat. At the cemetery gate, the undertaker got down nimbly from beside the driver of the hearse, and, with three assistants all in suits of rusty black, bore the coffin, covered with white roses, its six silver-plated handles flashing, to the grave. There, it was enclosed in a pine box, and lowered, by means of ropes, into the pit. Two rough-looking fellows, armed with spades, turned sheepishly to Felix.

His lips trembled; he designated the undertaker.

"Go to work, boys," that functionary ordered, softly, with an apologetic cough.

A rhythmic rattling began.   The grave was filled with earth.

Felix walked back heavily amid mounds and tombstones.   In the distance, men and women were moving slowly, sometimes stooping, with a lingering gesture, to lay a blossom on a grave, sometimes standing, in lax attitudes of melancholy contemplation, before a sculptured monument.   The ground, covered with last year's grass, bore patches of melting snow.   Here and there, appeared wreaths and memorial devices, shrivelled and sodden, the rusty wires of their frameworks protruding through discolored rubbish.   Brilliant sunlight shone on this deterioration and decay of things which had been fresh, blooming, and alive.

The same sunlight, penetrating the flat in Second Avenue, glinted on the backs of the hand-painted chairs, on the dozen photographs of Emma in her finery of other days, on the foot of the brass bedstead.

There Felix stood motionless, listening.   But no sound reached him from the kitchen.

He fell upon his knees.

"Oh, Pat, that poor little thing!   That poor little thing!"

PART FOUR

NINA

CHAPTER XVI

ANXIOUS to escape at once from that environment, he sent for an auctioneer, who asked:

"Do you want a public sale?"

Felix recoiled from the thought of strangers tramping through her home. The auctioneer, accordingly, explored the rooms, appraised each article, and, after letting fall some words about "hard times" and "the scarcity of cash," offered the young man seventy-five dollars down for everything. Felix made a gesture of resignation. The other, looking surprised and discomfited, went off for his porters.

They stripped the flat. The bare aspect of the parlor recalled to Felix the day when he and she had come house-hunting. Just so others would come now. It seemed to him that the little, garish room ought to express, somehow, in perpetuity, the tragedy it had enclosed. And yet, the next tenants would never see, as he did whenever he turned round, a chimera dissolving in the shadows.

Now it took shape beyond a succession of open doors, in the kitchen; again, from the kitchen he saw it float before a parlor window. Lacking outline and substance, vaguer than any apparition of conventional report, less like a wraith, indeed, than a mere fall of shade at the passage of a cloud before the sun, it was, for Felix, indefinitely suggestive of her person—as if one had there some unfathomable analogy to the echo, lingering after the voice has died away. But when, taking his departure in the twilight, he laid hand upon the door-knob, did she not stand there, barring his exit in a well-remembered pose, her large eyes peering up at him, as who should say, in apprehension, "Where to?"

The snow had melted from the streets; the breeze was temperate: Spring seemed to have drawn near under cover of recent storms, now, with her imminence, to surprise the city weary of its winter. Soon, in the parks, the trees would weave their pale green webs above the tulip beds, bright song-birds would sail down adventuring, and the fragrance of magnolia and hawthorn blooms would cause the eyes of lovers to turn wistfully toward incompletely foliated bowers. Felix recalled a speech of Emma's, "When spring comes, I want to fly away, to some place far off, where I have never been."

Returning to the cemetery, he saw the marble headstone set in place, and strewed fresh blossoms on the grave. But, despite his previous materialistic theories, he felt she was not there. Such cares soon appeared as futile, as those of a devotee who tends a spot sanctified merely by tradition, where nothing has ever happened, or will happen. So, presently, he found himself thinking of her as translated to some region beyond the sunset or amid the stars; and the offerings that he made to her thereafter were of contrition and belated tenderness. He pored over the dozen photographs of Emma, prim in her various provincial-looking gala costumes: and the details in each portrait which, once on a time, had amused him, at last brought moisture to his eyes. He packed those souvenirs away; he could not bear them round him in his new lodgings.

Miss Qewan, meeting him one day in Union Square, had made bold to recommend the boarding-house where she was living. Situated on Thirteenth Street, between Second and Third Avenues, it was the dwelling where he had seen her standing on the doorstep.

The brown-stone front, four stories high, was scaling off in patches; the shutters, all askew, were losing their green paint. Draggled lace curtains hung in the lower windows; and the weather was not yet warm enough for the upper sills to lack their rows of milk bottles. The front door, raised three steps above the pavement, in a small vestibule, and surmounted by a rickety iron balcony, was so narrow as to make one wonder how the landlady, looming in the hallway, got out and in.

Mrs. Snatt was a worried-looking woman, clad in a loose wrapper, thin in the face but elsewhere corpulent, with a mop of almost colorless hair, and indistinct eyes and lips. Formerly a theatrical costumer, she had married, "when old enough to know better," a musician. Her husband running through her savings and confronting her with the necessity of bringing up some children, Mrs. Snatt had opened a house of board and lodging for "the profession."

Still, as she informed Felix in her most elegant manner, on seeing him she knew of no reason for drawing the line at the footlights.

By a "singular coincidence," the "second floor back" was unoccupied. Felix contemplated apathetically a square apartment, with a faded ingrain carpet considerably stained round the washstand, a folding-bed that imitated by day a chest of drawers, a bureau with initials scratched on the mirror, and some spring-seated chairs from which the padding was nearly gone. A what-not of ebony, originally supported by three legs, leaned in a corner, and bore on its top shelf the tinted clay figure of a matador who lacked a nose. The pallid walls, with some vertical, brownish streaks on them, were set off by two or three oil paintings that Mrs. Snatt had seen, with her own eyes, done "by hand," in the window of a shop where soap wrappers were exchanged for premiums.

The apartment overlooked the rear walls of buildings fronting on Fourteenth Street. Below, the yards, their board fences crumbling from the top, displayed their kitchen entries, garbage pails, and rubbish heaps. In some, old mattresses lay doubled up in puddles; the relics of chairs and sofas were sinking to the ground, battered bird-cages, stoves without feet, and broken bottles were piled up in masses, while here and there, over the débris, some fathoms of rusty wire spread large, erratic coils and angles, like the flamboyant signature of ruin. Along the fences, cats, flat as lathes, their shoulder bones accentuated, paced with a suave and furtive gait.

A bath adjoined the apartment; and if one desired only a light breakfast served in the room, the price would be six dollars a week.

Felix shrugged his shoulders. It would do till he "got upon his feet."

He removed the oil paintings and the clay matador, unpacked his books, set his mother's photograph upon the bureau. He repented having disposed of all Emma's furnishings. His dissatisfaction was not reduced when he found in the closet an old copy of *The Open Air Magazine*. It contained a picture of "Mr. Mortimer Fray's new country house"—an excellent specimen of Tudor architecture in brick, with lawns, some groups of clipped box-trees, a fish-pond lined with stone, and, in the foreground, a Russian wolfhound couchant beside a sun-dial.

But, to his surprise, he could not conjure up his old rage against the man. Other humiliations had intervened; and animosity against a single object had given place to a general rancor, because of its diffusion at once vaguer and more bitter. He wished nothing, now, of Fray except that the latter should never learn of this deterioration.

It was a house of slamming doors, of shrill outcries, of shaking chandeliers, and a monotonous booming of bass voices engaged, apparently, in histrionic declamation. Strong odors of fried bacon, of onions, and of cabbage were wafted up the narrow staircase; and one could not issue into the corridors without smelling cigarette smoke and cologne.

At night, he sometimes woke with a start, under the impression that the ceiling was coming down. This rumpus, he learned, was created by some acrobats who roomed above him, and whose artistic fervor drove them out of bed, apparently, from time to time—perhaps to practise feats which had occurred to them at that moment, between waking and sleeping, when so many seemingly brilliant thoughts flash through the brain.

Every morning, before Felix was ready to arise, a clatter of pianos began up and down the block. Then one heard "the latest popular airs" repeated a hundred times, the interminable scales of aspirants for concert honors, the shout of hopeful barytones, and the guffaw that punctuated the low comedian's song. It became a competition, that uproar. Felix, with an oath, got up and rang the bell.

His breakfast was brought upstairs by the servant, an angular drudge named Delia, with big feet in broken shoes, and displaying, under frowzy hair, a pair of dull eyes and a patient smile.

She stood at the foot of the bed, twisting up a spotted apron in hands that appeared already to have sifted tons of ashes, scrubbed acres of floors, and washed a myriad greasy pans: and with one foot advanced toward the door, and her body half turned, she seemed continually ready to take flight. When she had recovered somewhat from her embarrassment before "so fine a gentleman," Delia enlightened Mr. Piers about his neighbors.

In the "ground floor front," a female, seldom seen, sat all day in a darkened room, behind a crystal ball, professing to bring back sweethearts grown indifferent, to restore lost articles, and to disclose the name of "the other woman." The rear was occupied by Mrs. Snatt and her three small children, of whose presence below Felix needed no announcement, since he heard them, at all hours, whining, bawling, and being spanked. Occasionally, he saw them in the back yard, wandering over an oblong plat of barren earth, beneath a net-work of clothes lines. The boy was a stupid-looking child with too large a head and spasmodic gestures. The little girl, pale and languid, walked unsteadily. Mrs. Snatt's third offspring, a babe in arms, of indeterminable sex, seemed, on the contrary, to judge from the redness of its face and the power of its lungs, excessively robust. Mr. Snatt was not at home. One gathered, from Delia, that the only time he gave his family this treat was when his wife had more than "cleared expenses."

On the second floor, directly in front of Felix's apartment, dwelt a theatrical couple somewhat advanced in years, known to the public as "The Delaclaires, King and Queen of Polite Vaudeville." Their son—a youth who, according to Delia, "wasn't much"—slept in the adjacent hall bedroom.

The upper regions were inhabited by various actors and actresses. Sometimes Felix encountered on the stairs a short, thin-faced damsel, always attired in the most girlish hats and dresses, a psyche-knot of straw-colored hair protruding backward six inches from her neck. She left behind her a trail of perfume of that sort which causes persons in the street to stop and look round in astonishment.

Miss Qewan also lived overhead; and Felix, one day meeting her in the vestibule, was curious to know why she had chosen this abode.

She assured him that when he knew the habits and ambitions of the other lodgers, he would change his mind about them.

"And yet you've not gone back to the chorus?"

"That's different."

She was now cashier in a restaurant on lower Broadway. This position she had obtained through the friendly offices of the "right sort of man"—a disinterested benefactor.

"He's a saloon keeper. But not what you'd expect."

"I know some excellent saloon keepers," Felix made haste to assure her. But she gave him a sad look that put him out of countenance.

"And you, I suppose, are writing?"

He responded, with a mirthless laugh:

"As you can see, I've found literature a poor crutch."

Nevertheless, next day he had a stroke of luck. He was accepted provisionally as a reporter on *The Torch*, an evening newspaper of revolutionary tendencies and a large circulation, published on Park Row. His salary was fixed at twenty dollars a week.

He breathed again the air smelling of printer's ink, paper, pipe smoke, and dusty floors; he was surrounded by a familiar clatter; he experienced the ennui that had beset him in the office of *The Evening Sphere*. But the two newspapers were intrinsically dissimilar.

In the pages of *The Torch*, accuracy was a negligible quality; mendacity which produced a thrill was an accomplishment; trivial facts were inflated recklessly by fancy in order that headlines a foot deep might shock the general eye; and, to excite the emotionalism of the masses, the part of criminals was taken in murder trials, the rich were crudely caricatured for their wealth and, at the same time, remarked obsequiously for their expensive entertainments, while the editorial articles, reduced to the simplest terms, bristled with praises of "the common people," and abuse of "moneyed tyrants." The reporters held their breath when the great man who wrote these essays, on a salary of thirty thousand dollars a year, stalked, with impassive visage, to his automobile.

After work, the young man stopped at the boarding-house for the bull-terrier, which the servant, from admiration of Felix, had been stuffing with scraps of food all day. In a restaurant on West Fourteenth Street he dined for a half dollar. Afterward, he entered Quilty's saloon.

For a while, he had remained away from this resort through delicacy. But other places in that neighborhood were not the same: and he had argued that, after all, the living were exculpated for indulging even in bereavement their habitual appetites. It was invariably with a faint tremor of anticipation that he glimpsed the bar, the mirrors, the pyramids of glasses which the bartender was always polishing and rearranging—a task never finished.

There, business was good. Situated on a thoroughfare where many cheap concert halls lured from surrounding districts crowds of humble pleasure-seekers, the dram shop caught every day new cus' tomers, youthful, vigorous, settled in employment, promising protracted patronage. As a result, Mr. Quilty was not troubled by the bugbear of saloon keepers operating in less populous regions—by the apprehension, namely, that incipient drinkers would not, sufficiently for continued profit, replace the worn out and bankrupt.

Clean shaven, carefully dressed, showing a gold watch chain and the emblem of a benevolent society, he received graciously, in his place between the cashier's desk and the cigar stand, the respectful salutations of the immature, and the trite flippancy of the middle-aged. Sometimes, closing the back room to feminine trade, he retired with corpulent, ruddy Irishmen in fancy waistcoats, to concoct stratagems, against constrictive legislation, of which mere customers could only guess the brilliancy. But despite his political importance, Mr. Quilty never failed to pass the time of day with Felix, whom he approached with an air at once propitiating

and self-conscious. At times, he referred to his
daughters. They ought to learn French and music?
He understood that there was a school in Connecticut where young ladies were taught everything
fashionable—even the proper way to enter a carriage. His apparent idea was to remove his children
ultimately from all associations that could readily
recall their origin. Meanwhile, they ought to have
some one in the position of a mother. And the saloon
keeper, after looking at Felix vacantly, remarked:

"I hear you're boarding at Mrs. Snatt's?" A
lady had told him so.

"Miss Qewan," ejaculated Felix. "Why, then
you must be——"

A blush brought into prominence Mr. Quilty's
scar. He made haste to explain that friendship.

He had seen her grow up on the "East Side," the
reputable daughter of a policeman. Left an orphan
while in her teens, she had suffered, as a result of
too much trustfulness, in a familiar manner. From
that time, life had been an uphill road for her.
Quilty, meeting her recently, had obtained for her
the position in a Broadway restaurant.

"And, mind ye, as good a woman as you'll find
anywheres!"

"Moreover, deserving of something better," Felix
assented, heartily.

Quilty rubbed his chin, and looked uncomfortable.

He was relieved by the appearance of a fat, good-
natured fellow of forty-five, in a baggy sack suit,
with a large mustache, and slightly protruding eyes.

"Mr. Piers, shake hands with my brother-in-law, Mr. Connla."

The stranger stared intently at Felix, suppressed a grin, and inquired of his relative, in a gruff voice:

"Where's Pandle?"

The bewigged habitué, of mysterious occupation, was not there. Quilty, with an expression of disgust, exclaimed:

"Has he been working again!"

"That's a question. I'll hunt him; but you warn him meantime, d'ye see, for I've nothing against him personally." Then, turning to the young man, with a twinkling eye,

"You'll not remember me?"

He identified himself as the detective who had rescued Felix, one night, from some negroes.

"And that was a good bull-terrier, too! Have you got him yet?"

Felix whistled to Pat, who was standing on his hind legs before the "free lunch" buffet. The detective, squatting down, made friends with the dog at once.

But he declared that the beast was too fat, that he was "losing his lines." Felix had to admit the justice of this criticism. Pat got too much food and not enough exercise; so that his neck and body were becoming heavy, while his white head, covered with the pink scars of many battles, was taking on that swollen, battered look noticeable in good dogs permitted to "run to seed."

"He's been neglected, that terrier," was the

detective's blunt comment. "He's done too much time loafing in kitchens and looking at ugly people. Faith, it's the truth—a dog gets to look like the place he's in, as a man does, too. He needs, now, exercise, and handsome faces round him. Leave me have him on Sundays: I'll take him for a twelve mile walk into the counthry, and he'll get both his requirements at once."

On several occasions, the detective returned to the saloon. Pandle, he confessed, had proved himself to be "temporarily an honest man." Felix found Mr. Connla an entertaining person.

Of a sanguine and impulsive disposition, he was better known for bravery than for such subtle talents as inform the traditional secret agent. He had, however, learned, from long contact with human nature in its crises, to be astonished at nothing, to regard without indignation the utmost depravity, to find in every delinquent, whether devoted to petty villainy or to great, something perhaps not alien to himself. In fine, he was a philosopher: and to stand beside him, on summer evenings, in front of Quilty's windows, while with one racy phrase he tore the mask, so to speak, from the visages of passers-by, was, in Felix's opinion, a "liberal education." Once, Mackeron, formerly the tenor of "The Lost Venus," now shabbier, sallower, and more nearly expressionless than ever, passed with a nod. Connla genially inquired of Felix:

"Who's your friend the dope fiend?"

"You can't mean that man!"

"Why, me boy, look at the wooden face of him, and them little points of eyes. It's cocaine or morphine, and, for my choice, cocaine. Ask him some day in his ear for a pinch o' the white stuff. I'll go bail that he'll projuice it."

Felix did not re-enter the saloon that night.

Was there not even a sinister similarity between his case and Mackeron's? Once more he woke to full realization of his predicament, like a wayfarer, wandering in the darkness, who, at a lightning flash, finds himself surrounded by the most appalling perils.

He sat down to discover the secret of this weakness, apparently unalterable.

He reviewed his innumerable revulsions from debauchery, his momentary states of continence, his relapses. He marvelled at the swiftness with which, in him, intense repentance had ever been followed by impatience of restraint. He tried to understand the rapid change from disgust to fresh desire, wherein, invariably, a host of arguments, ingeniously evolved, to prove his vices detrimental, had with well-nigh inconceivable rapidity lost all value. He asked himself "Why he was not like other men," who could restrain themselves from ruinous excesses.

But he remained without an answer to his query.

Thereupon, he attempted to alarm himself with the direst of forebodings. He followed vagabonds reeling along the curb, to impress upon his mind the picture of their degradation. He got his associates to recount stories of lives wrecked by drink. He listened to evangelists preaching temperance on street corners, and, departing, with homely exhortations ringing in his ears, swore that he had stood for the last time at a bar. Also, he repudiated tobacco, which seemed to increase his thirst for liquor. For an hour or two, he would observe men streaming in and out of cafés and tobacco shops with feelings of commiseration.

Or perhaps, walking at night, beneath the moon, in parts of town where no such temptations were to be met, he experienced, all unexpectedly, a belief, in the beginning faint and tremulous, that he had finally left his frailty behind. From the wide-spread fulguration of the clouds, on the path of the moonlight, through the breathless ether, serenity flowed down into his heart; and an exaltation that drew value from the beauty, the immensity, and the purity of space, raised his whole body toward those heights which the soul instinctively informs with an eternal holiness. Then a presence, impalpable and yet undeniable, was closer to him than the nearest human being: and it needed apparently but a short continuation of this ecstasy to disembody forever the spirit already half released. His gazed roamed the heavens; his lips parted; the words broke from him, "Yes, I feel it now! I have been wrong. You are there! You have been there all the while! You will be there forever!" And stretching out his arms, he pleaded:

"Save me now!"

Could one sink again, after soaring to such altitudes? He went home sure that his nature had been altered to its depths.

But afterward, he could not avoid wondering at the simplicity of his release. He asked himself, "Is it not strange, that I feel none of my old desires?" His condition soon seemed to him almost too good to last: he was expecting, at every sight of swinging doors and tobacconists' effigies, other sensations, as one expects, at the tridiurnal sight of a dining-room, a recurrence of hunger.

"They will return, no doubt, those cravings. Well, I must be on the watch, and, at their approach, spring to arms."

Then, while wondering at their delay in laying siege to him, he felt their onslaught. At once, his contemplated manœuvres all forgotten, he was like a warrior, enfeebled by the remembrance of innumerable defeats, who sees at hand the crest of an enemy that has always worsted him.

"How weak I am!" And each confession of weakness made his next overthrow the easier.

Sometimes, pausing in a deserted street at midnight, he raised his burning eyes toward the stars. "What a fool I was! Of all living things, only man is so fatuous, so conceited, as to believe himself worthy of immortality and the attentions of a god. A god, indeed! Well, supposing that there is one, a pretty world he has made, this time!"

With distorted face, he shouted, ironically:

"I say, up there! This is a sorry mess, this particular job! May a tenant, who didn't seek his accommodations, presume to enter a complaint?"

Silence fell. A chill ran down his back.

Everything in life irritated him—the commonplace remarks of strangers, the stupid conduct of persons with whom he had nothing to do, the injustice of acts which harmonized with public opinion. When he read the newspapers, he growled at "the imbecility and vulgarity of humanity at large." An obstruction of traffic enraged him. A collar that did not button easily he tore into shreds.

The disgust that he felt for everything connected with the boarding-house resulted in unprecedented outbursts. He would have liked to wring the necks of Mrs. Snatt's children screeching at one another in the back yard; the noises that re-echoed nightly through the corridors excited in him an intense longing to "cut the throats of the whole gang."

But such violent moments were all solitary; his savagery, from cowardice, died out at the first word of ordinary intercourse: and none would have suspected, from his conversation, that he was often shaken, in secret, by a homicidal frenzy.

It must have been generally observed, however, toward the middle of summer, that he was growing eccentric.

While talking with an acquaintance, he became absent-minded, gazed into space, finally uttered an inappropriate comment. At Quilty's, he would leave a gathering of revellers without excuses or farewells; and, at times, in the midst of a silence, he would raise his head abruptly, as if some one had called him. Truth is, he was frequently obsessed by this belief, particularly on a day following an exceptional drinking bout. He heard his name pronounced behind his back, but, on turning round, found no one near him. These voices usually resembled those of his companions of the previous evening. Once, though, he was frightened to hear a treble intonation like Emma's.

"Am I losing my mind?"

Connla, to whom he confessed, in guarded language, this delusion, assured him, with a hearty laugh, that it was a natural concomitant of "the morning after." Then, putting on a look of concern and approaching his protruding eyes to Felix's, the detective added:

"As a matter of fact, if you'll excuse the liberty, you'd do best by letting up a bit on Quilty's stuff, relation of mine though he may be. Take a run into the counthry. It'd do that terrier a world o' good, besides. Or, at least, get some business that'll occipy all your time."

This was what Felix was attempting to do; for he had just been discharged summarily from *The Torch*.

He visited the editors of Sunday newspapers, with "special stories," of a kind that could be illustrated by sensational pen-pictures reproduced over tints. These were tales of half-forgotten "soldiers of fortune," tragical histories of famous jewels, romances of old ships, anecdotes of Revolutionary landmarks. For such work, he received eight dollars a column;

but the demand was limited, and "one did not think of a new theme every day." He still had too much spare time on his hands.

If only he could gather energy and wit enough to begin "that masterpiece!" He picked up Pierre Buron's book. "Oh, fortunate wanderer in the labyrinth, who did not lose himself before leaving behind his relic!"

When he took pen in hand, an excruciating restlessness possessed him. He rose to pace the floor; he saw his hat lying on a chair; on approaching the door, he could not restrain himself from dashing out.

Through byways in the district where he lived, he pursued, with the same wistfulness as in the past, the mirage of pleasure, now exceedingly dilute. And yet, just before his every disillusionment, when he seemed on the point of holding fast that which he was attempting to embrace, he discovered in the most uninspiring material something winsome—the tenuous charm that may lurk, for the inordinately desirous soul, beneath the meanest of superficies.

Again, in desperation, reduced to a state of flaccidity that shamed him, he frequented vaudeville shows, "smoking concerts," and dime museums where, in the midst of languid men, he stood before the lecturer's platform, listening to pompous absurdities with a feeling that he was already wasted, finished, thrown away.

At last, the monotony of familiar places became almost unbearable. Since the days were growing shorter, he walked, for a change, uptown.

One evening, at Fifth Avenue and Thirty-fourth Street, his notice was attracted by a sign in the window of an art dealer's shop, which read, "View of M. Paul Pavin's 'Portrait of Lady and Child.'"

Passing through an exhibition gallery, where the walls were crowded with many oil paintings in gilt frames, he entered a room hung with curtains of maroon velvet, and containing but one picture, revealed, straight ahead, beneath a flood of yellow light. A woman in a Nile green, iridescent evening dress was leaning forward, with a fluid movement, toward a cradle which occupied the foreground.

It was Nina.

The automobile was at the door; some scene of gayety—a dinner party, or, maybe, a dance—was waiting; and now, before setting out, the mother had entered the nursery to bid her child good-night. Bending over the cradle, with hands half unclasped before her breast, she was portrayed as her attitude of caution melted into a movement preliminary to a caress. For the baby, its small, round head half hidden by the swelling of the pillow, had opened its eyes; and on its face was displayed an expression of rapt wonder, at sight of the vision, exquisitely shining, that hovered over it.

She had changed, perhaps. Her face had taken on the aspect of completion which sometimes, with motherhood, enriches intricately a beauty previously simple. And, thanks to a painter better known for cynicism than tenderness, there was exhaled from the canvas, notwithstanding the glamour of the ball dress, something of the atmosphere that pervades, in cathedrals, certain pictures of maternity.

Felix let his hands fall to his sides.

This, then, was what he had lost!

CHAPTER XVII

Dɪᴅ her child content her? Did her husband please her? Where was she now? What was the tenor of her life?

He seemed to see her, clad in a dress of dull-blue silk, stooping to tend, with curling fingers, the flowers in a garden border. Or, ruddy and with wind-blown locks, she sat her horse in a gray skirt and a white linen waist, while from the hand encased in a stained glove there dangled a riding-whip. Again, her neck was bare, and decked with turquoises; her hair pressed down about her brows in a thick braid, like a fillet; and nothing could have been more vivid than his visualization of her face— the alert eyes that searched his countenance, the upper lip lifted to a point as if inviting kisses, the softness and the candor of a look that he, on a night of smothered stars and perfumed foliage, had finally understood.

"It is true: once upon a time, she offered herself to me!"

That thought amazed him.

For she inhabited a gentle and luxuriously furnished world, to which rumors of ignobility and of shabbiness penetrated no more distinctly than the whine of a mendicant's accordeon filtering through the window draperies of a ball room.

He fell to pondering the various stages of his withdrawal from that sphere.

Eileen, Marie, Emma! In each of these he should have perceived, before the irrevocable step, an instrument formed as if expressly for his deterioration. And yet, toward the last as toward the first, he had been impelled by a longing both subtle and irresistible.

To love, to be loved, not tranquilly, but intensely, not once, but often! Perhaps this desire was not to be separated from his other craving? No doubt the two, symptomatic of an unquenchable appetency for inordinate emotions, went hand in hand?

Still, if the gratification of his sentimental yearnings had been painful, the reminiscences that lingered held a tenuous charm. Often, in moments of relaxation, he had a quick thrill of memory: he recalled a period now strangely sweet to think of, but in experiencing which he had known only mental confusion and distress. Whenever he lamented, "If only I could begin again, and escape my follies!" the remonstrance was intruded, "But, in that case, what reveries I should miss!"

Now, however, his life again lacked a romantic object. And thoughts of Nina began to occupy his mind.

She, though possibly even in the same city, was as far removed from him as are the princesses of children's fairy tales in their palaces fashioned out of one mammoth pearl; and her very inaccessibility soon evoked an interest enriched by pathos, of a bewitching novelty because necessarily idealistic, absorbing, finally, all Felix's habitual considerations of the horizon that could not be approached, the mirage visible only from afar, the dream one never attained.

Had she forgotten him? Surely, at times, a chance word, a sound of long-familiar music, the tint of a sunset from a hilltop, or the odor of tuberoses, made her pause and think of Felix. And who could say but that into such reveries intruded some regrets? When familiar presences lost their attractiveness, when repetition induced sensations of monotony, did she never send conjectures winging forth into the unknown, with the query, "What if it could have been otherwise?"

Then there was a bond between them still!

Besides, the white bull-terrier was a gift of hers. Putting his arm round the dog's neck, Felix whispered into an ear made ragged by the teeth of many a four-footed enemy:

"I must take better care of this old fellow!"

He forbade Delia, the housemaid, to feed Pat. He laid in a store of dog biscuits, bathed the brute every morning, and kept the brass-bound collar polished. On Sundays, he frequently relinquished his pet to the detective, for a run through the fields, along the New Jersey Palisades.

Connla—on his "day off" an enthusiastic pedestrian—inveigled Felix, once or twice, on autumn afternoons, into a ten-mile tramp to the north of the city. But the young man came back from such jaunts exhausted, with the appearance of a person who, in the detective's phrase, had been "chased by the Indians." In fact, the degeneration of his muscles, the disability of his lungs, and the irregular action of his heart, prevented Felix from continuing those excursions. His wanderings rarely extended far from Fourteenth Street.

There the signs of penny arcades, shooting galleries, and "medical museums" were spread out above bemirrored doorways; dirty awnings everywhere let down their scalloped edges; the thoroughfare was obstructed by cubical showcases containing nickel-plated toilet sets, false teeth, flimsy waistcoats, and roughly printed post-cards; while shop-keepers in slack trousers stood on their thresholds, the "pullers in" of clothing merchants paced back and forth with predacious eyes, the door-keeper of a concert hall, armed with a club, drove ragamuffins from before the bill-boards, and, amid the crowd, women of various ages, with bobbing plumes and switching skirts, exhibited their complaisant faces, their draggled petticoats, and their shoes run down at the heels.

The October rains came to wash this avenue: then winter reached town; and, an hour after every fall of snow, brown slush, churned into mud by a multitude of feet, covered the pavements. The street where stood Mrs. Snatt's boarding-house was, apparently, of too little importance often to be cleared. Heaps of snow, accumulating along the gutters, were buried under dirt and rubbish; grocers' wagons, drawing up in front of doorways, sank to their hubs; and, whenever thaws set in, a chilly dampness was exhaled on the night air. Old men, with their hands pressed against their throats, went along coughing. Mrs. Snatt's two eldest children fell ill.

For that matter, she was usually worried about both of them.

The boy, six years old, suffered from nervous irritability, and slight, involuntary muscular contractions. He would sit for hours with his large head lowered, his mouth open, his eyes vacant; then, abruptly looking upward, he would give vent to a prolonged howl. Talking a jargon comprehensible only to his mother, he could not be made to study his primer, and, indeed, seemed incapable of learning anything. When crossed, Willie went into fits of rage, threw himself upon the floor, beat his face with his hands, and screamed. Besides, he was almost as badly off as Job for boils.

The four-year-old girl did not enjoy the chubbiness usual in children of her age. With wan eyes and a fixed, listless smile, she dragged her spindling legs along; and the hairless doll that she fondled was scarcely less responsive than Jennie to surprises. Her face brightened, however, when Pat appeared before her with grinning jaws; and once, when Felix brought home a new doll with taffy-colored curls, he was rewarded by a slowly gathering expression of beatitude.

But the baby, its cheeks round and rosy, its tiny

mouth continually blowing bubbles of saliva, crowed, winked, and beat its short arms against its bib from lustihood.

"By George," Felix complimented Mrs. Snatt, "this little chap is vigorous enough."

"Oh, yes," the landlady assented, with an uneasy look.

She was harassed, in addition, by business cares. Her tenants, for the most part transient, sometimes disappeared leaving behind a battered trunk full of newspapers and bricks. The clairvoyant, in the ground floor front, a specialty of whose it was to direct patrons toward the road to wealth, contemplated the abandonment of her profession. This soothsayer, it appeared, was eaten up with chagrin because she did not have "the luck of some people" —of a woman, for instance, who, with great profit, was establishing a fashionable trade uptown, "an interloper"—in fine—"that called herself Mme. Babbage."

Then, too, "The King and Queen of Polite Vaudeville" were likely, at any time, to receive the most flattering offers in respect of a long tour.

Mr. Delaclaire, a short, bow-legged, bull-necked person of fifty, with the lineaments of a Roman Emperor in hard luck, had made his neighbor's acquaintance by the simple expedient of "borrowing" a match. An introduction to his wife was inevitable; so Felix made his bow before a stout, domestic-looking woman of middle age, whose hair had nearly all reassumed its original brown, and whose shape, in corsets that sank inward just below the breast, recalled the fashion plates of other days.

When young, Mrs. Delaclaire had carried a spear in theatrical productions full of good and wicked sprites, of transformation scenes, of disappearing demons, and of red fire. In her hours of relaxation she had met the Thespian, who, at that time, by the aid of thickened shoe-soles, had even played such rôles as *The Ghost of Hamlet's Father*, and *An Old Fellow Set Up to Personate Vincentio*. Though they earned their living, nowadays, by performing farces in cheap vaudeville theatres, he had not entirely abandoned his belief that he was a pattern for a Shakespearian actor; and, occasionally, carried away by glimpses of old visions, he threw himself into an attitude, humped his back, put on a distracted look, and bellowed, in a way to shake the window-panes:

> "I think there be six Richmonds in the field;
> Five have I slain to-day, instead of him:
> A horse! a horse! my kingdom for a horse!"

Of mornings, when he heard Felix moving about, Mr. Delaclaire frequently shouted through the partition for "a loan" of the newspaper. Then the young man found the Thespian still in bed, with his bristly dewlaps resting on the upper hem of the counterpane.

"Aha! Salutations! Is it cold to-day? Good! Then I can wear my fur coat!"

He had, indeed, such a garment, between brown and green, cut in at the back, boasting a wealth of ravelled frogs; while the pelt with which it was lined—of some yellowish animal unknown to Felix—had not given out before furnishing a pair of cuffs.

The couple cooked late breakfasts in a saucepan, over the gas jet, kept bottles of beer on the outer window-sill, sent two shirts and a petticoat to the laundry every week, maintained a high state of negligé so long as they remained indoors, sailed out arm in arm, with all their finery on their backs, lived from day to day, were fond of each other.

Their offspring was named Edwin Booth Delaclaire. Felix sometimes saw a lean youth of seventeen, pale, loutish, with elusive eyes, who spent his time consuming cigarettes before saloons, in the company of hoodlums wearing lavender stockings and green glass cravat pins. As a child, the son had assisted his parents on the stage, disguised in velveteen suits, lace collars, and angelic wigs: he had thrilled audiences by reconciling husband and wife about to part, by awakening with his innocent prattle the conscience of a burglar, by expiring with a long speech advising his father to be a better man. But now, too old to be spanked into submission, he rebelled against that occupation, refused, moreover, to work at anything, drank cocktails, kept questionable company, seldom came home except to sleep or to demand money from his parents, of whom he was obviously ashamed. Mr. Delaclaire confessed to Felix that "Eddie" was a source of worriment to him.

"The career we expected of that child! The newspaper clippings I can show you! The talents he ought to have inherited!"

And Delaclaire launched into family history.

His own father, long a member of the theatrical company of Edwin Booth, had been the most fiery *Tybalt*, the fiercest *Laertes*, of his day. "Not to mention that he was a wild one off the boards, as well as on them. The whiskey he could get away with! To tell the truth, if it hadn't been for that, he might have played *Romeo*—yes, or *Hamlet*, under Booth's very nose."

"Such a heritage of talent should be valuable," was Felix's polite comment.

"And yet," mused Mr. Delaclaire, "others manage without it. Look at Miss Vinnie Vatelle, upstairs. She does song and dance, with three changes, in the vaudeville circuit: her act goes big; and yet her father was quite an ordinary feller—a plumber, I think."

Miss Vinnie Vatelle was the thin-faced damsel with the straw-colored psyche-knot. Felix made her acquaintance through Mrs. Delaclaire, who professed that "the poor girl was dying to meet him."

Though her cheeks were rouged, she appeared tired; and the rice powder which she had rubbed under her light blue eyes had settled at the roots of her lashes.

Looking up at Felix coyly, she inquired, in a flat voice:

"You don't eat in the house, I notice, Mr. Piers?"

He explained that his affairs took him too much abroad.

"I don't blame you. The food's nothing extra, and all my instincts goes against basement dining-rooms. They're so—I don't know—so——"

She shrugged her shoulders in an imitation of patrician haughtiness.

Nearly every night, thereafter, he met her on the stairs. She hesitated; he paused in his ascent; they leaned against the balustrade to talk. If he was sober enough, they sat down on the landing, their feet stretched across the second step below them. Her shoes, with fawn-colored cloth tops considerably soiled, and crumpled toes of patent leather, were short and broad. The perfume that she wore was of so flagrant an aroma as to make Felix dizzy. While conversing, Miss Vatelle munched chewing gum.

She was always ready to talk about "her art," her struggles, and her early life. She gave him to understand that she had been married when "very, very young." That relationship had soon ended on account of incompatibility of temper. He was a clerk in a provincial hotel: she had met him while travelling the vaudeville circuit. Soon she was going to start off again on tour; and one evening, her departure being imminent, when Felix met her in the corridor, she burst into tears.

At first, she would give no explanation of this grief. Finally, however, she stammered:

"Hasn't a woman always got the right to cry about a wedding?"

"A wedding!"

Miss Qewan, he was informed, had just been married quietly to her benefactor. They had gone, for their honeymoon, to Niagara Falls.

That night, in Quilty's saloon, champagne was served to the habitués. The merry-making was marred by only one incident: Mr. Pandle, relaxing his pessimistic visage to essay some seasonable quip, had his wig knocked off his head by the bartender.

When Quilty returned, the young man was among the quickest to offer him congratulations.

"And Mrs. Quilty's little sister, who is away at school?"

The bartender, after scrutinizing Felix for a moment, responded, briefly:

"She'll live with us."

But Mrs. Snatt now had another room unoccupied. Besides, her husband unexpectedly returned.

At nightfall, Delia, wringing her grimy hands, brought the news upstairs. One knew what to expect thenceforth! Bills would be run up at wineshops; money paid out by tenants would pass into the prodigal's pocket; the landlady would economize still further; the boarders would rail against the food; and, in the midst of threats, altercations, departures, tears, infantile wails, and general frenzy, the author of these misfortunes would continue to indulge an insatiable thirst.

"But why doesn't she throw him into the street?" inquired Felix.

"Ah, sir, that's not so aisy, either, the way things is in this house. Bad cess to him! Would you just listen to that?"

A shout rose from the back yard.

"Delia! You come downstairs this minute and run my errand! Am I the master here, or ain't I?"

In the failing light, beneath the stretched clothes-lines, a squat figure oscillated clumsily. A broad face was upturned, with dyed side whiskers running into a mustache, a face on which Felix thought to perceive a narrow mask, dull red, extending across the nose. But this proved to be an eruption from alcoholic poisoning.

Mr. Snatt was the ex-drummer of the Trocadero Theatre.

He soon fulfilled the various predictions made of him. And, not unlike Nero, plucking at a harp while Rome burned down, the inebriate, with his wife's venture tottering about his ears, occasionally got out his snare-drum and a tattered score of "Poet and Peasant," the drummer's part of which opera he rehearsed from overture to finale, rocking in his chair, compressing his large lips, rolling his eyes in their inflamed sockets, and, no matter how far gone in liquor, not omitting so much as a flourish. At last, Mrs. Snatt overcame her delicacy and asked Felix for eighteen dollars due her.

He was nearly beside himself for lack of money.

So slowly did his brain evolve ideas, that it took

him a week to write a "special story" for the Sunday newspapers. Then, too, his time for such performances was limited: the middle of the day was generally the only period when he could set pen to paper with profitable effect.

But in Quilty's saloon, he met the proprietor of an establishment where moving pictures were devised. This person needed the services of a writer endowed with sufficient imagination and dramatic instinct to construct brief scenarios appropriate for performance, in dumb show, before the camera. Fifteen dollars was the price paid for the average manuscript.

It was, at least, a chance.

Felix, reflecting that the patrons of Fourteenth Street theatres rarely paid an admission fee of more than ten cents, recollected melodramas the crude "situations" of which had formerly filled him with pity for their authors. He dismissed from his mind his last aspirations toward subtlety, poetry, and technical excellence in exposition; he invited, instead, those motives of inordinate heroism, villainy, and self-sacrifice attaining the excessive climaxes so satisfactory to the leaders of dull lives, who, untroubled by an access of logic, glimpse, in the feverish adventures of protagonists exquisitely valiant and magnanimous, something of their own secret longings.

So, in Felix's scenarios, the heads of convicts were surrounded by halos of nobility, the hero stopped the heroine's runaway horse, "the papers" were discovered in the nick of time, the villain was hand-cuffed by half a dozen policemen, the lovers fell into each other's arms, and, in the midst of large gestures, revolver shots, and disguises thrown off instan-taneously, virtue triumphed, and vice grovelled in dismay. The young man was able to pay Mrs. Snatt, to buy new shoes and an overcoat, to see more money disappear into Mr. Quilty's till.

His expenditures in the saloon had resulted in a trifling economy elsewhere. He was no longer under the necessity of paying for breakfast, as he could swallow no food till mid-day.

It had become for him a matter of course to relapse after good resolutions. His hours of con-tinence, grown shorter, now, than ever, were fraught with apprehensions.

The sight of bars, of café signs, even of advertise-ments, in the trolley-cars and the newspapers, lauding an especial brand of whiskey, were to him all sym-bols of the power that had mastery over him. He would have tried to flee them; he averted his eyes; but they, unavoidable, like a hydra in a nightmare, multiplied about him at his every turn: on dead walls, in glittering windows, overhead—at night—in brilliant signs that vanished but to spring forth immediately against the stars, or above doorways illumined by a warm radiance, the portals of which seemed to give inward, on their well-oiled hinges, at the slightest pressure, as do the mechanisms of pitfalls.

Still, in the depths of his heart, there languished part of the aspiration of his early youth, which inebriety resuscitated. His surroundings rendered vague, his decline forgotten, he reproduced, to some extent, old ardors, dreamed of recovery, found the thought of quick reform not unreasonable. Raising his head, to cast round him a look both wavering and proud, he bade farewell to the scenes that he was enduring "for the last time." Next morning, however, that self-confidence had failed.

When he went out, a threnody as if of supernatural voices dominated the noises of the street, while familiar sounds seemed to reach him from a great distance. Pedestrians floated past like shadows; and all faces, appearing to him through a sort of haze, assumed an unnatural aspect. Was it a real world through which he took his way, or was his the only actual personality extant? At times, the countenance of Emma, now difficult to recall in its entirety, was not more ambiguous than the visages that loomed round him.

His depression relieved by his morning drinks of brandy, he thought, perhaps, of a hilltop spread with flowers, where he had bade farewell to happiness.

Did she still spend part of her summers there? Then the garden at night, the hillside at sunset, the narrow roadway through the woods at noon, recalled to her a dead romance. Did she travel? Then, in Swiss valleys and before antiquated French chateaux, she missed the response of an enthusiasm once quick to complete her own. Was she in town? Then she found sadness inextricable from some ball, and, at the opera, listened to familiar arias with a pang.

One day, while reading a newspaper, in a list of guests at a fashionable assembly he found her name. She was in New York!

Frequently, thereafter, when similar entertainments, scheduled in the newspapers, took place uptown, Felix was standing in a vestibule near by.

A striped canopy extended from the lintel to the curb, where a tall footman reached out to open the doors of automobiles as they glided to a standstill. Beneath the arch of canvas many women, cloaked to the ears, showing white satin boots, with diamonds flashing in their coiffures, appeared, and immediately vanished. If she was there, he did not recognize her. When all had entered, he turned homeward. Rain began to fall; and the dog, pattering ahead, seemed at each step to pierce, with elongated legs, the glistening pavement.

Mrs. Snatt, announcing that "a gentleman had called to see him," produced a visiting card with a dirty thumb mark on it.

"Oliver Corquill. So he has run me down!"

Next afternoon, the novelist appeared at the boarding-house.

He made no remarks about Felix's behavior at their last meeting, the young man's disappearance from Washington Square, or the means by which this last pursuit had been consummated. But, after glancing round the bedroom, he remarked:

"A very snug, secluded little nook, I should imagine, for literary work."

Felix's cheeks began to burn. He stared, with a

feeling of animosity, at the celebrity, who wore underneath an overcoat lined with sealskin a suit of dark brown cheviot, who displayed, above patent leather shoes, stockings of brown ribbed silk, and who had in the buttonhole of his left lapel a white carnation.

"Spare me your sarcasm!"

Corquill assumed an expression of surprise.

"Why, my dear fellow, I thought that I was falling in with your ideas! Isn't this retreat your deliberate choice? What else can one suppose, when you conceal yourself from friends who have other plans for you, when you refuse, indeed, the most exceptional opportunities to effect a change?" He had received a letter from Pavin, who was travelling in Algeria.

Felix lowered his head.

"It's true: I must cut a miserable figure before both of you! But it wasn't altogether my fault."

"Well, then, I must remind you that I have never yet enjoyed your confidence."

"What use would it serve to recount a history of errors?"

"When two become allies, both must know the characteristics of an enemy, to attack him with success."

An ally! Was it, indeed, in such a guise that Corquill, his sealskin coat-tails flapping, his white carnation an oriflamme, sallied into an all but stricken field?

They dined together, in a restaurant near Union

Square. Corquill made no objection to a bottle of champagne, or to entering, afterward, a café in the neighborhood. The young man, his reserve abolished, finally, by his potations, talked of himself.

Once started, Felix did not find it difficult to relate his troubles. He felt, indeed, in his parade of past experiences, a sensation that had something in common with the relief of a wrong-doer, too weak to rectify his misdemeanors alone, who whispers through the grille of a confessional. Some of the blame seemed to fall from his offences, when two minds shared the knowledge of them.

The other, turning his glass continually between his fingers, listened with impassive face. His first comment was:

"It's a puzzle!"

And, after a minute's thought,

"Our friend Wickit, the lawyer, was thoroughly conversant with your family's affairs?"

"Of course. What then?"

Apparently, Corquill did not hear that question. At last, staring at the table-top, he pronounced:

"There is an answer to everything."

They left the café. In Union Square, lamps shed their yellow rays upon expanses of white snow, which were transected by black, asphalt paths. Near a circular fountain, on a wooden bench, a man in mean clothes was leaning forward, his head lower than his body, one hand resting on the ground to keep him from toppling over, while, with a little piece of ice, he traced in unsteady fashion upon the asphalt some disconnected numerals. The two pedestrians stopped. The stranger slowly raised his head.

His thin, white face was covered with a straggling beard, half black, half gray; from either side of his delicate nose the flesh had fallen away; and, beneath brows abnormally projecting, eyes sunken and veiled in shadows regarded, with a sort of mournful blankness, the two witnesses. In his effort to straighten himself, he recoiled violently against the bench back: his hat fell off; and one saw a bald skull shining, covered with protuberances.

He gazed at Corquill. His eyes wandered to Felix. The young man and the derelict regarded each other solemnly. At last, both smiled.

"What are you making there?" asked Felix, in low tones.

"*Pardon?*"

And Felix, staring down at him in surprise, repeated his inquiry in French.

The stranger answered naturally, though somewhat thickly:

"I am writing figures of 5, that look like wolves at bay in the forest, and figures of 2, that make me think of the smile of Aphrodite, and figures of 4, that resemble knights in German armor riding to a tourney."

Abruptly standing up, he reeled. The young man caught him by the arm.

"Where do you live?"

The other fixed his shadowy eyes on Felix.

"You could never find the way."

"On the contrary, I can find it easily."

"Twenty-seventh Street, then, beyond Sixth Avenue. Is it far?"

They set out northward, the young man and the derelict proceeding slowly, arm in arm, Corquill pacing beside them silently.

On Twenty-seventh Street, beyond Sixth Avenue, they entered a French quarter. The windows of little shops were inscribed with the legends: *"Coiffeur Français," "Pharmacie Française," "Manufacture de Tabac."* They halted before a four-story brown-stone house that looked as if it were sinking into the ground. A plumber's shop occupied the basement; all the windows contained old shades of dull blue cloth; a flight of thirteen steps ascended to the doorway, which was sheltered by a little porch of rusty metal-work.

"It is here, is it not?"

But the Frenchman, rocking on the young man's arm, was peering down the street, westward, toward a bright, low-hanging star.

"A beacon that, for its lustre, might surmount the Pharos, guiding in the painted sails, making clear, on the long jetty, the wilted wreaths of revellers returning home, and the faces of Greek women loitering in robes of painted gauze. A beacon that might surmount, for us, to-night, the Pharos! But, alas, no Alexandria underneath!" His face sank forward. Tears, issuing from the shadows in which lurked his eyes, dripped upon the ragged beard.

The door above them opened. In the hallway, loomed a female figure, of formidable proportions, wearing a species of dressing gown in front considerably shorter than in back. A hoarse, contralto voice called out, with a menacing accent:

"Is it you, at last?"

The derelict, developing a nimbleness that surprised his escort, scrambled up the thirteen steps. The hallway engulfed him: the door was immediately slammed shut.

"One might pray," said Corquill, "never to know the state of that poor devil."

Felix, the blood rushing to his head, turned upon the novelist, with curling lip.

"Save your pity! As for you, rest assured that you will never become like him. One does not exceed his own mental limitations!"

Corquill stood motionless. Then, his face pale, he made the other a bow, presented his back, departed.

CHAPTER XVIII

ONE afternoon in March, Felix found himself ascending the thirteen steps of the dwelling house in West Twenty-seventh Street. The door—its small pane of ground glass covered with an iron grating—was opened grudgingly by the virago who, at the time of Felix's previous expedition thither, had received the intoxicated Frenchman.

Unkempt, extraordinarily fat, with a neck of several folds, a dingy face, and black mustaches, she had, nevertheless, a pair of brilliant eyes, provocative of conjectures, like a hint of bygone splendor discovered amid ruins.

After scrutinizing the young man from head to foot, she assumed a promising look.

Felix, asking himself what excuse he had for that intrusion, was inclined to run down the steps. However, he blurted out:

"The gentleman with whom I came here the other night—is he in?"

Her features immediately expressed truculence.

"What gentleman?"

Felix attempted to recall the occasion to her. Perhaps she would remember the dog? He pointed to Pat, who, seated on the topmost step, was looking up at her without sympathy.

"I know of no such person, Monsieur. You went somewhere else."

He was leaving, when she detained him.

"Who sent you here?" she inquired, violently.

Disconcerted, Felix fell back upon the truth. He had been actuated by interest in a stranger who, during the brief moments of a chance meeting, had said "some remarkable things." He had to confess an anxiety to renew that acquaintance—no doubt a presumptuous inclination. "My excuse, Madame, is the allure of intellect. But that, I fear, is scarcely an excuse to offer others; indeed, it no longer seems plausible to me."

Then, reflecting that there could hardly be need of further apologies to this slattern, he straightened his back, raised his hat, and again turned away.

Her face softened.

"So he can still play the spendthrift? Eh, that is a Fortunatus's purse he carries, the old incorrigible! There, pardon me, Monsieur: we all have our bugaboos. He is across the street, in the café."

Directly opposite, a small dram shop, painted yellow, seemed, with its squat bay-windows bulging outward, to be succumbing gradually beneath the weight of a four-story building. A plate-glass pane displayed, in letters of white enamel, the information, "Café de la Patrie."

The café ceiling, long and narrow, covered with sheets of stamped metal, hung low: owing to this, and to the dull hue of the walls, the place was shadowy. On the right, extended a row of tables·

on the left, the bar presented its worn woodwork
and perforated brass beer tray. No customers were
visible.

"Monsieur desires——"

It was the bartender, or, rather, the proprietor.
A plump little fellow, with white hair parted in the
middle, and gaining jauntiness from a dyed and
waxed mustache, he looked as if some one had just
told him a questionable anecdote. This was his
habitual expression.

He directed Felix to the rear of the café.

There, two pool tables, one behind the other,
announced their past popularity by the raggedness
of their pockets, and the amount of sticking plaster
on their green cloths. Beyond them, a diffuse
light entered between iron bars—through which one
saw a yard replete with empty bottles—and penetrated an alcove to the right, there to make poly-
chromatic a goblet half full of absinthe and water,
to touch a hand as narrow and of nearly as cadaverous an exility as the hand of an Egyptian mummy,
and to set shining a bald head, large and lumpy,
raised above a copy of the *Messager des Etats-Unis*.
The newspaper sank from before the pale countenance, the straggling beard, and the sunken eyes
surrounded by wide circles, that had remained in
Felix's thoughts.

Again he was inclined to make his escape. But,
while saying to himself, "What a ridiculous proceeding," he advanced.

"Monsieur has forgotten me? We returned together to his house, one evening not long ago. The Pharos was illuminated."

The stranger, after taking thought, smiled apathetically.

"I do not remember. So the Pharos was illuminated?"

His voice, high and unsteady, drifted into a half hysteric laugh. Then, apparently in an access of curiosity, peering at the other, he said, nervously:

"Sit down, Monsieur."

They drank, that afternoon, half a dozen glasses of absinthe together; and, since Felix then had his first experience with tobacco of Algerian manufacture, they consumed between them as many packets of cigarettes.

The other, it seemed, was a Parisian. They talked of Paris—of the boulevards, the buildings, and that indefinable "soul" which distinguishes a city no less than a human being, and which, at recollection, brings to the wanderer a nostalgia not unlike a longing to perceive again the charms of a once beloved individual. But Felix's companion, to whom few corners of the earth were unfamiliar, had not seen Paris for many years. Spots named by him stirred no memories in the mind of the young man, who, for his part, alluded frequently to resorts and institutions that had sprung up since the Frenchman's day. So, from time to time, they fell silent, both touched, no doubt, by the sadness which the disappearance of old landmarks causes—to those who remember them, and to those who have not known them.

The elder, however, disclosed some compensating reminiscences.

He led the way, as it were, out of the dram shop in West Twenty-seventh Street—where twilight was creeping through the window bars—and into a region of constricted, tortuous alleys, of old, rickety houses with mansard roofs and many chimney pots, of oriels, carved by workmen of the seventeenth century, that adjoined blank walls made bright with frivolous bill boards advertising public balls at the "Mabille," of mediæval dormer windows overlooking butcher shops where grisettes in their dressing sacks came yawning to buy a chicken wing—in short, to that traditional district seething, once upon a time, from cobble-stones to attics, with artistic ardors, iconoclastic frenzies, licentiousness, and momentary prodigality, in recalling which old men say sadly, "The Latin Quarter is no more."

And the cafés! Their doors opened: straightway appeared the long mirrors, the white-topped tables, the garnet-colored plush of their settees; and, through a mist, one saw characters with unconventional beards and flowing bows, the pioneers of æstheticisms once new, but now discarded, leaning forward in all the febrile poses deemed necessary for the synthesis of artificial lives.

But Felix was not used to drinking absinthe in such quantities, and his expectance of a singular result from it induced intoxication rapidly. The pictures conjured up by his companion gradually faded; the sound of a high-pitched monologue reached him but at intervals; and he woke, next day, in his own bed, ignorant of the episodes which had terminated the adventure.

Relishing this taste of congenial history decanted at first hand, he returned to the Café de la Patrie for a deeper draught.

The proprietor informed him that the Parisian had not yet arrived. "It took an old fellow of his sort some time, every day, to find his legs."

He was called Monsieur Pierre. For two years—in fact, ever since the virago's appearance in Twenty-seventh Street—he had been "a fixture" across the way. It was the general impression that he got his spending money from this Mme. Wargla, whose name, the proprietor admitted, was, at least, not French. She took in lodgers; but such was her temper that she often deluged with abuse a stranger who rang her door-bell.

"And yet, he is a highly educated man? He has seen the world. He has known interesting persons."

The café keeper shrugged his shoulders.

"Who knows? He has been somebody, maybe?"

Nowadays, however, it was an "off night" for him if he got up the thirteen steps without assistance.

The clock struck four. They fell silent. A hand, narrow and fleshless, trembled against the door; and Monsieur Pierre, his eyes blank of all expression, feebly entered the café. He had come for his "resuscitation."

Felix had, at first, some difficulty in identifying

himself. But a gleam of intelligence appeared in the absinthe drinker's wandering orbs.

"Ah! ah! It is you? You have come back, then? In the alcove, eh? We shall be very comfortable. More comfortable than in my house, where there happens to be no room."

The proprietor accentuated his habitual expression.

Felix became familiar with the shadowy resort, with the street full of foreign signs and faces, even with the establishment of Mme. Wargla, whither he sometimes went when the "diverting old type" did not appear on time in the café.

In this house, the staircases and the floors of gloomy corridors were covered with oilcloth; doors creaked on their hinges; steps resounded on the landings; then there brushed past a man with a smooth-shaven, oily face and the aspect of a waiter off duty, or a woman with a fringe of hair, dark and heavy, falling over her brow beneath headgear of singular style. Monsieur Pierre issued, at an infirm gait, into the hallway, hid his bald scalp beneath a black felt hat, and straightway accompanied his visitor across the street.

Between these two grew up, presently, a species of regard—in the younger engendered by a feeling that here, beneath depravation, existed a congenial spirit, in the elder roused, possibly, by the realization that he had, at last, company in his intellectual ramblings. It was when Felix succeeded in following him, one night, into the half-discovered country of Greek criticism, that Monsieur Pierre made no bones of embracing the other in French fashion, with the words:

"My dear Pierce! There is an oasis in every desert, after all!"

That was his pronunciation of the young man's name.

They had their own corner—the alcove near the back window. Many patrons of the café, inured to that Anglo-Saxon mode of drinking devised as if for a greater benefit to liquor sellers, stood at the bar, their attitudes conducive to a restlessness which bore fruit in orders more frequent than if suggested by a natural desire. Others, in their shirt sleeves, played pool upon the lacerated baize. In a corner, usually, sat an octogenarian with a fringe of fluffy, white whiskers round his chin, his glass of absinthe at hand, and, at his feet, a brown, mongrel dog so old, and of a mien so wretched, that Pat was evidently ashamed to bite him. After finishing his drink, the ancient folded his hands, let his head sink forward, and took a nap. A shaft of ruddy light crept up his neck and seemed to set fire to his whiskers: the sunset, in fact, had even thrust a little of its glory into the back yard. There, above the piles of empty bottles, a small ailantus tree, its pinnated leaves anod, heralded, with a rank odor, the advent of spring.

They talked of spring in Paris. But Felix would say, presently:

"Let us talk, rather, of the Café François Premier."

It was there that the artists and the men of letters had gathered, three decades before. Monsieur Pierre could recall their faces, their mannerisms, their discussions—the combats of the impressionists and the conservatives, the wars of stippled paint against square brush strokes, the derision in which the realistic novel writers held the naturalists, then the manias for symbolism, for diabolism, for ghastliness, for anything that could shock by its novelty that democracy which, in art, "is always reactionary." Or one was transported to studios of a bizarre complexion, where painters, poets, and women whose faces reappeared, thereafter, on the walls of the Luxembourg, sat listening to the sighing of a violoncello played by a musician whose work no public would accept. And, afterward, "What colors did the sounds of different musical instruments call to mind? What hue had the vowels? Was Friday violet, and Sunday yellow?"

"And among all these, Monsieur Pierre, you, too, played your part?"

"My part was quickly played," the other responded with his hysterical laugh.

But he had known, among that assembly of Parisians, Afro-French, and Belgians, Villiers de l'Isle Adam, and Mallarmé, the wistful and evasive symbolist, Catulle Mendés, and De Banville, who sang just because he loved the sound of limpid vocables, Leconte de Lisle, and that reincarnation of François Villon, Verlaine.

Drinking off his absinthe, Monsieur Pierre burst forth, with a wild manner, into some poem by

Hérédia; and his listener gazed on a brazen world, on caravans splashed with ochre, seen through quivering air, on a mirage of crumbling mosques, and on green moonlight drained through palm leaves into a pool.

"Buron should have been among these," thought Felix, and asked his companion if he knew that writer. The other set down his glass.

"You know him? You have read him?"

And, after a pause, smoothing his beard with trembling fingers, he replied, in his cracked voice:

"No! About that fellow, I have nothing to say! He played me many a dirty trick. In truth, he was an enemy of mine."

If he could not be brought to criticise that one, he was quick enough, when his intelligence had been sufficiently revived by liquor, to bestow praise or blame on others.

"Baudelaire? Yes, always sitting alone, at midnight, with a theatric sneer on his face, methodically dropping into an ice-cold crystal cup a venom that is going to poison no one. Gautier and Zola, the two extremities of human endeavor—the Mona Lisa and an old, dirty woman by a copyist, in imitation of Franz Hals. Coppée? Why, one night he seduced Romance up to the Butte Montmartre and there stabbed her in an alley. Hugo! He reminds me of a well-trained Russian artisan who has set himself the task of covering, with every color, in every formal combination, the walls of a building a hundred times the size of St. Basil's Church in Moscow."

Then he would stop, his head would droop forward, and his beard would rest on the soiled frill of his shirt. He would mutter:

"After all, what difference? We are all sitting together in a dark room, blindfolded, waiting, and, while waiting, stringing chaplets. Suddenly we fear these are not pearls that we are stringing, but beads! We have a moment of anguish; to reassure ourselves, we snatch at the string. The string breaks, the beads patter upon the ground. But we grovel for them; we bruise our fingers searching for them: among them there may be a pearl! This one? Ah, to see, to make sure! But a hand falls upon our shoulder. It is that for which we have been waiting. One must rise quickly, at that touch. 'Drop your chaplet. Follow me.' And we follow. Whither? Who knows? As we go, we hear the rest moving in the dark, and the industrious clicking of chaplets, and voices saying proudly, 'Mine are pearls,' and other voices moaning, 'Mine are beads.'"

He would fall silent, with his cadaverous hands spread out on the table-top.

At other times, when in the act of losing contact with objective things, he showed more spirit.

To the hallucinations gathering round him he stretched out his arms, with a smile at once vacant and cunning, as if he were escaping, at the cost of reason, an unsatisfactory world. Sometimes, at night, finding himself in such a condition, he insisted upon a promenade.

Resting his pointed shoulder against Felix, he

swayed through dark streets, in plebeian parts of town, which were, for him, the purlieus of regions antipodal and ancient. "It is not far, now, to the gardens of Naucratis," or, "We are nearly there: one can catch the sound of Phrygian flutes, and smell incense, ambergris, and camphor."

Felix, on hearing such speeches, all delivered with an accent of conviction, felt a thrill throughout his body; and, focusing his swimming senses on those thoughts, himself was able to respond in the same vein. For had not the commonplace and the monotonous been swept away, so that desires previously grievous because no longer satiable seemed more imminent than reality?

"Yes, we are nearly there. Courage; we will reach that place together!"

And, arm in arm, they wandered at random through the darkness, striving to find the unattainable.

But the awakening was different.

From the depths, Felix raised his eyes, to see far above him, as it were, a goddess of the heavens, a Madonna. Her unalterable aloofness clothed her in some of that vague splendor which is divinity's chief allure for the imaginative worshipper. Indeed, he found it impossible, finally, to think of her as being like other women: his association with her had been too nearly idyllic to facilitate comparisons; and so far had the whole period receded, that he was moved, occasionally, when more distraught than usual, to question its reality.

But, not infrequently, at thought of her his fever was abated, his agitation ceased, he held himself motionless, saying, "I will put away all this stress, and sit down to the thought, 'She has loved me.'" He was soothed immediately, and went on contemplating, in tranquil happiness, the attachment of a bygone time, which now had for him a charm so tender.

This satisfaction was often able to pierce his most profound melancholy.

Still, in those hours, now rare, when his brain resumed exercises wholly rational, a cynicism, exhaled like an acrid vapor from all the sentimental ferment that he had endured, threatened to corrode his idol. In his career, contact had always prefaced disillusionment. What if her well-nigh ethereal singularity were visible only from afar, as is the remote, half phantasmal vista of a landscape which, at one's approach, resolves itself into a scene resembling many others?

He tried to drive this thought away; but, in the manner of every thought that he endeavored to exclude, it returned to pain him. And his heart cried out, "Must I lose my last ideal?"

One evening, when he came home with such feelings, he met, in the vestibule, Mr. Quilty's new wife, tastefully dressed. She had called, as it transpired afterward, to tell Mrs. Snatt some news that would have gained in detail by a delay.

They scrutinized each other. Felix reflected:

"So you have found the happy ending!"

He made an effort to compliment her.

"You look very young to-night. Your little step-daughters will have in you an elder sister. They must adore you already. How is Quilty, by the way?"

"That's so: he mentioned the fact that you rarely go there now." She added, in a whisper, "How glad I was to hear it!" And, looking down, she confessed:

"I think I shall end by persuading him to sell his business."

"Do you know," said Felix, "that I divined your nature long ago, up there? Every time I saw you in those surroundings I felt surprise. My intuition didn't play me false in your case, at any rate."

They were silent, both thinking, no doubt, of the same woman.

Presently, he ventured:

"Do you ever hear of her?"

"Now and then."

Montmorrissy's extravaganza, "Poor Pierrette," had been a failure at the Trocadero Theatre: Marie Sinjon, in the opinion of the critics, was not "up to" the Broadway standard. She had retired from the stage. Noon had married her; and, as he was in a serious way from nervous debility, they were travelling, by automobile, through northern Europe.

"She, too, has her desire!"

He entered the boarding-house. A sound of angry voices reached him from the "ground floor rear." Through an open doorway, he saw Mrs.

Snatt and her husband engaged in one of their altercations.

Felix paused on the staircase, to contemplate this picture.

The drummer, with his dyed side whiskers and inflamed face, looking not unlike an undersized Spanish brigand in a red mask, sat rolling up his eyes in an attempt to draw from his wife's purse by pathos the money that he would demand, when drunker, with artificial sternness. She, towering in a wrapper, with curl papers sticking out round her brow, compressed her indistinct lips and bade her spouse defiance. In a corner, Jennie, hugging the doll with taffy-colored curls, sat apathetically at gaze; by the window, the boy, his large head bent, was examining his fingers as if he had never previously seen them; the baby, in a short dress, was crawling with a jolly air over a carpet full of large green and crimson flowers.

Mr. Snatt, attempting to gulp down his grief, stammered:

"Nothing but cruelty and harshness . . . a man ain't never understood by his wife . . . what a curse, this artistic temperament!"

Fixing her with his watery eyes, he sighed:

"It won't be long, now! You'll feel sorry, maybe, when they fish me out of the river, to-morrow morning."

"Oh, no such luck!" was the retort.

He relapsed into silence. A baneful expression appeared, presently, on his splotched visage. When the baby crawled toward his feet, he shouted:

"Take that brat away! I have nothing to do with him, d'you hear?"

Mrs. Snatt turned, with twitching face, to look at her other offspring. The words burst from her:

"That's why he's healthy!"

And, her bosom heaving, she came forward to close the door.

Next day, she asked Felix "if he could conveniently pay up his back rent."

His scenarios for the kinetoscope were no longer accepted with enthusiasm. He had exhausted all the conventional situations. Besides, the manufacturer of moving pictures now wanted "comic skits—jaw-breakers." But Felix was in no state of mind to invent laughable episodes.

Though desperate for a more lucrative employment, he was incapable of working steadily. With the utmost travail, he finished a page or two of writing, then considered that he had earned a rest. Finding his room a prison, and every necessary act a burden, he did not touch his pen till confronted by the most pressing need of money. Still, the twilight of day deliberately wasted was a melancholy hour!

Perhaps he might be able to write a new sketch for the Delaclaires?

The Thespian regarded this idea favorably. He and his wife had dragged their old farce across the boards of vaudeville theatres so long, that generally, when they appeared, the audience, recognizing them with a hum of resignation, settled back to doze. There were even managers "so dead to art" as to

refuse the couple further booking until they had
"freshened up their act."

Felix sat through several performances in a Fourteenth Street theatre, for the purpose of studying
their requirements.

Into a rococo boudoir—or whatever other interior
"set" came handy—Mrs. Delaclaire precipitated
her large person, wearing a low-neck dress that caved
in just below the bosom.

She announced that "she didn't know what to do!"
A gentleman whom she had engaged as "leading
man in her new tragedy" had failed to appear.
Meanwhile, she would, at least, rehearse a song or
two. "A song or two" was the cue for the piano-
player, lolling in the orchestra pit.

Encouraged by him, Mrs. Delaclaire essayed a
ballad about "colleens," "the gate below the
meadows" and "the Irish moon," concluding with
the ear-piercing asseveration, "He will come back!"

Thereupon, a crash of glass was heard, and Mr.
Delaclaire entered, looking behind him, in the
costume of a messenger boy.

When he had explained facetiously that he was in
the wrong house, he espied a piano in a corner.
"Would she play a jig for him?" "What, was he a
disciple of Terpsichore?" "Hold on! The lady had
no right to call him names!" "But if he could
dance, possibly he could act?" "Acting was his
greatest pleasure." "How fortunate! What a coincidence!" He took his place, and they gave a
parody of "Uncle Tom's Cabin." Then, when Mrs.

Delaclaire had performed the sleep-walking scene from "Macbeth," and Mr. Delaclaire had moaned forth a recitation entitled, "The Old Actor," they finished in front of a drop curtain, with a lively song and dance, to disappear glistening with perspiration.

The Thespian suggested that Felix "dash off" a more serious composition—a piece in which he could wear evening dress, create an atmosphere of wealth, say something about "other days," and recover the affections of a lady who had the fashionable world fawning at her feet. "You ought to be able to do that sort of stuff," was Delaclaire's conclusion, with a sidelong glance. Then, rubbing his bristly chin reflectively, he exclaimed:

"I'll tell you the style! Have you seen a sketch called, 'His Past'? It's made no end of money on the vaudeville circuit. A dame named Nuncheon wrote it about a lot of swells."

Sometimes, arrayed in rumpled pajamas, he entered Felix's room before the young man was awake: in the night he had "thought up an incident that ought to go into that sketch." His mind relieved of those lucubrations, the Thespian filled the other's pipe, sat down on the counterpane, and spoke of Eddie, his son. The boy had not come home to sleep. Moreover, though nothing was missing from the Delaclaires' apartments, he had been seen by Miss Vinnie Vatelle going into a pawnshop.

The soubrette had returned to town with the spring flowers. She was playing a short engage-

ment in the Bon Ton Music Hall, on Eighth Avenue.
Applause clattered round her when, in a pink dress
reaching to the knees, pink stockings, and gilt
dancing shoes, she uttered the refrain:

> "I don't care if she has yellow hair
>   Or hair of darkest black;
> I'll take it red, piled upon her head,
>   Or hanging down her back;
> I can be true to eyes of blue,
>   Or eyes of gray or brown:
> I'm not hard to suit, you see,
> For it's all the same to me
>   If she just hails from New York town."

Her room in the boarding-house was overflowing
with souvenirs of her successes. The walls were
covered with photographs of Miss Vatelle in every
variety of coiffure, in every sort of costume ranging
between the poles of children's dresses and tights.
Bright-colored post-cards, scrawled over by waggish
correspondents with all sorts of pleasantries, filled
wire racks; the mirror had a border of visiting cards,
newspaper clippings, and envelopes bearing curious
addresses; on the bureau top, amid rouge brushes,
powder boxes, pots of cold cream, false curls, hairpins, soiled handkerchiefs, and broken combs, two
elderly faces, one male, the other female, surveyed,
with a look of bovine self-complacency, their environment. It was a portrait of the soubrette's parents.

To the young man, there was an interesting artlessness about her. Living for the most part in a
sphere of thin dressing-room walls, sleeping cars,

and hotel accommodations sometimes verging, necessarily, on promiscuity, she had forgotten many of the strictures set upon conversation in circles more conventional. Her confidences were, occasionally, as generous as if Felix had been an intimate relative: her facial expression, however, so neutralized her words that one could not easily find in the latter anything immoderate. On concluding tales of the provincial hotel clerk, "the baby that died," and "the hard luck that a poor girl is born to," she looked at him mournfully from under her powdered lashes, with her mouth relaxed, and a few brown freckles showing through the "make-up" on her short, thick nose. He got used to her perfume, no longer remarked her soiled shoe tops, and more than once forgot entirely his earlier impression of her.

There was little to choose between his mental and his physical deterioration. He ate at irregular hours, without ever feeling hunger. Now and then, on approaching a mirror, he did not immediately recognize his face. He had continually a nervous agitation near the solar plexus; sudden noises made him start; his eyelids twitched by the hour; and it was not unusual for him to make his bed upon the floor, because of a horror, that seized him as he fell asleep, of falling into an abyss.

His distress was accentuated whenever he "went broke." He understood, finally, the impulse which drives footpads to their business.

Mr. Pandle, meeting him in Union Square, on such a night, listened attentively to a rambling plaint.

Then, raising one of his imitation eyebrows significantly, he inquired if Felix would care "to take a car ride."

"What for? Besides, I have the dog with me."

"All the better. We get on; the conductor objects to him; we get off again. There's the Twenty-third Street crosstown line, for instance. It catches a good transfer crowd at Broadway—theatre-goers from the suburbs."

Felix turned cold. He had an impulse to dash his fist into the other's face. But, after all, he did no more than turn on his heel.

Nevertheless, a few nights later, when he saw a stranger drop something in a deserted street, Felix halted, then stealthily advanced, picked up a wallet, made his escape. In his room, breathlessly he examined his find. It was worn out, and empty.

One afternoon, while he was sitting at home, racking his brains for some way to get money, a knock sounded on the door. It was Monsieur Pierre, who, wondering at the young man's recent neglect of him, had made the journey from West Twenty-seventh Street. He fell into a chair, exhausted.

"You see," he gasped, passing a handkerchief over his lumpy brow, on which the veins stood out in knots, "thus we must gratify the habits we acquire. It is lonely over there, these days, in the Café de la Patrie."

He soon rose, and began to move round the room.

"So you live here, eh?" he inquired, with an almost foolish chuckle. "Not bad, not bad! Have you cigarettes?"

Standing by the bureau, he picked up, with his shaking fingers, the photograph of Felix's mother.

"Who is this?"

When he had gazed long and earnestly at that portrait, he laid it gently in its place. Smoothing his beard, he wandered from before the bureau.

"How do you spell your name?" he enunciated carefully.

Felix, with a smile, informed him.

"Ah!"

The Frenchman, having reached the door, stood still, as if in a daze.

"How old are you?"

"Thirty."

"Where were you born?"

"In Paris."

An expression of fright was stamped upon the absinthe drinker's face. He stumbled out into the corridor.

"What an original! No doubt he is going to explore the house!"

But when Felix went to look for him, the corridor was empty, and the street door stood open.

"Gone! This is evidently one of his bad days."

The same evening, Felix, while rummaging a bureau drawer in search of a collar not broken at the edges, found a cardboard box half full of headache powders.

CHAPTER XIX

FELIX, on his next visit to West Twenty-seventh Street, did not see Monsieur Pierre. The café keeper shrugged his shoulders. Mme. Wargla, however, invited the young man into the hallway. There, holding her dressing-gown together at the neck with a plump, dingy hand, she scrutinized the caller earnestly.

"He is not able to receive his friends."

"Then he's ill?"

"He is always ill. Besides, at times he has curious notions. One does not live that life—you understand. We pay, *hein?* As the saying goes, 'each pleasure costs a thousand pains.'"

"You quote François Villon, Madame?" cried Felix, in astonishment.

Her face lost some of its churlishness, as she replied:

"Eh, like all the young and well-favored, you think the old and ugly have always been so. When one has been smothered in gold dust by the improvident, a grain or two may stick long afterward."

But a bell jangled, and she went to hold parley at the front door.

"*Oui, oui, oui! Entrez.*"

There entered a delicate-looking youth with an

incipient mustache and the trace of a bifurcated chin beard. On seeing another, he hesitated; then, affecting a bold air, he leaped up the staircase. Mme. Wargla resumed her scrutiny of Felix.

"How comes it that you speak French so well, Monsieur?"

"That language has always interested me."

A sound of creaking boards reached them from the rear end of the corridor.

"Well, as I have told you once, he is able to see no one! What more can I say? Are you satisfied? Good-by, Monsieur!"

And she slammed the front door.

A week later, returning to West Twenty-seventh Street at an unusual hour, Felix discovered him in the alcove of the Café de la Patrie. Monsieur Pierre set down his half-empty goblet, as the other exclaimed:

"My dear friend, how glad I am to see you recovered! Maybe it was partly selfish, that concern of mine? I have missed our expeditions to the Latin Quarter, our evenings in the Café François Premier, not to mention our association with Xenophanes and Empedocles."

"I, too," was the low response.

"But we shall resume those hours?"

The Parisian raised timidly his large, vague eyes, which seemed about to overflow into their encircling rings of reddish brown.

"Yes, yes; why not? By all means. We shall not deprive ourselves of that!"

"Two absinthes," called Felix, to the café keeper. So their companionship was resumed.

Those were days of early summer, when the first intense heat brought forth, simultaneously with the geraniums in public parks, light-colored, filmy dresses, bright parasols, palm-leaf fans, and straw hats which an army of punctilious toilers had not presumed to wear until the day appointed by some forgotten arbiter of style. In fashionable parts of town the doorways of dwelling houses were boarded over; in the principal thoroughfares, trenches swarmed with Italian laborers; everywhere dirt, pulverized by the sunshine, whirled toward the cornices in clouds; and the fumes of sewer gas mingled with street smells accentuated by the humidity. Then, round the Café de la Patrie, fat foreigners appeared without coats, in wilted collars, bareheaded women wheeled perambulators wherein babies restlessly kicked up their naked legs, garbage buckets remained too long at the curb, while few windows thereabouts lacked their tableaux of dishabille that bordered on indiscretion. In the rear of the café, an intermittent breeze wafted through the barred window odors of sour wine lees from the mass of empty bottles in the yard; and the ailantus tree dipped its long leaves above a scabrous wooden fence which radiated too effectively the prevailing warmth.

They sat in the alcove, smoking cigarettes, and staring at the two goblets. The sunlight, stealing across the table top, finally pierced the absinthe, to wake in that fluid a soft, nacreous splendor. There, straightway, was a cup glowing with fires of a subtle and unearthly beauty—a chalice brimming with enchantment. Their fingers embraced the glass with a tenderness almost voluptuous; the bland concoction trickled down their throats: and, presently, the lustre of that essence seemed shed on the surroundings—as a refulgence from the Grail, so one is told, transfigured the dark walls of its hiding place.

But the complexion of their intercourse had undergone a change.

The young man missed that sense of spiritual intimacy which had first attracted him to the Parisian. He had become less the listener, and more the talker; his revelations of temperament were now met by silence more often than by concurrence; and occasionally, when he had finished some rambling speech about "the only means whereby the inadequacy of the actual world might be evaded," a silence fell between them, as depressing as if freighted with an enormous sadness. The elder, passing a tremulous hand before his eyes, would stammer:

"Let us not stay here any longer."

Thereupon, to Felix's dissatisfaction, they would go out, to walk the dusky streets.

Soon, however, Monsieur Pierre, who had been wont on other evenings so swiftly to traverse space, was forced to a standstill by exhaustion. Under an arc lamp, slowly he removed his black felt hat.

Large drops of perspiration trickled down his temples, over a vermiculate network of distended veins.

"Lend me your shoulder, Félix. Let us turn back."

And, at the foot of Mme. Wargla's steps, he bade the young man good-night.

"You are going home now?"

"I suppose so."

"Good, very good. Home and to bed. That is the best. I, too. *Au revoir.*"

"He is changed since his illness," thought Felix.

But once, after making a pretence of departure, the young man stepped into a doorway. He was rewarded by seeing the absinthe drinker descend the thirteen steps, cross the street, and re-enter the café.

"So it's a trick! He is tired of my company?"

He determined never again to set foot in the Café de la Patrie.

But five days later, the Frenchman accomplished the journey to Felix's abode.

"What!" he ejaculated, while holding fast to the door jamb, in order to catch his breath. "You are up and about; you are as well as ever! Then it is because you no longer find anything of interest over there."

"On the contrary, because I thought that you preferred it so."

"Why?"

Felix, unwilling to confess his espionage, replied:

"An impression cannot always be expressed."

At these words, delivered in a chilly manner, an agitation seized upon the Parisian. Sitting down in the nearest chair, he mopped his head distractedly with a handkerchief.

"*Mon Dieu!* Are we going to quarrel, you and I?"

By that speech the young man's heart was immediately touched.

"Forgive me! I ask nothing better than to continue a relationship unique, for me, in this—that it is perfectly congenial."

"*Embrassons nous!*"

And Monsieur Pierre would not be denied the satisfaction of saluting Felix with a kiss on either cheek.

Thereafter, he returned frequently to the boarding-house in Thirteenth Street.

He insisted on examining every article that the other had got published. Displaying a sort of trepidation, he received into his arms the books of clippings, the sheaves of manuscript, all the literary souvenirs of a period signalized by self-confidence. With a pile of torn magazines balanced on his knees, he deciphered, word by word, the English prose. Occasionally he paused, with a look as if he himself had accomplished something admirable.

"Ah! Ah! There is a thought, charmingly expressed, that I have not met before!"

"Let me see it . . . . Did I write so well?"

"It is not for a young man to say such things!"

The Frenchman approached the window. There, standing beside the bureau, with his thin shoulders bent forward, he gazed out, apparently, on the back yards.

He haunted Felix, did this old wreck with the crapulous body and the head of a mystic who has lain desiccating for centuries in Roman catacombs. Invariably, his mournful eyes brightened at sight of the young man; he reached out a hand to pat the other's arm; he assumed, in fact, an air that was a caricature of the paternal. And, in the paternal manner, he commenced to bestow on Felix good advice.

But the words "resolution," "continence," and "emancipation" fell inaptly from his lips; a salutary philosophy, which he, erstwhile so eloquent in cynical discourse, developed as if expressly for his companion's benefit, had all the speciousness of a creed promulgated by an unbeliever; a quotation to the effect that "the object of life was, after all, the education of the will," obtained, because he uttered it, the flavor of a sorry jest. The result of all the Frenchman's feeble homilies was Felix's thought, "If he is, indeed, sincere in this, if, thanks to growing intimacy, one has finally perceived the secret yearnings of his soul, what a mockery is human aspiration!"

Nevertheless, Monsieur Pierre continued to harp on that tune, but with variations somewhat more practical.

While visiting the young man, he ignored all suggestions that they sally forth to "have a drink"; in the Café de la Patrie, he made anything a pretext to "take the air." They had arguments, in tenor

verging on acerbity, before swinging doors of glass;
Felix was drawn by the arm past many a saloon;
when a café sign appeared ahead, Monsieur Pierre,
with a quivering forefinger, designated some interesting object across the way. But, at every approach to dram shops, the feet of both began to lag;
two pairs of eyes turned furtively askance; and the
appetent expression of the one was mirrored in the
visage of the other. Thus walking the streets—
from which, because of these pedestrians' sobriety,
all interest had been withdrawn—each found, no
doubt, the other's company a burden. Felix, for
his part, was bored, exasperated, and disgusted, so
that the Parisian had to endure not only the discomfort of desires unappeased, but also the ill-nature of a
cherished comrade.

Indeed, excursions of this sort reduced him to
a pitiable state. Worn out by unwonted exercise,
beside himself from lack of customary stimulation,
rendered, moreover, half imbecile by the depression
of his mind, he gave in, finally, with a groan. They
retraced their steps to West Twenty-seventh Street.
On the threshold of Mme. Wargla's house Felix
went through the stale burlesque of seeing his companion safe indoors.

"And you, Félix?"

"Oh, I, like you, am for bed."

The absinthe drinker, rallying for a last effort his
expiring will, made his appeal in broken accents:

"Come, while I believe you, something might
happen; so let us make sure. Let us swear a little

oath together, eh? Even by our hope of heaven, by all saintly intercessors, by the Virgin? No, one breaks such oaths too easily. By what? *Tiens*, you will swear to me by the memory of Madame your mother?"

"My poor friend, I have no memory of my mother."

Then, as Monsieur Pierre continued to stare at him, he added, with a return of gentleness:

"Rest assured, I shall go straight home."

He no longer waited in a near-by doorway, so confident was he that, when his back was turned, the Parisian would scramble down the steps and make for the Café de la Patrie.

"He means well enough: it is, of course, a proof that he is fond of me. But as if such hocus pocus could effect what I have tried so desperately to accomplish!"

One night, after such a departure, having got himself thoroughly intoxicated elsewhere, he wandered back to West Twenty-seventh Street. In the alcove of the café, he found Monsieur Pierre enjoying a condition at least no less elevated than his own.

When the Frenchman had succeeded in focusing his gaze upon the new arrival, he gave vent to a vacant laugh.

"You are late! Where have you been, all day? Have you ever seen the treasure house of the Sassanian kings, in the heart of an unknown jungle, split open to the moon? There rubies and emeralds speak to one another of the secret sins of

long-dead begums; square sapphires that have
mirrored the eyes of monarchs devour with their
scintillations, still thus infected, the white skins of
pearls that peris wore; the topaz and the chrys-
oprase, the diamond and the chalcedony, once
learned, through many centuries, in marble pavilions
inlaid with arabesques of *pietra dura*, a variant of
royal procreation: their spawn is a blended miracle
of light—but, over all, there hovers to this day a
mist of blood." While speaking, he was looking
out through the window, to where moonshine, passing between the leaves of the ailantus tree, glinted
on the heaps of empty bottles.

From materials apparently as slight they could
construct, at such moments, the fabric of their most
entrancing dreams. A street, a building, a figure, a
chain of arc lamps, or a fall of shadows, suggested,
then, a picture wholly strange and, in suggesting it,
produced it. As each visionary, moreover, sure of
comprehension, immediately related his perceptions
to the other, in nearly every scene developed by the
overtaxed imagination of either they were able to
participate.

That night, under cover of an opalescent haze,
places familiar to them turned extraordinary; forms
took mysterious shapes about them; the air of other
worlds caressed their faces. The street lights
changed readily to flaming cressets; the windows
one and all unrolled long draperies of cloth of gold;
and over pavements deep with flowers moved capar-
isoned chargers, heralds blowing fanfares, and, after

them, pell-mell, a river of damask, steel, precious
stones, chiselled ivory, and velvet banners, amid
which, in a white hand heavy with ecclesiastical
finger rings, quivered the Golden Rose. The pair
doffed their hats, with mocking smiles, to a caval-
cade of work-horses, bound for sale, rope halters
round their jaws, and ragged stable boys astride
their backs.

So it was Rome: the Borgias' palace blazed with
light; robes rushed across bridges; blonde damsels
with jewelled foreheads leaned insidiously from casements, and an odor of musk was stirred into the soft
air at the swift passage of cardinals tricked out, like
revellers, in violet-colored masks. The two, raising their voices, implored the casement dwellers:
"Maddalena! Angelica! Pomona! Drop down, if
not the key, at least a kiss!" They moved on, however, when threatened with an appeal to the police.

It was Corinth: the salt waves lapped the prows
of Punic galleys; a faint murmur issued from the
Temple of Venus Pandemos; and, on the windy
quay, one wept to see an old drunken woman turn
up a face which had belonged, when fair, to Laïs.
"Where was her statue, fashioned by Myron," they
asked her, grinning through their tears. "What
had become of Diogenes and Aristippus?"—Nor
did they cease till flooded with scurrility in a dialect at least not Corinthian.

It was Troy: and Helen was in yonder "topless
tower," gazing out, with who could tell what reveries,
toward the camp fires of the Greeks.

But as Papal Rome shredded into the commonplace, and the salt breeze swept away the classic glamour from warehouses and moored schooners, so Helen's tower, when approached too closely, became a "sky-scraper." Perhaps the night air somewhat cleared, at last, the absinthe drinker's brain. He muttered:

"Reality is hanging the very sky in mourning weeds, against the burial of Romance. Let me, too, be buried, as a figment no more substantial." And presently, quoting from Empedocles:

"'Men, wrestling through a little space of life that is no life, whirled off like a vapor by a quick fate, flit away.'"

Then, turning up his eyes:

"Yet in my time, I have lived a hundred lives, to discover the especial thrill of each. I have soared—ah, and I have fallen! But I was wrong to think that I had sounded every depth."

At the Frenchman's door, Mme. Wargla, roused from slumber, turned on Felix with the ferocity of a tigress.

"So, the café is not enough: when that is closed, you must drag him through the streets! Look at him, now, asleep against the jamb! *Belle affaire!* His clothes: *cristi*, what a mess! And he who was so spick and span—no Bohemian, but a gentleman of the grand world. There, poor old boy, come in. Didst thou find out who cared most for thee, in the end? Thou wilt be ill enough to-morrow. As for you, Monsieur, cut your stick!"

Felix found his way home.

It was not thought that Mrs. Snatt's boarding-house could last much longer. Half the rooms were empty, while most of the lodgers now preferred to eat their meals elsewhere. But often, in the evening, Mr. Snatt's snare-drum could be heard rattling downstairs. He was remaining, this time, evidently, to play the dirge.

One morning, Delia, the housemaid, appeared before Felix with a frightened look. After rubbing her broken shoes together in embarrassment, she managed to get out the information that her mistress had an opportunity, which she could not afford to lose, to rent the room. As he owed, at that time, for five weeks' board, the young man's consternation was quickly followed by relief.

The Delaclaires insisted on giving him a "send-off." A delicatessen shop furnished the collation, which was composed of sardines, Italian sausage, rye bread, pickled pigs' feet, Swiss cheese, and beer. From this beverage, Mrs. Delaclaire obtained a certain sentimentality: her bosom heaved above her caved-in corsets; she spoke, in moving tones, of "ties made but to be broken," and "auld lang syne." The Thespian, not to be outdone, recollected a few appropriate quotations; and, at the last, summoning to his assistance a melancholy and decrepit look, declaimed, with that intonation called a dying fall:

> "Bid me farewell, and smile. I pray you, come.
> While I remain above the ground, you shall
> Hear from me still; and never of me aught
> But what is like me formerly."

Miss Vinnie Vatelle was unable to be present at that ceremony. The soubrette was confined to her room by a "sick headache."

Next morning, Mrs. Snatt came out of the "ground floor rear" to bid him good-by. Blushing, she fixed him with appealing eyes. Apparently, in her belief, not he, but she, had cause to plead excuses.

Felix declared that he would not forget her.

"At the earliest possible moment, you shall have your thirty dollars."

"It's not that. But we can't always do as we would like. I'm sorry. You sort o' gave the house a tone."

Jennie even insisted on a kiss. The baby, a marvel of intelligence for his age, achieved the words "Da—da!" and "Doggie!" Willie, his large head cocked, stared at these demonstrations as if some mysterious perfidy were going on.

From the end of the street, Felix, looking back, saw Delia on the doorstep. Her hair was in wild confusion; one hand shaded her eyes; an angular elbow glinted in the sunlight.

He went to a hotel in Houston Street—a nine-story, white-brick structure with a projecting roof—which an altruist had built for the decent and cheap accommodation of men.

Marble staircases and floors, walls of white tiling, elevators, and an administration bureau fitted out in oak, gave the young man, at his first glance, encouragement. But the bedchambers, each furnished with a narrow cot, a chair, a locker, and a strip of rug, were small as cells; the dining-room had long tables like those used in public institutions; and the shower baths were all situated downstairs. A night's lodging, however, could be obtained for thirty cents; and a meal was elaborate which cost more than a quarter of a dollar. On the other hand, one was forbidden to occupy his room from nine in the morning until five in the afternoon, dogs were excluded, and no liquor was dispensed.

Felix, confiding Pat, every night, to an attendant in the basement, remained there for some weeks: it was a place to sleep. In courts, nine stories high, white and glistening, roofed with glass, old men of boundless leisure, seated at square tables, played checkers interminably; in the library on the second floor, others turned languidly the pages of "Ivanhoe" or "Lorna Doone"; and Felix, when entering the lavatory for his morning bath, often saw honest-looking fellows rinsing undershirts and handkerchiefs at stationary washtubs provided for that purpose.

In time, the restrictions which obtained in the hotel, his loneliness, at night, for Pat, and the long faces that greeted him when he came home intoxicated, drove Felix to seek other quarters. He inhabited hostelries over cafés, where the carpets were covered with spots, the window-curtains torn, and the beds dirty; he made the rounds of lodging-houses "catering to a transient trade"; he dealt with hotel proprietors and landladies who surrounded their untidy persons with an atmosphere of mystery.

Those were domiciles full of battered furniture, broken washstands, door-knobs quick to turn in the hands of strangers who had "mistaken the number." His homeward road lay through streets by day alive with Jewish clothing makers, fruit-laden push carts, Italian brats, "kosher" restaurants—at night deserted save, perhaps, for some one lurking in the shadow of an entry, a policeman on his beat, or a drab skirt disappearing over puddles. He had come into a place where factories squeezed between their walls the ramshackle dwellings of an earlier period, where street lamps seemed to burn less brightly than elsewhere and the windows to give forth a sheen more wan, where, high over excavations, there remained large squares of wall-paper, pallid in moonlight—the blanched backgrounds of forgotten scenes enacted in the rooms of houses finally razed.

His address was known to Monsieur Pierre, who sometimes, smoothing his beard in agitation, stammered:

"I do not ask you to live in my house."

But he now insisted on loaning the other small amounts of money.

Such transactions, at first made difficult by a squeamishness which neither wanted to exhibit, soon became easy. It was, in fact, the Parisian—at what cost to his self-indulgence Felix did not venture to surmise—who kept the young man's head above water.

To others whom he chanced to meet, Felix

answered that he was "living with some friends uptown."

On Fourteenth Street, one afternoon in October, at a stentorious halloo he turned to see the Thespian, posing beside a poster, of late overlooked by the bill-stickers, that portrayed him. They shook hands. Mr. Delaclaire remarked that Felix looked very bad.

Mrs. Snatt, it seemed, was now "on her last legs." But there was no chance of the ex-drummer dying: "he was too thoroughly pickled." "Such fortunate situations, my dear boy, only happen on the stage."

As for the Delaclaires, they were, just for the moment, "at liberty." And lowering his jowls in a regretful manner upon a frayed cravat, the actor said:

"By the way, we never done that sketch!"

"That's true."

Felix changed the subject.

"What of Vinnie?"

"On the road again. Always working! A nice little thing, don't you think? She used to talk a lot about you, after you left."

"And Edwin Booth Delaclaire?"

Gloom pervaded the Thespian's Neronic countenance.

"That boy will be the death of me!"

He had even been arrested, on the charge of throwing a brick through a jeweller's window as a preliminary to stealing some gold-plated watches. Though the blame had been fastened on his companions, the youth had not escaped without leaving his picture in the "Rogues' Gallery" at Police Head-quarters.

"You understand? It makes him a marked man for life. If only there was a way to get it out!"

Felix promised to petition "a friend of his on the force."

With this in mind, he took the trouble to wait in Quilty's saloon for the detective. The saloon keeper had become the father of a son. He asked Felix what college was the best.

Connla came in. Pat's condition put him, at once, in a bad humor: "He had never seen a good bull-terrier so run down!" When Felix broached the object of his visit, the detective answered:

"Better leave that boy alone: you'll only dirty your fingers. One of these days, he'll be wheeling a barrow full of rocks, like Pandle."

Then, sucking his teeth reflectively, he added:

"Yestiday, I seen your friend the dope fiend go-ing into Chinatown. Faith, I could read fine print through him! He'll not see the winter out, and that's the truth."

"So near the end of his rope," thought Felix. "And what of me?"

Every day, he advanced farther into an opacity which hid, as it were, the simultaneous approach of something terrible. A feeling of material un-reality had so increased in him that he gazed some-times at his hands to find them strange, while his voice often sounded in his ears as if issuing from another's lips. The city had become a place of half a dozen familiar points: these, shrouded continually in a sort of mist, no longer represented anything important. His capacity for feeling, when in his sober senses, delicate or deep emotions, seemed dead; he could no longer call forth either violent or gentle impulses; his thoughts of Nina were distinguished only by sadness, as fleeting as the shadow of great wings, because he had lost, in that respect, the power to evoke a sweet regret. It was as if an inner intelligence had crumbled there, leaving no more than a fragile shell. This, scarcely able to bear the most trivial frictions, was liable, at any hour, to disintegrate.

One afternoon, early in November, he set out, by way of Sixth Avenue, for the Café de la Patrie.

It was a day of lowering clouds, of cold winds, of livid window-panes and dejected faces. The encompassing depression of nature penetrated his heart: how desolate the world, for all the footfalls round him!

Those footfalls accompanied his own; they intruded on his dejection; when he listened to them, they became the tread of a multitude, amid which he was lost, and by which he was being borne along to an unknown destination.

He raised his eyes to the housetops.

Tall, dull against the gloomy sky, slowly they changed their altitudes before his gaze: those in front were seen to rise, and those behind to sink gradually from view. It was a descent. The multitude was flowing, like a stream, down hill.

It flowed past columns black and straight, all alike, interminably reiterated. From time to time, a sound as of thunder burst forth overhead, at which the columns seemed to shake, as do tree trunks at the breaking of a storm. Were they not, indeed, tree trunks? They had that aspect. They were innumerable tree trunks gathering on the outskirts of a forest as tenebrous as oblivion.

Between them the human stream continued to flow downward.

He examined his company.

There pressed round him countless wayfarers with eyes fixed straight ahead. Save for their rapt expressions, they displayed a bewildering dissimilarity.

Some showed through tatters their emaciated flanks; to the shoulders of others hung strips of rotten mail; the rags of sacerdotal fillets dangled over the transparent temples of a few; and amid naked bodies, both tender and withered, all frail and covered with old scars, appeared, here and there, the muddy remnant of a purple robe. Senile old men in grave clothes, wearing a wreck of laurel leaves, rested their weight on youths whose lips were covered with a green froth of poison. Blind women, from whose necks were slipping sacred amulets, supported girls with bleeding breasts, their cheeks well nigh washed clear of paint by tears. Fathers, transfixed by rusty swords, still dragged along their lifeless children; and one who had been, perhaps, a king stumbled onward, though decapitated, hugging against his breast a head that wore a crown bereft of all its jewels.

Melancholy murmurs, sobs, moans, and snuffling rose from this host, to blend in a diapason like the sea's. He knew, at last, the source of those supernatural voices which had long haunted him.

But the shadows deepened; the tree trunks were multiplied; the stream had penetrated the forest. And, forthwith, all that company, with brandished arms and heads thrown back, melted, by a hundred paths, into the darkness.

Running forward, he cried:

"Must I stay here?"

A hand dragged him back. He was in the grasp of a tall spectre, decked with plates of silver, but beneath the visor of whose helmet no face appeared.

"They have all left me here alone!"

"I'll take you to where there's lots of them," was the reply.

He fell upon this guardian's neck with tears of gratitude.

His trust was not ill bestowed: for presently the threnody of mournful voices fell again upon his ears.

He listened to tales related by invisible mourners—of marriage beds covered with a pall, of treasure trove grasped finally by the dying, of love that stood smiling beyond an abyss perceived too late, of diadems from which the fangs of snakes whipped forth. As he heard these various accounts of baffled lives, he set them all down, word by word, upon an endless scroll.

Once, a voice reached him:

"This is an interesting case."

And, when he paused in his labor, he was asked:

"Why do you move your forefinger, day and night, as if you were writing?"

He replied:

"I am copying everything I hear: all the grief of the world shall be in my pages. Then I shall burn the book at the foot of a great altar; and the words shall fly up like little flames, to warm the heart of an angelic figure that sits overhead. But if I am sly enough to slip my own grief in among the others, it shall fly aloft like the rest, mingled with them; and the angelic presence, confused by so many flames, may feel for me also."

His questioner laughed gently.

"An educated man is sometimes able to get up a very picturesque D. T."

One morning, when he had been at his task "for centuries," he saw above him a ceiling of stamped metal that recalled the Café de la Patrie. He turned his head on a pillow. He was in a hospital.

In a long room were aligned against white walls a score of iron beds, all occupied by men. The rough chins of these invalids were upturned; their ignoble faces were flooded by the sunshine, and the same stupor seemed to dull every pair of eyes. Here and there moved orderlies, in white jackets and black trousers. By the door, a physician—a bland youth, clad in a suit of duck, with yellow hair and spectacles—was pressing the point of a hypodermic syringe into the shoulder of an old, idiotic-looking waif who leaned forward, on his mattress, in a sitting posture.

The physician, when he had finished the operation, came over to Felix. Seating himself on the bed, he inquired, with an amiable grin:

"How do you find yourself?"

"Where am I?"

"Well, if you must know, in the alcoholic ward."

Felix lowered his eyelids, to escape the other's smile.

"How long have I been here?"

"Three days. My dear fellow, I have to tell you that you've had a serious time. You are full to the neck with bromides and ergot—so, of course, you feel depressed. All the same, I take this opportunity to read you a lecture. One man has died in this room since you came into it. Perhaps you would not have got off so easily without special care. We did our best for you. To be frank, patients of your class don't come in here often."

"Many thanks," said Felix, with an effort. "But when shall I get out?"

"To-morrow, probably."

All day, he lay abed, watching his neighbors.

Their large, rough hands, spread out on the coverlets, twitched from time to time; their heavy eyes rolled slowly in discolored sockets; some displayed on their foreheads the violet-colored marks of blows, and a negro had his face so thoroughly bandaged that only his nose and mouth appeared. From between their restless lips, they puffed out, occasionally, low exclamations, incomprehensible phrases, fragments of querulous complaints. Or else, peering intently at the ceiling, those most recently arrived cried out in fear; and one, whose arms and legs were bound to his bedstead, expressed continually a belief that he was going to have his throat cut. He shrank back, with the look of an animal at bay, whenever an orderly approached him carrying a hypodermic syringe.

At nightfall, their condition grew worse.

From one corner rose a sound of weeping; elsewhere an unnatural chuckle was repeated at intervals; sharp ejaculations resounded: "Officer, stop that man!" "That's how they killed him!" "Your honor, it wasn't me!" "When it sticks its head out, shoot quick!" "I am in hell," thought Felix, and himself began to sob. The young physician injected morphine into his arm. He fell asleep.

Next afternoon, he was "discharged as cured."

On legs that bent under him at every step, he issued into the sunlight. A large rectangle of gray buildings surrounded him: in this enclosure stood some leafless trees; and, beyond these, on iron galleries rising in tiers against stone walls, one saw convalescents sitting in bed gowns of faded blue. To the right, a gate appeared. He was let out, by a watchman, into the street.

A white bull-terrier sprang at him with a whine, and Monsieur Pierre came hurrying forward.

The Parisian did nothing save wipe his eyes and press the young man's arm.

"But," faltered Felix, trying to collect his senses, "how did you find me?"

That had been due to Pat. Monsieur Pierre, searching everywhere for Felix, making, finally, the rounds of all the hospitals, had found the dog at this gate. Grimy, half starved, and fierce, Pat had attempted, whenever any one passed in or out, to penetrate the enclosure. He had been pelted with stones; and when the Frenchman arrived, the gatekeeper was consulting with a policeman as to the advisability of putting a bullet into the brute's head.

"I took him home. It was not easy: I got a bite or two. But he was fed—yes, indeed, on the best. And ever since, we have come here, twice a day, to wait."

He added, in beseeching tones,

"It is all over now, is it not? It is the end of all that?"

"Yes; I have learned my lesson."

"Let us pray to that effect."

The hospital was situated near the East River. They turned westward, and, at a slow pace, passed between tenements. But where were they going?

Not to the café, or to Mme. Wargla's house; not to Quilty's saloon, or to Felix's mean room!

"Monsieur Pierre, I am grateful for your solicitude and your kindness to the dog. But there are times when one should be alone. Maybe I shall feel better in Central Park."

The other, looking down, at last nodded.

"You are right, no doubt."

Before departing, he slipped ten dollars into the young man's hand.

"Let us say that this money shall now come to good uses."

And he shuffled away, with his hands clasped behind him, and his black felt hat tipped forward.

Felix found himself too weak to walk uptown. His dog, however, would not be permitted in a trolley-car. He hailed a hansom cab.

The cab driver, leaning down from his perch, inquired:

"And who's to pay for the trip?"

Without animosity, Felix displayed the banknotes.

At Central Park West and Seventy-ninth Street he left the cab. An entrance to the park was there. He went in.

The day was clear and cold. The sunshine had never been more brilliant.

CHAPTER XX

At this entrance to the park, a path, taking up
its eastward course, crossed a bridge with granite
parapets. Beneath the arch thus formed, some
thirty feet below, meandered north and south a
bridle path. Felix paused by the northern parapet
to look down at the equestrians.

Now and then, they appeared unexpectedly below,
on bay horses: rising clear of their saddles, they
departed rapidly up the incline of the perspective.

A hundred yards ahead, the gray flow of the
bridle path was cut in twain by an islet, so to speak,
of twiggy trees. Behind, extended a skyline, pur-
plish and undulating, of commingled branches.

The riders, turning to the right, skirted the islet,
to vanish amid bare thickets. But, on the left,
others came swiftly into sight, approached at a trot,
grew larger. Their white stocks, and the bits of
their steeds, became discernible; their faces were
soon hidden by their hats; the horses' backs were
elongated; the cropped tails disappeared beneath
the bridge.

He recalled the period when he had ridden so
with Nina.

For the first time in many months the tremor of
his nerves and the confusion of his mind had ceased:
as he gazed through air that seemed more limpid

than a celestial ether, he seemed to be sinking into absolute serenity. Round him a horizon of soft tree tops supported the edges of a flawless sky: the earth commingled with the heavens, and part of the golden brilliancy shed upon the ground floated upward immediately to its source. How beautiful this world, of which he was a part! Languidly he closed his eyes, the better to appreciate the purity of nature's exhalation. He was a boy again—the memory of past transgressions blurred, so that there remained to him only a vague wonder at the mystery of the sun, of the whispering grasses, and of the answering heart.

Ah, to have such feelings always, always to have had them! He remembered well the spot where he had parted from them.

It was not hard, perhaps, to keep the heart bright on hilltops where sweet breezes blew, and flowers blossomed, and sunlit vistas stretched far away to meet the sea?

But for youth, alas, the immaculateness of hilltops did not suffice. From such eminences did one not glimpse, at a twilight that was like all other twilights thereabouts, a distant flash, a beacon burning who knew where, a flame "that might surmount for one the Pharos?" So down from the summit, in the gathering darkness, to adventure far, with beating heart—through fields and cities, past palaces and hovels, till, at last, lost and fainting in black alley-ways, one said: "What I sought was never here; but it was always there."

He felt, however, no acute regret. His melancholy was so calm as to seem to him, after his long turbulence, pleasant. It was enough for him that he had regained, from abstinence without desire, from sedative medicines, or otherwise, the power of extracting enjoyment from the slightest materials. He could have shed tears, in weak happiness, at the aspect of the distant skyline. As he turned from the parapet, he paused to gaze tenderly at the withered petals of a bush.

He descended the path which led into the park.

A broad driveway appeared before him; beyond, was spread out a lake. The water, of a leaden hue close by, soon changed to a steel blue that joined, at length, in soft encroachments overlaid with scintillations, the olive-green reflection of a distant shore. There saplings, which began to rise directly from the water's edge, were gilded by the declining sun: in their upper branches was caught a fulvous haze; and between them one could see bare earth—in color a rich and luminous brown where not transected by long shadows—sloping upward till it vanished reluctantly behind the lowest horizontal limbs. Overhead, the eastern sky, too mellow to be blue, too azure to be yellow, trembled as if at contemplation of the radiant west.

Crossing the driveway, he walked north until he saw, on the right, a wooden bridge that spanned a little inlet from the lake.

The banks descended abruptly; smooth bowlders, half immersed, were each bound round, where they

entered the water, with a ribbon of moisture; amid
ripples, some swans continued to turn phlegmatically
in circles, and to plunge their bills toward the bottom.   Two or three men, leaning over the rail, were
watching these manœuvres.   A large, dark blue automobile, furnished with a "limousine," stopped
abruptly in the driveway.

But the bull-terrier, at sight of so many large and
obviously succulent fowls, became excited.   Felix
called him on, to a path beyond the bridge.   It
wound up a hillside, past steep rocks, and toward a
thickly wooded region.

To the right, overhead, roots projected from the
summits of crags; to the left, the tops of trees were
thrust up from a diminutive valley.   Across the
path, Australian firs let down their clumps of russet
needles; a birch, perhaps, sent up a waving white
column, and the way was lined with rhododendron
bushes, all their long leaves adroop.   These, in fact,
continuing ahead, at every withdrawal of the cliff
spread out in masses, then reappeared above, and,
at a turn of the path, filled the middle distance with
sun-drenched undulations.   Farther on, where many
trees swam together into a background at once confused and bright, here and there an oak or a beech
had retained some remnant of its leafage, to disturb,
with flecks of ochre and burnt umber, a fuscous
monotone.

Felix, however, discovered, to the left, a sloping
lawn on which a few magnolias showed their pale
trunks in incipient convolutions.   He turned aside;

though nearly exhausted, he began to climb among the rocks, by a path which at least should lead to solitude. Through a screen of rhododendron leaves, he saw a blue dress also moving upward, though by another way. The bowlders rose on either side of him, to form a rugged pass.

They were seal-colored and glossy, but overlaid with patches in the most evasive shades of green and mauve; they were dull as iron, and full of infinitesimal corrugations, like old lava; or, all at once, becoming rough, they were covered with a sheen of mica. They composed not only the walls of this ascent, but the footpath also: the irregular steps resembled the worn bed of an old torrent. And it was steep, this acclivity between rocks so high that sunlight no more than touched their tops. But above the shadows, straight ahead, trees, towering in an amber mist, marked a splendid summit.

Felix, gasping for breath, with failing limbs, was actuated by an irrational determination to win that goal. The crags fell away on either hand; a timbered landscape spread out below; directly before him, a woman clad in blue cloth and gray fur awaited his approach.

His heart leaped into his throat.

Inarticulate, he sank down upon a wooden bench half hidden by some laurel shrubs. Nina, advancing slowly, seated herself likewise. With gloved hands clasped in her lap, she regarded him.

She said:

"How you have changed!"

He succeeded in replying:

"And you, too."

She seemed to him an elder, fairer, consummate sister of her former self. The virginal charms which formerly had bestowed on her a somewhat tenuous allure, in this wife and mother had attained luxuriant development. Her beauty, indeed, appeared to him more complex and superb than that of a marble image clothed in gems: a thousand solved mysteries trembled in her gaze; and the familiar perfume which she still wore was more moving than a curtain of frankincense rising before a sanctuary.

But he saw her again; she had approached him of her free will; he heard her voice! What fate was to be thanked for this encounter?

Passing in her automobile, she had glimpsed him watching the swans. She had got out at once, had sent the automobile home, and, following him up the hillside, had deliberately contrived their meeting. "So much time had passed; one should not hold animosity forever; besides, even from a distance she had noted an unhappy alteration in him."

He thought it would do no harm to say:

"As for that, I have just left the hospital."

He was rewarded by a look of pity.

"Tell me about it."

"It is not worth relating. But do you tell me about yourself, if you are willing." He was aware, he added, of her marriage, and that she had a child; he had even seen her portrait by Pavin, whom he knew well. She showed no surprise at this announcement.

They still kept the farm in Westchester County. Denis Droyt's town house lay just east of Central Park. They had often travelled, until the birth of the baby. It was a boy, who resembled his father. When he was older, no doubt they would start off again, returning to New York for part of every winter season.

"In short," Felix ventured, frightened at his audacity, "much the sort of life that you and I once planned."

She looked down at her clasped hands. A pause ensued.

"Tell me," he asked, finally, "who was it that brought you word of me, that time? A man named Fray?"

"Mr. Tamborlayne wrote a letter to my mother."

He felt dizzy, at this sudden uphcaval of an old conviction.

"How little we know, of the past and of the future!"

"That's true," she assented in a low voice, her glance flashing over him from head to foot. Then the dog attracted her attention.

He came to her readily. His jaws wide open, his small, triangular eyes beaming with good-nature, he wagged his tail, made a wriggling motion, and suddenly put his forepaws on her lap. She did not repulse him.

"It is Pat; do you remember? You gave him to me."

"Is it he? I should not have known him."

And leaning forward, passing her hands over the bull-terrier's ragged ears, she murmured, with a tremulous smile:

"So many scars!"

Felix watched her while she continued those caresses, with fingers deft, as he remembered well, to soothe and pet dumb brutes.

Her blue cloth dress was plainly made; a simple toque of blue velvet did not conceal her thick brown hair; round her neck, and brushing her ear lobes, was a gray fur scarf. But each part of her attire was informed with an ineffable importance; a holy mantle could not have been more significant than the fabrics clothing her: her slightest movement swelled, as it were, the costume of a divinity.

Looking up, she surprised an expression of wonder on his face.

"What are your thoughts?" she inquired.

"I am trying to convince myself that it is you. This is the sort of meeting that one experiences in dreams—a scene in which the impossible becomes natural, a situation never to be expected in reality. Then, too, I find in you a marvellous change. Or perhaps an accumulation of past thoughts of mine has given you a different aspect?"

Once more it was the inevitable duo—but this time in a form how rare, how plaintive, how well attuned to variations in a minor key!

"When we had our falling out, you thought, I suppose, that we could never be farther removed from each other? But ever since, I have been widening the gulf between us. You stayed on the heights, and I descended, step by step, into the depths. Your world remained the same, but mine, always changing for the worse, became, at last, a place such as you could not imagine. So, when you meet me here, of your own accord, I recall the angel that visited the pool."

Perceiving moisture in her eyes, he was filled with a profound satisfaction. He felt acutely the dramatic difference between them; he appreciated the ideal quality of their surroundings; he saw in himself the classic prodigal laying bare his soul before some exquisite personification of compassion. However, the poignant touch that should complete the episode was lacking. He furnished it.

"Yet I have always struggled! An intuition, perhaps of moral origin, warned me of every pitfall: I hung back; but an irresistible force invariably drove me forward. And if that first transgression brought me, from the beginning, only misery, so it has been with all the rest. Still, I could gain nothing from experience. While yearning for the best, I had to choose the worst. I was like a man who staggers out of a fire only to be thrust back into the flames by an invisible hand. It was fate, that predestined for me a life of failure."

She replied, softly:

"Some time ago I ceased to blame you."

Presently, she went on:

"Do you remember old Joseph? He is still with me, very feeble, and sometimes childish. But he talks of you; and, when he grows garrulous, he relates tales that he would keep to himself, if his mind were stronger. Then, too, it was Paul Pavin who painted my portrait."

"I suppose you mean that Joseph told you of my loss of patrimony, and that Pavin had something to say about my subsequent life?"

For a moment she looked at him searchingly. Then a flush covered her face, as she replied:

"That's it."

All the same, he found it difficult to understand how such information constituted an excuse for his career.

They remained silent, gazing over the laurel shrubs.

The sunshine had nearly left the tree trunks; but it lingered, in an accentuated effulgence, amid the branches. The firs spread out their countless soft tufts of needles as if for a final and more thorough blazoning, the oaks showed a few leaves like scraps of beaten gold, while the whole wide-spread mesh of limbs and twigs seemed ready to dissolve its myriad intricacies and pervade the still air, in a shimmering vapor.

"What time is it, Felix?"

"I don't know."

She cast round her an uneasy glance which reached the farthest haze of tree tops. There, to the east and to the south, towered the "sky-scrapers" of the city. So their solitude had limits! She exclaimed:

"It will be twilight soon. It is growing colder. And you have no overcoat!"

Reaching forward, she felt the thickness of his clothing. Tears brimmed her eyes. He caught her retiring hand in his.

"Don't take your hand away. Something passes through your glove straight to my heart. All sorts of forgotten images reappear before me. The blind who were made to see must have had such sensations."

When he had bent down to kiss her fingers, he continued:

"I went on and on; I believed I had lost myself in the shadows: but no—you were always there, far overhead. When spring came, I remembered the lilac bushes through the woods. When it was winter, I saw your face across a glow of candles. Or else I heard leaves rustling in the summer breeze, at night, and dreamed of the garden."

She closed her eyes.

"Maybe you were not alone in such thoughts."

"All my aspirations were, in the end, attempts to win your secret praise; and your mute reproach seemed to intensify all my remorses. There were even moments when it seemed to me that you were present, if not in person, at least in spirit."

"Perhaps there was cause for that belief."

She turned away her head; but he could see, above the gray fur scarf, her trembling chin. Then, facing him, she let her eyes rain tears.

"We have been very unhappy!"

He had never been happier than then.

"No, this repays me for everything! What does the rest matter, now?"

And he added, with the thrill which comes to one who unexpectedly interprets, in a phrase, a principle of his life:

"If it had turned out as we anticipated, the joy of our happiness might not have equalled the joy of our distress."

While she understood this speech, she did not assent to it.

"On the contrary," she protested, "to have been promised so much, and to have lost it all! To have had this meeting, and to part!"

"Yes," he agreed, gloomily, "I suppose that is what we must do."

In fact, she was already looking eastward apprehensively.

"And what about you?" she asked, while pressing a handkerchief against her cheeks.

"It will be different with me, henceforth."

"Ah, Felix, if you will make that promise good! Perhaps it was not for nothing that I used to think of you as standing on a wonderful threshold. I have read somewhere, 'To become a saint, one must have been a sinner.' It is true, no doubt—at least, I know that I could find in a man who had fought his infirmities and conquered them a hundred times the worth of another, born to security."

Did she not have in mind her husband? A keener thrill pervaded him.

"You shall see!" he cried. "And afterward?"

She hesitated. But finally, with the look of a woman brought, despite herself, for the first time in her life to the commission of a subtle treason, she whispered, with averted eyes:

"Who knows?"

Then she rose quickly. He was shocked to find their parting imminent.

"But the sun has not set!"

"And yet we've said too much!"

She put out her hand.

"I have your promise, Felix."

"Yes."

For a while they looked at each other through a mist.

"Good-by."

"Good-by."

She departed.

He watched her descend the hillside by a narrow path that wound eastward between rhododendron bushes. Her blue dress vanished behind tree trunks; it reappeared farther on, diminished. A shaft of sunlight illumined her for an instant. She flitted through deep shadows. He could see her no longer. She had not looked back.

The white bull-terrier peered up at Felix inquiringly.

The latter cast his eyes toward the confines of the park.

And he felt that the horizontal sunbeams were bathing him in a sublime lustre. The earth was merged into the sky; the light, like an unalterable assurance smiling from afar, impartially benefited all it touched; and every substance in the universe, whether volatile or solid, growing or inert, revealed to him its meaning, its destiny, its harmony with all other substances and with the eternal. Was not he himself included in this synthesis? He seemed to share the will for evolution that pervaded everything existent; and he thought to recognize, deep in his nature, something of the inflexible determination which holds in place the firmament.

He faced the west. The sunset seemed to be consuming all the cornices: the city that had been his prison was in process of dissolution. He gazed to the south-east. The windows of tall buildings, flashing forth great rays, were like the trophies of a conquered host suspended on the walls of temples.

Finally, he went down the path by which he had ascended—between the rocks, past the rhododendrons, beneath the firs, across the wooden bridge, the driveway, and the arch above the bridle path. He was no longer exhausted. As if in a trance, he set out, walking southward.

On his right, roofs turned red: on his left, beyond a boundary wall, lamps showed among the branches points of clear yellow. Gradually, a whiteness filled the eastern sky, invaded the zenith, and descended toward the west. There, far beyond every cross street, was to be seen for a while, low lying, a thin strip of evanescent rose.

Twilight gathered in the busy thoroughfares. **He reached** Union Square.

The traffic threaded its way through a dusk studded with a confusion of lights. Close at hand, acetylene lamps blazed forth abruptly; trolley-cars rumbled past; horns and gongs sounded on all sides; and those afoot rushed forward, at intervals, between motormen straining at their brakes and automobiles halted with a wrench. Felix woke, so to speak, to find himself hemmed in by swiftly moving vehicles.

A shout reached his ears. He turned to look for Pat. The dog, scampering toward him, disappeared beneath an automobile.

Felix jumped forward with a cry. The automobile struck him, knocked him down, and, gathering speed, made off.

But immediately he was on his feet.

A crowd had already assembled in a ring, through which Felix pushed his way. In the midst, the white bull-terrier lay on his side, covered with dirt, his legs stretched out, his mouth closed. He did not move.

Felix lifted the body, and held it to his breast. He stared round him blankly. Each face expressed commiseration. A man in a battered hat began to curse the rich. Another, his cheeks swelling with fury, demanded "a law for the regulation of speed maniacs." One asked the rest if the automobile number had been taken. All turned to cast impotent glances into the dusk. Three policemen appeared simultaneously. Their spokesman, wearing a belted overcoat and a flat cap of blue cloth with an enamelled visor, lifted the dog's chin. After scrutinizing the small, three-cornered eyes already glazed, he pronounced:

"He's kilt, all right."

Then, laying his palm on Felix's shoulder,

"Will you be wanting to dispose of him yourself?"

Felix nodded.

"All right, then. I'm sorry. I've got a dog of me own."

And, turning on the crowd, the policeman shouted, violently:

"Now then, get out of here, the whole of yez! What do yez think this is—a show?"

The spectators, however, reassembling on the pavement, were not to be denied the excitement of following Felix eastward along Fourteenth Street. The van of this procession with difficulty escaped treading on his heels; the line was continually re-enforced, and ragged youngsters ran ahead to look back at the body slipping from his arms. Dizzy and faint, Felix no longer knew where he was going. Debility seized on him again; his limbs seemed ready to resign their offices; he expected every moment to plunge forward on his face.

But there rose before him a round, familiar visage, like the countenance of a dumfounded Vitellius. It was Delaclaire sent, by chance, to the rescue.

"Your dog! But not hurt?"

"Run over. Dead."

"Great heavens, what news to take home! I feel that I'm going to be a touching messenger to-night!"

Felix, once having come to a stop, was on the point of sinking with his burden to the ground.

"I am just out of a hospital. This has nearly finished me. I must get somewhere at once."

"My dear boy! Forgive me. I know what you need."

And the Thespian drew Felix to the door of Quilty's saloon.

The younger man shrank back.

"No, no!"

Delaclaire wore the look of a benevolent old physician whose patient exhibits a deplorable ignorance of his requirements.

"Nonsense! You are in my hands."

He saw the foil-wrapped chandeliers, the mirrors, the pyramids of glasses. Quilty's scar attracted his attention. The Thespian, while supporting Felix with one arm, was pouring out to the saloon keeper, with a wealth of florid gesticulations, "the tragic story." Moreover, Connla was taking the dog's body from him.

The group entered the back room. There the detective laid Pat upon a table. Confronting Felix, he inquired, angrily:

"How did it happen?"

The other, sinking into a chair, buried his face in his hands.

Delaclaire embellished his tale, this time, with several dramatic and entirely fictitious incidents.

"The mob stormed the automobile! They threatened the chauffeur! But my friend, mastering his sorrow, restrained them . . . ."

In short, facts no longer mattered to the actor. He was carried away by his imagination. Possibly he even "saw himself in the part."

Connla patted Felix on the back.

"It's just one of them things that can't be helped, that hits us when we least expect it. It's what we have to get used to."

Felix, raising his head, with difficulty got out the words:

"He never left me. He never deceived me. He was never ashamed of me. I think he understood, all the while, what I wanted to do."

He collapsed in a paroxysm of grief.

Delaclaire, who had darted out to the bar, returned, from caution more bow-legged than ever, bearing a small glass overflowing with whiskey. Distributing between the detective and the saloon keeper a sapient look, he addressed the young man in coaxing accents.

"You'll feel better when you've had some of this."

The liquor was beneath his nose; the fumes penetrated his brain. He took the glass, and emptied it down his throat. Soon, he experienced a delicious relaxation.

Another glassful intoxicated him.

The Thespian, his anxiety relieved by the obvious effect of his prescription, was relating to Connla and to Quilty, in a mournful manner, an appropriate anecdote.

"It's not as if I couldn't feel for him! I've had my own experience. Mine was a French poodle,

Gyp—the most intelligent animal! We put her in
an act that was a knockout from end to end of the
country: just before the curtain, she tore open a
sofa pillow and discovered the missing will. But
one day, she et a piece of bacon rind covered with
rat poison."

Connla, paying scanty attention to this chronicle,
stroked the bull-terrier's head. At last, clearing his
throat, he said:

"I remember well the first night I ever seen him.
How he stuck his teeth into them niggers' ankles!
But, at that, I think it kind of went against the
grain. He was a thoroughbred!"

"A man gets attached to a dog," was Quilty's
contribution. Moved, perhaps, by a variation of
that impulse which results in "wakes," he ordered
the bartender to bring in another "round of drinks."
The saloon keeper's own choice of beverage proved
to be, as always, "a little lithia water."

Felix no longer shed tears. His bereavement had
blended into a cloud of rapidly escaping thoughts.
Leaning forward, with his hands dangling between
his knees, he listened to the remote voice of the
detective, who assured him that the dog should have
a decent burial. There was a man uptown, it
seemed, who made a business of the interment of
pets. "And, as he's broke the health laws once or
twice, we'll make him do the job for nothing. I'll
see to it."

"You are too good. You are one and all too
good."

Was it not fortunate that he should be solaced by three friends so considerate and so sympathetic?

Later, he was bewildered to find eight dollars in his pocket.

He parted from Quilty, Delaclaire, and Connla. The detective suggested seeing him home. They stood in the open; the stars were thick; a cold wind was blowing.

"It's not worth while. I live close by."

"But where?"

"In this neighborhood."

"Well, just as you say. We'll meet at Quilty's, then, to-morrow morning."

"To-morrow morning."

He wandered through the streets. Whenever he saw the illuminated windows of a saloon, he pushed back the swinging doors. For the benefit of many strangers whom he met at bars, he began a sad monologue, which he was unable to finish; while trying to remember its conclusion, he sent a wavering glance round the floor, beneath the tables, into corners.

But the stars drew near, to give him news of all that they had ever seen; the trailing clouds held pictures of steel-covered armies, like mirages lingering long after the ancient battles which they seemed to have reflected; and the earth whispered to him of all that it contained, deep down, where man had not been. Then the shapes of women moved before him, lighter than thistledown, and fairer than the moon. Their red lips parted; their tresses fluttered back; enlaced, they darted upward; their laughter fell in showers; they shredded away.

He woke with his head on a table, in the back room of a dram shop near the river—a resort for longshoremen. The sun shone through a dusty window. A shabby fellow was preparing to sweep the floor.

Resting on his broom, the stranger favored Felix with a wink.

"There you are! A night's lodging, and no charge."

"What time is it?"

"Six o'clock, and a fine, crisp day."

Felix explored his pockets feebly, then pressed his hands against his head.

"I feel very ill."

"Indeed, you look so! And no money? Well, now, suppose I take a chance, and stake you to a drink?"

"Thank you."

When he had swallowed some fiery brandy, he found himself able to start homeward.

He was living in a four-story "hotel" that surmounted a café, on Fourth Avenue below Fourteenth Street. His week's rent was overdue; and, as he had not been home for four days, it occurred to him that he must have been evicted. He found his room, however, as he had left it.

An iron bedstead leaned against the wall opposite a wooden mantelpiece, painted to resemble oak. The washstand, its varnish nearly obliterated by many splashings, supported a basin and a pitcher. A small bureau by the window, and a straight-back chair, completed the furniture. His trunk stood behind the door.

When he had closed and locked the door, he inspected his surroundings carefully. An alarm clock on the mantle-shelf attracted him. He began to wind it. Soon, a smile crossed his face, and he set down the clock but partly wound.

In the bureau drawer, he found a box half full of headache powders. There were six "doses" left. He unfolded the papers, one by one, and emptied them into a glass tumbler.

But he stopped short. Some one was knocking at the door.

He held his breath. The knock was repeated, the door-knob rattled, and a voice called:

"Félix?"

Presently he heard Monsieur Pierre shuffle down the corridor.

The contents of the six papers made in the bottom of the tumbler a little mound of powder. He added water from the pitcher on the washstand. Then he drank the mixture off. As he set down the tumbler, he asked himself:

"What have I done?"

With a feeling of scepticism, he approached the window. Through soiled Nottingham curtains, he saw the sun shining as brightly as before, the drays full of bales and boxes, the people hurrying to work.

These passers-by were talking, laughing, full of life. He could not convince himself that he was on the point of leaving them.

Suddenly, he perceived Monsieur Pierre on the opposite corner, in front of a saloon.

The Parisian's clothes were too large for him. With his knees bent, his shoulders stooped, his arms dangling, he turned his piebald beard repeatedly from north to south. Even at a distance, his anxiety was perceptible. He was awaiting Felix.

After he had peered into several hundred faces, he removed his black felt hat with a gesture of hopelessness. His bald head flashed. His shadowy eyes were raised to Felix's window. But the Nottingham curtain prevented a discovery.

When he had again looked up and down the street—though this time more furtively than expectantly—the Frenchman edged toward the saloon behind him. He put out his fleshless hand. The doors swung ajar. Monsieur Pierre, with surprising agility, slipped between them.

"Poor old rascal!" thought Felix.

His headache was gone. The serenity of the day before had returned to him. Leaning against the sash, he continued to look out, listlessly, at the pedestrians.

They made haste, as if matters of great moment awaited them. All their faces showed a matutinal animation. It was the beginning of a fresh day for them. It was the world that hurried by.

So it would be to-morrow, next year, a century hence, a thousand years from now! He found the thought wellnigh incredible, that everything would go on the same as ever.

And she, too, would remain!

He saw her with children coming to adolescence round her; in the fulness of her maturity, in the rich autumn of her life, in an exquisite old age. "Her charms can never fail; they can no more than change. She will attain, at last, that fineness of the aged who have been fair. She will appear in lace and silk and white hair. She will sit on a hill-top, her gaze roaming far away, while the leaves flutter down upon her hands. She will be lost in dreams."

Oh, to have been, before departure, the close witness of such a progress—to have reached, with one so dear, such a culmination! Others were destined to those delights, but he must miss them.

Surely, if he desired another chance, there was still time?

A determination, strong beyond his previous experience, kept him motionless by the window.

"That illusion shall not cheat me again. Life is a struggle that I am not fitted for."

Weakness descended on him. He turned to the bed. The floor moved beneath his feet. His skin was bathed in a cold moisture. Weighed down by an immense lassitude, he had difficulty in stretching himself upon the counterpane.

"Then I was not deceived. It is here!"

And after a pause,

"Why am I not afraid?"

He lay still, breathing with difficulty, curious to find the room so bright, and listening to the ticking of the clock.

Confused images trembled in mid-air.

He saw, at the same time, the Delaclaires gobbling sandwiches in their room, Pavin by the "north light," old Joseph fashioning paper hats, Emma rolling up her large eyes, Marie posturing on the stage of the Trocadero Theatre, Eileen entering his room with parted lips. Mr. Snatt seemed to exhibit his nose in the dismantled chambers of a college student; while Noon showed his dusky visage in a parlor hung with the Ferrol family's portraits. Then the Parisian's bald head bent forward, and a pair of shadowy eyes pored over a pile of tattered magazines.

All these figments were in some way related to one another: they were like portions of a tapestry which, read aright, should form an intelligible whole. But for him that decipherment was a task too arduous. A labor more important engaged his every faculty.

He was at great pains to catch his breath.

"How one's instincts persist!"

Was not this effort to breathe as futile as his countless past endeavors?

"Yet if one might only be sure of achieving, elsewhere, the ideal . . . ."

The ideal! He could not recollect in what it had consisted. It was as if a guiding beacon had gone out.

At nine that night, the clock on the mantel-shelf stopped ticking.

Afterword

By Alden Whitman

The author of *Predestined: A Novel of New York Life* was a remarkably conscious literary artist who possessed a keen sense of what he sought to achieve in his book, the careful research that established its veracity and the discipline to bring his ideas together in fictive form. Stephen French Whitman published his novel through Charles Scribner's Sons in February 1910, about a month after his thirtieth birthday. The following June he was interviewed for the first time, and the resulting article, two closely printed columns, appeared in the *New York Evening Sun* of June 11th. The interviewer was an anonymous, but obviously adept, reporter with some knowledge of books.

Referring to *Predestined,* the reporter taxed Mr. Whitman as to "whether or not you believe a man has to pass through an experience before he can describe it." The question was a natural one, for the irony and candor of the novel, with its intimately portrayed cityscape, sliced the roofs off many New York houses; and the writer "permitted his face to radiate with a pervasive smile, pushed his straw hat well back on his forehead and spoke after this fashion:

" 'There was once a man named Flaubert who wrote a novel called *Mme. Bovary*. The story was the study of the character of a farmer's daughter unhappily married to a country physician. Flaubert's work in composing the intimate character of Mme. Bovary could hardly be surpassed. And yet is it quite fair to assume that Flaubert was ever an unhappily married farmer's daughter?'

"It began to be evident . . . that Mr. Whitman possesses none of the shadows that surround the central character of his book.

" 'I mention this,' he continued, 'to illustrate my opinion that it's easier to describe the sensations of a neurotic person approaching a mental breakdown, for instance, by reading in a medical library and by spending a night in a hospital ward as a spectator than it is by getting the ailment in person.'

" 'And how far do you carry this spectator viewpoint?' he was asked.

" 'All the way through in one way,' was the answer, 'and yet, well, the whole point is—but, say,' and he dropped his voice to a cautious whisper: 'Remember I'm not setting up any beacons of light.'

"Having been presented with any number of reassurances, Mr. Whitman went on:

" 'What I mean is that to write about one man and what he thinks and feels you have to get into the viewpoint of that man. You have to see everything as he sees it and only the things that he sees.

" 'Gustave Flaubert, it's true, didn't keep to the one character viewpoint in *Mme. Bovary*. But that was his first novel, and in *L'Education Sentimentale* he caused everything to happen as if Frederic Moreau had seen it, heard it, or heard of it. I think that this method in such a case usually gives much more of an impression of unity and reality.'

" 'But if you haven't been that sort of man, don't you find it pretty hard to get his viewpoint?'

" 'After you have been writing for a little while it's surprising how easily you fall into the habit of looking at things the way he does—while you're writing. They're keen about calling it the psychology thing these days, and I suppose that's what it is. Anyway, it's entirely different from the manner in which Thackery, for example, stood off and looked at his people as an outsider who was privileged to be on the inside track of their minds.

" 'But when you are doing it, as I tried to do, it's a case of a one man story in the—well, the right name is the realistic school's style,' he ended with a smile.

" 'How about utilizing the experiences that you happen to have had?'

" 'Certainly, that's the idea,' he answered, 'in so far as you share the experiences of that character.

" 'Now I wanted to start out my young man with an education about like that any fellow is apt to get. I went to Princeton and I knew about things down there better than about other places.

" 'Perhaps you couldn't recognize the portrait, but that was the place I intended to describe, because I believe it's pretty poor policy to try to describe things you don't know about.' "

Later in the interview Mr. Whitman was pressed to tell how he had acquired his close knowledge of New York's many sides.

"Some of it came in the four years after he left college, when he worked on *The Evening Sun,* but most of his work, he said, was writing sketches for the back page on Saturdays. He had looked around a good deal more since he left newspaper work.

" 'There's very little romance about getting material for a book,' he said. 'You go about it as you go about anything else. You figure out just what episodes you want your characters to go through and then you find the best places for those episodes.

" 'I wanted to get a French restaurant for one part of my book, so I went over to the West Thirties and found just the sort of place I was after and looked at it a few times and then came back and wrote about it. It was the same way with a boarding house.

" 'I went to see places of the type I wanted. The little vaudeville actress who comes into the book sat on the seat ahead of me in an open car one day. She was talking to a couple of hams and all I had to do was to listen and my material was wafted right to me. Nothing easier.

" 'I remember one day I went to see a flat in Second Avenue. That was where I was going to have Felix and the widow he married set up housekeeping. I found a building with just the right kind of outside that I wanted and I went in to see the agent. I told him I had come to see about renting a flat.

" 'In this place?' he asked, and when I told him that

I did he looked at me as though he knew I was a liar.

" 'He took me upstairs just the same and showed me a furnished flat which was precisely what I wanted to see. There it all was, the way I had hoped to find it, dogs' heads painted on the chair backs and all.' "

Later in the interview Mr. Whitman defended the somberness of his novel, saying: "Of course, if *Predestined* is largely in twilight, it must be, because it is so that Felix Piers soon comes to see the world. If it soon leaves many gay things behind, that's because the young man has left them behind.' "

Another novel, the writer went on, " 'would not be so, and yet could be quite as much in the realistic style. In my next book I hope to prove that brilliant sunshine is not out of place while flooding a realistic novel.' "

Although Stephen French Whitman was extraordinarily revealing of his literary attitudes, he left only a meager deposit of biographical facts. When he died December 28, 1948, in Los Angeles, he was so far out of public notice that no obituary article appeared in the *New York Times*. From records at Princeton University it is known that he was born in Philadelphia January 10, 1880, to Rowland and Jeanette Tresize Whitman. Their ancestry is a matter of speculation, but since most Whitmans in the United States trace their lineage to John and Mary Whitman who migrated from England to Weymouth, Massachusetts, in 1636, it is likely that Stephen French Whitman was part of that John Whitman's genealogical tree.

The occupation of Stephen French Whitman's father is not known, but it is evident that the family was prosperous for Steve, as he was called by his friends, was sent to Exeter and Lawrenceville to prepare for Princeton, all institutions then open ordinarily to young men of well-to-do families. His Princeton class was 1901, and in his senior year he was editor of the *Tiger*, the college humor magazine.

According to the *Evening Sun* interview, "he didn't bother a lot about the academic side of things, and upholds all the regular traditions by regretting it now.

"Mr. Whitman had the time of his life in his senior year when he edited *The Tiger*," his interviewer wrote. "In this sort of monthly, it appears, one phase to be noted is that the same old jokes come back into the fold with great regularity. Mr. Whitman explains it as the result of the same incidents recurring each year and having the same effects on minds of the same sort.

" 'There was one about wearing paths on the campus, I remember,' said he. 'You know that one which comes with spring and the Keep Off the Grass signs, and derives its mirth from the idea of a path as a costume.' "

The writer was asked, with the tact that interviewers then employed, if, to make up for his classroom delinquencies, he had done a good deal of reading outside the curriculum.

" 'No I didn't,' he replied cheerfully, 'except when I had to do it to work off a pensum. What is a pensum? Well, that's a little task inflicted when you don't go to class often enough. My task was extra reading in French.'

" 'Ah, you must have been great chums with the French faculty?'

" 'No, I wasn't; perhaps because I read a novel different from the one they suggested. Whatever I have read and absorbed of French authors has been almost altogether since I left college.' "

Evidently, he did read widely in French and Russian literature, for, after expressing his admiration for Flaubert, he continued: " 'Remember, now, I haven't one derogatory word to say about the American reading public or about the American writing public. Nor have I the vaguest idea of suggesting that the American author can't write. But I do believe that only in France and Russia were there great writers who in groups had practically attained perfection of form for the novel.

" 'Of course it isn't necessary to add that sooner or later we all wake up to the importance of form. Substance, and by that I mean plot and everything like that, is all very well to begin with, just as a piece of marble is very well for a sculptor to begin with. But both plot and marble while they have to be sound at the start must be approached with great pains and patience if they are to result in anything of moment.' "

"Pains and patience" aplenty went into *Predestined*, Mr. Whitman explained. He worked regular hours— from 9 to 4—in the two years it took him to compose the book. " 'I blocked out the whole book by parts and chapters,' he continued, 'with all the episodes I wanted in each chapter, and later on I added a schedule of the number of words I wanted in each episode. Now, about mapping it out. A good book is of course just as carefully balanced and composed as a good painting. You should know before sitting down to write what every character is to do at every point.

" 'It has been said by some writers that at a certain point the characters [in *Predestined*] seemed to sweep me aside and take the action into their own hands. There is nothing mysterious in that; it happens only because the writer hadn't made up his mind what to write before he sat down or because if he had made up his mind his plan didn't afterward appear logical to him.

" 'I allow a certain number of words to each episode, and generally a number that seems inadequate, so that I'll be forced to compress my matter to the utmost. The smallest number of words tells the story most effectively. Stevenson said in substance, "If I know what to omit, I know all I need about writing." Perhaps that was an exaggeration, but verbosity makes no points to speak of.' "

Stephen French Whitman's self-developed "pains and patience" emerged in his immediate post-Princeton years. "On graduating," said a death notice in the *Princeton Alumni Weekly* of February 18, 1949, "he worked for several years on *The New York Sun*, traveled around the world and settled down to a literary career." Initially, this took the form of short stories, one of which, *The Wife*, won a *Collier's Magazine* award. Over the years he produced some fifty short stories, according to the death notice. The earliest of these were collected in *Shorty & Patrick, U.S.S. Oklahoma*, which was published October 1, 1910, by P. F. Collier

& Son (cx), and reprinted in 1913 by McBride, Nast & Co. under the title of *The Happy Ship*.

Predestined was his first novel. There is no surviving record of how much he was paid for it, nor has a search turned up reviews or notices of its publication. The lengthy interview in the *Evening Sun* attests, however, a public familiarity with the novel and suggests that it was well received and much discussed. The book was still enough in the news to warrant a news story about Mr. Whitman in the *Sun* of December 2, 1911, which said, "Stephen French Whitman, who wrote *Predestined*, sailed yesterday [for Italy] after a month's stay in this country."

The article went on to relate that the visit was Mr. Whitman's first for a year and a half and that he had gone to Italy in 1910 to write another book "he had well outlined in mind at that time." He was deflected, however, "and he devoted himself to getting to know Italy, the country about which his second novel will be written."

This novel was *The Isle of Life*, published by Scribner's in 1913. Critical reaction to it and to *Children of Hope*, a third novel issued by the Century Company, in 1916, may well have survived, but I have not been able to find it. *Predestined*, however, continued to circulate and to be read by, among others, F. Scott Fitzgerald.

In a letter to the late Charles Scribner, head of the publishing house, in 1922, Fitzgerald proposed that the firm establish a Scribner library.

"Take for instance *Predestined* and *The House of Mirth,* Fitzgerald wrote. "I do not know, but I imagine those books are kept upstairs in most bookstores, and only obtained when someone is told of the work of Edith Wharton and Stephen French Whitman. They are almost as forgotten as the books of Frank Norris and Stephen Crane were five years ago, before Boni's library began its career."

In a list of eighteen books Fitzgerald suggested for a Scribner library, *Predestined* was ranked second after *The House of Mirth* or *Ethan Frome.* His own *This Side of Paradise* was third.

Mr. Whitman apparently remained abroad, probably in Italy, until after the outbreak of World War I. He may have returned to the United States in time for publication of *Children of Hope,* but it is certain that he was here in May 1918, when he joined the Navy as an ensign and was posted to the Navy Intelligence Bureau in Washington, where he was assigned to duty with the Office of Chief Cable Censor. He resigned as of April 13, 1920, according to Princeton alumni records.

Two years later he published a novel called *Sacrifice* under the imprint of D. Appleton & Co. Again, and tantalizingly, no reviews of it have been found. By this time, his Princeton obituarians wrote, he had gone "to Hollywood to write for the motion pictures."

"But," added his memorialists, "fate had already struck and it was only the empty shell of the old Steve that arrived in Hollywood. His life had become a tragedy—a hopeless fight against hopeless odds and he fought it in the brave way—without complaint."

The "fate" was described by his college classmates as "a thyroid condition which burned and seared him with its hidden fire." Nonetheless, Mr. Whitman worked at his craft during the twenties and thirties, producing, in 1931, a final novel entitled *Here's Luck: A Social Footnote,* which was published by D. Appleton & Co. Reviewing it in the *New York Evening Post* of April 13, 1931, William Soskin said: "It's been rather a bad weekend and not the least of its woes was caused by a little disillusionment in reading a new novel by Stephen French Whitman, the author of *Predestined,* a book which, years ago, stirred considerable excitement in the hearts of a considerable number of newspapermen. . . .

"But what is it that happens to a man to turn such sincere and powerful writing as went into Mr. Whitman's tragedy of a newspaperman's drunken failure into the glib, competent stuff of *Here's Luck.* In *Predestined* you had an author whose warmth and ability to project human realism onto the printed page made a novel the equal of anything of Theodore Dreiser's in the same field. In *Here's Luck* you have a story that could be turned out in any one of a hundred factories."

The novel concerns the bootlegging and racketeering career of Nick Sassotti, a swashbuckling liquor king, and his two-gun sister, Lucrezia. It is, as Mr. Soskin remarked, slick but not distinguished. A newspaper photograph of Mr. Whitman published in connection with his novel (but not necessarily taken in 1931) shows a man with a fairly thin face, which is dominated by bulging eyes—often a symptom of thyroidism.

The only other clues to Mr. Whitman's life that I have been able to unearth are as brief as they are piquing of the curiosity. All are from the *Princeton Alumni Weekly*. One, for January 2, 1939, notes that "Steve Whitman is in Washington with the present session of Congress" but is silent on details. Another note, for May 5, 1939, says "Steve is busily writing shorts, longs and movies." A third, in the issue of March 24, 1941, recounts that Mr. Whitman had a story in the February edition of *Esquire*.

This story, *The Great Preparedness Parade,* was characterized as a satire and was a fictive account of the writer's Uncle Hilary and his unintentional involvement in a New York parade in 1916. It is an amusing and facile piece, but hardly profound.

It is, so far as I can determine, Mr. Whitman's last published fiction, although there was a hint in the Princeton alumni notes in late 1941 and early 1942 that he was then working on a new book "and is much improved in health." But apparently not sufficiently to complete a manuscript. He was then living in Santa Barbara, California.

Earlier, in 1940, he had relinquished his rights in *Predestined* for reasons that cannot now be recalled by Charles Scribner's Sons. In a holograph letter dated May 1, 1940, to Whitney Darrow of Scribner's, he wrote, "Dear Whitney: In return for $10 paid me by

AFTERWORD 477

you today I hereby transfer to Charles Scribner's Sons
all rights of whatever sort in 'Predestined.' Very truly
yours, Stephen F. Whitman."

At various times in his life Mr. Whitman was a
member of the Players Club; the Coffee House; the
University Club of Los Angeles; the Nassau Club of
Princeton, N.J.; and the Princeton Club of New York.
At his death, ascribed officially to a heart attack, he
was living at 2000 Arlington Avenue, Los Angeles. He
never married and he left no known relatives. In their
memorial notice for the *Princeton Alumni Weekly* of
February 18, 1949, James H. McLean and Jasper E.
Crane, president and secretary, respectively, of the
Class of 1901, said, "In his youth, he was vital, bril-
liant and dynamic. In his later years, he was a kindly,
thoughtful gentleman. He did not complain."

Although *Predestined* was not the first American
naturalistic novel, it was a pioneer in that genre whose
practitioners at the turn of the century were most
notably Theodore Dreiser and Frank Norris. The
Whitman book, in breaking with the prevailing gentility
in letters, is clearly not an edifying romance. On the
contrary, the dissolution of Felix Piers is carefully
traced. At the outset he is a man of promise and
potential, but becomes enmeshed in a series of setbacks
and failures that ultimately lead to his death, which is
virtually a suicide. There is a complex interplay between his personality and his milieu, between the fading
of his talents as a writer and the unrelenting forces of
an uncaring society. Some of these forces are represented by the women in his life and some by the nature

of his occupation as a newspaperman and freelance writer.

Both Piers and his women are painstakingly drawn. Stephen French Whitman was a keen observer and a shrewd psychologist, for he delineates, in the personal sphere, how failure breeds on failure. In describing slatternly newspaper rooms, sawdusty saloons, cheerless roominghouses, and musty hotels, Whitman was reflecting an unidealized New York; nor was he less faithful in his depiction of life in the *beau monde*. His perception was pitiless as well as trenchant. But not necessarily condemnatory, for *Predestined* is not a judgmental novel. Indeed, the reader comes to have a certain empathy with Felix Piers—and finally to understand him.

Predestined is eminently worth this revival in the Lost American Fiction series not only for its historical significance, but also for its literary merit. With a little more luck *Predestined* would have been kept in print, as *Sister Carrie* has been. Perhaps it might have been, if Whitman's creative light had not dimmed so soon and if he had gone on to other masterpieces. But he was not lucky.

But we are, for this republication of *Predestined* gives us access to an important and influential novel in the development of American realistic-naturalistic fiction. It is part of the linkage between Dreiser and Lewis and Fitzgerald and Hemingway and their successors. Moreover, it is a good reading book, which is to say that it still speaks to us in the 1970s. Like all thoughtful novels, it transcends its immediate time.

I am indebted to Helena S. D'Atri of the Princeton University Office of Printing, Mailing and Alumni Records, Alumni Records Section, for data on Stephen French Whitman's affiliations with Princeton; to Mrs. Harriet W. Angulo of Arlington, Virginia, for her kindness in searching the Union Catalogue of the Library of Congress for Whitman references; to Charles Scribner for searching his files for Whitman material and for providing me with a copy of Mr. Whitman's letter to Whitney Darrow; and to Prof. Matthew J. Bruccoli of the English Department of the University of South Carolina for drawing my attention to Fitzgerald's letter to his publisher.

Textual Note: The text of *Predestined* published here is a photo-offset reprint of the first printing (New York: Charles Scribner's Sons, 1910). No emendations have been made in the text.

M. J. B.